The HOLIDAY FAKERS

EVIE ALEXANDER

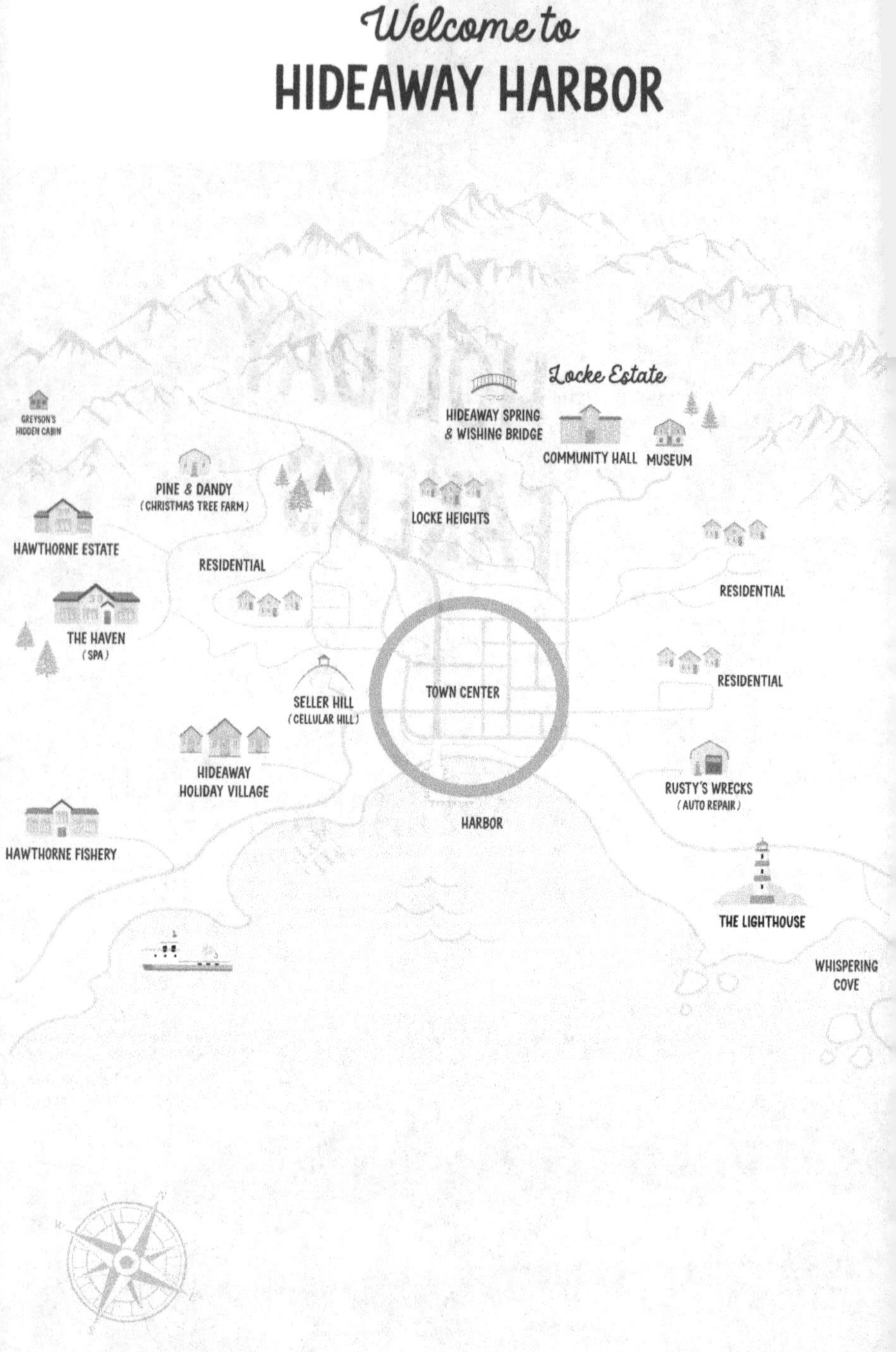

Welcome to
HIDEAWAY HARBOR

GREYSON'S
HIDDEN CABIN

Locke Estate

HIDEAWAY SPRING
& WISHING BRIDGE

COMMUNITY HALL   MUSEUM

PINE & DANDY
(CHRISTMAS TREE FARM)

LOCKE HEIGHTS

HAWTHORNE ESTATE

RESIDENTIAL

RESIDENTIAL

THE HAVEN
(SPA)

RESIDENTIAL

SELLER HILL
(CELLULAR HILL)

TOWN CENTER

HIDEAWAY
HOLIDAY VILLAGE

RUSTY'S WRECKS
(AUTO REPAIR)

HARBOR

HAWTHORNE FISHERY

THE LIGHTHOUSE

WHISPERING
COVE

The town center

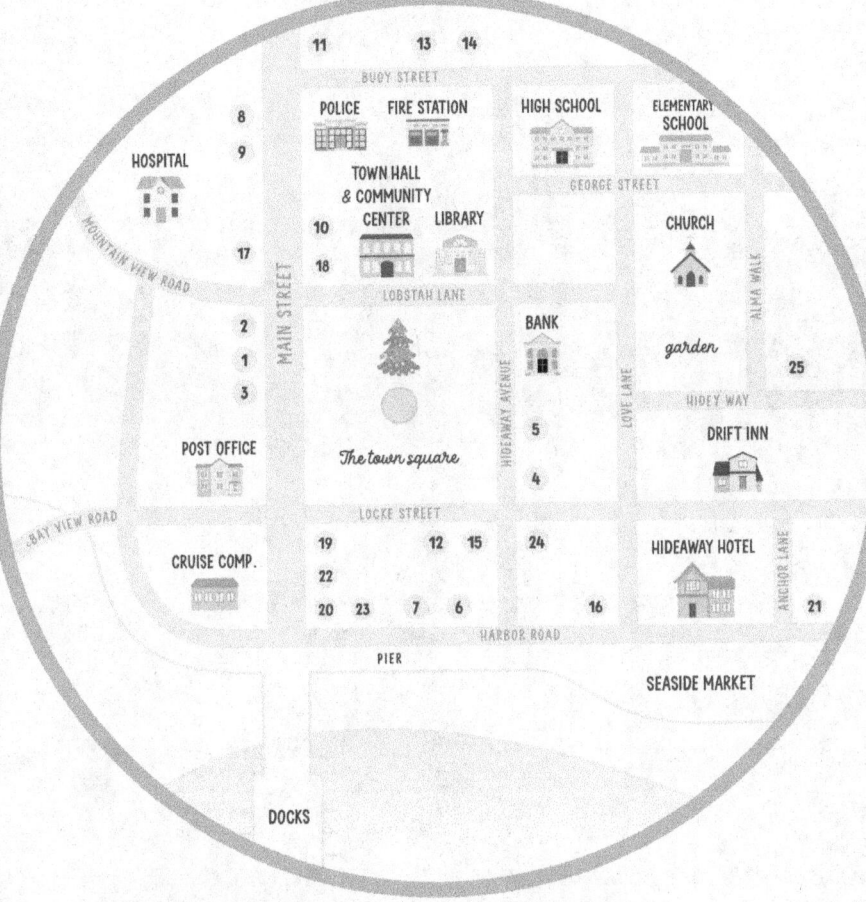

1   LOVE AT FIRST SIP (CAFE)
2   HIDDEN ITALY (RESTAURANT)
3   MAKING WHOOPIE (BAKERY)
4   HARD TO FIND (BOOKSTORE)
5   CHRISTMAS WONDERLAND (POP-UP STORE)
6   HOOK, WINE AND SINKER (RESTAURANT)
7   THE SHORE THING (BAR/RESTAURANT)
8   THE PERFECT PACKAGE (ADULT TOY STORE)
9   SCENTS AND SENSIBILITY (PERFUME SHOP)
10   THE WILDE KETTLE (TEA SHOP)
11   HIDEAWAY GROCER (GENERAL STORE)
12   PAPER MOON (OFFICE SUPPLIES)
13   LOBSTAH LIFTS (GYM)

14   HIDEAWAY CLINIC
15   HIDEAWAY TREASURES (GIFT SHOP)
16   THE CHOWDER HOUSE RULES (RESTAURANT)
17   ALMANAC (TOWN PAPER)
18   KIPPIS (SMALL BAR)
19   THE SWEETEST THING (CANDY STORE)
20   BEAUTY PARLOR
21   SALT & EMBER (RESTAURANT)
22   HOUSE OF PEARL (CLOTHING BOUTIQUE)
23   THE MASTER BAITERS (BAIT & TACKLE SHOP)
24   HAMMERTIME HARDWARE
25   OFF THE BEATEN PATH (ADVENTURE COMPANY)

THE HOLIDAY FAKERS

EVIE ALEXANDER

EMLIN
PRESS

First Published in Great Britain 2025 by Emlin Press

ISBN (eBook) 978-1-914473-85-2

ISBN (Print) 978-1-914473-86-9

ISBN (Audiobook) 978-1-914473-87-6

A CIP catalogue record for this book is available from the British Library.

www.emlinpress.com

EMLIN
PRESS

For Enni Amanda

ALSO BY EVIE ALEXANDER

THE KINLOCH SERIES

Highland Games

Hollywood Games

Kissing Games

Musical Games

Wedding Games

Christmas Games

THE FOXBROOKE SERIES

One Night in Foxbrooke

Love ad Lib

An Unholy Affair

The Upper Crush

The Love Position

Christmas off Script

One Night Only

Righting Mr Wrong

Under the Influencer

Foxbrooke Extras

By Evie Alexander and Kelly Kay

EVIE & KELLY'S HOLIDAY DISASTERS SERIES

Cupid Calamity

Cookout Carnage

Christmas Chaos

Get Evie's books in all formats as well as special offers, early releases, and exclusive deals direct from her website:

www.eviealexanderbooks.com

CHAPTER 1

PIPER

"*B*rody King and Secret New Woman Caught Loved Up at Hipster Hangout!" screams the Google Alert on my phone.

My thumb moves faster than you can say *clickbait*, but when the photos accompanying the headline flash onto the screen, my heart slams to a stop.

Whuhhht?

The chaos of the Brooklyn coffee shop is drowned out by the roaring in my ears.

I can't breathe.

The world around me shatters, crashing me into a new reality. One where Brody King, famous model, infamous actor, and the man who walked out of my life twelve years ago, is loved up with ... me?

"Piper, you okay?"

The barista's dark brows are slanted with concern.

I gape at her.

"Bad news?"

Shoving my phone away, I force the corners of my mouth up. My fake smile doesn't work, because she immediately thrusts the empty coffee cup with my name on it behind her at a colleague, then leans forward.

"What the hell happened to you?"

I move closer, my thick scarf toppling a pile of cellophane-wrapped Christmas cookies at the edge of the counter.

"What's the date?" I whisper urgently.

"December thirteenth. Have you missed an appointment?"

"Do I look the same to you?"

I spin in a circle, my purse swinging wildly, knocking one of the cookies to the floor.

"Uh..."

I rescue the cookie and pop back up again. "Do I look any different?"

"I don't think so?"

"Are you sure?"

I turn again, slower this time, like I'm my five-year-old niece showing off a new outfit.

Her nose wrinkles. "Did you do something with your hair?"

I shake my head, then a flash of adrenaline shoots through me, stronger than any caffeine.

"Wait a minute. Do elves exist? Wizards? For real? I mean *really* real."

Her eyes snap wide. "No, no, definitely not. You got lost down another online rabbit hole?"

I scan her face. "Is the world the same as yesterday?"

"That's kind of a deep question. It's not possible for it to be exactly the—"

"Hey! This gonna take all day?"

I whip around at the biting tone of the woman standing behind me.

"Sorry. I—I'm sorry," I say, then turn back to my favorite barista as I fumble in my purse for my wallet.

She leans in, folds her hand over mine, and gives me a sympathetic smile.

"It's on the house," she says quietly, then yells over her shoulder, "don't forget the extra cinnamon!"

"Thank you," I manage, my eyes prickling at her kindness, then push a ten-dollar bill into the tip jar before she can stop me.

It's lunchtime, and the place is filled with worker bees. They jostle one another like they're in a roller derby as they hurry inside, stand impatiently in line, then rush back out into the cold with steaming coffee and the panini of the day. Pigeons flap and fight over dropped crumbs on the icy sidewalk.

Grabbing my gingerbread latte, I weave through the press of bodies and find a free booth at the back. I slide to the far end, facing the wall, and pull out my phone. No one can see me, yet I still cup my free hand over the screen as I stare at the images.

A photo of me exiting Espresso Yourself, smiling. I know exactly when this picture was taken. My fantasy drawing of an elvish warrior had just gone viral last week. Well, fifty-seven likes and ten comments *is* pretty memorable to me.

But who snapped it? And why? Do I have a stalker?

In the next photo, Brody is going into the shop. He's got a baseball cap pulled low over his face, but I would recognize his mouth and the line of his jaw anywhere. And then there's one of the two of "us" embracing right outside.

Which didn't happen. Not in *this* universe, anyway.

My heart is still pounding in my chest, but I'm seated, so it doesn't matter how jelly-like my legs are. I gaze at the pictures playing *spot the difference*. The woman he's hugging is dressed in a red coat and brown hat and boots, my exact clothes.

Hold the front door.

3

I run my fingers through my wavy blonde hair, checking where it ends, then consider the length of my coat. The one the girl's wearing definitely falls an inch lower on her legs, and her hair is a fraction shorter than mine.

Now that I've started analyzing, I can't stop. The woman's standing on her tiptoes to wrap her arms around Brody's neck, and he's bending down. Unless he's grown since I last saw him, she's definitely smaller than I am.

My breath rushes out, and I sag into the banquette seat like a deflated red balloon. It's just a coincidence that Brody came in to my favorite coffee shop with his latest squeeze, who happens to have blonde hair and almost the same clothes and bag as I do.

And because the photographer didn't get a good shot of her, he hung around, saw me and thought we were the same person.

See? Perfect sense.

I close my eyes with relief and take a sip of my latte, letting the flavors transport me to my happy place—my family home in Hideaway Harbor, Maine. Mom's cinnamon cookies are cooling on a rack, and Dad has just brewed a pot of coffee.

Sighing happily at the memory, I gulp my drink, then choke as it goes down the wrong pipe. I slap a hand over my mouth, dropping the cup, and cough violently, coffee spraying through my splayed fingers and splattering across the table.

My eyes are streaming, my lungs heaving as I struggle to suck in air before coughing again. My chest burns, my cheeks are on fire, and I'm wheezing and hacking like a donkey.

A hand appears, holding a pile of napkins, each finger weighed down with massive gold rings. I snatch a couple of napkins and cover my mouth as I take in my rescuer. He's a short man in his sixties, with thinning hair dyed a reddish-black and slicked back over his head. I clock his camel-colored coat and brown silk scarf as he pats the surface of the table. He looks like he's just stepped out of a 1970s mafia movie.

"Thank you," I manage, finally getting control of myself.

"No problem," he replies in a nasal accent, then slides into the seat across from me and extends a hand. "Marvin DeVille. You can call me Marv."

I take it, wondering again if I've dropped into a parallel world where weird shit just keeps on happening. "Uh … Piper."

He nods, not looking the least bit surprised. "You're perfect. Even cuter IRL. And let's stick with the minimal makeup. Right on brand." He grins, revealing four gold teeth, two of which have diamonds embedded in them. "This is gonna be great!"

I blink. "What's going to be great?"

He glances over my shoulder, toward the entrance of the coffee shop, and his eyes light up. "Right on time!"

Marv stands again, his arm outstretched, a smile so wide it looks almost painful.

Scooting to the edge of my seat, I peer around the corner, my heart leaping into my throat as Brody strides toward us like a dark angel. His broad shoulders are hunched, and his face is partly obscured by a black hoodie, but it's not enough to hide how movie-star hot he is.

Oh my god. He's here.

His glittering deep brown eyes are fixed on Marv, promising vengeance, but then they descend on me and narrow with a furious intensity.

I scurry back into the booth, hitting the far wall with a thud as my pulse pounds in my ears. I've had plenty of daydreams about bumping into Brody since I moved to Brooklyn, but in them, I was always poised and confident, never sideswiped and covered in gingerbread latte.

Brody slams his hands down on the table and leans toward me.

"What the hell do you think you're doing?" he snaps, his tone low and harsh.

My mouth opens, but my brain has taken my ability to speak and left the building.

It's all too much. *He's* too much. I'm not prepared to have the living, breathing Brody King up in my business after all these years. Sure, I may have a Google Alert set for his name, filtered to catch only the big stuff, but it's one thing keeping tabs on an old friend from the safe distance of curated headlines, and quite another to have him here, in the flesh, stealing all my air.

A nervous, stammering laugh slips from my lips, cutting off with a squeak as he leans closer.

"Is this a fucking joke to you?"

My head whips from side to side. I still have no idea what's going on, but I've never seen Brody this enraged before. I struggle to reconcile the controlled, composed person he was back in Hideaway Harbor, even when everything was going wrong, with *this.*

Marv pats him on the shoulder. "Hey, kid, it's all good." His gaze darts around like he's assessing for threats. "C'mon, sit down." He steers the much bigger Brody into the booth, then slides in next to him, blocking his exit.

Brody sits directly across from me, his hands clasped on the table, knuckles white.

"How much?" he asks, as if he can't even bear to look at me.

"What?"

"*How. Much. Did. He. Pay. You?*" Brody enunciates each word like I'm a toddler.

Hang on. He thinks *I'm* part of whatever the hell is going on?

"And how much of *my money* will it take for you to go away?" he continues.

Fingers trembling, I reach into my purse.

Brody exhales sharply and shakes his head. "You're seriously going to write out the number? Un-fucking-believable."

6

"Take a breath, bud," Marv says, turning the rings on his left hand like they're the number wheels on a combination lock. "Be cool."

I take out my phone and show Brody the screen, pointing to the picture of him and the woman. "That's not me."

He huffs again. "No shit, Sherlock."

Fury burns in my belly, spreading up into my chest. I can't figure out if I want to scream, burst into tears, or punch him in his sanctimonious face.

"F-fuck you."

His eyes widen.

"Fuck you," I repeat, my anger fueling me. "Get out of my face and out of *my* coffee shop. Fuck off all the way to Fucksville. And when you get there, keep going."

"Excuse me?"

I brace as the image of Brody I've carried all these years shatters in front of me. I don't know this guy. He's a cold stranger, staring at me in disbelief behind the mask of a familiar face.

Inhaling deeply through gritted teeth, I attempt to keep my voice steady.

"I found out about these photos ten minutes ago, and have no *idea* what's going on. And now, because *you're* so famous and important, *my* face is all over the internet."

I'm shaking so badly that the phone slips from my grip and falls onto the table.

Brody stares blankly at me, frozen.

"I have a career, friends, my own *happy* life," I say. "The last thing I want is to be famous, or *infamous*, because of you."

There's a flicker in his expression, as if my words have touched a nerve, and guilt needles my gut. My words are a low blow, but I'm still hurting too much to take them back.

Then Brody's head slowly swivels toward Marv, like a serial-killer cyborg zeroing in on his prey.

Marv's hands shoot up in surrender. "Bud—"

"You're fired." Brody's voice cuts like a knife through the hum of voices around us.

Marv ignores him.

"You told me to think outside the box," he says, his words clipped and urgent. "Well, I didn't just think. I brainstormed. I had a cerebral cyclone. A mother-fucking thought tornado. I tore that box to shreds, and then the sun burst through the clouds, and I could *see!*"

I blink at the marketing-executive-on-steroids declaration, already picturing how I could draw it as an infographic.

Marv stabs his index finger in the air, emphasizing each point. "I'm talkin' rainbows, choirs of angels, the aurora-freak-ing-borealis."

In my mind I'm now adding colors to the drawing as my imagination takes me away from the weirdness of my reality.

"And guess who's shining down from heaven with the answer to all our prayers?"

Suddenly all his fevered attention is on me.

"*She* is."

"Who *are* you?" The words stumble out like I'm a one-line extra in a bad soap.

"Marv DeVille. Brody's agent." He flashes me a toothpaste-commercial smile and extends his arm towards me. "But you can call me Marv."

This time, I don't take his hand.

"*Ex* agent," Brody growls, and all the tiny hairs on my arms lift in excitement.

"But why would you dress Brody's girlfriend up like me?"

"I don't have a girlfriend," Brody mutters.

My heart skips several beats and now I don't trust myself to reply without it coming out as another squeak.

Why, oh *why*, does he still have such an effect on me? He's not the man I remember *or* who I've built up in all my fantasies. The real Brody King is an arrogant, surly, ego-centric asshole.

I'm saved from having to speak by Marv, who addresses me as if presenting a pitch.

"Here's the deal, Piper. Can I call you Piper?"

He doesn't give me a chance to respond.

"Great, thanks, Piper. So, here's the lowdown. No time for an NDA, and besides, you're like family to Brody."

I *am*? Then why hasn't he reached out to me in the last twelve years?

"This is inner-circle shit, Piper, and we trust you. The—"

"Marv," Brody cuts him off. "I said, you're fired. It's time for all of us to get up, walk away, and pretend this never happened."

"Hey," I say sharply. "I think it's about time you told me what the hell is going on and why I've been dragged into it."

Brody opens his mouth, then shuts it again, his perfectly soft lips now a hard line before he slumps back into the seat like a petulant teenager.

"Thanks, Piper," Marv says, as if we're the only adults in the room. "The thing is, Brody's been going through some ... er, difficulties. It's been having a suboptimal effect on his career. Are you aware of any of this?"

I sense Brody's eyes on me, his unspoken question hanging in the air: *How much do I know?*

The answer? A lot.

"I'm not interested in the lives of celebrities," I reply, my cheeks heating at the half-truth. Right now, I'm pretending Brody is just an old family friend, not someone whose face is used to sell gossip magazines at the bodega down the block.

Marv lets out a breath and smiles, then leans closer. "There's this job. A TV series. I've hustled hard to even get his name in the mix. It's different from anything he's done before and he wants it more than anything. Ever."

My eyes flick to Brody, wondering how a job could be the most important thing in his life.

He stares at the table, his shoulders hunched like he's trying to disappear.

"The showrunners," Marv continues, "they're not convinced. Think he's a loose cannon. Unreliable."

Gaze still lowered, Brody shakes his head.

No matter how angry I am, my stomach still twists. Growing up, he was the sweetest, most—

"The clock's ticking, Piper, and that's why he needs *you*. We've tried everything else to mend his image and it ain't worked. So I ran a full-brand audit, flipped the narrative funnel, spitballed until the walls were dripping with ideas, and then—bam! It hit me like a freight train of authenticity."

He slaps the center of his chest.

"We don't need more glam. We don't need another A-lister girlfriend or a TikTok apology tour. We need *roots*. Nostalgia. Americana! We need Brody King reconnected with his origin story. And that means Hideaway Harbor—and *you*. You're a slice of good ol' American sweetness and charm that we need to rub all over Brody until he shines again."

And I'm gone, imagining rubbing against Brody. The heat of his body. The friction between us creating sparks that turn into flames. Our inconvenient clothes no longer exist. They're burned to ash by the fire of our desire. We're naked. Rubbing. He—

"It won't take much, just a few well-orchestrated photo ops and plenty of candid shots from fans."

I'm frozen, horrified at where my thoughts just took me. I don't want to fantasize about Brody. I want to settle down with a nice guy. Someone who's reliable. Present. Not some overpaid actor who's so attractive they don't need to bother with kindness and respect.

"It'll be in the bag by the time the Christmas decorations

come down," Marv continues. "It has to be, since they start shooting in the beginning of January. We've got a good window of time as you're home for the holidays longer than usual this year."

"How do you know my travel plans? How do you know *me*?"

Suddenly I don't feel safe. At all.

Marv shrugs, like it's nothing that he's been stalking me. "Harper's socials."

"My *sister*?"

"And Brody."

What the—? My gaze shoots to him, expecting him to tell me Marv's talking shit.

He doesn't. But his cheeks darken, and a muscle ticks in his jaw.

"Brody's told me about his childhood in Hideaway Harbor, and your family. Hell, he's even got a—"

"Marv!" Brody half-shouts.

Marv seems unperturbed.

"I've booked you a suite at The Hideaway Hotel with two rooms, so you'll have your own space," he continues confidently. "And I'll be on hand with my assistant and a stylist—"

"Stop." I hold up my hands to halt the barrage of insanity. "You want me to go back to Hideaway this Christmas *with Brody* and pretend we're *dating*?" My voice is rising in pitch. Soon only dogs will be able to hear it. "Lie to my *family*?"

"We can fill them in if you want?" Marv replies like it's no biggie.

"None of this is happening," Brody cuts in. "Marv, I don't need you, and I don't need this. I can make the deal on my own."

Marv raises his eyebrows. "No, you can't. You don't have any of their contact details, and I'm the one who's been handling the negotiations. And even if you do get in touch with them, how's it going to look when you don't have an agent? You think it'll be easy to find another one this quickly? Sure, a new, hungry one. But you won't get one of the big boys."

Brody shifts in his seat but doesn't reply.

"And besides, you need to get away from the city. Take some time off. Reconnect with your roots—"

Brody lets out a huff and shakes his head.

Hurt is metabolizing into anger inside me. Growing up, Brody was practically one of the family, but then he left the moment he could, and never came back. Not even for my brother's wedding where he was meant to be the best man.

Was that all my family was to him? Just a convenience? Before moving onto the bigger, better, celebrity life he has now?

"Piper." Marv turns back to me. "You're in, right?"

"W-what? No, I most definitely am *not* in!"

"I'll make it worth your while," Marv continues. "How much do you want? A couple grand? Plus all expenses, new wardrobe, nice presents for the fam?"

Grabbing my purse with shaking hands, I shuffle out of the booth.

Marv stands. "There must be something you want?"

I don't dare risk glancing at Brody.

"I need to get back to work," I mutter, my words thick in my throat.

Suddenly, I remember with a shock that I'd only come to Espresso Yourself for a quick pick-me-up before the big meeting.

Shit! I'm going to be late!

Marv takes my arm as I stride off, stopping me in my tracks.

"Call me. Any time." He thrusts a business card into my hand.

I turn around, meeting Brody's gaze.

He lets out a heavy breath. "Piper ..."

I wait for him to finish, time ticking in my head like a bomb countdown as I imagine my colleagues filing into the conference room.

"Look, I ... it's just ... I don't ..."

I shake my head.

"Good to see you, Brody," I say coldly. "Been a while."

Then I turn away, striding out of the coffee shop as fast as I can.

Once outside, I break into a run.

CHAPTER 2

PIPER

The biting winter wind burns my cheeks as I sprint down the sidewalk, weaving around people like it's an Olympic sport. I can't think about Brody right now. Grabbing a coffee was supposed to take ten minutes, not twenty. It was meant to clear my head before the very secret, no agenda, company-wide meeting.

Closing down? Buyout? Diversification? Stanley finally retiring?

Possibilities circle my brain like runners on a track with no finish line. The only thing that makes perfect sense is my boss tapping into his 401(k) and finally taking that cruise he's always talked about.

The thought of him leaving is bittersweet. Stanley Parker is one of America's finest, a good-hearted family man who took a chance on me straight out of college and has done his best to keep the business he inherited afloat during times no one could've predicted.

I slow my pace as the brick building comes into view,

Parker & Overton Office Products—the first letter of each word far larger than all the rest—painted across the entire side in white over eighty years ago, now chipped and fading.

I shake my head. How did they not think that name through? The brown "POOP" building is famous throughout Brooklyn, and even though Mr. Overton left the business entirely to the Parkers in the fifties, the name never changed.

I take the stairs to the second floor. It's quicker and more reliable than the elevator. The only incentive to step inside that creaking metal box is the hope that the fire department gets called when you get stuck, and that your rescuer is single, drop-dead gorgeous, and asks you on a date.

Of course, if that hunky firefighter were to break up with you after a few months, you'd better not risk getting stuck again unless you want him thinking you did it on purpose to win him back.

Which I would never do, and definitely didn't happen. Okay?

Tentatively pulling open the conference room door, I step in. Luckily, the meeting hasn't started yet. I scan the room, checking for any unfamiliar faces.

None. Is that a good or a bad thing?

A moment later, the door opens behind me, and Stanley Parker enters with his oldest son, also called Stanley. I don't think they mean to dress the same, but they're almost always wearing beige slacks and white button-downs. With their identical bald spots and rosy cheeks, they look like twins separated by thirty years.

The room falls silent as they make their way to the front.

This feels bad. *Really* bad.

Stanley Parker Sr. gives us a confident smile, but his fingers twist in front of him. He shoves his hands into his pockets and takes a breath.

"I know you're all wondering what this is about, so I won't

drag it out. I'm retiring, and Stanley is stepping in to take my place."

A collective breath is released, then the room breaks into spontaneous applause.

Thank God. My job's safe.

Stanley raises his hands, quieting us. "But you know, folks, the market is changing, and times are tough."

Uh-oh.

"I'm not gonna lie. It's been challenging, but Stanley and I have been determined to keep the company going."

I glance at my colleagues, a sea of tense postures and frowns.

"And to do that," Stanley continues, "we're partnering with another company."

I swallow as alarm stabs at my stomach. A merger usually means half of us will lose our jobs.

"I don't want anyone to worry. This is a good thing," Stanley says, raising his voice above the murmurs rippling around the room. "There will be generous voluntary redundancy packages on the table, and a six-month transition period during which we'll work side by side to figure out the best fit for the new company."

Six months to fight for my job while sitting across from someone doing exactly the same thing. *Ugh.*

"What's the other company?" someone asks.

Stanley smiles. "Turner's Office Supply Solutions."

I stop breathing. This can't be happening. Not them.

Not *him*.

People murmur around me as the full horror of the situation sinks in.

Come January, I'll be fighting for my job against Colin Turner, the owner's son.

And my ex-boyfriend.

. . .

"Piper? Can I have a word?"

My head jerks up from the computer screen.

Stanley Parker Sr. is standing at the entrance to my cubicle, a perk of an unintentional promotion after the lead graphic designer retired two years ago and was never replaced. No hike in salary, but hey, have some screens around your desk!

He lifts his chin toward my computer. "Working on the new printer ad?"

"Yes." I follow his gaze back to the stock photo of smartly dressed women standing around an office printer, laughing like it's more hilarious than salad.

"Looking great!" he says enthusiastically. "High energy!"

I clench my teeth as I formulate my response. Sure, the printer is apparently so advanced it could cook a three-course meal and pick your kids up from daycare, if you could program it correctly, but this ad is generic and dull.

I may have the skills and creativity to match my job title, but by the time my work has passed through three layers of corporate approval, it's been sanitized of anything original. So, I have to put my digital stylus aside and focus my energy on vetoing the use of Comic Sans.

I force a smile. "Thank you. And congratulations on your retirement."

His face lights up. "It's been a long time coming, but I'm excited now."

He hesitates, then pulls a folded piece of paper from the pocket of his slacks. "I'm here because I want to talk to you about something very important … It's not just me that's retiring."

"But you said there would only be voluntary redundancies!" I stammer before I can stop myself.

His eyes widen, and his hands fly up. "No, no, this is a good thing for you, Piper! The last thing I want for the company is to see you go."

I slump in my seat, breathing heavily.

He looks stricken. "I'm so sorry I gave that impression. It's Stanley who's retiring."

"Your son?"

"No, the other Stanley."

My mind goes blank. How many Stanleys *are* there?

"Stanley the Stapler."

Oh yes. The company mascot I drew a few years ago—a project that had *literal* legs when I was then tasked with creating a full-body costume—and given the dubious honor of wearing it at the company summer barbecue.

"I wanted to recognize your work for us, Piper," Stanley continues, fiddling with the paper in his hands. He lowers his voice. "And I also thought it might strengthen your position after the merger."

I nod and he beams.

"So, I wanted to be the first to tell you. We have a new company mascot."

Unfolding the piece of paper, he holds it out to me. "You! Meet Piper the Pen!"

I stare at the picture. It looks like one of those inflatable tube men you see outside car dealerships, with a manic smile and flailing arms. But this one has bright yellow hair that sticks out like overcooked spaghetti after an electric shock, and eyelashes that reach halfway up its forehead.

"My granddaughter drew it," Stanley says proudly.

No shit ...

"You'll have to tidy it up a bit. But don't lose any of the energy. You know, she worked from a photo of you!"

Is this how people see me? No wonder I can't find a boyfriend.

Stanley pushes the picture into my hands. "Congratulations!"

"Thanks," I manage, my mouth dry.

"Put the printer job aside and work on this today," he says, grinning. "It'll be fun. Help take your mind off things."

He leans in, like we're part of some secret office clique. "Boss's orders!"

Another rosy-cheeked smile, then he's off, leaving me caught between a printer, a pen mascot, and the looming battle with my ex for my job.

"ARE you sure they'll only keep one graphic designer?" my best friend, Mia demands over the phone that evening. "The other company will bring in their own clients, so they'll need the extra resources when you merge. And surely, *He-Who-Shall-Not-Be-Named* will take a management position?"

I haven't moved from my couch since I got home from work. I need to pee, and I'm starving, but my body feels too numb to move.

"I don't know. Maybe?" My voice is drained of any energy. "Colin isn't interested in the admin side of things. He really loves drawing, just like me. Do you remember how we met at that conference and bonded over a game of Pictionary?"

"Yes. All very cute, but he still had the gall to leave you for—"

"No ..." I groan. "I can't believe I forgot his new girlfriend is the receptionist at his dad's company."

"That's currently the least of your problems."

"What do you mean?"

"Uh ... Isn't there another Colin-related issue you're forgetting?"

A chill runs down my spine. Mia's right. There's something very important that's been momentarily buried under the chaos of today. An elephant hiding in my one-bedroom that I can't yet see.

"What you promised your mom?"

The elephant leaps out from behind the drapes and trumpets loudly.

Oh god.

I make a strangled sound as the full magnitude of the situation hits me.

A boyfriend.

I promised Mom I was bringing one home for Christmas.

"At least you never gave her Colin's name."

"I thought I'd have time to find a replacement," I wheeze.

"You still can! I have faith!"

"What have I done?" I wail.

"Put other's feelings before your own as per usual," Mia says breezily. "And we all know what your mom's like. The more her excitement grows, the harder it is to let her down."

"But what am I going to dooooo?!"

"Okay. We need to prioritize here. Strategize. One problem at a time."

Mia's words rattle out like she's calling the Kentucky Derby.

"First, we need to get you a boyfriend or lay the groundwork for crushing your mom's hopes and dreams to dust—"

"Gee, thanks—"

"Then we need a plan to make you indispensable at work. A way to make you golden. Teflon. Un-freaking-touchable. Boyfriend first. Have you gotten stuck in the elevator yet to catfish that hot firefighter who ghosted you after three dates?"

"Didn't work," I mumble. "He went back to the truck and sent his colleague to help me."

"Was *he* single?"

"Wife and four kids."

"Dammit. And still no luck on the dating apps?"

"No, and it's too late now. Christmas is almost here. I'd look unhinged if I asked a guy to come home for the holidays with me on the first date."

"There must be someone you can find! You're the best! Hot, clever, kind. What the hell is wrong with city guys?"

I shrug, even though she can't see me. I've been steadily losing confidence over the last couple of years. Maybe there *is* something wrong with me.

"I've even stopped telling my dates about my drawing," I tell her.

"Why?"

I don't immediately reply. I haven't told Mia everything about my experiences sharing my art online. I once made the mistake of posting some pieces to an art forum, only to be told my work wasn't original, that it was just derivative "fan art."

And then there was the time I went with Colin to an artist's collective meeting in Brooklyn he was part of. That was even worse because I could see the look in people's eyes when they judged my work as somehow lesser, just because it wasn't like what any of them did.

So I settle for, "I don't want them thinking I'm some elf-loving weirdo."

Mia grunts her frustration loudly in my ear. "Own it! You're insanely talented. And anyway, there are people online who love what you do. Surely you can see that?"

A handful of them, sure, but there are so many more haters out there …

I take a fortifying breath. "Colin told me I should direct my talent elsewhere."

"Where? Staplers and photocopiers?"

"Animals. He really loves dogs, so he thought I should do pet portraits."

"*Pet* portraits?"

"So I did."

"Wait … what?"

"Hang on, I'll show you." I pull up the picture I drew shortly after Colin ended our relationship, a snarling wolf chasing him. I quickly crop out the left-hand side of the image, and send it to her.

A ping sounds, followed by a raucous screech of laughter.

"Oh Piper, that's hilarious!"

I smile for the first time in hours and gaze at the uncropped image of Brody as a warrior elf, standing with his arms crossed as he watches his pet send Colin packing.

Should I tell Mia about what happened today?

"Did you send it to him?"

I gasp. "What?!"

"Colin. Did you send the picture to him?"

Oh.

Relief rushes out with my breath. "No. It was just for me."

"Well, that's a missed opportunity. You should at least post it to your art account."

"Hmm," I reply noncommittally. I've never posted any of the pictures I've drawn of Brody. They're my guilty secret, and I don't want the world to know he's been my muse since I was a teenager.

Once, when I was fifteen, a sketch I'd done of him fell out of my bag at school and was found under a desk. Luckily, it wasn't good enough for people to realize it was Brody, and I denied drawing it. But the crawling fear and anxiety caused by the laughter and cruel comments made me determined that no one would ever see one of my Brody drawings again, accidentally or otherwise.

At least now I know he's turned into an asshole and I can move on from this silly crush …

"So, what are you going to do about a non-existent boyfriend?"

"Huh?"

Mia huffs. "Should I tell your mom he's sick? His granny's on her deathbed?"

"She'll only want to send a care package."

"You could just say you broke up?"

I rub my temples, feeling a headache coming on. "It doesn't matter whether I say he dumped me or I dumped him. It'll have the same result. She'll fuss over me, then drag me to every Christmas party in town to set me up with any single guy under fifty."

"She'll probably force you to Eileen's so she can offer her advice."

Closing my eyes, I groan. According to her and my mom, it's their civic duty to give love a helping hand.

"There's no way I'm subjecting myself to that. Last year she tried to set me up with the guy who sat behind me in English class in eighth grade. He used to throw spitballs at me."

We fall silent, but it's a comfortable silence. Mia and I have been best friends since forever, and even though I left Hideaway Harbor and she stayed, our friendship is just as strong as it's ever been.

She lets out a breath. "You don't think that this might be the universe telling you to finally go freelance?"

Forgetting she can't see me, I shake my head.

"Better money, more control, more interesting projects?"

I score my fingernails across my scalp, trying to relieve the tension.

"It's not worth the risk in this market." My voice sounds flat and empty. "Not when so many people in my industry are out of work and the rent on my place keeps going up."

She doesn't respond.

"I've just worked so hard to get where I am. I don't want to throw it all away."

"Okay!" Mia says brightly, knowing when to move on. "Let's brainstorm. How can you make yourself indispensable?"

My heart swells with love for her.

"I honestly don't know right now. It's going to take something pretty spectacular for them to see me as more valuable than the boss's kid."

"When do you have to start working with him?"

"New Year."

"Hmm, we can put our heads together over the holidays. You still coming on Friday?"

"Yeah."

I scroll through my apps to my sister's social feed. No wonder Brody's agent knew everything about me. There are photos documenting Harper's last visit, complete with every detail of my everyday life and future travel plans, as if the whole world should be as interested as she is.

"Great. I'll pop in and help soften the blow if you don't find a boyfriend between now and then."

We say our goodbyes, then I pull up the pictures of Brody hugging someone dressed like me. Marv wants me and Brody to fake a relationship, however Brody seemed to like that idea about as much as a hole in the head.

My phone pings, and my heart sinks when I see who it is.

> Mom: YOU MUST TELL ME IF YOUR BEAU
> HAS ANY DIETARY RESTRICTIONS XOXO

My mom lives for my happiness, and I want to protect hers. It's a dynamic that landed me here—promising a boyfriend for Christmas like a gift I now can't deliver.

> Mom: AND EILEEN WANTS TO MEET HIM!

> Mom: EVERYONE WANTS TO MEET THE
> LUCKY GUY!

> Mom: LOVE YOU, HONEY! XOXO

I slip my hand in my coat pocket, feeling the sharp corner of Marv's business card. I need to stop thinking about his crazy idea and stop thinking about Brody. So, I force my mind back to the problems at work: how to sell a printer, how to avoid being the company mascot, how to save my job.

An idea jolts through me like an electric shock.

Fingers trembling, and mild hysteria fizzing in my veins, I take out the card and dial the number.

It connects after one ring.

"Marv DeVille speaking."

"Hi, it's, uh ... Piper."

"Piper! Hey! Great to hear from you! You been thinking about my idea? Got an answer for us?"

I bite the inside of my cheek. "Um, yeah. I'll do it—"

"Yes!" I swear I can practically hear him fist-pump.

"On one condition."

"Name your price."

"I don't want any money."

"You don't?"

"No. I want Brody to do something for me in return for me being his ... his fake girlfriend."

"Anything. What can he do for you Piper?"

I tell him.

Silence.

Then Marv exhales. "O-kay ... Let me run it by the big man and get back to you."

I stare at my phone, my pulse thudding in my ears.

There's no way Brody would agree to this.

Right?

CHAPTER 3

BRODY

"She said *what?*"

Cara, Marv's assistant, takes a step back, her face paling.

I raise my hands in surrender. "Sorry. It's just been—"

"No, I'm sorry," she cuts in, her red eyes refilling with tears. "I would never have—"

"You're sorry, he's sorry, I'm sorry," Marv interrupts testily. "But this pity party ain't gonna solve the bigger problem."

He steers Cara to the front door of my apartment.

"Why don't you get some fresh New York air, huh? Do a bit of Christmas shopping. Use my card. Treat yourself. I'll message you when we're done."

Marv pulls her woolen hat snug over her blonde hair and wraps her scarf around her neck like a protective dad. Even though my anger still simmers, I see what drew me to Marv when I was eighteen and what Cara sees in him too: a steady, fatherly presence neither of us had growing up.

Cara's gaze flicks to me, uncertain. I've only known her for two years, ever since Marv realized he couldn't handle me on his own and hired an assistant, but she already feels like a little sister. She reminds me so much of Harper, the youngest Locke sibling, and my inner big brother steps up.

"It's okay," I say. "I promise I won't harm a hair on his head."

Marv gives her a broad smile and smooths a hand over his thinning locks.

"Can't afford to lose any more!" he jokes.

The corners of her mouth twitch, and the tightness in my stomach eases.

"Okay," she says. "I won't go far, and if you need anything, just call."

Marv hustles her out of the apartment.

"Yeah, yeah, all good. Go have fun."

As soon as he closes the door behind her, I'm on him.

"How could you use her like that?" I growl, keeping my voice low so Cara won't hear if she's listening outside. "It's one thing getting her to reply to emails pretending to be you—"

"I don't—"

"C'mon, Marv. She's polite and knows how to spell. You're fooling no one. But to dress her up as *Piper*? And not tell her why?" I shake my head. "That's fucked up, even for you."

He makes his way over to one of the giant leather couches, the tap-tap-tap of his Italian shoes on the parquet floor echoing around the open-plan space. His shoulders hunch as he sits, his posture signaling defeat.

Without an adversary, the fight leaves me too. I take a seat opposite him, the silence between us filled with police sirens, traffic noise, and all the other noises that make up the Big Apple soundscape. I once used to love it. It was the sign I was somewhere exciting, where dreams come true.

Now? It grates on my nerves.

"Look, I'm sorry, man. Genuinely." Marv rubs a hand across the deep grooves in his forehead.

"I just … I don't know. Panicked? Things have been snow-balling in a bad way, and it's a motherfucking avalanche of shitty press right now. This job … it's still possible, but we need a new story out there. Something good."

He's not wrong. My career is sliding into a chasm, and I can see the bottom I'm headed for. Soon, all I'll be offered are bit-parts. The low-rent thug who gets offed in the pilot episode, the guy who doesn't even get a name.

The job I want isn't a lead role, but it's different and complex. An opportunity to show what I can really do. But Marv's right. The chance of the showrunners wanting anything to do with me right now is slim-to-none.

"Bro, can I be real for a sec. Like, *really* real?" Marv's voice is hesitant.

I brace myself, a sick feeling settling in. I'm pretty sure I know exactly what he's going to say.

Marv takes my silence as an affirmation, leaning forward, his hands open.

"We've been together twelve years. That's longer than most marriages. I see your hunger, your talent, where you want to go, and who you want to be. But you're running on sand. There's no foundation because you won't deal with your past."

My jaw clenches, holding back emotions I don't even want to acknowledge.

"I know how much the Locke family means to you. How much Pi—"

The ferocity of my gaze cuts him off and I spring to my feet, wanting to run away. I'm still reeling from seeing her again yesterday. All those feelings I thought I'd buried, leaping out of the ground and smacking me in the face.

"The longer you leave this, the worse it's gonna get. The Lockes are family to you. They—"

I sit back down and hang my head. "It's been too long now," I manage, my voice scratchy and raw. "I'm too late."

"You're not. I've never met them, but I know they're good people. Sure, this fake-dating thing isn't real, but your relationship with the Lockes *is*."

"*Was*."

"You need to go back to Hideaway Harbor this Christmas. Yeah, I hope the good press will land you this gig, but that's not the most important reason. You need to remember who you are under all this famous actor crap. Right now, you're lost."

I shake my head, even though I know he's right. How the fuck did I get so caught up in the fame game that I let my true friends go?

My stomach twists like I've got an ulcer. I can't face Piper and her family after so long. I'd be like the prodigal son on steroids, and I doubt even the Lockes would celebrate my return.

"And anyway, Piper's on board."

Marv's words cut through the fog of regret and self-disgust, and my heart misses a beat.

Piper.

I clear my throat of the remorse that's clogging it and deflect.

"A printer? She wants me to advertise a fucking *printer*?"

Marv shrugs. "She works for an office supply company."

"Doing what?"

"Graphic design." He takes out his phone, jabs at the screen, then hands it to me. "She even drew the company mascot, Stanley the Stapler."

"Huh?"

Marv keeps talking, but I'm not taking any of it in. I'm just staring at the photo of Piper on the company's website. Her smile. Like she wants to be there. Is proud to be there. Has a purpose.

"They're in the Poop Building."

I tear my gaze from the phone. "The *what*?"

"You must know it. The big brown building with 'POOP' painted across the side?"

Marv throws his hands in the air at my confusion. "What the fuck does it matter, anyway? Just say yes, for Chrissakes."

"And how do you think that's going to help my reputation? My career? Standing next to a printer with a stupid grin on my face?"

Marv gets to his feet, pacing like he's got ants in his pants. "You won't *actually* do it. Just say you will. Once you get the job, you'll be on the other side of the world. It's not like she's gonna produce a contract. And even if she does, I'll find a loophole."

"No, I'm not lying to her."

"Then you'll do it?"

I stare back at Piper's face, my heart pounding so fast I think I might faint.

"You'll go back to Hideaway Harbor and fake-date her?"

Could I? The thought feels like madness. Like standing on the edge of a precipice with no parachute or safety net. And what would fake dating involve? Even the thought of holding Piper's hand makes my breath stutter to a stop.

"Brody?"

"I can't … We can't … I'm not sharing a room with her," I say decisively, even though my body thinks otherwise.

"I told ya, I've already booked rooms at the Hideaway Hotel. A few photo ops and a catch-up with old friends. It'll be a piece of Christmas cake."

Marv grabs his phone back from me and taps the screen. "Gotta call her."

"Who? Piper?"

But he's already stalking across the living space, the phone clamped to his ear and one arm outstretched behind him like he's already pushing me away.

"Hey, Piper? It's Marv. Brody's in."

Palms sweating, I jump to my feet and follow him, a million thoughts and questions running through my head: What's our backstory? Will we tell her family the truth? How are we getting to Hideaway? When are we leaving? Can I really do this?

It's just another acting job.

So why am I in full fight-or-flight mode with my mouth as dry as a desert and my heart racing at VO2 max?

"I need to talk to her," I say, the words feeling like gravel in my mouth.

Marv ignores my outstretched hand. "Yeah, yeah," he says into the phone. "Separate rooms."

At least we're on the same page about that. So why does the thought make my chest ache?

"You just need to act like you're into him in public," Marv continues. "Hold his hand and shit. Y'know, as if you like him."

The pain in my chest moves up into my throat. Piper doesn't even *like* me anymore?

What the fuck did you expect after the way you spoke to her?

"Nah, you don't have to kiss him … But if you want to?" Marv sounds hopeful.

I don't realize I'm holding my breath till I let it go at Marv's next words.

"Okay, no problem. I get it. Remember, you just need to *look* like you're into him. If you don't wanna hug him, I'll use Cara for those shots."

"Marv!" I hiss. "No!"

"Cara's my assistant." Marv pauses, and I strain to hear what Piper's saying. But the phone is pressed so hard against his ear I can't make out a word.

"She wasn't a part of it," he continues. "The photos online. Cara's a sweet kid, so go easy on her when you meet, okay? I'm the asshole here, not her."

Another pause, then Marv laughs. "Yeah, I know."

My foot taps impatiently on the wooden floor as I wave my hand in front of his face.

He frowns at me and turns away. "You got it ... yep ... yep ..."

Panic rises inside me. I'm so out of control of my own life right now.

"Give me the fucking phone, Marv!"

"Huh? Oh, don't worry about him," he says to Piper, like I'm a rugrat having a temper tantrum. "He'll be cool. Okay, speak—what?"

There's a beat, and Marv's eyes move to me, as if unwilling to acknowledge that I'm an integral part of this charade.

"Uh ... you sure?" Another pause. "Yep, okay."

He presses the phone against his chest, muffling the microphone. "She wants to talk to you. Don't fuck it up."

I shake my head, as if this situation isn't already totally fucked up.

He reluctantly passes me the phone, and I bring it to my ear. I can't hear anything on the other end.

"Brody?"

Adrenaline and guilt spear my heart at the sound of her voice, and my free hand tightens into a fist as I will myself to hold it together.

"Bro—"

"Yeah, I'm here."

Silence.

"Are you—"

"Look—"

"You go—"

32

"You speak—"

Fuck's sake! I repress a growl of frustration. How can this be so difficult?

Marv's in my face now, his palms upturned, his expression one of utter incredulity at my incompetence.

"Piper, I'm sorry," I say quickly. "I'll shut up and let you speak."

More silence, then she takes a breath. "I … I just want to check that you're okay with this."

Her voice is hesitant, and that makes me feel even shittier about myself and this whole ridiculous mess she's been shoved into.

"I'm fine," I reply, sounding anything but. "Don't worry about me."

Marv throws his hands in the air and stomps over to the window, staring at the street below. I wish he would just fuck off. It's impossible to have a conversation with him listening in.

"Should I buy you a ticket?" she asks. "For the train and the bus? Or should we hire a car?"

"I've got a car. I'll drive us."

Marv spins around. "Good idea. Me, Cara, and the stylist can ride with you, too."

"No, we're not fucking carpooling," I grit out.

"I don't think I can handle him for six hours," Piper says.

"You and me both."

"And we need to talk, to get our stories straight."

What does she mean by that? We're not going to tell her family we're faking it?

"Yeah, sure," I reply. "Can you message Marv with your address and what time to pick you up on the sixteenth?"

"Oh … okay."

I hear the hurt in her voice. What have I done now?

"Piper?"

"Yes?"

"Have I said something wrong? Not at the coffee shop, where I said everything wrong. I mean just now."

Again, there's a painful silence before she finally speaks.

"Am I not important enough to know your number?"

"What?"

"Well, you changed it years ago and didn't give any of us the new one. And now I have to go through Marv to get in touch with you?"

Oh fuck. "No! Of course you can have it. I just didn't know if you wanted me to have yours. Hang on. I'll message it to you now."

I don't wait for a reply, immediately bringing the phone down and sending her my contact details.

"Call me anytime you want," I say. "Okay?"

"Okay."

Christ, this conversation couldn't be any more stilted and awkward if we tried.

"I'm gonna go now," she says quietly. "I'll send you my address."

"Okay."

"Bye, Brody."

"Bye."

She hangs up and I stare at the phone screen.

A slow hand clap breaks the silence.

"And the Oscar *doesn't* go to … Brody Fucking King." Marv jabs his finger in my direction. "You'd better up your game when you get to Hideaway Harbor. You've got to sell it, or people will know it's fake, and you'll be in even deeper shit than you already are."

I head back to the couch and collapse onto it, simultaneously wired and exhausted. I feel my thirty-one years like they've been doubled. What the hell am I doing? Who even *am* I anymore?

The couch shifts as Marv sits down. "It's gonna be okay. I promise."

"You're still fired."

He pats my knee. "Yeah, yeah. Just wait till the New Year, huh? When you've got the job and everything's coming up freaking roses again."

I huff. If roses need shit to bloom, then my life's got more than enough right now.

My phone buzzes in my back pocket, and I pull it out.

Unknown: This is Piper. You can pick me up
the day after tomorrow at ten

Just under forty-eight hours till I see her again.

My heart's beating too fast, my mind racing with questions I'm not sure how to answer. Should I bring gifts for the Locke family? For Piper? What is she into now? Does she still draw? Outside of designing office company mascots, of course.

And what the fuck am I going to say to Ethan? *Hey, buddy! Sorry I missed being the best man at your wedding because I was doing some dumb fashion shoot. And shame I couldn't make the birth of your kid or your wife's funeral because I was too chickenshit to ask for time off.*

Nausea rolls in my stomach. I can't do this. I can't face him.

Wanting to block everything out, I close my eyes. But in the darkness, all I see are the tabloid headlines gleefully chronicling my fall from grace. Then Piper's face as I lived up to my reputation as an unpredictable asshole.

"The last thing I want is to be famous, or infamous, because of you."

Fuck. I need to apologize.

To her. Ethan. The whole Locke family.

Opening my eyes I gaze at the slate-gray clouds, wondering what the sky is like over Hideaway Harbor right now. What Ethan is doing. What his kid looks like.

Marv's right. Going back will give me closure. Then I can move on. Hopefully with the acting job of my dreams.

"Cara, sweetie, I need you to pick up some gifts when you're out, okay?" Marv's on his phone and pacing again. "For Brody to give Piper and her family."

"No," I say, rising to my feet. "I'll do it."

"Fifty to a couple hundred bucks each. Ask the assistants what are the most popular gifts this year."

I grab the phone from him. "Don't get anything. I can do it."

"You sure?" Cara asks. "If you tell me what you want, I can pick them up now."

I press the fingers of my free hand to my forehead. I have no fucking clue what to buy them.

Cara's a smart cookie as well as kind, because she continues, "We can go together. I'm around Harper's age, and I've seen her socials, so I can suggest a few things she might like. And perhaps something for Piper, too."

Relief floods through me. "Thanks. Can we do this now?"

"Of course! I'm a block away, so I'll meet you at the front of your building."

Marv pulls up the collar of his coat as I make my way to the elevator, following me.

"You're not coming with us."

"Nah, I'm gonna find a stylist to come with us. Get them to sign an NDA."

"No stylist."

"They can do the whole family."

"What the fuck, Marv, just stop!"

The elevator doors open, revealing a prim old lady from the floor above, holding a toy poodle dressed in as many layers as she is.

Did she hear me?

Marv nods at her as he steps inside. "Ma'am."

The woman gives me a filthy look.

Turning away, I gaze at my reflection in the polished chrome walls. Despite the designer clothes and expensive hair cut, I look like I haven't slept for days.

I force my mouth into a smile as fake as the relationship I'm going to have with Piper. But my heart still flutters.

I'm going to see her again.

CHAPTER 4

PIPER

*H*e's not coming.

I'm standing outside my apartment building, my bags at my feet, and it's a quarter past ten o'clock. I've heard nothing from Brody since I sent him my address, and now I feel like the world's biggest fool.

The wind whips my cheeks and stings my eyes. Part of me expected for this to happen. I haven't even told Mia yet. I didn't believe that Brody would actually follow through and I don't want her thinking I'm stupid for trusting him after so long.

I'm pretty sure if Brody *did* help advertise the printer, then I'd keep my job, but I also wanted him to come back to Hideaway to make things right with Ethan. This has nothing to do with my crush. No, my feelings for Brody are now officially as dead as a doornail.

It's a relief really. The rose-tinted glasses are off and I can finally move on.

Via public transportation to Hideaway Harbor with a story for my mom about why I'm traveling alone …

Dammit!

I will *not* cry. I refuse to ruin the "barely there" makeup I've just spent the last hour fussing over. I'm just going to put on my big girl pants, hold my head up high, and look like a woman in complete control of her life.

I check my phone one last time, then make a move for the subway. I want to exude confidence, but I've forgotten how much I've packed. So, I end up dragging a heavy wheeled suitcase with one hand, balancing a smaller one on top of it, while trying to keep an enormous duffel bag over my shoulder and my purse in my free hand.

I make it a few yards before grinding to a halt as the Jenga tower of luggage collapses. How on earth am I going to manage stairs with all this?

Turn around. Re-pack. Start again.

Suddenly, I just want my mom. Like a little girl with an owie, I want to cry on her shoulder and let her tell me everything's going to be all right. I love going home for the holidays, but right now, there's a lump in my throat so big I can't even swallow.

I take out my phone and dial the one person who will understand.

Mia answers on the first ring. "Did you find him?"

"What? Who?"

"A new boyfriend. I know you had the office party last night."

I smile as her optimism pushes the tears away. "You honestly think I could have asked *anyone* from work?"

"I dunno? Desperate times and all that?"

"Well, I did have a plan, but he never showed up."

"Holy crap. Did you hire an *escort*?"

"What? No! Jeez, Mia, I'm desperate, but I'm not *that* desperate."

"So who was it, then?"

I take a steadying breath.

"Piper!"

A huge black SUV screeches to a stop on the other side of a row of parked cars next to the sidewalk.

"Sorry!" Brody calls from inside. "There was an accident. My phone's in my bag and I couldn't reach it."

"Who's that?" Mia demands.

I don't reply, caught in a guppy moment. The winter wind blows my hair into my open mouth and I splutter as I pull it out.

Cars are already honking at where Brody's double-parked and blocking the street, but he ignores them, rushing out to help me with my bags.

"Piper! You still there?" Mia asks.

"Um …" I reply as I dash toward Brody's ride. Out of the corner of my eye, I see people leaning out of their car windows.

"Hey, asshole! Move it!" a guy yells.

"Is that Brody King?" a woman asks.

Brody opens the passenger door. "Lock it behind you," he says urgently as I climb in.

"What's happening? You being mugged?" Mia asks, her voice rising in panic.

Brody slams my door shut, and I lock it. A millisecond later, a young woman is tugging on the handle, her phone raised as she films me.

"Ohmygod!" she screeches. "It's Brody King's secret girlfriend!"

"Have they stolen your phone?" Mia is saying.

My mouth is bone dry, a strand of hair stuck to my tongue. I pick at it and swallow as Brody leaps into the seat beside me and pulls away, cutting into the traffic like he's driving a rental tank and insured up the wazoo.

"Listen to me, you piece of shit!" Mia snarls. "You give Piper her phone back right now. I don't know who you are, but she has a brother with a particular set of skills. Skills he's spent a long time acquiring. Skills that make him a nightmare for people like you—"

"Mia," I say, but my voice is a croak she doesn't hear.

"If you give Piper her phone back now, that'll be the end of it. But if you don't, he will look for you, he will find you, and he will ki—"

"Mia!"

"Piper! Jesus Christ, what's going on?"

I glance at Brody. His face is locked in fierce concentration as he weaves through the traffic. I can't talk to Mia now. I can't tell her what's going on in front of Brody.

So instead, I laugh nervously. "Did you just do the speech from *Taken*?"

"Yep."

"And you know Hudson's 'particular set of skills' involves putting out fires for a living?"

"You cannot tell him I said that, or I'll never hear the end of it."

The car settles in one lane, and I sense Brody's eyes on me. "Is that Mia?"

"Who's that?" Mia demands.

"Can't talk now. Okay, gotta go. Bye, bye." I end the call and send her a message.

Piper: As soon as we stop for a break, I'll call you and tell you everything

Mia: WTAF? You can't leave me hanging like that!

41

Piper: I'm perfectly safe

"Is that Mia?" Brody repeats.

Shoving my phone in my purse, I nod. My heart's still pounding so hard there's not enough room for my lungs to work properly.

I want to look to my left and stare at him. Trace the lines on his face that time and experience have etched. I want to know who he is now, and if any part of the boy I once knew remains.

But I'm not a creeper. *Much.* So instead, I look ahead, my forward gaze unfocused, as my peripheral vision gets all the attention, zeroing in on his right arm as he shifts gears.

Brody's running super-hot in all senses of the word, dressed in a cream Henley with the sleeves rolled up to reveal a muscular, tanned forearm dusted with dark hair. Around his wrist is a silver bracelet made from tiny shackles that I know is from Tiffany & Co, and a leather braided bracelet with a Dolce & Gabbana clasp.

Pretending to look for something in my purse, I sneak a glance further left, noticing the vintage Rolex on his left wrist and the tailored navy pants that cling to his thighs.

Gone is the slightly scruffy teen who loved hiking with Ethan, and in his place is a very rich, well-dressed man who probably hasn't seen the inside of a Target for over a decade, and whose life is several tax brackets above mine.

Brody clears his throat, and that's all the excuse I need to face him. He's clean-shaven today, his dark brown hair freshly cut but still long enough for me to run my fingers through and—

"So … who knows I'm coming back to Hideaway with you?"

I swallow, then reply, "Well, no one … yet."

He frowns. "Why haven't you told anyone?"

"Um …" *Because I wasn't sure you'd show?*

"You might as well let them know now. Give them a chance

to get their head around it," he continues. "And explain why we're faking it."

Well, shit. Now I've got to fess up that we're faking it for real.

At my silence, his gaze quickly flicks from the road to me. "Piper?"

I'm suddenly too hot. But it's not horny hot. It's guilty and embarrassed hot. Shuffling out of my coat, I toss it onto the back seat along with my scarf.

"I'm going to tell Mia the truth," I say, then lapse into silence, brushing invisible lint from my jeans.

"*And ...*" Brody draws out the word, expecting a reply.

I don't know what to say, so I approach the final destination of my answer from far away. *Very* far away. "You know the founding story of Hideaway Harbor?"

"Ye-es ..."

"When my fourteen-times great-grandparents fled their warring families to be together during the Puritan era?"

"And when they made it over the mountains, dehydrated, and at the edge of death," Brody continues in a sing-song voice as if reciting a children's story he's heard too many times before.

"They were saved by the waters of the Hideaway spring, decided to stay in this corner of paradise by the sea, and founded a town that was the most perfect place to live. A town where everyone finds their one true love, unicorns fart rainbows, and nothing bad ever happens."

I'm silent, listening to the bitterness in his voice. Brody didn't have a particularly happy childhood, and no, Hideaway isn't perfect, but it's still pretty darn special to me.

"And what has any of that got to do with us, Piper?"

He's right. We're not in love. At least, he's never been in love with me. As my older brother's good-looking and kind best friend, Brody was always dazzling to me, like a first celebrity crush.

Now? My hormonal body still wants his in every sexual position I know the name of, but I'm just fangirling because God gave him too many sexy genes, not because I'm still in love with him.

"Well?"

Just rip the Band-Aid off.

"I had a boyfriend, but he dumped me for someone else a few months ago."

My cheeks are burning with embarrassment. It's like being in high school all over again.

"I didn't tell my mom," I plow on, "I didn't want to disappoint her. She was so happy. You know how she is about love."

Brody's eyes are focused on the road ahead, his posture rigid, but he gives me a small nod in agreement.

"I promised to bring him home for Christmas. And I thought I could find a replacement. I never told Mom his name because I didn't want to jinx it."

I let out a huff and shake my head. "But I haven't been able to. So, when I thought about Marv's idea … I …"

"So … you need me to pretend to be your boyfriend." Brody's words aren't a question but a statement. He delivers them slowly, as if tasting their truth.

I shrug.

"And getting me to advertise a printer is, what? Just to fuck with me?"

"No! I actually really need you to do that," I reply quickly as his tone sharpens with anger.

"My company is merging with another in the new year, and we'll be competing for our jobs. The new owner's son is also a graphic designer, and my ex."

"And you think using me to promote the printer will make them choose you over him?"

"I don't know! Maybe? But it's the best bargaining chip I've got."

Brody doesn't reply, so I gaze out the window at the road ahead. Cars stream out of the city, wipers flicking as a flurry of sleety snow hits us. My mind starts throwing out scenarios for how the next few days might play out, like a stylist trying to satisfy a picky client. But every idea, even the sexy ones, sends a prickle of nerves through my stomach, and with each mile closer to Hideaway, my anxiety builds.

"Have you thought about a backstory?" Brody asks, jolting me from a vision of Ethan dressed as a Puritan, challenging Brody to a duel while I swoon dramatically in my mother's arms.

"About us?"

He nods, a muscle ticking in his jaw.

Stop asking stupid questions!

"Not yet. Probably best to keep it simple. Maybe you were dodging fans and came to hide out at the coffee shop, not realizing I was in the far booth until you slid in and saw me."

Brody's jaw is so tense and chiseled, I almost wish I had a match to strike against it.

"That'll do," he finally replies.

Feeling a nervous ramble coming on with the speed of a bullet train, I continue, "I mean, as far as meet-cutes go, it's not the most exciting. Not like I was being mugged and you saved me. Or like you were rappelling down a waterfall when carnivorous birds cut the rope, sending you a thousand feet into the swirling waters below. And I was kayaking nearby, observing said birds' feeding habits, dragged you onboard, then used my ninja paddle skills to protect us."

"In New York?"

"Well, King Kong was once up the Empire State Building."

The corner of his mouth twitches. "Any other ideas?"

Even the tiniest sign of his amusement is enough for me to keep going.

"Mercury went so retrograde that the Earth spun into an alternate reality where dragons and elves roamed, and you were a warrior elf searching for the lost sword of Tlygonne. Instead, you found me, a plucky mortal, held captive in the tower of Khlessid-dhug, and you knew I was the key to your quest."

Brody frowns, as if recalling something he'd rather not, and I stop talking.

"You've got quite the imagination … Do you still draw?"

I nod, my mental eye flipping through the hundreds of sketches I've done of the man sitting beside me. I feel like an obsessive stalker right now, even as part of me yells, "It's his fault for being so gorgeous!"

"What do you most like to draw?"

I can't admit the real answer, so I just shrug like a moody teenager being asked about their hobbies.

"And what media? Pencils? Paint? Watercolor?"

Again, I don't answer.

"Guano? Blood?"

My head whips around. "What?"

Brody grins. "Just checking you're actually listening."

My heart skips a beat. "Rest assured, I don't draw with blood or poop. I either use a digital stylus or pencils if I want a break from the screen."

"Can I see any of your pictures?"

My insides lurch so violently I'm surprised I don't throw up. There's no way he can see any of the drawings I've done of him, so I fumble for an answer, my skin clammy with dread. I forget entirely that I have plenty of pictures that don't feature him at all.

"It's okay, you don't have to if you don't want to."

46

I'm torn. I want to show off what I can do, but Brody's a super-cool superstar, and I'm a super-nerdy fantasy fan artist.

Any negative comment online about my art sticks to my soul like super glue. No matter how many positive comments there are, they can never outweigh the shitty ones. I know I shouldn't pay the haters any heed, and most likely they're just jealous, but I can't shake their words. They erode my confidence like drops of acid.

And it's not just the hate, but the silence that also breaks my spirit—only hearing crickets in response after I've spent so long crafting a post.

"Maybe. I'm just a bit private about them," I say, omitting the fact that I post the ones not starring him publicly online.

"Well, I can't draw for shit, so whatever you do, I'll think is great."

I smile.

We're quiet for a few more minutes, then Brody clears his throat again. "So, we bumped into each other at Espresso Yourself, got chatting, and then started hanging out?"

As I imagine the scenario, my eyes sting with longing at the thought of it being true. Even just hanging out as friends. Because he *was* my friend when we were growing up.

"Sounds good."

"And how long ago was this?"

"I told my mom in April that I would be bringing someone home at Christmas if things worked out."

"Okay. April. Got it."

I cast my mind back over my Brody King Google Alerts that have been pinging into my phone for the past nine months to check if he's been linked with any other women. Luckily, he hasn't, but his ex has been throwing out cheating allegations.

"I wasn't unfaithful to Marisa."

Are you reading my mind?

"She cheated on me but didn't want the press finding out, so she said I was the unfaithful one."

"I didn't believe it," I say firmly, playing the part of loyal friend.

"Thanks. That … means a lot. But most of the other stuff is true. I don't know how much you've heard, but you should probably be prepared for when your family starts grilling you about why you're with someone like me."

"They would never do that."

He huffs. "If I were them, I would. I wouldn't want you with me."

I want to jump to his defense, and my family's, but I don't want Brody to know how much I really know about his recent escapades. And I'm not sure I trust Ethan's response when he sees Brody with me. It's one thing for Brody to show up unannounced after so long, but sharing Christmas with the family? Dating his little sister behind everyone's backs?

So instead, I say, "I'm a grown woman, capable of making my own decisions. And anyway, my family loves you."

He shakes his head. "I don't deserve their love."

"That's not true! You can't say that!"

"Oh yeah? Where the fuck have I been for the last twelve years, Piper? Chasing my dreams and leaving my best friends behind."

I don't know how to reply, because I have the same thoughts.

"I should have been at their wedding," he continues, his voice aching with regret. "I should have come back for …"

He can't say Olivia's name or "the funeral," and I understand. It's been four years, but there's still a hole in our family that will never fully heal.

Without thinking, I reach across the center console and touch his thigh. I want to comfort him, but he stiffens, glancing down at my hand as if it's diseased or on fire.

"Sorry," I say, jerking it away and sitting on it, lest it decide to go rogue again.

"This is really hard for me, you know, going back," he says, haltingly. "And I want you to know that I'm grateful you agreed to Marv's crazy idea."

He gives me a quick glance and I see a glimpse in his expression of the old Brody. The one who was vulnerable. Real.

"I'm glad you're here to hold my hand through this," he continues. "Metaphorically, of course."

Oh ... so no hand-holding then in this fake relationship.

Frowning, Brody rubs his jaw. "Although I expect in public, we probably should. At least when Marv's taking photos." The frown deepens, and he shoots me a worried look. "If you're okay with that?"

"Yeah, sure," I say, trying to keep my voice light, while my fingers itch to practice hand holding immediately.

I distract them by checking my phone and the constant stream of messages from Mia. I need to talk to her before she explodes, or even worse, she calls my mom.

"Can we take a quick break at the next rest stop?" I ask.

"Sure. I brought food so we can eat on the way if you want to save time."

"Does that mean I can do some of the driving?"

He smiles. "If you want."

"Yeah. It'll get us there quicker."

Although it also means I get to sit in the same seat he's been sitting in ...

What is wrong with me?

Give it ten minutes, and I'll be doodling a heart with "Piper King" inside it on my arm. I may look like a twenty-eight-year-old, but right now I'm thinking like a teenager who needs to grow up.

Half an hour later, Brody pulls into a service plaza in Darien, Connecticut, and parks at the far end of the parking lot. I'm about to ask why when he pulls a baseball cap and sunglasses from the glove box, puts them on, then reaches to the back seat to get a coat.

"You don't want our first public sighting to be outside a Chick-fil-A?"

Brody gives me a tired smile. "I'd just rather get to Hideaway without any drama."

He gets out and makes his way to my side of the SUV, opening the door and offering his hand.

I'm not as small as Harper, but it's still a fair way to the snowy ground, so I take it. A spark of electricity travels up my arm at the contact of his skin on mine.

Brody doesn't seem to notice, releasing my hand as soon as I make it safely to the tarmac.

Buttoning my coat, I head toward the building, Brody matching my pace. He holds the door open for me, and a rush of hot air meets us as we walk in.

"I won't be long. I just need to use the restroom."

He leans forward, and for a wild moment, I think he's going to kiss me.

"Say hi to Mia from me," he says, then turns toward the mens' room.

My face hot, I head to the ladies' room, fully aware I need to have this conversation somewhere private. It's empty, but I still check every stall, and place myself outside the one furthest from the door so I can see if anyone comes in.

Then I call Mia.

It doesn't even ring once before she picks up.

"Shoot," she says. "I'm standing by."

"Okay. Don't freak out."

"What the hell, Piper! That sentence is literally designed to freak anyone out. What are you going to ask me to do next? Calm down?"

I giggle. "I'm sorry. It's just that I don't know how you'll react."

"Just tell me then! It can't be any worse than the thousand scenarios I've been running through for the last hour!"

I glance around to make sure no one's nearby, then quickly tell her everything that's happened since the Google Alert about Brody being caught "Loved Up" pinged on my phone.

To give Mia credit, there's only a few seconds of silence before she's off again.

"Okay, first up, this is freaking amazing, and it's like your teenage fantasies are coming true—"

"What do you—"

"Come on, Piper, I bet you're as hot for him now as you were when we were sixteen."

"I'm not—"

"Second, props to his agent for the idea. Brody needs to come back to Hideaway to see Ethan, and the longer he leaves it, the harder it's gonna be."

I nod, even though she can't see me.

"Third, this solves all your problems vis-à-vis your non-existent boyfriend. I bet your mom lays an egg when she finds out it's Brody."

I snort. She's not wrong.

"Fourth, you can't tell anyone else apart from me it's fake or someone will blab. I'll be your wing woman and help manage the situation. Just put me in touch with this Marv dude, and I'll coordinate your couple sightings and keep him away from you if he gets too much."

"Are you sure?"

"Of course! I'm going to have a riot. I'll tell him I'm taking the photos. That way, I can sell them *and* make sure you look hot AF. If you're cool with that?"

"Absolutely." Mia's a photographer, and I know how hard it is for her to make a decent income.

She squeals down the phone so loudly that I have to hold it away from my ear. "This is gonna be so much fun!"

Having her on my side makes me feel a whole lot better, like this crazy scheme might actually work.

"Okay, when will you get here?"

"If we only take quick pee breaks, we should hopefully arrive by five thirty. We'll pop in briefly to see Mom and Dad, then check into the Hideaway Hotel. It'll just be us and my folks for dinner, so come on over and say hello."

"Will do. I'll pop by around six."

"Perfect. I'd better get going."

"Sure, and one other thing …"

"Yeah?"

"I give it three days before you're banging."

"Mia!" I cry, but she's already hung up.

I quickly take care of business, then head back outside to where Brody is waiting in the car for me.

"I forgot to say hi to Mia from you," I tell him as he starts the engine and pulls away. "But she says she's going to help us. She'll keep Marv in line and take the photos to sell to the press. She's a photographer, so they'll be good."

He nods, then inclines his head toward the back of the car. "There's food from a deli behind your seat."

"Ooh! What did you get?" I lean around and bring the bags to the front.

"No idea. I didn't have time to look."

On top of one of the bags is a handwritten menu on a gilt-edged card.

"A selection of charcuterie and meats, including Wagyu roast beef, prosciutto di Parma, French duck rillettes, smoked organic chicken, and truffle salami from Seville. Cheese: Cave-aged Swiss Gouda, Roquefort, twenty-four-month-old Manchego, and limited edition Ossau Iraty. Freshly baked baguette, San Francisco sourdough rolls, Parmesan lavash crackers, and raw, cultured butter."

Holy shit.

"Accompaniments, truffle honey, whole-grain Dijon mustard, cornichons, and fig and walnut jam. Salads and sides: lobster salad, deviled eggs with Osetra caviar, and Peppadew peppers filled with whipped ricotta and prosciutto."

I turn the card over.

"Desserts: éclairs covered in Valrhona dark chocolate and filled with Madagascan vanilla bean cream, assorted macarons, and mini-Basque cheesecakes. To drink: a half bottle of Dom Pérignon and a half bottle of aged, biodynamic Bordeaux. San Pellegrino sparkling water, Badoit still water, organic cold brew coffee, and freshly squeezed blood orange juice."

"Is that okay?" Brody asks.

"Um, no. Unfortunately, I'm a teetotal, sugar-free, grain-free, gluten-free, lactose-intolerant vegan …"

CHAPTER 5

BRODY

*W*ell, fuck.

I thought I couldn't go wrong, leaving my credit card with the deli owner and telling him to go to town. I wanted to impress Piper, but I never thought to check what she could or couldn't eat.

And what the hell do I do now? Turn around and see if Starbucks has anything that'll do?

My eyes stay on the road ahead as I merge back onto I-95 heading north, but at the edge of my vision, Piper's head is bent and her shoulders are shaking.

Shit.

"We can go back. See what we can find," I say quickly. "I'm sorry. I should have run it by you first."

She makes this weird noise, halfway between a sob and a shriek, and panic stabs me in the gut. Is her blood sugar crashing? What the hell does an everything-intolerant vegan even eat? Cardboard? Air?

I speed up, scanning the road ahead, looking for the next place I can exit, praying she's going to be okay.

"Piper, I—"

"Bro—Bro—ahahaha—"

She's hyperventilating, and I'm freaking the fuck out. Slamming the car into the right shoulder, I screech it to a halt, unclip my seatbelt, and grab her shoulders.

"Piper! Look at me! Breathe!"

Tears stream down her bright red cheeks.

I reach for my phone. "I'm calling 911."

Her hand closes over mine. "No! I'm—I'm fine."

I take a breath and pause, gazing at her more critically. "Are you *laughing*?"

She's now alternating between snorts and whoops like a pig in a cage fight with an owl.

I slump back in my seat, a wave of relief crashing through me. I've been on edge for months—scratch that—*years*, and over the last few days, the tension inside me has ratcheted up to heart-attack levels.

The SUV rocks slightly as cars whiz past with a roar. I listen to the thunk-thunk-thunk of the wipers, the rapid thudding of my heart, and Piper's breathing as she gets herself under control.

"I am so sorry," she says, sniffing through her tears of laughter.

I don't open my eyes, still trying to calm myself down and not rebound into rage at how much she frightened me.

"I was expecting, I don't know, a pre-packaged ham and cheese sandwich wrapped in plastic, or a couple of mystery meat hot dogs in foil. Or maybe a slightly squashed Hostess cupcake and a couple of cans of room temperature soda. Not the fanciest food in New York."

"Gee, thanks for the vote of confidence."

I open my eyes and skewer her with a look. "I wouldn't even buy that for Marv, and he's at the top of my shit list."

She plays with the clasp of her purse. "It's just so fancy, that's all. I'm not used to it."

You should be used to it. You deserve the best.

Huh? Where did *those* thoughts come from?

Turning my gaze away, I fiddle with the air vents. The interior of the car feels too small right now.

"Would you prefer we stop and get something else?"

"No way!" She settles back in her seat. "I want to try everything."

"So you're not really a gluten-free, sugar-free, whatever-free, vegan?"

She giggles. "God no. You should see me at Thanksgiving. I eat *all* the food."

I smile, but the image of her around her family's table is tinged with sadness. After my mom, my only family, died, I should have spent every Thanksgiving with the Lockes. Instead, I left Hideaway and never came back.

I merge back into the traffic, dreading what I might be walking into.

"Do you want me to feed you?" Piper asks as she rummages through the bags. "Pop chunks of cheese or some charcuterie in your mouth? I think most of this is finger food."

"I'm not hungry right now. I might have something later if you want to do some of the driving."

I skipped breakfast because of nerves, and now my stomach's in knots thinking about returning to Hideaway.

So, I focus on the road ahead as Piper eats. Her obvious enjoyment lifts my spirits, but when she starts to make unconscious sex noises, my dick jumps to attention, wanting to play.

What the fuck?

I should have dated again after I broke up with Marisa.

Hooked up with the first woman who flashed her eyes at me. If I'd been getting some then maybe my dick would get the memo that Piper's a friend. Nothing more.

It's bad enough that I'm using her to help my career and build bridges with Ethan. There's no way I'm crossing a line with her.

As if she'd want you anyway.

I meant what I said to her earlier. I wouldn't ever put her with someone like me. Taint her by association and have people tear her to pieces online.

She's got a happy life in Brooklyn that doesn't include me or my celebrity bullshit.

I just hope that once Christmas is over, she can go back to that life in peace.

So why does the thought of saying goodbye again hurt so much?

I press a little harder on the gas. I just need to focus on getting us to Hideaway. A few carefully curated photos and difficult conversations with Ethan and the rest of Piper's family, then we can both move on.

WE STOP A COUPLE MORE TIMES, and Piper takes a turn at the wheel. We don't talk much, and when we do, it's surface stuff. But after I take over driving again and we get closer to Hideaway Harbor, we both clam up, lost in our thoughts.

The town is by the coast but completely encircled by mountains. For years, it was difficult to access until the original mountain pass was widened. Snow covers the jagged rocks around us and drifts onto the road as we climb higher. It's pretty, but I know how treacherous it can be. As we go over the pass, I pull into a viewpoint by the side of the road, the spot tourists always stop to take pictures.

Piper gets out, and I follow, standing by her side as we look down at Hideaway Harbor below us. The winter sun dips toward the horizon, heading into the golden hour, when everything is still visible, but there's an illusion of darkness, with the lights twinkling like stars below.

I see the colored lights along Main Street, the town square, the Christmas decorations covering people's houses like they all want to be seen from space. It's like Who-ville, but I can't be a total Grinch when Piper's by my side. My childhood wasn't all bad—it had its moments of joy, and I'd rather people went all in for Christmas than not at all.

"It's so beautiful," Piper murmurs.

I gaze at her, her eyes bright and cheeks flushed. Her hand hangs loose by her side, an inch from mine. Some crazy part of me wants to take it, but I know I can't. Not unless Marv is about to leap out from behind a tree and shout, "Action!"

Piper glances at me. "Thank you for doing this."

She's talking about our fake relationship arrangement, but I play dumb. "Taking my car?"

Her head shakes, her loose blonde curls catching the dusky light.

"Pretending to be my boyfriend, and not saying how stupid I am for not telling Mom the truth."

"You've never been stupid. I'm the one who punches the wrong people and makes friends with troublemakers. And I know what your mom is like. She just wants everyone to be as happy as she is with your dad."

"I know."

"I just hope we can bring her down gently after Christmas," she continues. "You know, when we 'break up.'"

The air quotes hit like a throat-punch.

There's no way her mom will take our "break-up" well. When I'm insulated on the other side of the planet, Piper will be stuck fielding her mom's questions and trying to find another boyfriend, a real one this time, to take my place.

I step back, feeling how cold the air is between us. "We should get going. Check into the hotel."

She looks away, nods, then gets back in the truck, and I start the descent down to the town.

My eyes stay on the road, but I can't help watching as Hideaway grows larger below us. The high school, the Locke Reserve, the harbor and lobster boats, every place triggers a memory, clear and vivid, like it just happened.

My chicken-shit self wants to turn around as the back of my neck prickles with sweat.

"I should call Mom and Dad," Piper says, staring at her phone. "Give them the heads up before we arrive."

"You don't want to check in first?"

"I do, but I'd rather let them know about you before that, and give them a chance to process before the evening meal."

She takes her time making the call, then puts the phone to her ear.

I'm holding my breath. Waiting to hear what she'll say.

"Dammit!" She shoves the phone in her purse. "I knew I shouldn't have left it until the last minute."

"Hideaway still hasn't got a new mast?"

"No. And people still think patchy-to-zero cell coverage is a good thing."

"Fostahs commoonity spirit," I say, putting on a Maine accent.

"Yeah. Some things never change." She huffs out a laugh. "Oh well, let's hope my folks don't have a heart attack when they see you."

There's a sharp silence, then Piper rushes to cover it.

"I'm so sorry, Brody. I didn't think. I—"

"It's okay. Honestly. It was a long time ago."

"But—"

"Seriously. It's fine."

I thought I'd dealt with it. But now, driving back into Hideaway Harbor, my mom's death from a heart attack at only fifty-two doesn't feel like a long time ago. It's as painfully fresh as if it happened yesterday.

Piper doesn't say anything else, and a lead weight settles in my stomach, growing heavier as I navigate on autopilot toward the Locke family home.

It's almost exactly as I remember—a big, three-story wooden house with steps leading up to the front door and a large wraparound porch. A double garage sits off to one side, and the front lawn and white picket fence are as immaculate as ever.

There are more Christmas lights than there were twelve years ago, an inflatable Santa, a pair of light-up reindeer, giant candy canes, and Christmas tree baubles the size of exercise balls. There's also a small snowman with a scarf around its neck, two lumps of coal for eyes, and a carrot for a nose.

Piper's quiet beside me, also making no move to exit the car and face her parents.

I take a deep breath and get out, meaning to go around the hood and open the passenger door for her.

But the moment my foot hits the gritted sidewalk, there's a cry.

"Brody?"

I pivot slowly toward the house.

Piper's mom is standing outside, one hand covering her heart.

"Oh, my Lord! It *is* you!"

My feet are frozen.

Erica takes hesitant steps closer, reaching out cautiously as if to touch a ghost.

Then her eyes widen even more. "Piper?"

Her gaze bounces between us, then the penny drops.

THE HOLIDAY FAKERS

"Oh, my!" she cries, her hands going to her cheeks. "Brody! And my baby!"

I'm caught like a fish on a line, wanting to escape but can't.

"John!" Erica yells, never once taking her eyes off me. "John! Get out here!"

Then she reaches my side, her fingers brushing my cheeks as if she can't believe I'm real, and bursts into tears.

CHAPTER 6

PIPER

"Thank you, Lord, for bringing our Brody back to us!"
My mom's a regular churchgoer, but I've never heard her invoke God so openly.

Brody's still as Mom touches him, but I notice the tension in the lines around his eyes.

I should have known this would happen. How could it not? My mom's the most loving and forgiving person I know. Not that any of us need to forgive Brody. We know why he wanted to go, even though it cut like a knife.

My feet finally get the memo, and I rush around the hood to rescue him.

"Mom—"

"Brody, Brody, you sweet boy. You're back. You're finally home!"

Tears are ruining my mom's makeup. Still caressing Brody's face, she reaches her free hand to my shoulder, pulling me closer.

"My baby. My baby and Brody. Oh, thank you, Lord. Thank you!"

"Son?"

My dad is still as strong and straight as an arrow. His face is severe under the porch light, but I know it's because he's holding back his own emotion.

"John! Look! Look who our baby girl has brought home!"

Brody clears his throat and holds out a hand stiffly as my dad approaches.

"Mr Locke," he begins. "Sir."

Dad takes his hand and pulls him into a hug that lasts long enough for me to know he's struggling to keep his own feelings in check.

"Call me John."

Tears flow fresh down my cheeks as Dad clears his throat. I've never loved my parents more than at this moment.

"I can't believe it! You're both here! This is going to be the best Christmas ever!" Mom continues, pulling Brody away from Dad so she can hug him again. "You're the most perfect gift!"

She wipes her eyes. "Oh, my, just look at me, crying on the street! John! Get their bags. Let's go inside. I need my glasses and a proper light to check that Brody's still as handsome as ever."

"Mom. We're not—"

"I can't see through these tinted windows." She peers into the back of the SUV. "Or are your bags in the trunk? Isn't this fancy, John?"

She's got one hand gripping Brody's arm, the other gesturing at the car as if Dad wouldn't have noticed it before.

"Mom—"

"Did you choose black to blend in? Avoid the paparazzi?"

Dad opens the trunk. "Let's get you both inside."

"Stop! We're not staying here!" I yell, a little too loudly.

The silence that follows is deafening. I swear I can hear each tiny snowflake falling around us.

"What was that, baby?"

Brody's mouth opens, but nothing comes out. He still looks frozen with shock.

"We're not staying here," I repeat.

Mom looks utterly confused, as if their house is the only building for a thousand miles. "But ... where *are* you staying?"

"The Hideaway Hotel."

Her jaw drops like we're electing to sleep in a barn, and not the fanciest place in town. "But why?"

Good question. "Because ..."

"But your bedroom has a big enough bed for the two of you," she continues. "We bought a new one, especially."

Oh no ...

"And it's right at the end of the hall, so there's plenty of privacy for snuggle time. We won't hear a thing."

I cringe. Mom's euphemism for sex is "snuggle time," and she's been using it since we were kids. I remember putting two and two together with Mia when I was about fourteen and shrieking for half an hour at the thought of what my parents were actually doing when Mom talked about needing "snuggle time" with Dad.

"Er ..." Brody tries, his voice scratchy.

"It's because of the press," I say quickly. "We don't want them camped outside the house. If we stay at the hotel, it's easier for everyone."

And we'll have separate beds ...

"Oh," Mom says, her shoulders drooping like she's a deflating floatie. Then she straightens and forces a bright smile. "Are you heading to check in now?"

I nod.

She glances between the house and the car. "Why don't I come with you? Show you the way."

"It's okay, Mom. We won't be long, and we know where it is."

Dad takes Mom's hand, and she reluctantly releases Brody's arm, like she doesn't really trust us to return.

I give her a hug and whisper in her ear, "We'll be home within the hour. I promise."

As Brody drives slowly away from the curb, the silence is deafening. It's only been a couple of minutes back in Hideaway, and I'm worried it's already too much for him.

It only takes a few minutes to get to the hotel, but the parking lot is almost full. God knows how Marv managed to get us adjoining rooms so close to Christmas, and rooms for him, his assistant, and whoever else he's going to spring on us.

Maybe he planned this months ago …

Inside the hotel, a huge artificial Christmas tree fills one corner of the reception area, and *Chestnuts Roasting on an Open Fire* plays softly in the background.

Between us and the front desk is a couple in their thirties, the man arguing with the receptionist as his wife jiggles a fretful toddler on her hip and tries to soothe two smaller children who are tugging on her coat for attention.

"But that can't be the case!" the man says. "I booked the rooms months ago."

"I'm sorry, sir, but I can't find any record of that," the young receptionist replies. Her cheeks are red and a film of sweat glistens across her forehead.

He taps on his phone, then shows her the screen. "Look, there's the booking confirmation for two adjoining rooms."

My heart sinks. *Marv.*

Brody's gazing at me, looking torn, wanting me to make the decision. Our conversation is wordless, but when I nod, he knows exactly what I want him to do.

He takes a breath. "Excuse me, sir, ma'am?"

The couple twist to face him, instant recognition making them freeze as if touched by the Snow Queen.

Brody gives them a reassuring smile, then turns to the receptionist. "There should be two adjoining rooms booked under the name Marvin DeVille?"

She taps on the screen, then nods like a bobblehead toy.

"Please give these rooms to this couple, but still charge Mr DeVille for them, plus any other charges that are incurred. You have his card on file?"

The woman nods again, her eyes bulging as she stares at him.

Brody gives the couple a heart-stopping smile. "My girl-friend and I were just coming in to say we didn't need our rooms anymore, so this is perfect timing."

"But the cost?" the woman whispers. "We couldn't possibly—"

"I insist. It's a Christmas gift." He hands the receptionist a credit card. "Please keep a copy of this in case there's any issue with Mr DeVille's card."

The woman stares intently at her husband, as if trying to communicate telepathically, her eyes darting to Brody every tenth of a second.

"Er … Mr King?"

Brody gifts the man another megawatt smile. "Yes, sir?"

The man slowly brings up his phone. "Would you … I mean—"

"A photo? I'd be delighted," Brody replies, seeming genuinely happy.

The man fumbles to unlock his phone, and I reach forward. "I can take it."

"Thank you," he replies, looking relieved.

The couple flank Brody, shyly moving closer as if not wanting to invade his personal space. He throws his arms around them, and the two kids stand in front, looking up at him in awe.

"Kids!" the dad whispers. "Look at the pretty lady!"

I make a big show of looking behind me, which makes everyone laugh, then snap away.

The toddler seems just as enamored with Brody as the rest of his family, stretching his pudgy arms toward him. Brody looks at his mom as if for permission, and she lifts her son into his arms.

Brody pulls a face, the toddler giggles, and my ovaries promptly explode.

Everyone's laughing now, and the sound makes the little boy laugh even more.

"You need to be in the photo, too!" the mom says, beckoning me forward, then glancing over her shoulder at the receptionist. "Can you take the picture for us?"

The receptionist rushes up, takes the phone from me, and gestures for me to step forward.

I move to the end of the line next to the mom, but she guides me into the middle, next to Brody.

"Say cheese!" the girl says, and I smile, hyperaware of Brody's hand on my back.

Still holding the toddler, who is now tugging on his hair, Brody takes his phone from his back pocket, unlocks it, then hands it to the receptionist. "Can you get one for me, too?"

Is this the start of our public fake-relationship? Why else would Brody ask for a photo of a family we're probably not going to see again?

"Sure," she says, moving back and framing the shot.

The toddler notices me and pulls a face. Obviously, I'm a threat to his one-on-one time with a Hollywood star. His little hand comes up and smashes into my face, pushing me away.

Brody and I crack up laughing as the parents apologize, horrified.

"I hope you got that," Brody says to the receptionist.

"Sure did!" She hands the phone back to him, and we all crowd around it like we've known each other for years as he goes through the photos from the start.

There's one of all of us, beaming smiles on our faces. Then one where the toddler notices the interloper. Another with me being pushed away, while the parents have comical looks of horror on their faces, and then one of Brody and me laughing, with the toddler looking put out that I'm still there.

"I think that's the best one of the lot," Brody says. "If you give me your email, I'll make sure they're sent to you."

"Thank you! That would be … awesome!" the woman says, utterly starstruck.

The receptionist produces a pad and pen as Brody hands the infant back to his mom, and the dad scribbles on a piece of paper, then gives it to Brody.

"Thank you, Mr King. You've made our Christmas."

"Your little one just made ours."

Ours … As if we're a real couple.

Brody must have a sixth sense for fans, because he turns to the receptionist and grins. "Want a selfie?"

She nods so fast I'm worried her head might fall off, and Brody moves closer.

"Here, let me," he says, taking her phone. "I've got a longer arm, and we need the distance for my enormous ego, I mean, head."

This is the Brody I remember. So kind even strangers feel at home with him.

A few more photos, then Brody says his goodbyes and we walk back to the SUV in silence.

Inside, I face him. "That was really sweet of you. You were amazing with them."

He lets out a slow breath. "It's the least I could do. Remind me to kill Marv when I see him next, would you?"

"You don't know—"

He gives me a look.

"Well, anyway, you made their whole life back there."

He fishes his phone from his pocket and sends them an email with the photos the receptionist took.

"I don't mind fans like that at all," he says. "They're nice. It's the other ones. Like from this morning. They're not so pleasant."

I nod. I was scared witless by the woman trying to get in the car.

"I'll make some calls," he continues. "Try to find somewhere else we can stay."

Finding a place this close to Christmas in Hideaway, which is famous for being the only place in New England to celebrate the season when the Puritans banned it in the 1600s? Not likely.

"I'll find something," he continues with determination, tapping on his phone.

I sit in silence, waiting for the inevitable.

Sure enough, after five minutes, he tosses the phone into his lap.

"It's okay, we'll make it work," I say.

"I'm so sorry I've dragged you into this."

"You didn't drag me into anything. I need you probably more than you need me. And anyway, my room has that pull-out bed Mia used to sleep on when she stayed over. I can use that."

"No, I'll sleep on it."

"Brody," I begin, in the patient tone of a schoolteacher. "You won't fit."

He opens his mouth again, but I hold up my hand. "We can have this argument later. Let's just get back to my folks and eat."

"Okay."

He reverses out of the space, and we drive back to my parents' house, lost in our thoughts.

No one comes out to greet us, which I see as a good sign. The excitement has worn off and we can all go back to normal.

Leaving our bags in the car for later, we walk up the path together.

The front door is open, but I still knock and call out, "Mom? Dad?"

"In the family room, sweetie! Just come on through."

I give Brody what I hope is a reassuring smile, and he follows me into the main entertaining room of the house.

"Surprise!" Mom yells.

I stop dead. Along with my parents are my little sister, Harper, my younger brother, Hudson, and my big brother, Ethan, who's holding his daughter Martha. Ethan's stony gaze shifts to Brody, and man, he looks pissed.

Oh shit.

CHAPTER 7

BRODY

*M*y mind attempts a reboot, then it short-circuits. It's like I've been woken from a coma after twelve years. Erica and John look a little older, and John's grown a white beard, but they don't look that different from when I left Hideaway.

But their kids? Harper was a dorky twelve-year-old with wobbly teeth, which she would twist and tug whenever she had an audience—a kid who would burp the periodic table to make people laugh.

Now she's an adult. A proper fucking adult.

Hudson? He was a skinny fourteen-year-old who was lifting weights smaller than my biceps.

Now? It looks like he lifts *all* the weights.

I thought I was in shape, but he's built like a tank.

And then there's Ethan. Taller, broader, older. Still a stupidly handsome bastard, but I can see the lines that life has left. The hardness that's now directed at me.

I can't hold his gaze, so I look at the child in his arms. And there it is, the sucker punch. The killer blow that slams the breath from my body.

Martha. With her white-blonde hair and big blue eyes, she's a little Olivia. It's like she's still in the room.

But she isn't.

She's dead.

"Surprise!" Piper cries, echoing her mom, the sound cutting through the heavy silence.

I've got to get out of here. I can't do this.

Piper grabs my hand, her fingers crushing mine, holding me in place.

I'm still staring at Martha, her shy smile now uncertain. She may be only five, but she can read a room.

This is all my fault. How the fuck did I think this would work?

An enormous belch reverberates off the walls and I can't help a snort, which immediately evaporates at Ethan's glare.

"Harper!" Erica scolds as Hudson rolls his eyes.

The youngest Locke sibling has a naughty grin on her face.

"Hey Brody." She burps again.

"Can you still burp the—"

"Hydrogen, helium, lithium, beryllium—"

"Harper!" her entire family yells, even though they're struggling to keep straight faces.

"Hydogen, hedium, lissium, beribibum ..."

"Don't you be copying Aunt Harper now, Martha-Moo," Ethan says gently.

"But Daddy!" she replies, her little hands holding either side of his face. "It's *science!*"

Ethan's trying to be stern, but one corner of his mouth twitches, and his eyes are full of love.

"And you think it's funny, too," she continues. "*Everyone* thinks it's funny."

Hudson steps forward, his arm extended. "Good to see you again, Brody."

"You too," I reply.

Piper lets go of my hand, and I reach out to take Hudson's, bracing myself for what's coming.

Jesus Christ. I know this is a test, so I grip back as hard as I can, my metacarpals screaming in protest. Piper told me Hudson was a firefighter, and judging by the strength of his grip, his job involves tearing burning buildings apart with his bare hands.

Just as I'm about to tap out, Harper pushes her brother aside and gives me a hug I'm not expecting, followed by a few loud sniffs, like she's a dog checking me out.

"Harper!" Piper cries. "Stop it!"

"I see you wear what you advertise," Harper says with a grin as she disengages. "Top notes of bergamot and a marine accord, heart of cedarwood and ambergris, with a base of smoked vetiver and labdanum. Good balance. Clean but dark. *Tempest* suits you."

"Honey," Erica says, drawing her youngest child away. "We don't smell our guests."

Sweat breaks out across my skin. Can Harper smell fear, too?

"I'm so sorry," Piper mutters. "I had no idea."

"You're Brody," Martha states solemnly.

I meet her gaze, forcing a smile.

"Don't be scared," she says. "Aunt Harper is very special."

Hudson snorts, and Harper elbows him.

"You've gotten old," Martha continues.

What the—

"Very, *very* old."

Harper bites her lip and looks away. Hudson stares at the floor, his shoulders shaking slightly. Even Ethan's grim façade seems to be cracking.

I glance at Piper. Her smile is strained, her eyes telling me she wishes we were anywhere but here.

"Just like Daddy," Martha continues.

Ethan's eyes widen as he gazes at his daughter, and Harper and Hudson laugh out loud. John clears his throat, attempting to disguise a chuckle, while Erica covers her mouth.

"Why are you laughing?" Martha asks, her little chin starting to wobble. "It's true!"

"Shhh, sweetie," Ethan says to her. "It's okay. They're only laughing because Daddy isn't really that old."

"But you're nearly as old as Grandpa!" she cries. "And you used to be much younger, like that." She points to a framed photo on the wall, and my heart stutters.

It was taken two weeks before I left Hideaway, at a graduation party Erica and John had thrown for Ethan, Olivia, and me. Even though Olivia and I weren't their kids, they'd included our names on the cake alongside Ethan's.

I remember everything about that moment as if it were yesterday. Mia had taken the picture. Ethan is in the middle, one arm slung around my shoulders, the other holding Olivia close. Harper and Hudson stand next to her, at that awkward, skinny stage of adolescence when they seemed to grow overnight.

And next to me, Piper. I wanted to put my free arm around her, but knew I couldn't. The backs of our hands were touching, though.

"See!"

"Yes, honey," Erica replies, "you're absolutely right. Now, are you hungry?"

Martha presses her lips together, an expression of intense concentration on her face, then looks at her father.

"Am I hungry, Daddy?"

Ethan lifts her out of his arms, pressing her tummy next to his ear.

"I think so, pumpkin," he says. "I can definitely hear the gurgle monster."

"What does he want to eat?" Martha asks, giggling between words.

Ethan glances at his mother.

"Mini lobster rolls, roast pork, and blueberry pie," Erica says in a growly voice from just behind her granddaughter.

"Feed the gurgle monster!" Martha cries, then wriggles in Ethan's arms to face her grandmother. "I want to be between you and Daddy." She looks at Piper. "And opposite Aunt Piper."

Piper presses a hand to her heart. "I am honored."

My heart feels too tight inside my chest as I watch Martha with her family. It's one thing to know your friends' had a kid; it's another to meet her face-to-face. It makes it real in a way I can't deal with.

A zing sparks through my fingers, as Piper takes my hand and squeezes.

Suddenly, I don't feel quite so alone. Her presence grounds me.

Just friends, remember?

I drop her hand and extend my arm towards the dining room. "Ladies first."

Her expression glitches for a second, like she's embarrassed, then she smiles and leads me into the other room, seating me next to her, with Hudson on my other side.

"Can we help?" I ask Erica as she brings a booster seat to the table for Martha.

She waves me away as I begin to get up. "Absolutely not, young man. You sit. We've got this."

The table is set with a garland of evergreens running down the center, with sprigs of pine and cedar nestled around the bases of the candles. Flatware sparkles in the light, and the linen napkins are neatly pressed. Nothing about this looks like the low-key dinner for four we were expecting.

"Mom …" Piper says. "I thought it was just supposed to be you and Dad this evening."

Erica ignores her, directing Hudson to the kitchen as Ethan lowers Martha onto her seat and pushes it toward the table.

"Gee, thanks," Harper says. "Love you too."

"You know I don't mean it like that," Piper replies, trying to keep her voice down as Martha leans closer to listen. "It's just … a lot."

"And so is this," Ethan says, gesturing toward me and Piper as he takes his seat.

Piper stiffens beside me.

"That's my fault," I say. I have no idea how it's my fault, considering this relationship was only invented a couple of days ago, so I leave it at that.

"How?" he asks, his tone deceptively calm.

I rub my free hand over my jaw, trying to buy time. "Because …"

Because I ghosted your entire family after my mom died, and needed to get away to prove I wasn't like her or my dad? And now I'm back and fake-dating your sister just so I can land a job?

Erica bustles back into the room, leading John and Hudson, who are carrying mini lobster rolls, wine, and a cut-glass crystal jug of iced water.

"You leave him be," she says to Ethan. "There's plenty of time for explanations. I've got my whole family with me, and that's all that matters."

"You want some wine, son?" John asks me.

My hand covers the top of the glass a little too quickly and I feel people's eyes on me. "Just water, thank you."

He moves on without acknowledging my choice, and I'm glad. I have no idea how much they've followed my life since I left Hideaway, or what they know. Our first meal together is not the time to spill the dirt, especially not with Martha here.

My mouth waters as the lobster rolls are passed around. I've eaten some of the best food in the world at the most exclusive and expensive restaurants, but nothing compares to the food at the Locke house. Yeah, I know it's a cliché, but food made with love just can't be beat.

"You okay with this, Brody?" Erica asks. "You're not on a special diet?"

Piper stops moving beside me, and I glance around the table, noting who else reacts. Harper and Hudson's expressions haven't changed, and Ethan's is inscrutable.

This is the part of fame I hate most. Waiting for someone to bring up your public fuck-ups like it's the only thing you want to talk about.

"No," I reply. "I eat everything."

I try and force my heart to calm but it's not listening. I need to man the fuck up. Say the words that are filling my chest.

"I want to apologize ... for running away ... and—"

Erica leans across Piper and touches my arm. "You don't need to do that, honey."

My jaw is clenched so hard I can hardly get the words out. "I do." My voice is gruff, with the kind of emotion actors wish they could access on demand.

"Son—"

That nearly breaks me. John Locke was the father I always wanted, not the deadbeat dad I got.

"I do," I repeat, a little forcefully. "There are a thousand reasons why I left Hideaway and didn't return, but it was the biggest mistake of my life. I can't take it back. I can't change—" Martha's enormous blue eyes are wide, taking in every word. "Even though I would do anything—"

Fuck! An ocean of grief I've ignored for over a decade is crashing through me.

Piper takes my hand and squeezes almost as hard as Hudson did earlier, making it even more difficult to hold it together.

"I'm sorry. I'm so, so sorry."

Through the blurred edges of my vision, I see Martha stretching her arms toward her father, and a lump rises in my throat.

The silence around the table is deafening, broken only by the screech of chair legs on the wooden floor and the patter of tiny feet.

Piper lets go of my hand as Martha pushes between us and throws her arms around me.

I lift her up and bury my face against her small chest while she strokes my hair.

"It's all right, Uncle Brody. Daddy says it's good to cry because you're ..."

There's a low murmur from across the table.

"Acknolging your feelings."

I hear the pride in her voice as she says such a big word, and the pain of her mom not being here hits me even harder.

I didn't cry when Olivia died. It was too much of a shock. Too unreal to accept. The logical part of my mind accepted the truth, but the rest of me refused to believe it. And if I never went back to Hideaway ...then maybe it didn't happen. She, Ethan, and their baby girl were still one happy family.

But now the tears won't fucking stop. I haven't cried since my mom died, not even for a role.

Piper's arms are around my back, helping hold me together, but her kindness is only breaking me further apart. I don't deserve it.

I hear more chairs moving, feel more hands being placed on me, their warmth telling me I'm not alone.

"We love you, Uncle Brody!" Martha says brightly. "Everything's going to be okay!"

I huff out a laugh even as the tears keep falling.

I see now why people want children. Why they adore them.

Hell, I love Martha enough to lay down my life for her, and we've only known each other for fifteen minutes.

Little hands pull my hair, and I raise my head.

Martha's lips are pressed together as she assesses me, her expression so strikingly like Ethan's.

"You need to blow your nose now," she says authoritatively. "Then eat your lobster roll."

"Yes, ma'am."

"Being hungry makes you cry," she continues. "Because the gurgle monster pinches your tummy."

I nod, aware of people around me. Erica is wiping her eyes and gazing at me and Martha with so much love that I have to look away.

"You can put me down now," Martha says.

I gently lower her to the floor, and she skips back around the table to Ethan. I can't look at him.

Piper hands me a wad of tissues, and I make for the hall outside the dining room. She follows me, closing the door behind us.

We both blow our noses, then face each other.

Tears make her eyes sparkle brighter, and the Christmas lights catch her hair, giving it a soft, golden glow.

"I'm so proud of you."

Her words cut straight to my heart, and I hold my breath, staring up at the ceiling, fighting the urge to cry again.

"Do you want a hug?" she asks tentatively.

I give a tiny nod, and then she's in my arms, and my whole body sighs, "*Yes.*"

I rest my head against hers, breathing in her scent like it's the air keeping me alive.

"Thank you," I manage, and she hugs me tighter.

Her touch isn't sexual. It's just … loving. Comforting. Kind.

But the longer we stand there, the harder it becomes for me to stay in the friend zone.

The edges of my grief soften and dissolve, and in their place, a steady beat of attraction builds, growing louder and louder.

My cock wakes up, and I panic. Piper's being nice, and I'm being … the biggest creeper on the block.

The hug is now officially too long and has turned, for me, into the opposite of platonic. If we don't break apart right now, she's gonna know exactly how attracted I am to her, and that is not what either of us wants.

We jump apart as the doorbell rings, and Piper rushes to open it.

"Mia!" she screams as her best friend grabs her in a fierce hug, and they jump up and down, squealing.

I close the door against the winter air, wishing I could roll around in the snow to cool off from Piper's touch. Then I gaze at her and Mia.

Mia's older, more grown up, but her curly auburn hair still reaches her waist.

Finally breaking away from Piper, she gives me the once-over.

"Welcome back to Hideaway Harbor, Brody."

She glances slyly at the light fitting above Piper and me, where a sprig of mistletoe is tied.

"Well, what are the chances?" Mia puts a hand on my shoulder. "You need to do the right thing, Brody."

I stare blankly at her.

She slowly nods and gives me a slight push. "You need to kiss Piper."

CHAPTER 8

PIPER

"*M*ia! Knock it off!"

I'm breathing too fast, my internal organs ricocheting around inside of me like they've just been caught doing something naughty and are scrambling to get back where they belong.

I was meant to be comforting Brody, but it turned, at least for me, into something else. Something so hot, horny, and addictive that I couldn't let him go.

Jesus. And after he'd just ripped open his chest and bared his soul to my entire family?

"I'm only trying to help," Mia protests, a cheeky glint in her eye.

"How, exactly?" I cross my arms, attempting a stern face.

"Is that Mia?" Mom calls from the dining room.

"Yes, give us a minute!"

"Have you kissed yet?" Mia asks.

Brody takes a step back, his palms raised, and a little piece of my heart breaks off.

"Of course not!" I whisper to Mia, then gesture at Brody. "He'd rather kiss a piece of furniture. It's fake, don't you remember?"

"*I* know that." She inclines her head toward the dining-room door. "But *they* don't. You need to practice so you can make it look real."

Brody shakes his head. "There isn't going to be any kissing."

Dammit!

I take a calming breath. "See? Now make sure you—"

"Aunt Mia!"

Martha runs toward us.

Mia scoops her up and whirls her around. "How's my favorite Martha in the whole wide world?"

Martha giggles, then pulls Mia's knitted hat off. "Hurry up! We're having lobster rolls and pie!"

"I'm glad I'm not too late for that," Mia says, then strolls to the dining room carrying her.

Brody and I follow. I want to take his hand again, but after Mia dropped the idea of a kiss on us like a bomb, I can't. I don't want him thinking that's what I want, because I don't. Well, not really. Although if—

He doesn't want to kiss you, so back the sexy truck up.

Back in the dining room, Dad is getting an extra chair, and Mom is setting another place next to Hudson.

"Mom, there's no room next to me," he grumbles. "Put Mia next to Harper."

Dad sighs with good-natured exasperation and moves the chair to the other side of the table as the show starts.

"I forgot how much extra room was needed for your ego," Mia says to my brother with a smirk.

Hudson rolls his eyes. "Muscles, Mia. Muscles."

I bite my lip to stop a laugh escaping as Mia squints and peers at my brother's arms.

"I don't think that's muscle. It looks to me like too many big meals down at the station."

She glances at Brody as he takes his place next to Hudson. "Now *Brody's* got muscles. He's seriously buff."

Hudson instinctively flexes as he flicks a glance at Brody's arms.

"See?" Mia says. "You should ask him what workout he does. He probably has some ex-Navy SEAL trainer."

My traitorous eyes roam over Brody's body. Unfortunately, most of it is clothed, but I've ogled his bare forearms long enough on the drive up—and felt his body against mine when we hugged, so I know Mia's right. He's solid in *all* the right places.

"Do you, Brody?"

Spots of color appear on Brody's cheekbones, and he nods.

Mia squeals. "Knew it! Is his name Bullet? Or Warrior?"

"Major Gains," he deadpans. "Or Major Ab Gains if he's being formal."

I giggle.

"Although after a session with him, I call him Major Ab Pains," Brody continues.

"Really?" Mia asks, looking delighted. "Please let this be true!"

Brody grins. "Unfortunately, not. His name's Weston."

She sighs dramatically. "Well, you should still give his number to Hudson. He needs all the help he can get in the personal fitness department, especially after his poor showing in Hideaway's Wife Carrying Championships last summer."

Hudson growls and shoves an entire lobster roll in his mouth. They're mini ones, but still.

Both Hudson and Mia are single. You don't actually have to

be married or even in a relationship with your teammate to participate, and Mia competes with her brother.

"Remind me who won this year?" Mia continues, an expression of pure innocence on her face. "And last?"

"Mia, honey, leave the poor boy alone," Mom chides. "He still hasn't processed the defeat."

Hudson tries to speak, clearly taking issue with the word *defeat*, but Mia holds up her hand.

"Not with food in your mouth." She turns to Harper. "How's your search going for a shop for your perfume business?"

"I haven't found the right place yet. But once Christmas is over and the pop-up shops are closed, there should be more choices." She looks between Mia and me. "You don't seem surprised about Piper and Brody. Did you know?"

Mia shrugs and finishes her mouthful. "Piper didn't want to tell you in case you freaked out. Also, she didn't want to jinx it."

"Jinx it how?"

"You know, how she's finally landed the—ow!"

A lifetime of kicking my siblings under the table means I know how to make contact with the right shin. And I also know exactly where Mia's motormouth was running.

There's no way I want Brody, or the rest of my family, to know I was head-over-heels for him all those years ago.

"How did they re-meet?" Harper asks.

I wave across the table. "Hello? We are here, you know."

"Yeah, but Mia will make the story way more exciting than it probably is," she retorts.

"One hundred percent. So, a few months ago—"

"Brody was dodging the paparazzi and slid into my booth at a coffee shop," I say quickly. "We started talking and hanging out. I didn't want to tell anyone in case it didn't work out."

Mia huffs dramatically. "See? Boring."

"Not everything has to be a big drama," Hudson says to her. "Nothing wrong with simple and straightforward."

Which, of course, is nothing like the situation Brody and I are actually in.

"Is that a line from your online dating profile?" Mia asks Hudson. "Simple, straightforward, excels at coming second."

Hudson raises an eyebrow at Mia and I watch her process the other meaning of *coming second*.

Her cheeks flush a deeper red than her hair, and she immediately changes the subject.

"Hey, Brody. You know you're not the only new celeb in Hideaway this Christmas?"

Hideaway Harbor has always attracted famous people. They might like the patchy phone signal, the stunning scenery, or the small-town vibe. But they stay because they're usually treated like normal people, and left alone.

"Amanda Willis is in town," Mia continues. "She was great as an astronaut in *Lift Off to Love*. Have you ever worked with her before?"

The actress is stunningly beautiful, and my evil mind conjures up an image of Brody kissing her on camera. The director yells "Cut," but they keep on going.

"No, we run in the same circles, but we haven't properly met."

"Well, if you run into her and have some kind of mwah-mwah-sweedie-dahhling moment, put in a good word for me, will you? I've always wanted to photograph her."

Brody grins. "I don't think I've ever had a mwah-mwah-sweedie-dahhling moment with anyone before."

Mia smirks. "When in Hideaway …"

"Do you have any interesting jobs coming up?" Mom asks Mia.

"I've been doing some social media work for the spa. That's been pretty cool." Her face lights up. "And the other day, they had this mysterious package turn up. A bag filled with carrots and candy canes, and a note that said, 'Healthy and not-so-healthy treats for the holidays.'"

"Who was it from?"

Mia shrugs. "No clue. Apparently, there's a secret do-gooder going about in the middle of the night doing things like leaving gifts and clearing snow from people's porches."

This is one of the things I love about my hometown; there's always something interesting going on. It also means the conversation can move away from Brody and me. My right arm is buzzing next to him, and when our elbows occasionally touch, I have to stop myself from jumping at the shock.

Dad collects our plates. "As long as good deeds don't turn into pranks, I'm happy."

He's been Hideaway's mayor for the past twenty-five years, and the town is like another one of his children.

"It's an elf," Martha says with the authority of a preschooler who's figured out exactly how the world works. "An elf who doesn't live on the shelf."

"But are you sure it's a good elf?" Hudson asks.

"He made a funny-looking snowman with a big smile in front of the school."

"You sure it wasn't the janitor?"

"I heard him talking to the principal about it. He said he didn't do it."

Hudson arches a brow, and Mia leans across the table toward him. "You gonna do a stakeout? Patrol the streets at night to protect us from a marauding elf doing good deeds?"

My younger brother ignores her and follows Dad into the kitchen.

"You never know!" Mia calls after him. "It might be me!"

"*Is* it you?" Martha asks.

"Sorry, I wish it were, but I only do bad deeds."

"Really?"

Ethan clears his throat.

"Only joking," Mia says quickly, hiding her smirk. "I'm ninety-nine percent good."

Dad and Hudson return carrying the main course, and from the size of the pork roast in my brother's hands, there's no way Mom planned this meal for fewer than the entire family.

"Wow," Brody says as Mom passes his empty plate to Dad so he can be served first. "This is incredible!"

Mom's cheeks flush at the praise. "It's basted with Maine maple syrup, Dijon mustard, and fresh herbs. And slow-roasted all afternoon. The potatoes are mashed with butter and buttermilk, and the winter salad is a mix of baby greens, crisp green apples, dried cranberries, toasted pecans, and a maple-Dijon vinaigrette to complement the roast pork."

"This …" Brody slowly shakes his head, "is the best meal I've eaten in years."

"Since you were last here?" Dad asks.

"Absolutely. There's no cooking that compares to Mrs Locke's."

"Erica," Mom says, leaning across me again to squeeze his arm. "Call me Erica."

"Yes, ma'am."

I start eating and follow the happy hum of conversation. Brody seems more relaxed now, laughing at Harper's terrible jokes, and the tension inside me melts away.

"Blueberry pie!" Mia exclaims as my mother places it on the table. "I have to take a picture."

The lattice design on top is so precise I think Mom must have measured each line. It looks better than anything store-bought, and I know it tastes better too, with a perfect buttery pastry that crumbles and melts in the mouth.

Mia gets to her feet to snap a couple of photos, then sits back down. "By the way, I'm having Hudson's portion. He told me earlier that he'd prefer a small, low-fat yogurt instead."

"As if," Hudson rumbles, and we all laugh.

Dad cuts the pie and hands it out. It's still warm, and when a scoop of Mom's homemade vanilla ice cream melts on top of my slice, my mouth waters even more.

My hand inches toward my spoon, but I force myself to wait until everyone is served.

"Eat! Don't wait!" Mom says to me and Brody.

"I don't need to be told twice," Brody says with a smile and we dig in as if we're starving.

As the cool creaminess of the ice cream and the slight tartness of the soft blueberries hit my tongue, I moan with appreciation before I can stop myself.

Brody's spoon makes a clanking noise as it crashes into his bowl.

"Yummy, yummy, in my tummy!" Martha shouts, breaking the silence.

Mia stares at me from across the table, a knowing smirk on her lips.

I glare at her and give a tiny shake of my head.

She gets the message and turns to Mom. "Are these the blueberries we picked on Labor Day weekend?"

"Sure are, honey. And we've still got nearly a hundred pounds left in the freezer in the basement."

As Mia and my mom chat blueberry recipes, I sense Ethan's eyes on me and Brody. It's the kind of scrutiny I'd rather avoid. He's a search and rescue pilot, but if he wasn't being a hero on a daily basis, I bet he would have joined the FBI.

"What are your plans now you're back?" he asks Brody.

"Just hanging out," I reply as Brody finishes his mouthful. "See what's going on in town."

"There's the Santa Fun Run tomorrow," Harper says. "Lots of guys from Hudson's station are doing it, so I'm going to cheer them on."

"Then there's caroling in the town square late afternoon,"

Dad adds. "Another live music event at The Shore Thing, and the ice carving competition up at the estate."

"Are you doing the fun run?" Mia asks Hudson.

His mouth is full of pie, so he shakes his head.

"Oh, I forgot, you don't do fun."

He finishes his mouthful and rolls his eyes. "I'm saving myself for the woolen sock running championships on Sunday."

"That's still going on?" Brody asks.

"Yep," Hudson replies. "I came in second last year." He shoots a look at Mia, and she lowers her gaze to her pie. "So this year I'm going to win it."

"Did you knit your own socks?" Brody continues.

"I did," Mom says proudly.

The sock-running championships are one of Hideaway's more bizarre traditions, inspired by the ones in Finland. The races are held either around the Locke Family Reserve or up in the mountains if there isn't enough snow. One of the rules is that participants must wear hand-knitted socks, or a pair made right here in Hideaway Harbor.

"You're not joining?" Hudson asks Mia.

"I'm taking photos for *The Almanac*."

"Then make sure you're at the finish line to capture my victory," he says with a grin. He glances at Brody. "You want in?"

Brody shakes his head. "I've never tried sock running before, but I'll be there to support you." He turns to me. "If that's okay with you?"

My cheeks heat. "Of course." It's weird enough that he's sitting here after all these years, but deferring to me as if we're a unit is even stranger.

Ethan's eyes narrow slightly as he looks at me.

Shit!

I catch Mia's eye, trying to communicate telepathically, and she claps her hands. "I need to take a family photo now that you're all here!"

"Doesn't that wait until Christmas Eve?" Hudson asks.

"This is an informal one. Do you need time to do something with your hair?"

Hudson's hand moves to his head, and he frowns as she giggles. His hair is short, with never a strand out of place. If he hadn't become a firefighter, he definitely would have joined the military.

"I think a photo is a lovely idea," Mom says, then dabs at her mouth with a napkin. "Let's clear the table first, and I'll put a pot of coffee on."

Brody leaps to his feet. "Please, let me help clean up."

Mom hesitates. She doesn't like giving up control around the house, but she's learning. "Okay, then. But I'll make the coffee."

"We can do it," Ethan says. "Why don't you and Dad take Martha?"

"Yes, Grandma!" Martha says. "We need to put our feet up."

"And maybe read a story, sweetheart?" Mom suggests.

Martha fist pumps, then lifts her arms up to Ethan, who lifts her off the booster seat and sets her on the floor. She takes Mom's hand and leads her toward the family room.

Brody and I go to the kitchen and start loading the dishwasher. He hasn't been in this house for twelve years, but he seems to remember exactly how Mom likes it stacked and where things go.

"Some things never change, huh?" Ethan says to him as he loads a serving dish in the top rack.

The words are mild, but with my older brother, each syllable is measured. He's never been one to waste words or run his mouth, so Brody knows, as do I, how this seemingly innocuous sentence is loaded with meaning.

Brody stills, then nods.

"You should come around to mine one night," Ethan continues. "Watch the game."

"Sure," Brody replies, his voice neutral. "I'd like that."

"Ooh, Ethan!" Harper says, grabbing his arm. "I forgot. I have a new creation to show you. I think it's the perfect men's cologne!"

She pulls him out of the kitchen, and Brody's gaze follows them, a frown on his face.

Hudson gives us a sympathetic smile. "He'll come around. It's just been a shock, that's all."

I nod, guilt eating at my insides, as Brody glances back at me.

We finish up in the kitchen, then Mia herds us into the family room in front of the fireplace.

"Think of this as just a bit of fun, informal practice for Christmas Eve, when I've got my proper camera," she says, steering Dad to the back row behind Mom.

He dips his head to kiss Mom's cheek, and she smiles, leaning back into him.

I know they're my parents, and I should be gagging, but seeing the love between them makes me happy.

They were lucky to find their person while they were still in school, and their love has only grown over the years. It's inspirational, even though it often feels like an impossibly high bar to clear.

"Brody, go behind Piper," Mia says.

We both hesitate at the same time, and I sense Ethan's pointed gaze on us again.

I quickly shuffle back until I feel the warmth of Brody's body behind me, but don't move any further, so we're not actually touching.

"Now put your arms around her," Mia continues.

I can't feel Brody moving. What should I do?

Mia huffs. "Call yourself an actor? You're not very good at taking direction."

I freeze, immediately paranoid that everyone knows Brody is only pretending to be my boyfriend. Then I grab his arm and put it over my shoulder.

"That's better!" Mia calls out. "Now the other one."

Brody complies, and suddenly the whole back of my body is flush against the front of his. I'm stiff at first, but the heat from him radiates through me, unwinding the tension in my muscles until I melt against him. It's the most delicious guilty pleasure, and I don't want it to end.

Mia's usually super-efficient when she works, but right now she's messing around with the people around us, rearranging them again and again while Brody and I stay locked together, a still point in the hubbub.

Only when Hudson pulls out his phone to take a selfie of us all does she stop fussing and step back to take the photo.

"Say 'true love,'" she cries.

"True love," Brody rumbles in my ear, and I shiver.

How can I make this moment last? It feels so right, even though I know it's so wrong.

Eventually, Mia finishes snapping pictures and dips her head to look at the screen.

"If I ignore Hudson," she says, grinning, "you all look gorgeous."

"What's wrong with Uncle Hudson, Aunt Mia?"

"Well, he—"

"Absolutely nothing," Hudson cuts in. "Aunt Mia just can't handle perfection."

"*Are* you perfect?" Martha continues, her eyes wide.

Hudson's "yes" is immediately drowned out by all our shouts of "no."

"I think that's our cue to get you home," Ethan says to Martha.

She pouts. "But Daddy! We've just got here!"

He gently sweeps a lock of blonde hair from her forehead. "It's way past your bedtime already, pumpkin, and you can see everyone tomorrow."

Her lower lip wobbles, but she nods. She knows Ethan loves her to the moon and back, but she also knows that when he sets a boundary, it's not going anywhere.

Before long, it's just Brody and me with my parents, and when they decide to turn in early, I know the inevitable can't be put off any longer. We've got to find a way to sleep apart without anyone knowing.

My folks are over the moon that we're no longer staying at the hotel, and they follow us all the way up to my childhood room. I'm small enough to fit on the daybed, which will help with any awkwardness, but when I push open the door and step through, my stomach drops.

The room has been completely remodeled. The old wallpaper, stained from where teenage me had stuck up posters, has been replaced with a delicate floral design that I can't help but love.

My old bed has been replaced with a queen-sized one, and the white counterpane is strewn with hundreds of pink rose petals.

And the daybed Mia used to sleep on when we were kids? The one piece of furniture my fake relationship with Brody can't function without?

Gone.

CHAPTER 9

BRODY

"*W*hat do you think?" Erica asks, her excited tone telling us there's only one acceptable reaction to her turning her daughter's bedroom into a honeymoon suite.

Piper makes a strangled noise that could either convey ecstasy or horror. I know which one to bet on, but her mom's racing a hundred miles an hour in the opposite direction.

"Oh, honey, I was just so excited you were bringing your beau home for the holidays that I wanted to do something special for you both!"

I glance around the space, half expecting to see a bowl of condoms on the nightstand. But then I realize the only reason Erica hasn't provided them is because she wants nothing to come between her and the prospect of more grandkids.

"M-mom ..." Piper manages. "What ... Where is—"

"And you've got the bathroom next door all to yourselves. I

wanted to knock down the wall and turn it into a private bathroom, but we didn't have time between Thanksgiving and now."

Erica moves to the dresser and lights—*actual fucking candles.*

What next? A bearskin rug? Oh, there it is, on the floor where the daybed used to be. Well, I suppose it's gonna be more comfortable than sleeping on the wooden boards.

"We brought up Hudson's old CD player from the basement," Erica continues. "And I've left some of my favorite music for you."

"Why don't we leave them to it?" John says from his position by the door. He's obviously supporting his wife, but I'm sure he's not as enthusiastic as she is about creating the ultimate shag pad for their daughter.

"Just a moment, honey," she replies, then presses a button on the CD player.

The opening bars of *Endless Love* fill the room, and I close my eyes, hoping that when I open them, I'll find myself back in my apartment in New York and that all of this would have been a fever dream.

Unfortunately, when I do, it's to discover Erica sashaying across the room toward John as they sing the lyrics to each other.

Kill. Me. Now.

I can't even look at Piper. Thankfully, she's facing away, her posture rigid, like someone turned her to stone.

"Happy snuggle time, kids!" Erica says, and I wonder if she's drunk or if there are hidden cameras recording our reactions.

The door closes behind them and it's just me and Piper, along with Diana and Lionel crooning about endless love.

Piper's shoulders shake slightly, and a brief flare of panic rushes through me, fearing she's crying.

Then she faces me, laughing hysterically.

I suppose it's a better choice than a mental breakdown.

"What … the fuck!" she whispers between silent laughs. "I'm so sorry!"

I relax a little and grin. "I think we should count ourselves lucky the pastor isn't next door, waiting to marry us."

She holds the side of her head. "Can you imagine if I were still dating Colin, and I brought him home to this? He'd be out the window and back to Brooklyn before the end of the song!"

My stomach twists at the thought of any other man being with Piper, even though it's nothing to do with me. Is she still in love with Colin? Does she wish he was here instead of me?

Piper swivels. "I mean, *candles*? In an old wooden house? Hudson would have a fit if he knew. And *rose petals*? Oh my god, Brody, Mom's lost her mind."

She goes to the nightstand and lifts a box from the top. "Tissues. Of course." Then she carefully opens the drawer, as if expecting a spider to leap out. "Oh, for goodness' sake."

"What is it?"

She holds up a box of chocolates.

"That's not too bad."

Then, she lifts out a small bottle.

"What's that—holy *shit* …" Yep, Mrs Locke has supplied us with a bottle of lube.

Now I'm laughing as hard as Piper is, my hand over my mouth to stifle the sound.

The fact that we're trying to hide our hysteria, rather than the sounds of sex, makes us laugh even harder. We end up leaning on opposite sides of the bed, doubled over.

"Thank … thank God I'm doing this with you," Piper finally says. "I don't think anyone else would be able to cope."

I straighten, wiping my eyes and smiling at her. "Likewise. We've got this." I hold out my fist, and she bumps hers against it. I'm no longer worried about what we're doing. We're friends, and we're on the same team. It's gonna be easy.

96

"I know the daybed's gone, but I'll be fine sleeping on Barry," I say.

"Huh?"

I gesture to the rug on the floor. "Barry the bear."

Piper kneels down beside it. "It's a sheepskin."

"Bear sounds cooler."

She grins up at me. "Barry, it is, then, but there's no way you're sleeping here. It's still hard as nails, and there's a draft from under the door."

I run a hand through my hair. "Do you think I could sneak into Ethan's old room?"

"No way. Can you imagine what Mom would do if she found out? We'd be in couples' counseling by the end of the day."

Piper sighs. "Look, this bed is crazy big, and I'm a really sound sleeper, so there's no way I'm gonna roll onto your side and accidentally feel you up."

"We're friends," she continues, "and if you pretend the last twelve years didn't happen, then we're actually really close friends. I don't even remember a time in my life when you weren't around, and I trust you as much as I trust either of my brothers. Actually, I trust you way more. If I had to share a bed with Hudson, he'd eat beans all day so he could fart all night."

"Nah, he'd only do that to Mia."

"True, they're gifted at annoying each other."

Piper unzips one of her bags and rummages around. "Do you mind if I use the bathroom first?"

"Go ahead."

She stands, holding a pair of pajamas and a wash bag. "I won't be long. Who knows what Mom's stashed in the closet or the dresser? But there should be enough room if you wanted to unpack."

"Sure."

"Okay, see you in a bit."

She quietly slips out into the corridor and closes the bedroom door behind her.

My gaze is unfocused as I stare at the door. I know I should be pleased that Piper's so matter of fact about this arrangement, like we're coworkers having to share a room at a conference, or like it was with Ethan when I used to stay over in his room.

But part of me wants more.

This is what happens when you go almost a year without sex.

I shake my head at myself and focus on unpacking. There's plenty of room in the closet, with only a few items from Piper's childhood.

My hand lingers on her cheerleading uniform like a creeper.

Turning abruptly away, I sit on the edge of the bed, a few petals falling to the floor.

If I survived seeing the Lockes again after all this time then I can keep my thoughts about Piper in line.

In my mind's eye I see Martha, the spitting image of her mother, and my heart squeezes. I'd never allowed myself to think of having kids, but if they could be like her? A sweet little girl who could comfort a grown man with such compassion?

An image of children pops into my head, *my* children. Two little girls and a boy, chasing each other around the Locke family yard, the three of them laughing and calling out, utterly absorbed in the moment. They all have Piper's eyes and her smile.

What the fuck?

Springing to my feet, I rub a hand across my face to try to erase the image of what will never happen, then go to the window and pull back the drapes.

Gentle snowflakes drift down, lit in every color by the Christmas lights on the neighbors' houses. It's picture-perfect, a scene movie directors spend a fortune trying to recreate.

I did the right thing coming back, even if it's many years overdue. It might be the season for forgiveness, but I know now that Piper's family would have forgiven me, no matter the time of year.

The sound of the door snaps me out of my funk, and I turn as Piper enters, dressed in oversized pink-striped pajamas. Her face is freshly washed and her smile hits me in the gut.

"There are fresh towels in the closet and also the bathroom for you to use," she says.

I nod, not wanting to open my mouth to reply in case I say something stupid about how pretty she looks, then grab my wash bag and nightclothes, and head out.

Inside the bathroom, the whole space smells of her—fresh and floral.

It's got to go.

Turning the dial to arctic cold in the shower, I wash myself with brisk efficiency.

Five minutes later, my body and teeth are clean and I'm headed back down the hall. I usually sleep naked, but tonight I'm wearing light gray sweatpants and a navy T-shirt, bought especially for this trip, to appear decent in front of Piper.

My heart pounds in my throat as I lightly knock on the door. I don't hear a response from inside, so I wait.

A few moments later, Piper opens it.

"Come in," she says, her eyes darting down my body before she quickly looks away and turns toward the window.

The music is off, and so are the lights. The only illumination in the room comes from the candles and the colored lights outside, reflecting off the falling snowflakes.

It's the most romantic setting I've ever been in, but then I see that the rose petals are gone from the bed, and Piper has placed a line of throw pillows down the middle.

This is good. We're on the same page.

Piper beckons me over to the window, her golden hair like a halo around her beautiful face.

My feet move slowly but inevitably forward, and I force myself to keep a little space between us.

"It's so beautiful," she says, her gaze on the snow silently drifting down like a rainbow broken into tiny pieces of colored light.

"Sure is," I reply, my attention solely on her.

"Thank you for doing this for me," she says quietly, her eyes still on the view outside.

I don't immediately reply, my brain struggling to process what she's saying.

"I appreciate it so much."

I huff out a laugh, and she gazes at me, her eyes questioning.

"Piper, any thanks owed are one hundred percent from me to you."

"But—"

"It's not just the job you're giving me a chance at getting, you're rebuilding my reputation, which is currently a dumpster fire."

She shakes her head. "It's not."

"It is. If you've seen half the press I've generated over the past year, you'd know."

Her cheeks flush pink, and I wonder how much she actually *does* know.

"I, er … You probably noticed, but I don't drink."

"Nothing wrong with that."

"There is. If I do, I can't stop. It gets ugly, and I don't want to end up like—"

I break off, and take a breath as Piper waits patiently for me to finish. I see the care and compassion in her eyes. It's how she's always been. Someone who always puts others before herself.

"You know how my mom struggled with addiction? Well I'm just like her."

"That's not true. You take care of yourself."

"Like living off sea moss smoothies and air-fried pizza made with cauliflower and cashew nuts instead of bread and cheese?"

I shake my head. "No wonder everyone thinks I'm a dick."

Her expression clouds and she reaches to touch my arm. "I don't think that. Nor do my family."

I shrug like I don't really care, even though I do, and take a step back, breaking the connection between us. "Is this going to be our first argument as a fake couple?"

Her smile is hesitant. "That's why I put a pillow wall on the bed."

"You could make me sleep on Barry?"

"I'm not that mean. You need to be properly rested for tomorrow."

"You got plans for me?"

Her eyes widen almost imperceptibly, then she moves further away. "I haven't, but if this—" she gestures to the room —"is any indication of how excited Mom is about us, we'll probably discover she's planned a parade in our honor. You'll be Brody *Snow* King, and I'll be your queen."

Piper waves regally, acting like she's on top of a float.

I give her a short bow. "Your majesty."

She curtsies. "My liege," she replies in a terrible British accent, and I crack up.

"Hey! It wasn't *that* bad!"

"Not at all," I say in a perfect British accent. "It was practically perfect in every way."

Her jaw drops, and she stares at me like I've just demonstrated I can fly.

"Oh, my god!" she whispers. "Do it again! Say something posh!"

I don't hesitate. "Being your slave, what should I do but tend upon the hours and times of your desire? I have no precious time at all to spend, nor services to do, till you require."

Her cheeks flush with color, and her mouth opens and closes like the cutest little fish at the fair.

"Shakespeare," I say, by way of explanation.

She takes a step back, fanning her cheeks. "Holy British shitballs, Brody. That was … objectively hot."

I don't know what to do. I want to say more. But I'm not using Shakespeare's gift of words and my ability to mimic any accent to make Piper like me.

So I bow as if I've completed a performance and turn to the window. "Should I close the drapes?"

She doesn't immediately reply, and I keep my gaze on the street outside.

"Could you leave them open for a bit? I'd quite like to watch it from under the comforter."

"Sure." I open them a little wider and join her on the bed, her under the covers, me on top.

My body aches just to hold her hand again, but she's tucked in like a child, only her head showing, propped up on two pillows so she can see the snow falling.

"I forgot to blow out the candles," she says. "But I kind of don't want to. They're so pretty, even though they're a massive fire hazard."

"I'll blow them out later."

She stifles a yawn. "Thank you. And you can get under the covers, you know."

"Maybe later."

"I told you, I sleep like the dead, so I'll definitely stay on my side, and there's the pillow wall as well. You'll be safe. I promise."

I make a non-committal sound in response.

The room is silent, save for the soft sound of snowfall on the windows.

At the edges of my vision, Piper's eyelids grow heavy until they close. I wait, listening to her breathing change. After a few minutes, she turns on her side to face me, shuffling further under the covers, as if the two pillows under her head are now too high.

I carefully pull the bottom one out and add it to the pillow wall between us.

Piper wriggles a little as she repositions herself, then lets out a contented sigh.

She's so cute right now, I can't stop smiling.

Her perfect little mouth opens. "Habajuh puh-puh," she mutters.

Huh?

"Jar bahjuh jup purrr?"

I press my lips together to stop a laugh escaping as she begins a garbled conversation with herself.

"Bah buh-buh *brum.*"

It's a letter salad and makes absolutely no sense, but it's too adorable for words, and I'm utterly captivated.

"Juh bruh, mahbrum—VISION!"

I nearly leap off the bed, but then she lapses back into mumbles and my shoulders shake with laughter.

She's moving about again now, and I wonder what's coming next. For someone who claims to sleep like the dead, it looks like she's dancing under the covers.

Then her arms flail free, and she grabs a pillow from the pillow wall, hugging it to her. She lets out another loud sigh, then falls quiet, sprawled in the middle of the bed.

I gaze at the sheepskin on the floor, wondering if I should sleep on it, then decide there's enough room here.

If I lie on my side at the very edge of the bed, and Piper's happy cuddling the pillow, we should be okay.

Getting up quietly, I close the drapes, blow out the candles, then carefully slip under the covers. I know I should turn away from Piper, but I can't resist facing her, watching her face in the half-light as she sleeps.

"Buh shh muh," she mutters.

"You too," I reply, then gaze at her until I can't keep my eyes open any longer and allow myself to drift off to sleep.

CHAPTER 10

PIPER

"*M*y lady ... I'm gonna fucketh you. Long and hard, till you screameth my name like a good wench."

Brody's topless above me, only wearing his thirst-tastic gray sweatpants, bracing his weight through his corded forearms as he murmurs Shakespeare into my ear.

Who knew English could be this hot?

We're lying in front of a log fire, my back cushioned by a bearskin rug with such a thick, soft texture it's like I'm floating. My pajamas are still on, which is annoying, and I twist beneath him to get more contact. I want him to rip them off with his teeth.

He chuckles. "You wanteth this?"

Then he grinds his perfect cock against my needy pussy, and I gasp.

"Verrily, sirrah! Right thereth!"

My orgasm is already so close, it's hovering at the edges of my skin, just waiting for the final spark to make me burst into flames.

I grab at my pajamas, but they're stuck in place. I need them off. Now. Or I'm going to lose my mind.

The fabric is hot under my fingers. And hard. Like warm skin stretched tight over muscle.

Now I can't move my arm anymore. Something's gripping my wrist like a vise.

My mind tumbles, falling through space and time as it struggles to work out where I am while still clinging to the dream as it rushes away from me.

Then I wake with a start, crashing into a reality so mortifying I want to die.

Right noweth.

I'm lying half on top of Brody. His T-shirt is pushed all the way up to his neck, and he's holding my wrist to keep my hand from grabbing his ...

"Oh, my fucking god!" I cry and leap off him so fast I fly off the other side of the bed and land with a loud thump on the floor.

A head appears. "You okay?"

"I am so sorry. Shit, Brody, I attacked you. I assaulted you. I defiled you!"

One eyebrow raises. "Defiled?"

He's so hot with his hair all messy and his eyes a little puffy with sleep. But I can't think about that right now. I did a bad thing. A very bad thing.

A thing he was trying to stop ...

"Yes! Verily!" I reply without thinking. "I mean, very. One hundred percent. Absolutely. I *mauled* you!"

The corners of his mouth twitch.

"It's not funny, Brody! I was out of control! Invading your personal space! Violating your boundaries like a ..." *Sex maniac?*

"You were asleep," he says. "You didn't know what you were doing."

"It doesn't make it okay!" I run my fingers through my hair and tug the roots with embarrassment and frustration. "Why couldn't I just sleep *talk*? Or walk? Why did I have to ... sleep *hump*?"

Brody's laugh is warm. "It's no biggie. And you do sleep talk."

Oh. My. God.

A memory of me asking him to fuck me surfaces from the jumble of my fading dream.

No. Oh no, no, no, no, no!

All the blood drains from my face as I stare at him, too petrified to ask what I said.

"Don't worry, nothing incriminating."

"Are you sure?" I whisper.

He nods. "It's just a stream of mumbled nonsense, punctuated by a few English words."

"What kind of words?"

His forehead furrows. "Last night, you yelled 'vision' really loudly."

"Vision?"

"Yep."

"Nothing else?"

"Nope, just vision. Do you know what you were dreaming about?"

I shake my head. "No clue. What else did I shout?"

"Nothing more last night. About ten minutes ago, you shouted, 'Right now!' and it woke me up."

I drop my head with a groan. "I am so sorry."

"Don't be. It was—" He clears his throat. "It's fine."

Scrambling to my feet, I hastily grab clothes from the dresser and head to the door. "I'm going to take a cold shower, then go downstairs," I say to the floor, unable to meet Brody's eyes. "Meet you there?"

"Sure. But it's okay, Piper. You didn't do anything wrong."

"I did." I meet his gaze. "What if it had been the other way around?"

His face falls, and he looks stricken. "I ... I'll sleep on the floor tonight."

"No way. Absolutely not. *I'm* the creeper here, not you."

"Don't call yourself that," he says, his tone sharpening. "You're not. And there's a massive difference in strength between a man and a woman. I had no trouble stopping you."

Stopping you.

"I'll see you downstairs in a bit," I mutter, then run away before he can reply.

MY COLD SHOWER lasts less than ten seconds before I relent and turn the heat up. But even though my body can't stand the punishment I want to inflict on it, my mind makes me suffer enough.

Eventually, I tell my brain to shut up. Yes, I'm embarrassed as hell, and yes, I'm annoyed that my subconscious is hot for Brody, but it's not going anywhere. He's not interested in me, and I have no desire—wrong word—*wish* to be with anyone who doesn't want what I want: stability, structure, a family.

My hormones just need to get with the program and remember what we signed up for—a fake relationship that suits *both* our needs.

Only now my other needs are screaming to be met.

I wish I'd packed my rechargeable toyfriend. However, there's no way I could have used him with Brody in the same room.

This is going to be a very long few days without an orgasm ...

Switching the shower off, I get dressed and carefully apply

makeup. If we're photographed today, then I need to be looking my best. Brody hasn't mentioned anything about Marv, so I'm hoping he's still in New York and we've got a few days to ourselves to just hang out and chill with my family.

But as I reach the top of the stairs, my hand pauses on the rail. There's a male voice downstairs that most definitely doesn't belong to my dad.

"So, I said to him, 'Ryan, you may be one of the biggest stars on the planet, but you don't have the magic of Brody King. He's gonna eclipse you like a freaking supernova!'"

My heart sinks.

"Oh my gosh," Mom replies. "Do you really know—"

"Piper!" Marv cries as I enter the kitchen. "The golden girl!"

"There she is!" Mom exclaims. "How did you sleep, honey?"

"Hopefully not *too* well," Mia says with a wink.

She's sitting at the breakfast bar next to Marv, with a pot of freshly brewed coffee and a plate of cinnamon cookies in front of them. On the other side of Marv, a young woman scrambles off her seat and stands, staring at me like I'm the firing squad. She's smaller than me, with wavy blonde hair a little shorter than mine, and looks like she's straight out of college.

"This is Cara," Mom says to me. "Marv's assistant."

I force a smile. "Nice to meet you."

"You too," she replies immediately. "I—" She glances nervously at Mom and Mia, as if not sure whether they know Brody and me are faking it.

"So," I say brightly. "Where are you staying?"

"The Hideaway Hotel," Marv replies. "It's cute, but the coffee's not as good as Mrs Locke's."

Mom preens. "You must call me Erica, Mr DeVille."

Marv throws his arms wide. "And you must call me Marv. I'm only Mr DeVille to lawyers and my enemies. Which, y'know, are one and the same in showbusiness."

Mom giggles like a teenager, and I look around for Dad.

"I'm so sorry we missed your husband, Erica," Marv continues.

"Oh yes, you missed him by less than a minute."

Cara blushes, which tells me they were waiting until Dad had gone before knocking on the door.

"You must stay for dinner tonight. Both of you," Mom insists. "You can meet the whole family."

"We'd love to. Wouldn't we, Cara?"

She glances nervously between me and her boss.

"Don't be shy, honey," Mom says, patting her arm. "I promise we won't bite."

There's a thundering of feet on the stairs, then Brody skids into the kitchen, his hair still a mess and his shirt untucked.

If Brody's eyes were lasers, then Marv would currently be lying in two pieces on the linoleum floor.

"What are you doing here?" he demands.

Marv, with the confidence of a man who knows he can play chicken with death and win, holds up a cookie. "Partaking of the best breakfast in Hideaway. Want one?"

"No. I said, what are you—"

"Brody, sweetheart, you and my baby girl must be hungry," Mom interrupts. "Let me make you some eggs." She picks a spotless apron from a hook on the wall and puts it on. "Bacon? Pancakes?"

Brody runs a hand through his hair and takes a breath. "Thank you, Mrs L, but I can cook it."

"Nonsense, honey. You're my guest. And remember, call me Erica. Piper, you want the same? Mia? You ate this morning?"

Mom doesn't wait for a reply, bustling around the kitchen with the efficiency of a short-order cook.

"Thank you," Mia replies. "I'll take whatever's on offer. It's going to be a long day."

"It certainly is with everything you and Mr De—*Marv* have planned."

"What?" Brody and I say in unison, glancing between Mia and Marv. Meanwhile, Cara is staring at the floor like she wishes a sinkhole would appear and swallow her up.

Mom comes up to us and places a hand on each of our cheeks. "It's okay. I know your little secret."

Brody and I exchange a look. How on earth is Mom being so cool about us faking a relationship?

"Mr—*Marv* told me you're having a little hiccup in your career and could use a bit of help landing a very important job."

Neither Brody nor I say a word. I'm still trying to process the fact she seems so happy about our subterfuge.

"He's explained everything," Mom continues. "And it makes perfect sense."

"It does?" I ask, my voice cracking.

"Yes, of course. The world needs to know who you *really* are. A small-town boy with the sweetest small-town girl on your arm. And where better to show you both off than here, in Hideaway, the town built on true love."

Oh god. She doesn't know.

"So, Marv and I are making sure you get seen at all the right places, and Mia will take the photos to share with the world. It's going to be so exciting!"

I can't criticize my mom when she's genuinely this thrilled to help Brody out. She lives for her family, Hideaway Harbor, and true love, so we're ticking all her boxes. But this also means that Marv just became Mom's biggest enabler.

Or is it the other way around? All I *do* know is that Brody and I are going to be followed everywhere by at least four people. More, the moment Mom gets on the phone to her friends.

She glances at the wall clock, then claps. "We've got just under an hour before your first appointment. Sit down and have some coffee while I whip you up something to eat."

The moment Mom goes to the refrigerator, Brody pins Marv with a fierce look. "And what *is* our first appointment?"

"You're tearing a page off the calendar," Mom calls over her shoulder. "Every day was booked months ago, but I made a few calls this morning, pulled some strings, and got you a slot. Saturday mornings usually draw a good crowd, and word's already out that you're today's star. Everyone's excited to meet you!"

She turns and winks at Brody. "Sometimes it pays to be the mayor's wife."

Brody gives me a questioning look.

"It's a relatively new tradition," I tell him. "To help local businesses. There's a wooden board and it has a giant flip-chart pad. Each sheet is numbered from December first to the twenty-fourth. Every morning they move it to a new location, and a local celebrity reveals the date."

"Every location is listed on the town website and in *The Almanac*," Mom adds, then addresses Marv. "That's the town newspaper. Great way to spotlight local businesses. *And* the bigger the celebrity, the better the exposure."

Brody's jaw is clenched, but he nods. It's the perfect way to get photos of him in Hideaway without it seeming staged, and if I'm by his side when he reveals the new date, all the better.

"What's the business?" he asks.

"A gift shop," Marv replies, smiling at Mom. "Erica, I appreciate what you've done. I think you're going to be our secret weapon over the next few days."

She blushes. "So glad to help. And I'll see what else I can do."

Mia's back is turned, her shoulders shaking.

Suspicious, I move to her side. Her face is contorted as she tries to stifle her laughter.

"What is it?" I ask, my voice low, as Mom clatters around the kitchen and Brody sets plates on the counter.

"I can't tell you yet. I really need this job."

"Is it really a gift shop?"

"Kind of," she replies with a smirk, that tells me it's probably *not* a gift shop.

"It's not the cat sanctuary at the spa, is it?"

She shakes her head.

"The yoga studio where they have goats?"

Her hand covers her nose as she snorts.

"Come on, Mia! The retirement home?"

"No," she whispers. "But I promise it's going to be the best publicity for the two of you, like ever."

She walks off, going to her camera bag, and I glance at Marv and Cara. They don't seem bothered. Whatever it is, it can't be *that* bad … can it?

After the stresses of this morning, I don't think I can eat. But as soon as Mom places a plate of crispy bacon, eggs over easy, and pancakes drizzled with blueberry compote and maple syrup in front of me, I realize I'm ravenous. Plus, I'll need all the fuel I can get to deal with the wintery Maine weather.

Brody, Mia, and I eat, then we get wrapped up and leave the house.

This is it. We're in public—well, there's no one on the residential street, but who knows who's watching from their windows?

Brody's ridiculously handsome, clad in a brown wool coat and a dark green cashmere scarf which probably cost more than I make in a month, and I'm wearing the same outfit I was photographed in leaving the coffee shop, just to double down on my "mystery woman" status. At least Cara isn't in the same thing.

"You need to hold hands," Mia hisses at us as we trail behind Mom, Marv, and Cara.

I stumble, and Brody grabs my arm to stop me face-planting on the sidewalk.

"Yep, that's it. You need to be actually touching each other," Mia says, then adds with a pointed look. "Like a real couple."

Brody hasn't let go of my arm. "Do you mind?" he asks, his voice unsure, like he's asking me to pick up dog poop with my bare hands.

"Not at all. I think we should," I reply briskly, then link my arm with his and set off after the advance party.

Brody matches my step, and I revel in the feeling of him so close to me. The calendar reveal is at ten and even though we're half an hour early, Main Street is already busy with tourists and locals. A few people do a double-take when they see Brody, but he doesn't seem to notice. Either he's immune to the attention, or really good at pretending it doesn't exist.

A few younger women recognize him, then their gazes slide to me. I look away, gripping Brody's arm tighter, unwilling to see any surprise or confusion in their eyes about why he's with me.

He isn't with you, my mind inconveniently reminds me.

Well, he is with me in public, I argue back.

It's not just the difference I feel in our outfits right now. The looks we're getting remind me that he's a somebody, and I'm a lucky nobody.

Across the road, a bunch of people are gathered outside a storefront. One of them spots Brody, and the squeals of excitement start immediately.

His arm tenses, and I give it a reassuring squeeze, even though I'm probably just as tense as he is. Time to step up and be the best fake girlfriend I can.

"Hey ladies! Here to meet the big man?" Marv calls out as we approach. "I'm Marvin DeVille, Brody's agent, but you can call me Marv."

Mia's already got her camera out, snapping away as we're instantly surrounded.

"Smile!" she mutters under her breath, and I make my lips turn up.

"It's okay," Brody murmurs to me, his voice low, before greeting the women in front of the store. "You here for the big reveal?"

"Hell, yeah!" a woman cries, as others screech with laughter. "I hope you rip it *all* off!"

Brody's forehead creases slightly as he glances at Marv and Mom.

Mom pulls an apologetic face and mouths, *"Sorry, this is all I could get."*

Marv's eyes widen as he stares at the front of the shop, still hidden from view by the women. "What the actual fuck?"

The women slowly move away from the entrance, and …

Oh shit.

"The Perfect Package?" Brody asks, still unaware of where his first official sighting in Hideaway Harbor is about to happen.

Then his gaze drops to the smaller lettering beneath the name, which reads, 'Hideaway's naughtiest little secret. For when size really *does* matter.'

Yep, Brody's about to promote Hideaway Harbor's woman-run and female-focused adult toy store.

I glance around for an exit, but we're surrounded by a wall of eager faces. There's no escape.

A shocking-pink door in the center of the building opens, and a voluptuous woman with waist-length powder-blue hair steps out.

"Brody King," she says, her voice sultry and as striking as her appearance. "I'm Lola Monroe. Welcome to The Perfect Package. Please, come right in."

CHAPTER 11

BRODY

I'm in a nightmare.

Erica's biting her bottom lip anxiously, Marv's face is set with fury, Cara is as white as a sheet, and Piper's staring at me, unblinking, her expression frozen.

Meanwhile, Mia is snapping photos at a mile a minute, and I'm surrounded by excited women who are acting like Christmas has come early. Multiple times. With squirting.

I can't run. There's nowhere to hide. I have to pull up my big-boy pants and turn lemons into lemonade. If only I could add vodka. And a Xanax. I always knew sobriety was going to be a challenge, but this is harder than a Hollywood party where you're forced to smile at everyone, knowing half of them are stabbing you in the back.

I reach my free hand toward Lola. "Great to meet you. Is this your store?"

"Sure is." She gives me a nod and a firm handshake, which is oddly reassuring. Lola Monroe may look like a cross between a mermaid and a '50s sex siren, but she's also a professional with a business to run.

She then extends her hand to Piper. "I'm Lola. Nice to meet you. I know your mom, of course. And Harper. She's told me all about you."

"She has?"

"Yes. I've been helping her look for a space for her perfume store, and she showed me your art. You're incredibly talented." She smiles at me. "You must be very proud."

I glance at Piper. Her cheeks are bright red. I don't have the first clue about her art. But I want to know everything. I want to know if she's still drawing dragons and elves, and the cartoon-style doodles she used to make in the margins of her math homework when she got bored.

She doesn't have math homework anymore, idiot.

Lola is staring at me, expecting an answer.

"She's way more talented than I am, always has been," I reply quickly.

"I'm sure your talents extend beyond the screen," Lola says, giving Piper a wink.

It may be only twenty degrees out here, but Piper's cheeks could heat the whole block right now.

"Let's go in," Lola says to us, then addresses the surrounding crowds. "Ladies, give us five minutes for me to show Brody around, then I'll bring everyone in for hot glögg, the grand reveal of today's date, and the raffle drawing, where one of you will win a gift bag guaranteed to jingle your bells."

The crowd oohs and giggles, and someone calls out, "Just stick a bow on Brody and I'll take him home now!"

I've never been inside an "adult shop" before, but as the door closes behind us, I take in the space and my shoulders relax slightly.

If I don't look too closely at the items on sale, it could pass for a high-end boutique, where customers are made to feel at ease before handing over their cash. Plush velvet sofas and chairs are dotted around between glass cabinets. There's soft lighting, a wall of gold-framed pictures of women, and phrases painted in calligraphy around the other walls, reading: "Consent Is Sexy," "Pleasure Is Your Birthright," and "Own Your Yes."

There's even a Christmas tree.

I move closer, fingering the oddly shaped ornaments. They're identical in shape but cast in resin, and in all different colors and sparkles. They look a bit like wishbones, but I have no clue what they're actually meant to represent.

"They're anatomical models of the clitoris," Lola says, then laughs as my hand drops away.

In the background, Marv's having a coughing fit, and Erica's slapping his back. I know Piper's beside me, but I can't look at her right now.

Lola takes one from the tree and points out the different parts, like I'm in science class.

"The first full anatomical map of the clitoris was only published in 2005," she says. "By Professor Helen O'Connell, an Australian urologist. Her picture is on our wall of icons over there. She literally changed the way science understands female anatomy. Did you know the clitoris has approximately eight thousand nerve endings?"

I shake my head.

"More than any other part of the human body," Lola continues. "And its only purpose is for pleasure. See this bit? It's the glans, where most of the nerve endings are. It's the area you're probably familiar with?"

Yes, I know where that bit is. My face is prickling with sweat, and I tug my scarf off, then nod at her questioning gaze.

She gives Piper a quick glance and smiles, seemingly reassured that I know how to make her come.

Even though I'm in public, with my soon-to-be-ex agent

and Piper's mom watching our every move, my mind suddenly gives me an image of my head between Piper's thighs, my—

Shut up! What the hell is wrong with you?

I tug my coat open, uncomfortably hot. I need to roll around in the snow right now. That, or jump in the frigid sea.

"This bit is the body, or shaft," Lola continues, "and it extends inward beneath the skin. The legs, known as crura, are about three and a half to five inches long and anchor the clitoris to the pelvic bone, transmitting sensations of vibration."

For fuck's sake, stop talking about a clitoris!

"These parts are the vestibular bulbs, which engorge when you're turned on and hug the vaginal opening. I cast them as keychains."

"Huh?"

Lola gestures to a glass bowl on a counter filled with them.

"Keychains. I include them free with every purchase. I want all women to understand their own anatomy. The clitoris is an organ that has been *hugely* underrepresented and misunderstood in medicine, education, and the media for millennia, and I want to change that."

"I've got one!" Erica calls over, jiggling a sparkly pink clitoris in the air to prove her point. "I had no idea they were this big in real life! I've got lots of spares and wanted to give them to you and Piper as gifts, but I didn't want you to feel uncomfortable."

Jesus Christ.

Piper makes a noise that's half wheeze and half strangled cry, and I'm wondering if she's also thinking of the lube her mom left in the nightstand.

There's a knock at the door, and an older woman pokes her head into the shop. "I've got the calendar. Can I bring it in?"

"Of course, Miriam. Come in. We're just setting up."

Miriam wheels in a trolley carrying a large wooden board

with the words "Hideaway Harbor Christmas Countdown," painted in red and green at the top. Attached via hooks is a huge pad of paper, the number sixteen painted on the top sheet.

"Hello, Erica, hello all," Miriam says, then turns to me. "You must be the famous actor who's pinched Dorothy's spot today."

I cringe. Dorothy is more than welcome to it. I'd rather be anywhere else than here right now.

"I'm sorry, I—"

She pats my arm. "Not a bother, young man. Lola's soothing her ruffled feathers with a goodie bag, so we won't be seeing her for a few days … if you catch my drift?"

Erica laughs loudly, and Mia snorts. Even Piper's mouth twitches.

Fuck it. I need to embrace this moment. If I resist, then it's uncomfortable for everyone, and the world will have a field day when they see the photos.

So, I smile at Miriam. "But when we do see Dorothy again, she's going to have the biggest smile in Hideaway Harbor on her face?"

Miriam hoots and slaps my arm. "That's the truth. Now, can you give me a hand with the calendar? It's heavier than it looks." She glances at Lola. "Where do you want it, honey? On the counter in front of the icons?"

"That would be perfect," Lola replies, as Marv steps forward and helps me lift the calendar off the trolley and into place, unfolding a wooden brace hidden behind it to prop it upright.

Erica takes out her phone and snaps a picture. "Doesn't that look good?"

"I'm just going to get the glögg," Lola says. "And the raffle tickets. Erica, can you give me a hand?"

"I can help," Cara says.

Mia puts her camera down. "Me too."

Miriam joins them as they follow Lola out the back, leaving me, Piper, and Marv.

"Bro," Marv says under his breath, "I had no freaking clue about this."

"It's okay," I reply. "Honestly, it shows I don't take myself that seriously, which is the message I want out there. And if you want me in the media, this is more likely to get me there than an appearance at a cupcake shop or Mom and Pop store."

Marv frowns. "But this ... a fucking *dildo* shop?" He glances at Piper. "Sorry."

What the hell have I dragged her into?

"You okay with this?" I ask her. "You can leave if you want."

She smiles, and it's like pop rocks are going off in my stomach.

"I've decided to lean into it," she says. "Pretend I'm totally cool with my mom shopping here more times than she's had kids. Remind me to murder Mia, though, for not giving us the heads up."

"I've got a veto on all photos," Marv says. "Don't worry. I won't release any that look like Brody's got a stick up his butt."

Piper giggles. "I'm sure Lola sells sparkly ones for that explicit purpose."

I huff out a laugh. "Thanks for being so cool about this."

She gives me a quick curtsy. "That's what fake girlfriends are for."

A smile hovers in the air between us, like it's ours and it's precious.

I break away, going to the back of the store as the women return with glasses, jugs of steaming glögg, and a book of raffle tickets.

"Please, let me help."

Two cats follow the women into the room, then spring onto one of the sofas and curl up next to each other.

"Clitopatra and Meowyoncé," Lola says with a twinkle in her eye. "This is, after all, a place that celebrates the pussy."

Piper laughs. "They're beautiful."

"They certainly are. Regal, self-assured, and used to being worshipped. Just like every woman should be." She smiles at me. "It's nearly ten. You ready?"

"As much as I'll ever be."

"Awesome, I'll let them in. Erica, Cara, Miriam, please, could you help me serve the glögg?"

"Has it got alcohol in it?" Marv asks.

"Yes, aquavit," Lola replies.

He presses a hand over his lined forehead. "Great. I'll take two."

"There's also a non-alcoholic one in the green jug, if anyone would prefer that."

"Not today, ma'am," Marv says. "But Brody'll have it."

Thankfully, Lola doesn't bat an eyelid. "Sure thing. Right, let's get everyone inside."

Lola welcomes everyone in, handing a raffle ticket to each woman.

I straighten my spine and go into schmooze mode, making sure to engage with each person while Piper greets old friends and acquaintances. I'm trying to focus on who I'm talking to, but in the background, I'm aware of Piper spinning the tall tale about our fake relationship. Thank God, we kept it simple.

My shoulders relax more as I interact with the customers. They're nice people, and my guard slowly drops.

Soon, I'm taking selfies with them and leaving voice notes for their kids, telling them to tidy their rooms, or for their husbands, informing them their wives are with me in The Perfect Package, so they'd better up their game tonight. The women are hilarious, and my cheeks ache from smiling so much.

I catch Piper's eye, and she grins at me, her face full of life and light.

"Okay, everyone," Lola calls. "It's way past ten o'clock, but what happens in The Perfect Package stays in The Perfect Package. Am I right?"

Glasses are raised as people cheer.

"Brody, Piper, let's have you up here!"

"Me?" Piper asks.

"Absolutely," Lola replies. "It's a two-for-the-price-of-one deal today!"

I hold my hand out for Piper, and she takes it, her cheeks pinking. We make our way over to the counter where the calendar is, and Mia gets into position for the shot.

Reluctantly, I release Piper's hand, and she stands on the other side of the calendar, holding the bottom corner of the top sheet nearest her.

"In three …" Lola counts down.

"Two!" everyone else cries. "One!"

At zero, Piper and I pull up the sheet to reveal today's date, and the crowd goes wild like we've just won the World Series.

I'm grinning at Piper, filled with the joy of the moment and a buoyant happiness I haven't felt for years.

"Now it's time to draw the raffle winner!" Lola announces. "And don't worry if Brody doesn't pull your ticket, as everything in the store is twenty percent off this morning, so everyone's a winner!"

There are more cheers, whoops, and a shout of, "If I don't win Brody, stick a bow on the little guy!" directed at Marv.

Lola holds an upside-down Santa hat out to me.

Closing my eyes, I affect a look of deep concentration as I fish for a ticket, then hand it to Lola.

"And the winner is …" Lola unfolds the ticket and then snorts. "Number sixty-nine!"

There's a shriek from the back, and everyone laughs as a

woman pushes through the crowd, holding her winning ticket aloft.

Lola presents her with a pink-and-white striped bag, and her friends crowd around to see what she's won.

"Don't forget it's twenty percent off *this* morning only, ladies," Lola reminds them. "And I've just taken delivery of some vibrating candy canes. They're the perfect stocking stuffer, all the pleasure and zero calories for every good girl out there!"

As people move to the shelves, Lola comes up to me and Piper.

"Thank you both so much for this morning. I know it was really last minute, but word gets around Hideaway fast, and I don't think I would have had half as many people show up if you weren't here. You can make a break for it now if you like. I just wanted to say thank you before I get behind the counter."

"It's our pleasure," I say. "And an education."

"I run workshops once a month, so the next time I do one for couples, you must come."

"Thanks," I say, even though I've got no idea what a workshop here might entail, and if I ever do come back to Hideaway, it won't be with Piper on my arm.

"And before you go …" She dashes behind the counter and returns with a gift bag, which she hands to Piper. "Toys for the two of you to use together. I think you'll have lots of fun with them."

Piper stammers her thanks, her cheeks once again telegraphing her embarrassment.

"And they're remarkably quiet," Lola adds. "The loudest thing coming from your room will be your cries of pleasure …"

"Ooh! A gift bag!" Erica says, coming over. "What have you got?"

Piper puts the bag behind her back, away from her mother's prying eyes.

"I just wanted to see if they're the same as mine," Erica replies. "I could give you my review."

"Mom! Please! Just no!"

Erica and Lola laugh, and before I can stop myself, I take Piper's hand and gently squeeze.

She squeezes back, then immediately drops my hand to say goodbye to Lola and doesn't take it again, instead leaving the shop.

I follow her out onto the street, not knowing if hand-holding is now off the table. I can't ask her, as Erica, Marv, Mia and Cara follow us out.

"I think that went very well," Erica says happily. "How do the photos look, Mia?"

Mia's gazing at the back of her camera. "Some really nice ones."

"Let's go grab a coffee and go through them," Marv says. "Where do you recommend, Erica?"

"Love at First Sip," she replies. "It's run by Eileen, one of my best friends, and the coffee is, dare I say it, even better than mine."

"Sounds great."

There's a ping from a phone, but it isn't mine.

Simultaneously, Piper, Cara, and Marv each pull out their phones and swipe them open.

Then three sets of eyes swivel to look at me.

This can't be good.

Piper's face flushes, and she jams her phone back in her pocket as if I weren't meant to see it.

Cara's looking at Marv now, waiting for his lead.

He looks stunned; I can't read him further than that.

"Brody ..." he begins, shaking his head. "You've done it now."

CHAPTER 12

PIPER

*W*hy, oh *why*, did I take out my phone? Now Brody *knows* I've been stalking him.

Of course, his agent would have a Google Alert for him. And so would Cara.

However, I doubt anyone thought *I* would have one, and Brody certainly wouldn't have pegged me as one of his biggest fans.

A muscle twitches in his jaw as he faces Marv. "What? What have I done?"

Marv grabs his cheeks like he's a little boy, not a strapping man who's a whole head taller than him. "You did it, man! All on your own!"

Brody shakes him off. "What?"

"Some good fucking—" he pulls a face at my mom. "Sorry, Erica. Freaking publicity for once! Some guy just posted this crazy-long post on his socials about how the sun shines out your butt. And there are photos. Look!"

He shows us the screen and Mom reads aloud.

"Brody King has to be the kindest guy in the world. He gave us his room and paid for it when the hotel lost our reservation." She gazes at Brody. "You're such a good man."

His cheeks darken.

"And look at those lovely pictures!" Mom continues, before turning to me. "My beautiful daughter."

"This is what I'm talking about!" Marv says, swiveling the phone back toward him to look at the photos again. "Christmas spirit, family values, cute kids, a fu—goddamn *baby*, and a wholesome, small-town girlfriend." He looks at me. "If only we'd brought you in sooner."

"Brought her in?" Mom repeats, and my stomach drops.

Marv's face freezes for a moment as he realizes he's put his foot in his mouth. Then he recovers. "Brody wanted to protect Piper from all the BS that comes with being famous, so he's never mentioned she's his girlfriend before."

"But now he needs this special job," Mom says. "So, we need to bring in my special girl."

"Exactly. Your daughter is our other secret weapon. After you, of course."

Mom places a hand over her heart, thrilled to be part of this subterfuge she doesn't know the half of.

Brody's gaze travels between Marv and my mom.

"You okay?" I ask him quietly.

He smiles. "Yeah, sure. I'm glad there's some positive publicity out there."

I blink. Is that why he gave the family our rooms? In the hope this would happen?

Marv claps his hands. "Right, let's strategize. Erica, where's this coffee shop?"

"Not far. Follow me!"

I hang back with Brody and let the others lead the way.

Almost immediately a pretty woman stops him, her hand on his arm.

"Oh my gosh, can I get a selfie?"

Brody gives her a dazzling smile. "Sure!"

I've never felt so invisible. The woman doesn't even acknowledge my existence as she tucks her caramel-blonde tresses behind an ear and cuddles up to Brody, her phone held out in selfie mode.

I rock back on my heels, waiting impatiently, and being reminded of yet another reason why I wouldn't want to date a celebrity.

"Oh my gosh, thank you!" she gushes after taking far too many photos. "How long are you in Hideaway for?"

Brody slings an arm around me. "We're here until the New Year."

Her gaze finally flicks to me. "Oh." Then her attention is back to the star of this show. "Well, maybe see you around?"

"That would be great. Happy Holidays."

She saunters off confidently and I bite back a sigh.

"What is it?" Brody asks. "What's wrong?"

"Nothing."

He rolls his eyes. "When a woman says nothing's wrong, it usually means there's a big, fat something wrong. Is it about that woman? She's just a fan."

"A fan who wants to bone you."

"She doesn't *know* me. It's a fantasy. It's not real."

And I don't know you either.

"And isn't the whole reason why we're out here to get candid shots from the public?" he continues. "To see me in a different light?"

"For the job."

"Why else would I be doing this?"

I rock back on my heels again as if I've just been shoved.

Yes, he's doing this in the hope he'll get a job, but what about Ethan, my family?

What about me?

I thought I was rediscovering the old Brody, but this is a stark reminder that he's Brody two-point-oh. And I don't know who that is.

"Did you give the family our rooms at the Hideaway Hotel to get some good publicity?"

"What?"

I cross my arms. "You heard me."

"I can't believe you would ask that."

"That's not an answer."

Brody shakes his head. "No, Piper, the thought that they would tell the world about it never once crossed my mind. Am I happy they did? Of course, I am. It's authentic reach. Organic amplification."

I feel my eyes bugging out as I stare at him. "*Organic amplification?* It's like that time at work when I had to design an ad campaign for a highlighter that's supposed to *embody disruption*."

"This is *my* work, Piper. It's part of *my* job. And why I'm out in public promoting a sex toy shop rather than chilling out in private."

My fingers tighten around the handle of the gift bag I got from The Perfect Package, utterly miserable and not knowing what to think or say.

"Hey, Brody! Piper!" Marv calls back to us. "C'mon!"

Brody waits for me to start walking, then we follow Marv into Love at First Sip.

"Piper! Brody!" Eileen cries. "Welcome, welcome, come in, come in!"

She takes our hands and tugs us over the threshold, dragging us through to the back where the corner booth is free.

I glance around and spot a barista helping a couple get re-seated with their drinks at another table. I cringe as the man shoots Brody a dirty look. It's all well and good getting special treatment, but not if it means someone else has to suffer.

"And this is my fault too?" he murmurs under his breath.

"Who else?" I snap back, then say to Eileen, "We can sit anywhere."

"Nonsense. I'm sure they don't mind one bit. There were only two of them, and there's six of you."

She herds us into the booth. Brody and I sit in the middle, Marv and Mia on one side of us, and Mom and Cara on the other. There's no escape.

"Everything's up on the board," Eileen says, "but I'll grab you some menus."

She hurries away, and my phone pings again at the same time as Marv's and Cara's. Why did today have to be a good signal day in Hideaway? Brody glances at me as they take their phones out, but I don't touch mine. I need to get to the bathroom ASAP and put it in silent mode.

Marv fist pumps. "That guy's social media post is going viral." His finger swipes fast across the screen. "And people want to know who the 'mystery woman' is." He nods at Cara. "We need to put out a statement about Piper."

"No," Brody says.

Marv rolls his eyes. "C'mon, man! Control the narrative! If we don't release something, some little schmuck she was in high school with will do it for us, and you can guarantee it'll be some dorky guy she wouldn't go to prom with or a mean girl who was jealous of her." He turns to me. "You got any enemies?"

"I don't think so."

"Mia," Marv says. "Anyone got Piper on their shit list?"

My best friend grins. "Well ..."

"Mia Grace Keye," my mom says sternly, "you know full well Piper is well liked. She was Homecoming Queen and voted 'Most Likely to Brighten Your Day' senior year. You don't win both unless people actually like you."

"Love it," Marv says, "Cara, you got that?"

She nods, her thumbs tapping on her phone screen.

Brody's hands are interlaced and resting on the table. His knuckles have already gone white. "Marv," he says sharply. "I want to protect Piper from—"

"It's okay," I say. "I don't mind." Then, snarkily I add, "It's part of the job, after all."

Brody tenses beside me and I suddenly hate myself. Why am I being such a bitch? This isn't like me at all. Of *course*, Brody should be happy about the positive publicity. It doesn't make him a bad person, and I know in my heart he didn't give our rooms away hoping the couple would tell the world about it.

"See?" Marv says. "Piper's cool. We'll include the usual 'please respect their privacy' bit, and you can both read it before it goes out. Mia, can you pull up the photos?"

Mia opens her laptop, transfers the photos she took onto it, then shows Marv.

"Delete. Delete. Keep. Delete," he barks over her shoulder as Eileen returns and quietly passes out the menus.

"Keep. Keep. Delete. Keep. Done."

"Can we see them?" I ask.

Mia pushes the laptop in front of me, and Brody and I slowly move through the images.

The pictures are amazing. Like, *really* amazing. Mia's an incredible photographer, and she's captured the atmosphere of the event perfectly. Everyone looks like they're having the best time, and Brody and I look … like a real couple.

"I'm sorry," I whisper to him as Mom and Mia loudly explain every drink on the menu to Marv and Cara.

"Me too," he murmurs in reply. "I'm trying to do the right thing."

His admission makes me then do the wrong thing, stroking my fingers over his white knuckles.

He unlaces the clasp of his hands and takes mine between his, rubbing his thumb across the back of my hand like a soothing caress as we gaze at the pictures of ourselves.

His touch is gentle, but feels like fire, heat that spreads up my arm and then flows through my body. I squeeze my thighs together to relieve it, but that only makes things worse.

Brody's being friendly. However by the time I reach the end of the slideshow, I don't think I can speak without it coming out as a squeak or a moan.

Brody clears his throat. "Thank you, Mia. These are fantastic."

She grins. "Not my first rodeo." She pulls the laptop back across the table and addresses Marv. "I'll send these to you now and the editor of *The Almanac*."

"Could you also send them to me, please?" Brody asks. "I can give you my email address."

Mia gives me a quick look, clearly trying not to smirk. "Sure. Type it in here."

"I'd like to post a couple to my socials."

"Sure." Marv replies. "Cara can set it up."

"No. I'd like to do it."

Marv and Cara exchange a look.

Brody sighs. "I can use Cara's phone."

Mia and Mom are watching the interaction, just like I am. We're all probably coming to the same realization: Brody is no longer trusted to manage his own social media accounts.

I think back to when Brody was friends with Casey Connors—a child star turned drug-addicted bad boy. The posts Brody made when he was drunk, only to delete them afterward. He acted nothing like the boy I knew in Hideaway, but a lot can change in twelve years, especially when you're as famous as he is.

Is he fully okay now? He looks fit and healthy, but I don't know enough about addiction *or* Brody to know if he might relapse.

"Do you have an account so I can tag you in?" Brody asks me. "Or would you rather I didn't?"

"Um ..." I rarely use my personal account. My energy is focused almost exclusively on the one I set up for my fantasy art, even though no one seems to view it anymore. But I'm not ready for Brody to see it, at least not with an audience.

"Use her artwork account!" Mom says excitedly. "Just think how many more followers she could get!"

Brody's fingers stop moving on the back of my hand as he gazes questioningly at me.

Heat temporarily abandons my panties, rushing to fill my cheeks. How does it look that I haven't shown my so-called boyfriend such an important part of myself?

"Piper likes to keep that one private," he says to Mom, trying to cover for me.

"Then why did you ask her if she had an account?" she asks.

"I meant to ask *which* account she wanted me to use," he replies, shrugging casually.

"Oh. Well, I think you should publicize her drawings, especially considering how much she's doing to help your career, honey."

"Mom," I say quickly. "It's more than enough for me to deal with going public with my relationship. I'm not yet ready to have my face associated with what I do in my spare time."

"It's not exactly an OnlyFans account for feet!"

"Mom!" I cry as Mia snorts with laughter.

"It's true! You're so talented, baby. You're wa—" She breaks off before finishing her sentence, the end of which I know is *wasted at your job.* "More people should see what you do," she says firmly.

Fortunately, a smiling girl who looks about high school age, comes over with a pad and pen.

"Have you decided what you all want?" she asks. "Any questions, just ask!"

Love at First Sip is famous for drinks named after romantic heroes and poets, and as it's run by Mom's best friend, I always make sure I come here whenever I'm back in Hideaway.

"Have whatever you want, guys," Marv says. "It's on me."

Brody leans a little closer to me. "What do you like here?" he murmurs.

You? With extra sprinkles? His voice is like liquid velvet, melting my insides.

"Um ... I always have the Lord Byron," I reply, sounding like I've just run up a flight of stairs. "It's a cinnamon latte."

"The Lord Byron?" he says in a British accent. "Hmm ..."

Our faces are nearly touching, but we're not looking at each other. Instead, our eyes are glued to the sight of our hands entwined on the table.

Brody takes a measured breath, then still in a British accent, starts reciting *poetry* to me.

"She walks in beauty, like the night, of cloudless climes and starry skies. And all that's best of dark and bright, meet in her aspect and her eyes ..."

Oh, my dear Lord ... I make a strangled noise as my throat just about stops me from yelling, "Do me already!"

Mom suddenly stops her monologue about what a dirty chai is in Hideaway. "You okay, honey? You got allergies?"

I take a breath but promptly choke on my own saliva and start coughing.

Brody rubs my back. "Can I get a glass of water?" he asks the barista.

"I'm fine!" I manage, mortified.

As I get a hold of myself, I catch Mia's eye. She looks at our hands, still clasped together, then winks.

The barista, meanwhile, has dashed to the counter and returns with a jug of water and a tower of glasses.

"Thank you, sweetie," Mom says, taking the glasses from her and distributing them.

My phone again pings with a notification at the same time that Marv's and Cara's phones go off.

I jerk my hand away from Brody's, grab my phone from my coat pocket, and turn it on silent.

Marv whoops, "Super viral!"

Brody's looking at me.

Please don't ask if I've got a Google Alert set up with your name on it.

My stomach twists with anxiety, and I'm also frustrated because I don't know how to take his hand again without it being a thing. So instead, I smile at the barista. "A Lord Byron, please."

Mom chuckles. "Always with the cinnamon!"

"I'll have the same," Brody says.

Everyone orders, and Marv adds a selection of pastries.

Cara passes her phone to Brody. "I've chosen some images. You can edit as you like and then add the caption."

Brody holds it so we both can see and flicks through the pictures. There's one of him with one of the clitoris ornaments, an eyebrow raised, while I'm laughing in the background. There's one of him in the middle of a group of women as he takes a selfie of them all, one of the two of us revealing today's date, one of him, Lola, and me, Brody holding a very happy-looking Clitopatra, and one of the two of us standing together as we chat with people. We look like a power couple on the campaign trail.

And there's one more that Cara selected, the one I would do anything for it to be real.

In the picture, I'm chatting with Mom, and Brody's gazing at me like I hung the moon. He looks content. Happy. Like a man in love. His finger moves away from the screen as we stare at the image.

"Are they okay?" Cara asks.

Brody starts as if woken from a dream. "Yeah, perfect," he says, his voice gravelly, then goes back to write a caption.

I know I should look away, give him some privacy. But I can't.

Cara has already tagged The Perfect Package, Mia, and Hideaway Harbor in the post, so Brody writes, "Not gonna lie, I had no idea what I was holding in pic one until about ten seconds later. Learned a lot today … Huge thanks to The Perfect Package (yes, that's really the name) for letting me crash their big reveal for Hideaway's Christmas Countdown. Special shout out to Lola, the amazing crew, and the ladies who made me feel so welcome. Best part? I got to do it all with my girl by my side, laughing at me, mostly. Now taking refuge at Love at First Sip, ordering her favorite: a cinnamon latte called the "Lord Byron." Guess I'll be learning poetry next. #SheWalksIn-Beauty #HideawayHarbor #ThePerfectPackage."

"You okay with that?" Brody asks softly.

The feel of his breath on my cheek makes me shiver, and I nod, words escaping me.

Brody hands the phone to Cara, who reads what he's written, a smile breaking out. "That's fantastic!"

"Lemme see," Marv barks and she passes it to him. He makes a grunt of satisfaction, then stabs at the screen with a finger. "Done! Nice work."

Eileen arrives with our order, and I know I'm in heaven. Sitting next to Brody, pretending to be his girlfriend with a cinnamon latte in my hands, everything is right with the world. Christmas music is playing, and my mom and best friend are along for the ride.

"So, what's next, Erica?" Marv asks.

Mom places her drink down and raises her hands like she's

about to conduct a choir. "Well, the Santa Fun Run starts in forty-five minutes on Main Street, and John is making a speech, so you don't want to miss it. The run is only five kilometers, so it's over in less than an hour, and then there's the prize ceremony. Amanda Willis is handing them out this year!"

Marv grunts his annoyance, as if Brody should be up there instead.

"There's also ice carving up at the Locke Reserve, then caroling in the town square at four. It's so pretty, and we always try to break our own record for the most people caroling wearing Santa hats. Do you and Cara have any?"

Marv shakes his head.

"Don't worry, I have lots to spare." Mom types a quick message on her phone. "I've asked Harper to bring more when she meets us at the start of the fun run in a bit. After that, it's the caroling, then back to our place for dinner."

"Looking forward to it, Erica."

"Absolutely! It will be our pleasure!"

Kindness runs through my mom to the marrow, but even though my dad has a soft heart, I'm not sure what he's going to make of Marv. And if Ethan's there? I have a horrible suspicion he's going to start asking awkward questions about why I agreed to promote our "relationship" in such a shameless fashion. *Ugh.*

"And tomorrow it's the woolen sock-running championships around the Locke Reserve," Mom continues. "And I've had a wonderful idea for a photo opportunity!"

Uh-oh ...

"Go on," Marv says, leaning forward.

"How about I fix some mistletoe in one of the trees? It'll look so pretty with all the snow, and I think there should be at least one picture of them kissing."

Marv glances at us. "Uh ... I'm not sure—"

"And they could also make out on the Wishing Bridge over

the Hideaway Spring! It's so romantic. It's where John and I first kissed." She sighs happily. "And where he proposed."

Her dreamy eyes snap into focus, and she looks at Brody, clearly hoping he will follow in Dad's footsteps. "You and Piper should kiss there. It'll make the most beautiful picture!"

Suddenly I'm having an out-of-body experience, one where my hormones have kicked out logic and common sense and taken over operations. "Yes, it would," I hear myself say. "Sounds like a great idea."

Marv's eyes light up, and he turns to Brody. "There we go. Piper's up for it. You on board?"

CHAPTER 13

BRODY

*A*m I on board?

"Hell, yeah!" my dick says, while my mind yells, "Fuck no!"

However my body refuses to listen to reason, and I shift in the seat, my leg that's touching Piper's pressing closer against hers.

She doesn't move away.

Why did she say it's a good idea for us to kiss? To help me out? Or because she wants to?

Is she feeling guilty for questioning my motives at the hotel? And is now going above and beyond what we agreed to?

I've noticed that a British accent is … appealing to her. But is *that* what does it for her, or does she actually like *me*? Am I going to have to change my name to Lord Brody of Hideaway and permanently speak like I've stepped out of a period drama with a silver spoon lodged up my butt?

My mind is whirling, trying to find a pattern in her

behavior that points to her seeing me as someone more than a friend. Does she have a Google Alert set up for my name? It sure looks like that. And if so, how long has she had it? And why? Research? Does she know every fuck up I've been involved with over the last couple of years?

If she does then there's no way in hell she'd want to have anything to do with me.

And it's why I can't entertain the idea of a kiss, or anything more than friendship. Every relationship I have turns to shit. Love is a luxury I can't manage and don't deserve.

"Hey man, you in, or what?" Marv says.

Say no!

"Yeah, sure. Why not?" I reply, going for nonchalant but coming off like I don't really give a shit either way.

Which isn't exactly the truth.

"Don't sound too excited," Mia says sarcastically, and I wince.

"It's okay," Piper says into her mug. "You don't have to if you don't want to."

"Of course he wants to, honey!" Erica cries. "He's in love with you. Everyone can see it. He's probably just a bit shy. Are you feeling shy, Brody?"

Jeez. It sounds like I'm a kid in kindergarten, being pushed to talk to a pretty girl.

"I just don't want it to look fake," I say. "Staged."

Mia snorts, then flinches as if someone's just kicked her under the table.

"We can't help it being a bit staged, honey," Erica says. "It's not like we've got hidden cameras in your bedroom to record your snuggle time."

Piper's mug hits the table with a bang.

Erica laughs. "Oh my goodness, you don't think I'd actually *do* that, do you?"

The image of rose petals on the bed and Piper lifting the bottle of lube flashes through my mind.

"Oh, wait till I tell everyone at the crochet and romance book club," Erica continues, still giggling. "They'll think it's hysterical!"

"Mom! Please!"

Before my brain can control my body, I loop an arm around Piper's shoulder, hugging her into me. I want it to be in a friendly way, but then I ruin it by dropping a kiss on the top of her head.

Abort! Abort!

Just as I'm preparing to let her go, Piper's free arm reaches around my chest.

My heart moves up a gear.

"Ahh, that's so cute," Erica coos, and lifts her phone to take a picture.

"Mom," Piper grumbles into my chest, but she stays where she is.

This is all wrong, but having her nestled in my arms feels like a kind of perfect that's utterly new to me. I no longer want to finish the buttery pastry or even touch my latte. I just want to nuzzle the top of Piper's head and drink in her scent.

Marv and Erica fall into an easy conversation planning every minute of my time here in Hideaway. Piper doesn't seem to want to move, so I break off a bit of pastry and offer it to her.

She smiles, her lips brushing my fingers as she takes it from me.

Holy shit.

Trying to keep my hand steady, I break off another piece and feed it to her.

This time, the tip of her tongue darts out to lick a flake from my finger, and I suck in a breath.

Mia brings her camera up. "This is gold. Hashtag relationship goals."

Piper gives a little hum as if in agreement and my mouth runs dry.

It's for show. It's what we agreed to do. Piper's okay with this. We're in public.

I keep the internal monologue of justification going until the plate is empty.

"Kiss her head again," Mia instructs. "The shot wasn't in focus the first time."

Determined to show willing, I drop another kiss into Piper's hair, this time allowing myself to make it last a little longer. *Just in case Mia needs time to frame the shot* I tell myself.

As my lips make contact, Piper hums her approval again, and the sound vibrates through my body, cracking the walls around my heart.

"Come on, kids, let's get going so we find a good spot for the fun run," Erica says as Marv throws some bills down on the table.

Piper pulls away and sits up, fussing with her coat like she doesn't want to meet my gaze. Is she embarrassed? Is she regretting what just happened?

I tug on my coat, and we make our way out of Love at First Sip, onto the street. People are already on the sidewalk heading for the start line, wearing Santa hats and drinking from paper cups.

"It's Glögg Appreciation Day today," Erica says over her shoulder as she leads the way. "Keeps us warm when we're outside."

Snow covers the rooftops and piles up along the edges of the buildings where it's been cleared from the sidewalks. Christmas lights hang across the street and the scent of spices and wine fills the air.

It's so different to LA or New York. There's a warmth here

that has nothing to do with my woolen clothes, and everything to do with the mood of the people around me. Everyone's smiling like they know this is the place they're meant to be.

I glance at Piper and shift my arm slightly outward, my hand extended in invitation. She takes it and my heart leaps.

"Mom! Over here!"

Harper's up ahead, standing next to a raised wooden platform. John and a few others are on it, talking and pointing as they arrange things for the race. Runners fill the street, held back by a line of bunting. All of them are wearing Santa hats, and most have gone for the full Santa suit.

"Did you bring them, honey?" Erica asks as we reach Harper's side.

"Yep." She hands Santa hats to all of us. Many look handmade and are embellished with bells or stars.

"I made these at the crochet and romance book club," Erica says proudly. "Right after we finished reading that scene in *Hooked on the Highlander*. Felicity gave us a choice between a vagina and Santa hat. That opening at the back is when I mixed up the instructions for a bit."

Marv pulls a face and gingerly tugs his hat onto his balding head.

"What?" he asks as I laugh. "I'm gettin' in the Christmas spirit."

"You look like a Mafia don at a school nativity show," Piper says.

His chest puffs up with pride. "That's what I'm talkin' about. Ain't no one gonna mess with Mobster Marv."

Piper laughs, and Cara joins in.

A tap-tap-tap comes through the sound system, then Piper's dad speaks into the microphone.

"Hey, everyone. I'm John Locke, Hideaway Harbor's mayor, and I'd like to welcome you all to the Santa Fun Run!"

People cheer and clap.

"We're raising money for the Locke Trust, so give generously, folks. It's also Glögg Appreciation Day—the perfect drink to keep you cozy on this December afternoon. The race follows a loop around Hideaway, so we hope you all stick around to watch the winners come across the line in about half an hour. There are prizes in all kinds of categories, including the best-dressed Santa, so make sure you show your support for the runners today. We're also delighted to welcome Hollywood royalty Amanda Willis to give out the prizes this afternoon."

"Should have been you," Marv grumbles under his breath to me, then lifts his chin toward a good-looking man standing by the stage. "Stuck-up little schmuck."

"Who?" Piper asks him.

"Jack Lourd," he replies. "Amanda's agent. Pah! Just look at him. Running off good looks and charm."

"You can be charming, too," she replies.

Marv's chest puffs up. "Don't forget good-looking."

"Absolutely," Piper says and I hide a grin.

"There's an ice carving event at the Locke Reserve running all day," John continues. "And caroling by candlelight in the town square at 4 p.m., where you can help us beat our own world record for the most people caroling while wearing Santa hats!"

More cheers, claps, and whistles fill the air. I can't believe how many events Hideaway Habor now has, and I'm sure a lot of that has to do with the energy Piper's dad pours into the town.

"And don't forget, we've got another night of live music across town, plus a full program of events tomorrow, including the woolen sock-running championships around the Locke Reserve, and children's story time at the library with hot chocolate, whipped cream, and marshmallows."

A few nearby kids fist pump.

"You can find all the information at hideawayharbor.com or on our event app. Just download it from the site. Any questions? Just find me or any other Hidie and we'll be happy to help. Okay, then, are we ready?"

People shout, "Yes!"

"I can't hear you!" John cries. "I said, are you ready?"

"YES!" people scream.

"Okay, let's get this race started!"

He blasts a bullhorn, the bunting across the start line drops, and the runners take off.

"Go, Cody!" Mia screams at her brother.

It might be a fun run, but the folks at the front are clearly in it to win it.

As the pack rounds the end of Main Street, John steps down from the stage, shaking hands and hugging people. His love for this town is unmistakable, and it's clear the residents love him right back.

"Has anyone stood against him for mayor since I've been away?" I ask Piper.

"Nope," she replies. "But you know him, he never rests on his laurels. He's always pushing for bigger and better."

I nod, then let myself be drawn into a bear hug by the man himself.

"You survived a trip to The Perfect Package, then?" he asks with a smile.

I raise my eyebrows. "It was educational."

John laughs and pats my shoulder. "Every day's a school day."

"Grandpa!" squeals a little voice. Martha comes toward us through the crowd, perched on Ethan's shoulders, Hudson by their side.

"Hey there, pumpkin! How's my favorite grandchild?"

Martha attempts an eye roll, but it makes her go cross-eyed. "I'm your *only* grandkid, Grandpa."

"And still the best," he replies.

All three are wearing Santa hats, and Martha's has her name crocheted in red across the white brim.

"How's it going?" Ethan asks. His tone is friendly, but I catch the guarded look in his eyes. And the way he notices me holding Piper's hand.

"Good," I reply. "I was given the honor of revealing today's date on the Christmas Calendar this morning."

"Where was it?"

"Um ..." I lower my voice. "The Perfect Package."

Hudson starts laughing.

"I know that place," Martha says. "Grandma has an orn'-ment for the tree she got there. It's a clitsuss."

Ethan briefly closes his eyes and lets out a heavy sigh as we all laugh.

"What's funny?" Martha asks.

"Your daddy," John replies. "You can't see him, because you're up there, but he pulls the silliest faces."

"Especially when he's mad," Hudson murmurs, then grins at me. "What's it like in there? Cauldron? Broom? I've heard she's got cats."

"You, out of all people, should pay that place a visit," Mia says archly as she joins us. "You might learn a thing or two."

"I don't need to learn anything," Hudson says, swaggering.

"You think you're a master?" Mia taunts him, a sly smile on her lips.

"Yeah? And?"

"Sorry, I meant a master ... bater."

Even Ethan laughs, and it's so nice to see his severe face soften into someone I remember.

"You're ..." Hudson shakes his head, then glances at his niece perched on Ethan's shoulders, tracking every word, and doesn't say anything else.

"Hilarious?" Mia supplies. "A genius?"

"A piece of work," he mutters.

Mia drops a curtsy. "Why, thank you."

Marv appears at our side and holds out his hand to John. "Mr Locke, I presume?"

Piper's dad shakes his hand.

"Marvin DeVille, Brody's agent. But you can call me Marv."

"Nice to meet you," John says. "Are you here for the festivities?"

"Yeah, kind of. Great little town you've got here. And this is Cara, my assistant."

Cara's eyes scan the six-foot-plus wall of Locke men, like she's trying to find an escape route.

"I see you've all met Marv and Cara?" Erica cries, swooping in to rescue the situation. "They're coming to dinner tonight, so I hope you all can make it."

"I'm on duty tonight, Mom," Hudson says.

"And I'm taking Martha to Eleanor and Garrett's," Ethan adds.

"Well, will we see you tomorrow then at the sock-running championships?"

"When I win," Hudson says, stretching his arms over his head.

Mia coughs the word, "Second place."

Erica gives her a side hug. "Will you ever let him be?"

"Probably not," Mia replies, then lifts her camera. "Huddle up, people, this'll make a great photo."

Marv steps to the side, followed by Cara.

"You both, too," Erica says.

Marv shakes his head. "This would be a good one for ... you know."

Erica winks, and I inwardly groan. She's about as subtle as a sledgehammer.

"Mom, what's going on?" Ethan asks, his tone sharp as a blade.

"Shush! It's a secret!" she hisses, then beckons everyone closer. "Circle of trust!"

"It's a secret!" Martha repeats loudly, even though she has no idea what's going on.

"Erica?" John asks, his tone making me want to stand up straighter.

"The thing is," she whispers. "Brody's going for a very important job, and … and he needs to look like, I mean, it's got to look like he—"

"Hasn't spent the last few years getting drunk, punching people, and talking shi—" Ethan's eyes go to his daughter's legs dangling over his shoulders as if he'd forgotten she was there. "So, he's using Piper and our family as a way of rebuilding his reputation."

His words are a knife to the gut, but he's not wrong.

"No!" Erica cries.

"That's not true, and it's not fair," Piper continues. "Brody's … He's …"

My stomach clenches. Even Piper can't defend the undefendable.

"Do you have any idea how hard it was for him to come back after all this time?" she finishes.

"Daddy?" Martha asks, knowing something's very wrong.

"Sorry, Martha Moo," Piper says, plastering a smile on her face. "Everything's okay, I promise."

But it seems Ethan's not done. "You're just using her," he repeats. "And what does Piper get out of it? Nothing except some publicity that won't—"

"Stop it!" Piper's voice is low but she still spits the words at her brother. "I need Brody way more than he needs me. Without him, I might not even *have* a job next year."

CHAPTER 14

PIPER

"*W*hat, honey?" Mom asks.

I let out a frustrated sigh. The last thing I wanted was to spoil their Christmas by telling them about my work situation.

"Piper?" Dad asks gently.

"Stanley Sr. is retiring, and the company is merging with another one in the new year. We'll be competing for our jobs, and—"

"But you're so brilliant!" Mom cries. "Of course you'll win."

I shake my head. "The guy who has the same job as me at the other company is the boss's son." I leave out the part about him also being the man I *thought* I'd be bringing home for the holidays.

"Oh."

"And how do you think Brody can help with that?" Ethan asks.

It's a valid question, but I don't like how he delivers it, like he's looking to find fault.

"I'm working on a campaign for an office printer," I reply. "And I'm going to pitch the idea of having Brody promote it."

Ethan scoffs. "Seriously? That's your plan? As if he'd—"

"Hey," Brody interrupts. "Piper's helping me, and I'm going to help her."

"Really? The famous Brody King, the face of a designer cologne, is going to put on a beige button-down and shill a *printer*?"

Brody hesitates, his eyes darting to Marv, and my heart drops. No wonder Ethan's so scathing. It's never going to happen.

"I don't care what people think," Brody continues.

"Really? But you care enough about what people think to be here playing happy families, don't you?"

"Son," John says firmly. "That's not fair. Brody's doing what he believes will help him land a job. It doesn't matter what anyone says about that online. We know the truth."

"Do we?" Ethan asks coldly.

I grip Brody's arm so hard, I'm surprised my nails haven't gone through the fabric of his coat. Why does my eldest brother always have to be so damn perceptive.

"Daddy," Martha says with authority, "you're being mean to Uncle Brody."

Ethan's expression cracks slightly, revealing the man beneath his gruff exterior, though it seems he's still overwhelmed with unspoken thoughts and feelings.

"And what happens when you get this job?" he continues to Brody. "What then? You'll just leave? Again?"

And there it is, the hurt beneath his harsh words. His best friend walked out of his life, and then his soulmate died.

Martha slaps both her little hands on the top of Ethan's head. "Daddy! Time out!"

"Yeah, pumpkin," he says. "You're right." His gaze passes over us, but misses Brody. "We'll see everyone tomorrow."

Without waiting for a reply, he strides away, Martha twisting around to look over her shoulder and wave goodbye.

We're on Main Street, surrounded by people, but a heavy silence has fallen over us.

"I'm sorry," Brody says hoarsely.

Dad rubs his arm, his brow furrowed. "No, son. You've done nothing wrong."

Mom is up on her tiptoes, still waving at Martha, her smile big but strained.

"Do you really think Brody can help you keep your job?" Harper asks me.

I shrug, feeling the weight of uncertainty press down on me. I haven't thought about my job today, but now reality crashes through me. Come January, Brody and I will have gone our separate ways. I'll be sitting across a desk from my ex, and his new girlfriend will be the face I see each time I enter and leave the building.

I let go of Brody's arm and shove my hands in the pockets of my coat. Ethan's right. There's no way he would advertise a printer. Brody's trying to rehabilitate his image, not ruin it.

I just can't believe I was so stupid to believe that I was going to get anything out of this deal apart from the reanimation of my teenage crush.

Mom finally loses sight of Martha and faces Brody. "He'll come around, honey."

Brody nods, but a muscle in his jaw ticks.

"I'm off to find some more glögg," Harper says. "Who wants the boozy one?"

Everyone raises a hand, except for Brody.

"I'll help," Mom says, before weaving through the crowds with Harper to the nearest stand.

"Do you think the crowds are as big as last year, Mr L?" Mia asks.

Dad's face lights up. "Even bigger!"

I'm grateful for Mia steering the conversation onto neutral ground, keeping Dad talking and asking the kinds of questions Brody might want to know the answers to. It means I can keep quiet and let my mind ruminate in peace on what a fool I'm being.

Mom and Harper return with the hot glögg, and Harper whispers in my ear that mine has extra Aquavit in it.

I rarely drink, and now that I know Brody doesn't, I'm hyper-aware of every sip of alcohol I take. However, when the Aquavit hits my bloodstream, it smooths away the rough edges of my mood.

But then it hits me—the memory of saying what a "great idea" it would be for us to kiss.

What the hell was I thinking? Clearly I wasn't, just wallowing in sex hormones and allowing them to run the show. Brody's a fantastic actor, and I'm … not. Just someone trying not to lose herself in the role of "fake girlfriend" like any other obsessed fan.

I squeeze my thighs together as I remember him kissing the top of my head, turning on nerve endings I didn't even know I had. Did he *want* to do it?

He's an actor.

The thought tastes bitter in my mouth, and I swallow it down.

We mill around as the race continues, then scream and cheer as Cody, Mia's older brother, crosses the line first. It bodes well for their team in the wife-carrying championships, and Mia delights in reminding Hudson that they're going to beat him again next year.

Then we wander through the town as the sun sets, heading into the main square for carols.

Hideaway Harbor is magical, but at Christmas, it's even more special. The enormous tree is as tall as the surrounding buildings and covered in multicolored lights.

"How did they decorate it?" Brody asks.

"The fire department did," Hudson replies. "We've got the equipment, and we're not afraid of heights."

"I don't remember it being this big when we were younger."

"It wasn't. I think Dad just wants each year to be bigger and better than the last."

A lump forms in my throat. *That drive for something bigger ... it's not just in Dad.*

After Brody left, a part of me left with him. I've never really acknowledged it until now, but it's true. I wanted to leave Hideaway, travel the world, and experience places and cultures completely different from my hometown. It wasn't that I didn't love it; I just yearned to see what else was out there.

But here I am, twenty-eight, and the only time I've ever left the country was a brief visit to see Harper in France last year. My job doesn't pay enough for that around-the-world ticket I've always dreamed of.

Maybe I should let the idea go ... even my New York dream, which ended up being Brooklyn anyway. I could move back here and go freelance from the financial safety of my childhood home.

I bite the inside of my cheek. Why does the thought of coming home feel like I've failed? And it just puts even more physical distance between me and Brody. At least when he's across the East River, he seems closer. But when we get back, we'll be as far apart as ever.

"Hey, what's up?" he murmurs, his mouth close to my ear.

I press my lips shut and shake my head. People are lighting candles all around us, waiting for the caroling to start. It's so freaking beautiful it intensifies the ache in my heart.

Taking my hand, Brody draws me to the back of the crowd,

beneath the awning of a shop. The windows are lit up with a display so big that it blocks the customers inside, and those outside are facing away from us. Even though we're in public, it somehow feels private.

Brody faces me, dipping his head as I lift mine. His eyes are a deep chestnut brown, the irises flecked with hints of gold.

"Please talk to me."

I cross my arms over my stomach. "Do you have any intention of advertising the printer?"

There's a pause, then he rubs a hand over his face. "Marv doesn't want me to."

"And you?"

He swallows. "I won't let you down."

"That doesn't mean you want to!"

"I … I'll do it. I promise."

"But it's stupid!"

"Not if it's to help you keep your job."

"But surely you can imagine what people will say?"

He shrugs. "It can't be any worse than what they've said about me already. And if I get this job then it won't matter."

That's true. I mustn't lose sight of the fact that the only reason we're both standing here is because Brody wants a new job and I'm desperately trying to hold onto my current one.

"I promise I'll do it," he repeats.

I nod, emotionally drained, as everyone behind us begins singing *Silent Night*.

Brody gazes intently at me. "Can I ask you a question?"

I swallow. There are so many he *could* ask, and a long list of ones I don't want him to.

"That depends on what it is," I reply, my voice wobbling.

He nods like he understands, then pauses, his eyes moving up and to the left as if sorting through his list of questions to find the one I'll most likely answer.

Then his gaze falls back to me. "Can I see your art?"

Unfortunately, my brain decides to hear, "Can I see your arse?" said in a British accent, and I gulp.

"Piper?"

"Oh my god, I thought you said ... never mind. I'm sorry. Um ... Maybe?"

He cocks an eyebrow. "What exactly do you draw? Because now I'm imagining ... well, I don't know."

"No! It's nothing weird!" *Much ...* "Or pervy!" *Apart from the pictures I draw of you looking so hot I have to break out my rechargeable toyfriend ...*

"Then why do you look so horrified? You know I'll think they're amazing."

You'll also know I'm borderline obsessed with you ... and have been since I was about twelve.

"I'm sorry about what I said in Love at First Sip," I blurt out, trying to change the topic of conversation, but immediately landing on an even more embarrassing one.

He frowns. "What did you say that you should be sorry for?"

Oh god. "Ahahaha!"

His lips twitch like he's trying not to laugh. "Piper?"

"When I said it would be a great idea for us to kiss ... Funny, right?"

He freezes. "Oh, that."

Then he waves his hand as if dismissing a minion. "Don't worry about it. We're cool."

I'm mortified. But rather than keep my mouth shut, all the anger spills out.

"Don't you care about me at *all*?"

"Huh?" He blinks. "What are you talking about? Of course I care!"

"This is just a means to an end. *I'm* just a means to an end."

"What? No! It's not like that."

"But what happens if people don't buy a bit of hand-hold-

EVIE ALEXANDER

ing? What if all this doesn't get you the job because we haven't put on a good enough show?"

I'm rambling but I can't stop.

"And if you don't get the job then you'll never advertise the damn printer, will you? I'm trying to help you here, but all you can do is swat your hand like I'm an annoying fly."

Brody pinches the bridge of his nose. "What are you going on about?"

"I can't kiss on demand, and I've got no idea if I can fake it like you're used to doing."

"Huh?"

"In your movies. Your TV shows."

"You think that's easy? Faking passion with someone I'm not attracted to?"

"Oh, puhlease. Those actresses were all hot as fuck."

"It doesn't mean I wanted to kiss them!"

The dreamy sounds of *Silent Night* envelop us but have no effect on our little angry bubble.

"Exactly!"

Brody gives me a wide-eyed stare of utter incomprehension. "*What?*"

To be honest, I'm not sure where I'm going with this word salad either, I'm just pissed that I offered to kiss Brody and he's not interested.

I put my hands on my hips. "It's simple."

"It is?"

"Yes. If you *really* wanted to convince people we're a couple, then you'd know we need to kiss in public. And if you cared about me *in the slightest*, then you'd know I can't do that without knowing what to expect."

"Piper, I'm not going to force you to kiss me."

"But you kiss other people you don't like all the time! What's wrong with me?"

"Huh? There's nothing wrong with you!"

156

"Then why won't you kiss me!"

He goes still, then his eyes flick down to my mouth and back up, his expression turning from confused and frustrated, to rather, *heated* …

"Okay. Let's practice."

For someone who just ran her mouth, I'm suddenly all out of words.

"Kissing," he continues slowly, making sure I understand *exactly* what kind of practice he's suggesting.

"Here? Now?"

He nods, gaze smoldering, then folds his arms and lifts his chin in challenge. "You think we should kiss, but you don't know what to expect. So let's do it. Let's practice."

I glance around. Everyone is facing away from us. No one's watching.

When I turn back to Brody, his arms are uncrossed and he's stepped closer.

"You said yourself it would be a great idea," he murmurs, his voice low and hypnotic.

I sway towards him until we're almost touching. "Funny, right?"

His hands skim up the outside of my arms until they frame my face. "Not particularly …"

"What?" I whisper.

"I don't think it's going to be funny."

I swallow. "You don't?"

"No." His voice drops even lower. "I think it's going to be very, *very* hot."

I make a noise that sounds suspiciously like a whimper as my nipples tingle and my panties flood. I'm so close to coming and his lips have yet to touch mine. This is a situation that needs to be rectified immediately or I'm going to explode and take the whole of Hideaway Harbor with me.

So I lift my heels to close the last bit of distance between us and press my lips against his.

Brody groans, and I swear it's the hottest sound I've ever heard in my life. It's like he's spent his life eating dry bread and water and now he's diving headfirst into a chocolate fountain.

My bag drops from my shoulder to the ground and I thread my fingers through his hair under his Santa hat. Now that I've got him exactly where I want him, I never want to let go.

Our lips are touching but not moving, like we're balanced on a knife's edge. One way ends chastely, the other with—

Brody slants his mouth over mine and kisses me like there's no tomorrow. I gasp as he takes control, his lips soft, then firm, his tongue licking fire into my mouth. There's nothing leisurely about it, no gradual ramping up. He's gone from zero to sexty-sex miles an hour in a heartbeat, and I'm so here for it.

I've spent almost a lifetime fantasizing about kissing Brody King, and reality is so much hotter than my imagination. With every sweep of his tongue, every nip of his teeth on my lower lip, he's ruining me for all other men.

I can't even analyze what's going on anymore or question his motives; all I can do is feel.

It's all too much and, at the same time, not enough. Brody's the god of kissing, his sinful mouth making me want to rip off all my winter layers and pull him deep inside me.

My breath is coming quicker and quicker through my nose, my hands clenched tight in his hair as pleasure explodes inside me. My clit is aching to the point of pain, and I shift my legs to anchor one of his muscled thighs between them, rocking my pussy against him.

Brody growls into my mouth and it's so hot I think I'm going to faint. Ripping my mouth from his, I suck and bite his neck, whimpering with desire and frustration.

Then he abruptly stops, and cold reality slices through me like ice.

The carol has finished.

People are clapping.

People are clapping *near us*.

I bring my face away from where I've been feasting on Brody's neck like a starving vampire to look over his shoulder

At Mom, Marv, and Mia.

Mom's still clapping, Marv's got a massive grin on his face, and Mia's smirking at us from behind her camera.

"That was beautiful!" Mom cries. "A little more passionate than I had in mind, but if you can dial it down a few notches, I think it'll be perfect!"

CHAPTER 15

PIPER

"*M*om?" I manage, hardly the first word I expect to say after having a panty-destroying first kiss from my fake boyfriend.

But she's already turned to Mia. "How are the photos, honey?"

"Not too X-rated," she replies, "and the start of the kiss was really quite sweet."

Mom and Marv crowd around her to look at the camera screen.

Meanwhile, Brody and I are still breathing like we just ran the Santa 5K at a full sprint.

"You okay?" he asks.

I stare at the rise and fall of his chest. I am so *not* okay right now. My mind and body are tumbling like a washing machine on a spin cycle with a hundred vibrators in the drum. I'm horny and also shocked, embarrassed, furious at the interruption, and terrified that it was all an act for Brody.

"Piper?"

"Yeah, fine," I say breathlessly. "Nailed it."

He raises an eyebrow in question.

"The practicing," I continue. "They seemed to buy it."

His expression stills.

I can't tell what he's thinking, so I panic. "Good job!" I blurt, like a deranged Little League coach, then give him two thumbs up.

Oh my god, just stop!

Mom bustles forward and takes my arm. "Come on now. Plenty of time for snuggles when you get home. You've got such lovely voices; you need to join in with the carols."

She draws us back into the crowd.

I'm on autopilot now, singing the tunes I've known since childhood while most of my brain relives and dissects the kiss that just turned me inside out and upside down.

Someone nearby is singing loudly and off-key. I turn to see the agent Marv dislikes, Jack Lourd, standing next to Audrey from the Making Whoopie bakery, doing his best to murder *The Twelve Days of Christmas.*

The jarring of his voice mirrors what's going on in my brain. Brody's an actor. I've seen him kiss women on screen. It looked believable enough to fool me, and every other fan he's got. Is what just happened the same thing? Another performance?

After the carols, we walk home, and Mom takes a casserole out of the crockpot where it's been simmering all day. There hasn't been a moment where Brody and I have been left alone, and as the minutes slowly count down toward bedtime, my trepidation increases.

Marv is in top form, regaling my folks with PG-rated stories from Hollywood, and even Cara has come a little out of her shell. Harper helps keep the conversation going, occasionally sending glances my way. She's a smart cookie and knows something's up.

Marv and Cara leave with Harper, who's staying with Hudson. Brody and I help clean up, then Mom and Dad send us off to bed, like we're kids and it's a school night.

As my bedroom door shuts behind Brody, I scoot to the other side of the room and hide the gift bag from The Perfect Package at the bottom of my suitcase.

"You don't want to see what you've got?" he asks.

My face heats. "To be fair, you were the reason we got the bag, so whatever's inside is probably yours."

"I'd rather share …"

His words are mild, but the message behind them certainly isn't, and it sends a flush of desire rippling up through my body.

Metaphorically pulling up my big-girl pants, I face him. "I'm sorry about Mom and Mia. Earlier."

"I'm sorry about Marv."

Brody's stance is relaxed, hands tucked into the pockets of his slacks. Meanwhile, I'm as jumpy as a cat in a dog pound. We're finally alone, with a bed. And I don't know how to ask him if any part of our kiss was fake for him, or if it was as real as it was for me.

Actually, scratch that. It was the most mind-and-body-blowingly *unreal* experience I've ever had.

"Can I see your art now?"

"Oh. Uh …"

I'm torn. Of course, I want him to see it and tell me I'm brilliant, but if I show him everything, then I'll also have to admit a whole lot more.

Come on! Big girl pants!

He raises his hands. "It's okay, I understa—"

"I'll show you." I fetch my tablet, sit on the bed, then pat the space next to me.

He gets onto the bed and sits beside me, his hands clasped in his lap, like he's being a good boy, here to admire my artwork, not feel up the creator.

I open up the library and start with safe images, the ones I've already posted to my fantasy art account.

"Holy shit, Piper! These are incredible!"

I hand him the tablet as I preen. "These are the best ones from my early twenties."

Brody scrolls through pictures of elves and wizards, dragons, witches, mermaids—a whole world of beings from my imagination, books I've read and films and TV series I've binge-watched.

Brody's taking his time with every image, his eyes tracking over the lines and the composition.

"Some of these are hand drawn and the others are digital?"

"Yeah. It depends on what mood I'm in or what kind of effect I want to achieve."

He swipes to the last one in the gallery, and an old pain resurfaces in my gut.

"This one is familiar," he says slowly, as if he's trying to place how he knows it.

I sigh. "Yeah. It was the first one to go semi-viral. A massive online store ripped it off, printing it on everything from blankets to mugs. I complained, of course, but nothing happened. It's just the same old bullshit when you're an individual creator. Your stuff gets pirated, and you can't do anything about it."

Brody's gone incredibly still, like he's a panther about to pounce.

"It's okay," I say brightly, even though it's not, and it's never going to be. "I'm over it. More or less. And there's no point in staying mad when it won't change the situation."

"Am I allowed to be mad on your behalf?"

"Honestly, I don't want you to waste another thought on it.

Yes, it's shitty, but I'd much rather you think about the pictures themselves, and that I drew them."

He takes my hand. "I'm so proud of you. These are incredible. I love them. You were always crazy talented growing up, but these are next-level cool."

I can't stop a smile taking over my face. "Thank you."

"Seriously, I want you to send them to me so I can always see them. Or do you have them online? Is this what your mom was talking about?"

I nod. "Most of these are online."

"Do you have any others?"

My cheeks flush with heat. *This is it, the moment I unleash the crazy.*

"I do," I begin. "But if I show you, you have to promise not to freak out."

He turns to look at me properly, and suddenly, I feel stupid. The best friend's little sister with a crush that never really went away.

"I'll do my best," he says gently. "And I promise you there's nothing you could ever say or do that would change my opinion of you."

But this *will* change his opinion. He's gonna think I'm just like every other super-crazed fan who can't tell fiction from reality.

I don't know what to do. It's like I'm made of tissue paper, and one word from him could tear me apart.

"You don't have to show me if you don't want to," he says, his voice so patient and understanding.

Even though my mind says, *"Don't do it,"* I still want to show him. It's a secret I've held onto for so long, it's practically begging to burst out. I just have to trust it won't make him run.

Taking the tablet from him, I open my secret folder, the one nobody else has ever seen, the one filled with drawings of the man sitting beside me.

The first image is of him as a warrior elf, striding toward the viewer, a bow in one hand, the other reaching over his shoulder to fetch an arrow from his quiver.

"Is that ... me?" he asks, his voice hushed like he's in church.

"Yeah."

"But ..." His eyes find mine, and he looks genuinely confused. "Is this online? Has anyone else seen it?"

I shake my head. "You're the first person I've ever shown these drawings to."

He looks stunned.

Panic is beginning to strangle me. I've miscalculated.

Brody turns back to the tablet, swiping through the pictures like he needs to know how many there are. He stops when he gets to the one of him sending his pet wolf after Colin.

"Who's that?"

"The guy who dumped me. The one who was supposed to be coming home for Christmas with me. The one I'm going to be fighting with for my job next year."

His jaw tenses. "I wish I had a wolf to hunt him down."

I stay silent. The elephant in the room is growing bigger by the second. I'm just waiting for Brody to notice it.

He takes a breath, like he's about to say something, then stops. I just know he's trying to work out how to ask, "Have you been in love with me for years?" or "Are you a mad, crazy stalker lady and I need to jump in my ride and head out of Hideaway, stat?"

"You've drawn me in every role I've ever played," he says slowly. "And every commercial."

"Yeah," I reply, not sure if he thinks that's a good or a bad thing. My palms are clammy, which tells me it's probably *extremely* bad that I've followed his career closer than anyone else.

"I have a Google Alert set up for your name," I say, as if that explains everything, although I'm sure I just made the situation worse.

A pause, then: "How long have you had it?"

"Twelve years."

Brody's silent, clearly realizing *just* how obsessed I am with him.

"So you know about every one of my fuck-ups," he says quietly.

Oh, shit. I never thought he'd be thinking about that.

He gazes at me, his expression bleak. "I didn't cheat on Marisa, but most of the other stories are half-truths."

"A half-truth is an untruth because it's not the whole picture. If you *did* hit that guy, then I bet he deserved it."

Brody nods. "He was sexually harassing female actors in the films his studio was producing. But it got hushed up and spun like I was the bad guy, then he blacklisted me."

"Well, there we are then," I say firmly.

How has it not clicked that I've been secretly in love with him for years?

"But the drinking, that's a fact."

My mind flips through a carousel of online images, each one worse than the last, all of Brody looking wasted.

"I never touched drugs, but the booze ..." He gazes at me. "I've been sober for over a year now. It makes some things harder, as there's no cushion between me and the world, but it's better. I don't want to be that guy anymore."

Relief washes through me. I know this is the truth and he's still the Brody I remember.

"How many years do you think you had an issue with alcohol for?"

He shakes his head, his mouth twisting. "Four years, maybe, if I'm honest?"

"Well, in terms of your adult life, that's less than a third."

"I …" Brody gives me a soft smile. "I never thought about it like that before, but you're right."

I smile back. "You're still you."

"That's why I did that interview about healthy eating and fitness," he says, and the happiness drains from his face. "But the guy twisted my words, made me out to be an out-of-touch Hollywood prick. I only mentioned the sea moss smoothie and the other stuff because I was giving a shout out to a friend's new start-up."

My gut twists with empathy. I knew Brody was speaking from the heart about wanting to take care of his body, but the journalist turned him into a laughing-stock.

"He was an asshole for what he did to you. I knew what you were trying to say, but it was like he was out to get you."

"Yeah, I think he thought it would get him a date with my ex." He sighs. "I'm sorry you've read about every mistake I've made since leaving Hideaway."

"Hey! Hudson or Ethan would have punched that producer too. You didn't cheat on your girlfriend, and it's not your fault that douche of an interviewer twisted what you said. You've done incredible things as well. You've worked without a break since you left Hideaway, and you're so talented. You need to take credit for everything you've achieved."

"You're the talented one. Always have been. I'm just a pretty face who can memorize lines. I mean, look at these. They're incredible."

He swipes to the next image on the tablet, then jerks like he's been hit.

"No way."

"What is it?"

He shakes his head. "You've drawn me as the Emberking of Draventhorne! From *The Chronicles of the Sword and the Flame!*"

"So?"

His eyes are alight as he looks at me. "That's the series I

auditioned for! I'm up for the role of the warlock of Zhash-Dhrog!"

"You'd be perfect for it!" I say excitedly, then swipe through to the next drawing. "I've drawn you as him too!"

"Wow," he says. "Warlock me looks badass."

I laugh. "I'm a huge fan of the books, and I read on the forums that they're planning a series next year."

"Yeah, the warlock's not one of the main roles, but it's still pretty cool, and he's in every episode of the first season."

My brain jolts as a memory awakens, one I know is bad.

Then it hits me.

"When do they start filming?"

Brody's gaze is still on my drawings as he flicks back and forth through them, like he can't decide which one to focus on. "January fifth."

"How long will they be shooting the first season for?"

"Nine to eleven months, depending on reshoots," he replies, his attention still on the tablet.

"And where are they filming?" My voice is barely audible.

"New Zealand," he replies, still staring at my art.

Time stops, and for a nanosecond the full force of my foolishness hits me.

Brody has spent the last twelve years building a career as a model and actor. His life is so far removed from mine, the only point of intersection is right here, right now. And I'm just another fan with a crush who let her imagination get the better of her.

That kiss earlier? It was part of the act, just a performance to help him land a job. He might have enjoyed it, but that doesn't mean anything between us has changed. He's still destined to continue a life that's light-years apart from mine, most likely on the other side of the world.

"That's fantastic!" I say, with cheerleader-level enthusiasm.

His eyes snap to mine and he blinks.

Once again, I can't read his expression, so I clap my hands and bounce on the bed like a tween at a sleepover. "I'm so excited for you!"

He clears his throat. "I haven't gotten it yet. I might still be in New York next year."

I shrug, trying to play it cool even as my heart cracks. "You're really talented. You'll get the job."

I take the tablet. "You wanted me to send you the pictures? No problem." I tap quickly on the screen. "Yep, there's your email address … sharing a Google Drive link now … And … done. You've got them."

Bouncing off the bed, I grab my pajamas and fake a yawn. "I'm going to take a quick shower and get ready for bed. It's been a long day."

I put the tablet to sleep, toss it into my open suitcase, then dash out of the room and down the corridor into the bathroom.

Inside, I sit on the seat of the toilet and hold my head in my hands.

It was a fake kiss for a fake relationship. To get him a real job.

Things couldn't be more different from when we were teenagers. Our shared history feels like a lifetime ago, and now we've got nothing in common.

Back then, I still had my whole life ahead of me. Now? I'm pushing thirty, and none of the dreams I had for adulthood have materialized, while Brody's achieved more than any of us ever imagined possible.

I didn't realize until the last few minutes how lonely I've been in Brooklyn. I've just been pushing the feelings down and getting on with life. But now, back in Hideaway with the people who mean the most to me, it only magnifies how alone I feel.

And the last straw? The kiss that sparked a bubbling, ridiculous hope that Brody and I could actually be a thing. All those future possibilities fizzing up inside me like Mentos in a bottle of soda, only for reality to come along and toss the whole thing straight in the trash.

Brody's a famous actor who dates other famous actors and works all over the globe.

Meanwhile, I'm scraping by in a Brooklyn one-bed and just got dumped by a future coworker for the receptionist.

I take a steadying breath, strip off my clothes, and step into the shower.

Everything's going to be okay.

I just need to manage my expectations.

Brody's helping me with Mom, and I'm helping him land an incredible job. I should be happy for him.

And make sure we never kiss again.

BRODY SPRINGS up from where he's been sitting on the edge of the bed as I enter the bedroom.

He runs a hand through his hair. "Er ... Are you ...?"

I force a sunny smile. "Yep! I'm done. Bathroom's all yours!"

I give him a wide berth as I make my way to the other side of the bed, grabbing earplugs and an eye mask on the way.

"Night-night, Brody," I say as I get into bed. "Sweet dreams!"

Then I jam in the earplugs, shove on the eye mask, and turn onto my side, facing away from him.

Even though my hearing is muffled, I still make out his heavy sigh, then the click of the door as he leaves the room.

I press my lips together to hold the fake smile in place and force myself to breathe evenly.

Exhaustion drapes over every part of me, and I silently pray I'll be asleep before he comes back.

CHAPTER 16

BRODY

"*K*ing of the Fuck Up!"

That's been one of the nicer headlines about me.

With "King" as my last name, and every mistake I've made in public, the press and internet trolls have torn me apart over the past few years.

Marv and Cara try to keep it from me, but they can't stop the social algorithms from thinking that's what I want to see when I'm scrolling—or when I'm paying for gas and catch sight of my drunken face plastered on the cover of tabloid magazines.

But you could take all the pain and regret I feel from every single one of my mistakes, amplify it by a million, and it still wouldn't come close to how I feel right now, lying next to Piper.

I've worked with enough inexperienced actors to spot when

someone's faking emotion, and Piper's smiling face just before bed last night rang hollow in my chest.

I know I've hurt her, but I don't know exactly how, and I don't know how to fix it.

Did she want to kiss *me*, or the versions of me she sees on screen?

And if she *has* held a torch for me, how can anything between us work when I've fucked up so much of the last twelve years, and I'm heading for a job on the other side of the world?

Maybe nothing happening is a good thing. Piper's sweetness and sunshine and I'm the rain cloud that would ruin her life. Marisa may have cheated on me, but she's not wrong about a lot of things. She accused me of not being present, emotionally as well as physically. I can't be like that with Piper. She deserves more.

It's still dark outside, but the time on my watch shows it's already morning. I've spent most of the night awake, listening to her unhappy mumbles, trying to find meaning in the occasional lucid word, while also trying to wrap my head around what happened yesterday.

We kissed.

I kissed Piper Locke and nearly came in my pants in the middle of a carols-by-candlelight attempt to break a world record based on the number of people wearing Santa hats. I don't know which was more surreal, the kiss or the setting.

It was hands down the hottest moment of my life. So hot that I forgot where I was.

Yes, it was supposed to be practice. It was supposed to be fake.

But there's a world of difference between kissing another actor on set and what happened last night.

The former always leaves me cold. At best, it's slightly weird; at worst, downright unpleasant.

Kissing Piper? It blew my mind.

But before I could talk to her about it, everything unraveled.

I've never been the sharpest tool in the shed, and I didn't understand the significance of Piper having a Google Alert for me until it was too late.

I was too wrapped up in my own story of public failure and embarrassment to realize it meant she had a thing for me, or at least for who I've played on screen. All I could think about was how she'd perfectly captured me in the role I was going for.

A role in a show filming on the other side of the planet for nearly a year.

"A King-Sized Ego and a Right Royal Mess." That's what the headline should be for this catastrophic fail.

I scroll through the pictures from yesterday in the half-light, gazing at a smiling Piper, reliving how it felt to have her on my arm. The way we worked as a team in The Perfect Package. It was the first time I'd ever been in public and felt truly safe and secure in letting my guard down. *That* was happiness for me. And I don't know how the hell to get it back.

How can I persuade Piper to talk to me? How can I fix this? And should I even try when I can't let anything happen between us?

Ethan's words from yesterday are also playing on a loop in my head. I hurt him. I hurt Olivia by not going to their wedding, not visiting after Martha was born, and now it's too late to say sorry.

Carefully getting out of bed, I go to the window, pushing back the drapes a little so I can look outside. It's getting light, and the sky is clear this morning, although snow is forecast later.

Piper stirs behind me, and I glance over my shoulder. One arm slowly creeps over to my side of the bed, like she's checking if I'm there or not. She pats the empty pillow, then lets out a sigh so heavy it's like a ball of lead in my gut.

I clear my throat, not wanting to scare her by saying anything.

She jumps up, ripping her eye mask completely off, then sags when she sees me and pulls out her earplugs, putting them on the nightstand.

"How did you sleep?" I ask.

She yawns and pins on another fake-looking smile. "It was okay. You?"

I don't know how to reply, so I make a non-committal noise.

Throwing back the covers and getting out of bed, Piper grabs some clothes, then heads to the door. "I'm gonna get ready, then go get coffee."

"Sure. I'll see you downstairs."

For someone who was asleep less than a minute ago, she's certainly awake now and can't get out of the room fast enough. I stifle a shout of frustration as the door closes behind her.

AFTER PIPER MAKES her way downstairs, I use the bathroom, then join her in the kitchen.

"Morning, son!" John calls out. "I'm just telling Marv and Cara all about the sock-running championships."

"And I'm making breakfast," Erica adds. "Same as yesterday? It's gonna be another long day."

"Thanks, that would be great," I reply, wishing a quick "good morning'" to everyone before going to Erica's side. "Can I help?"

She bats my arm away. "Absolutely not. And anyway, you don't know where anything is."

"What are you getting out next?"

"The eggs and bacon."

I know this is a trick question, but I move to the refrigerator first.

"See!" Erica crows. "You don't know."

I take the bacon out, then reach up to a cupboard where I know she keeps the eggs in a ceramic bowl because she says they should always be kept at room temperature.

"You were saying..."

She laughs. "Okay, you got me there, but you're still sitting down. Go! Scoot!" she says, shooing me away with a wooden spoon.

I can either sit next to Cara at one end of the breakfast bar or Piper at the other, and I know how weird it would look if I chose the wrong end. So, I pull out the chair next to my fake girlfriend as she sprinkles cinnamon into her coffee, then adds half-and-half.

"But *socks*?" Marv is saying, like people need to get with the program and use proper footwear.

"Hideaway has lots of Nordic roots," John replies. "It's like running barefoot, but warmer. Want to have a go?"

Marv chokes on a mouthful of coffee, and Cara whacks him on the back.

"No thank you, Mr Mayor," he finally manages. "I spent a lot of money on these shoes and they're staying on."

"You'll both need snow boots if you're coming up to the reserve," John continues.

"Don't worry, we've got plenty to spare that'll fit you," Erica adds. "I'll get an old pair of Hudson's. And a warmer coat."

"Thanks, that'd be great," Marv replies, although he doesn't sound enthusiastic about swapping his handmade Italian shoes for Hudson's cast-offs.

My stomach rumbles as the scent of breakfast fills the air, and I try to think of something, *anything*, to say to Piper.

"You're awfully quiet this morning, honey," Erica says to her. "You coming down with something?"

Piper sits up straighter. "I'm fine, Mom."

"You sure?"

"Yeah, yeah. So, what's the plan for today?"

Erica breaks eggs into the sizzling pan. "We've got it all arranged. Marv, why don't you fill them both in?"

Marv leans forward. "It's Christmas story time for kiddies down at the library. Erica's worked her magic and got you a slot at the end, so fingers crossed the rugrats aren't too hyped up on sugar by then. Then there's the sock race in the woods—"

"And I've got extra mistletoe to hang in a tree for your kiss," Erica interrupts.

Piper's coffee mug stops halfway to her mouth at her mother's words.

"We don't have to do that," I say.

"Why not? It's so pretty up there. I've got it all planned out."

"What about the photos Mia took last night?" Piper asks. "You know, of us ..."

"But that was at *night*, honey. We need them during the day, too. Don't we, Marv?"

"Er ..." Marv has clearly picked up on the vibe between me and Piper this morning.

"But we've got it all organized!" Erica's voice is plaintive, like a little girl who's just been told her party's canceled because all the guests are sick.

"The forecast says it's going to snow later, so it might not photograph well," I say. "It can always wait for another day."

"Okay," she replies, seeming slightly mollified, then dishes up our breakfast.

It's delicious as always, but my stomach is too tangled to enjoy it.

Marv's one-man show continues for the next hour as we clear up and get ready to leave the house.

After John heads out to the Locke Reserve to oversee preparations for the sock-running championships, and Erica and Piper go with Cara to find boots that fit her, Marv rounds on me.

"Whatever you've done to screw things up with our golden girl, sort it," he hisses.

I don't even bother arguing with him.

"What did you do? For the love of all that's holy, please tell me you didn't turn her down?"

"I—"

"Because that girl's in love with you. The way she looks at you? That ain't acting."

"You don't know that."

Marv whacks my arm with the back of his hand. "Seriously? Give me a break."

I rub the lines on my forehead. How the fuck can I fix this mess?

"So, what the hell happened last night?"

I take out my phone, pull up the images she's drawn of me, and show them to him.

"What the—" He swipes through them. "Holy shit, man!" He gazes up at me, his eyes wide. "Did she do these?"

I grab the phone from him and shove it in my back pocket. "Of course, she fucking did."

"But how did she know you were going for the part?"

"She didn't. That's the point. She loves the world of *The Sword and the Flame* and imagined me playing everyone from the Emberking of Draventhorne to the warlock."

Marv rubs his chin as he stares off into the middle distance. "So, I was right."

"Huh?"

"She *did* have a thing for you when you were kids, and it looks like it never went away."

"She might be like one of those fans, in love with the character, not the real person."

"Have you lost your frikking mind, Brody? Piper's in love with *you*," he says crossly, giving me another slap.

"Hey! Cut it out!" I rub my arm, even though Marv's about as effective in a fight as a damp sponge. "We've spent the last twelve years apart. We're different people now."

"On the outside, maybe a bit," he replies testily. "But in here —" He pokes the center of my chest. "You're still the same kid I met all those years ago. Trust me on this. People don't change. I'm twice as old as you and I know what I'm talking about."

I shrug as if I don't believe him, and his nostrils flare.

"Are you gonna man up or what? Faint heart never won fair lady, and you need to make a decision about whether to be happy or not."

"What?"

"Tell Piper how you feel."

"But I don't know how *she* feels."

Marv growls with frustration. "You kissed. It was real. Time for the happily ever after, numnuts."

"But how? If I get the job, I'll be in New Zealand?"

"So?"

"What do you mean, '*so*'?"

He shrugs. "She can come with you."

"Are you insane? She's got a job in Brooklyn. A life there."

"A job where her talent is used to design a stapler mascot? A job she might not have anyway in a few months' time?"

"I can't just expect her to drop all that and follow me! What about her career? What *she* wants? This isn't the 1950s, where her needs take second place to mine."

I score my fingernails across my scalp. "Besides, she said she was excited for me. She acted like she was cool with me leaving. Like the kiss didn't mean anything."

"*Acted*. She's protecting herself. You need to sort this. She's a sweet kid and I want this thing between you to be real."

"Huh?"

He looks at me like I'm too dumb for words. "You think this is just about the job? I care about you, dipshit, and I want you to be happy. Marisa didn't make you smile like Piper does. No one has, not even me, and I'm the funniest guy in the room."

"All ready then?" Erica enters the hallway and Marv and I move apart.

"Sure," Marv replies. "Cara all sorted?"

"Yes. She's the same size as Harper, so we've got her kitted out to cope with any weather Hideaway can throw our way. Hudson's old boots fit you okay?"

"Yeah, sure," Marv replies. "With his coat and muffler, I'm gonna look like—what do you call yourselves again? Hidies?"

Erica smiles. "Yes. You're a Holiday Hidie at the moment, but if you move here, you become a full-fledged Hidie like the rest of us."

"Hidie ho, hidie ho," Marv replies. "Off to the library we go!"

Erica laughs, then hustles us out the door and down the street.

The sky is a crisp, pale blue, and the sun glints so brightly off the snow I squint. Piper and I fall into step behind everyone, but she doesn't take my hand, keeping hers in the pockets of her coat.

"Piper, I—"

"Looking forward to story time?" she asks, cutting me off.

"I ... uh ... Look, can we talk about what happened last night?"

Her gaze is fixed straight ahead, as if I'm not even there, another tense smile on her face.

"No need," she says brightly.

"About our kiss."

She stumbles but quickly recovers, then shoots me a quick look. Her lips curve upward, but her eyes don't look happy.

"I think we did what we needed to do. And ... that's enough."

I don't know what to say next. I may be passable at acting out lines other people have written, but I sure as shit can't seem to write my own.

Faint heart never won fair lady.

I shake my head at my chickenshit self as we walk down Main Street towards the library, past decorated shops, and smiling people enjoying the morning sunshine.

I nod or wave automatically as people call out to me, my mind fully focused on finding the right words to say to Piper when I get the chance. I still don't know whether to tell her the truth or not. I want what's best for her, and I'm not sure that's me.

The library is an old stone building, full of warmth, polished wood, and the smell of old books and freshly made hot chocolate. I haven't been here since I was a kid.

I remember my mom letting me loose in here for hours, then sitting on the couch at home with popcorn and a beer while I acted out the stories. I spent so many years angry that she didn't take better care of herself, but therapy has helped me see her as a loving mom who did the best she could. Plenty of people eat badly and live long lives. She didn't know about her underlying heart condition, and it's not her fault she died. Nor is it mine for not being able to stop it.

"You okay?" Piper asks, snapping me back into the present moment.

"I was thinking about my mom," I answer truthfully.

Piper's gaze is full of understanding and compassion.

"The library was great because it was free," I continue. "So I could read as much as I liked without feeling guilty."

"Ethan was always telling us at dinner about books you'd recommended to him."

I smile. "Usually ones about boys going off into the wilderness and having adventures, fighting giant crocodiles or going back in time to see the dinosaurs."

"Yeah." She smiles back at me, and my heart lifts a little. "Do you remember when you both decided the stairs at home were Mount Everest?"

"And we had to use crampons, ropes, and ice axes in order to scale it?"

"I thought Dad would have a fit at the damage to the wood, but do you remember what he said?"

I nod, still amazed at his calm reaction. "He said it was better we were doing something fun than sitting around playing video games."

"I was convinced you'd both be grounded forever."

"He never even told my mom about it."

"Really?"

"I think he knew it would be a worry she didn't need. He's a good man."

"Yeah. I'm lucky."

The silence fills with the ghostly presence of my father who only showed up in my life when I was famous.

"I suppose you know he got in touch," I say. "My dad."

She nods.

"Of course, all he wanted was money."

"I'm sorry."

I lift a shoulder like it's nothing. "I thought I'd feel more for him, especially since he looks like me. But I saw him for who he really is. A flawed man who couldn't be there for his kid, and someone I never want to become."

"You'll never be like him."

"I hope not."

I gaze into Piper's endlessly blue eyes, trying to communicate everything I can't yet say out loud.

"Right," Marv says, striding up with a thin book in his hand. "*The Night Before Christmas* is taken, along with *How the Grinch*

Stole Christmas, *The Polar Express*, and *Olive, the Other Reindeer*. *A Christmas Carol* is too long, as are all the versions of *The Nutcracker* they've got, so there are only slim pickings left for you."

Mia enters the library behind us. "Morning, everyone! Am I late?"

"Nah, plenty of time," Marv replies. "Brody's on last, and he's only got five minutes, so be prepared."

"Cool. What's he reading?"

Marv looks at the front of the picture book with disgust. *"The Yeti Who Got Stuck in the Chimney."*

CHAPTER 17

BRODY

*M*ia snorts. "Never heard of it. What's it about?"

Marv turns it over.

"*Deep in his cave, a lonely yeti watches families celebrating Christmas, wishing he could join in but thinking he doesn't belong. One magical Christmas, a wise luna moth, who had once been a caterpillar, shares an important secret: it's not about how you look, but who you are inside.*"

He shakes his head. "Sheesh. It sure as shit ain't Shakespeare."

Clearing his throat, he continues. "*Inspired by the moth's words, the yeti sets out to become Santa. But when he gets stuck in a chimney, it's a brave little boy who comes to his rescue. Together, they discover the true spirit of Christmas is all about kindness, love, and finding where you truly belong—yada yada yada.*"

Marv slaps the book against my chest. "Good luck, man. If you can't sell this sappy garbage, then no one can."

"I think it's sweet," Erica says.

"That's because you're the nicest woman on the planet. You even make me feel like I'm redeemable."

"Oh, honey," Erica says to him as if he were a kid, not a man older than she is. "There's nothing to redeem."

Marv gives me a quick glance, as if I might tell her about the stunt he pulled with Cara that brought us all to this moment, but I keep quiet.

"Is Martha coming?" Mia asks.

"Not this time. Ethan and her are spending the morning with Eleanor and Garrett, then joining us up at the reserve for the race."

A smartly dressed young woman with bobbed black hair and a lanyard around her neck identifying her as a librarian comes forward to say hello.

"Mr King, welcome," she says warmly as she shakes my hand. "I'm Alice."

"Great to meet you. I haven't been here since I was a kid, reading every adventure story I could get my hands on."

"And do you still read them now?"

"I'm ashamed to say it's been a long time since I picked up a book."

"Nothing to be ashamed of. However, if you want, I can recommend some titles that might interest you."

"Thanks, I'd like that," I say, meaning it. Being back in Hideaway Harbor, even if just for a short time, has shown me there's more to life than work, and I like the idea of reading for pleasure rather than trying to memorize lines.

Alice bounces on the balls of her feet. "Awesome! This is one of the best parts of my job, so thank you for the opportunity."

She walks us through the library to a corner area at the back, where low bookshelves surround a carpeted section filled with bean bags and child-sized sofas. Two walls are covered in paintings of Christmas trees, snowmen, and Santa, with children's names at the bottom. The space is filled with kids, their parents standing around the edges, proudly watching their offspring.

Nerves prickle in my stomach. With more adults than children in the audience, it suddenly feels like a higher-stakes performance.

As a young couple, introduced as Lucy and Enzo, read a story together, I stand at the back and open the yeti book, reading it through for the first time. It's a cute little tale, and like most kids' books, has a message of love and acceptance that most adults seem to have forgotten.

Piper stays near me, watching people reading the stories. The kids seem enthralled with the whole experience, although I think the hot chocolate was the biggest selling point.

All too soon, it's my time, and I step forward to loud applause from the adults and muted claps from the kids who don't have a clue who I am.

The seat they've left for me is one of those small plastic ones designed for people half my height. I gingerly lower myself onto it as everyone goes silent.

It gives a loud creak that sounds suspiciously like a fart, and I say, "Pardon me," to the kids, who burst out laughing.

Okay, good start.

"Hi, everyone," I begin. "I'm Brody, and I'm going to be reading to you *The Yeti Who Got Stuck in the Chimney*."

I show them the cover of the book. "Do any of you know this story?"

I'm met with blank stares and a few shaking heads.

"Okay, well, I hope the title doesn't give any of the story away."

A little boy with a chocolate mustache pipes up, "Is it about a yeti who gets stuck in a chimney?"

I act like I'm shocked. "How did you know?!"

"It's in the title!" he says, like I'm a dummy, and a few kids giggle.

"Ah, but do you know how it begins?" I ask.

He scrunches up his face. "Once upon a time?"

I open the book. "*Once upon a time—*"

"No way!" the little boy cries, as a few of the other children gasp like we've just performed a magic trick.

"Yes way." I show them the first page so they can see I'm not making it up. "You were right."

I begin reading again. "*Once upon a time, in a cold, snowy cave high on a mountain, lived a yeti. He was all alone and always had been, staying hidden and watching the little village of Hideaway Harbor down in the valley below.*"

"Does it really say Hideaway Harbor?" the boy pipes up again.

"It actually says the village is called Heartwood, but I think we should change it to Hideaway Harbor. What do you think?"

"Change it!" a few of the children yell.

I sneak a glance at Piper, standing off to the side. She's smiling, but when she catches my eye, she blushes and looks down, fiddling with a button on her coat.

"Okay, democracy has spoken. Heartwood is now Hideaway Harbor." The little boy leads the cheers, and his wholehearted enthusiasm for such a small thing makes my heart swell.

"*Every Christmas, the people of Hideaway Harbor hung twinkling lights on their houses, sang songs that echoed up the mountainside, and spent time together, laughing and having fun. The yeti wished he could join them, but he knew he didn't belong. He was too big, too furry, and, most of all, too different.*"

I continue with the story, trying to inject as much drama into it as possible. Some of the kids seem more interested in trying to scoop out every last drop of hot chocolate from their mugs with their hands, but the little dude near the front is hanging on my every word.

"He squeezed down the chimney headfirst, his big, furry hands clutching the sides as he tried to wriggle down, his mind full of dreams of Christmas cheer. But something was wrong ... The chimney was too narrow, and no matter how much he wiggled, he was stuck halfway. His large, fluffy feet kicked helplessly, his furry belly wedged tight.

"'Oh dear,' he mumbled, his voice muffled by the bricks. 'This wasn't how I imagined it at all!'"

The kids laugh, and I sneak another look at Piper. Her attention is solely on me, as if I'm reading the most captivating story in the history of literature, or if we're the only two people here. She doesn't look away when I catch her eye and I want to hold her gaze. But I'm in the middle of the book, so I clear my throat and read on.

"The little boy peered up the chimney and saw a big, furry shape wedged tightly. 'Hello?' he called. 'Is someone stuck?'

"A muffled voice groaned from deep inside. 'Ho, ho, ho! It's me, Santa! I tried to squeeze down the chimney, but I ate too many Christmas cookies, and now I'm stuck!'

"The boy furrowed his brow, walking closer to the fireplace. 'You don't look like Santa. You look like a yeti!'

"The yeti's head popped into view, his furry face stuck halfway out of the chimney, looking embarrassed. 'Can I be a yeti and Santa?' he asked with a sheepish grin.

"The boy laughed. 'Yes! You can be both!'"

I keep my eyes glued to the page as I finish the story, with the yeti spending his first Christmas with the little boy and his family, and making his first friends.

"As the snow fell gently outside, the yeti knew he had found the one thing he had been longing for: not just a family, but a place where he truly belonged."

There are still two lines left, but I pause. Where do *I* belong? New York? Here? I glance at Piper again, and the answer arrives like a neon sign in my brain.

I belong wherever she is.

"And from that day on, every Christmas, the yeti would return, because sometimes, it's not what you look like, but who you are inside that makes all the difference."

I close the book, and that's the cue for the applause, which I lap up, because at the end of the day, I'm a needy actor who lives for validation.

The boy who's taken such a keen interest in the story leaps to his feet and comes forward, his arm outstretched. "I'm Billy."

I shake his hand. "Nice to meet you, Billy."

"I've got a puppy. Her name is Lucky, and I'm training her to be a hunting dog. We're gonna hunt a yeti."

"Do you know where yetis live?"

He points at the book in my hand. "In caves. The book says so. High up in the mountains."

"And how do you track one down? They're pretty shy."

"You have to look for *signs*," he replies. "My grandpa is teaching me to track animals." He leans forward like he's about to impart a big secret. "And one of the signs they leave is *poop*!"

I try to smother a grin and fail.

Billy seems delighted with my response. "Big, stinky poop!"

This time, I snort with laughter.

A woman rushes up with a worried expression. "I hope he's not bothering you, Mr King."

"Not at all. Billy's been teaching me how he tracks animals with his grandpa."

"Poop!" Billy says happily to his mother.

"Billy!" she replies, but her stern expression is cracking.

"See! It's funny!"

"Say thank you to Mr King, then let's get you to Grandpa's."

"Please, call me Brody," I say with a smile, then hold out my hand to Billy again. "Good luck with the tracking."

"Thank you." He shakes my hand firmly, then lets his mother draw him away. They're just about to exit the carpeted area when he turns his head and mouths the word "*poop*" at me again.

"What are you laughing at?" Marv asks as he comes to my side.

"The kid. He's got my sense of humor."

"Jeez, God help him. Anyway, you did great. Mia got some good photos, and Piper has perked up a bit. We're off to the Locke Reserve now for the sock running thing. There'll be hot dogs and spiced cider, because apparently that's the drink we're all supposed to appreciate today. Don't worry. Cara checked, and there'll be hot spiced apple juice for you."

"How long are you both staying in Hideaway?"

"However long it takes."

"You're going to keep Cara working over *Christmas*?"

Marv doesn't respond.

"Seriously? For fuck's sake, Marv! Let her go home to see her mom and sister. You don't need her here."

He shrugs, not meeting my eye, and I wonder if he's keeping her around because he's lonely and likes the company.

"Marv!"

He throws his hands up. "All right, all right. I'll get her on a plane back to Milwaukee."

"Do it now. She'll have to connect somewhere like Philly or Newark from Bangor, so make sure you sort it today while there are still flights."

"Yeah, yeah."

I still don't trust him, so I go over to her.

The moment I arrive at Cara's side, Piper heads off to her mom. The move looks natural, but I can't help feeling it's to put distance between us.

Alice smiles at me. "I've emailed Cara a list of books you might like to read."

"I appreciate it, thank you."

Alice is drawn away and I turn to Cara.

"I've told Marv to get you on a plane back to Milwaukee by tomorrow," I say to her. "You need a holiday from the Brody circus."

There's a pause, and I can guess she's forcing herself not to insist she stay to help. "Are you su—"

"Yes. Make sure you book it yourself. Don't wait for him to accidentally-on-purpose forget."

The corner of her mouth twitches. "Thank you. I haven't seen them for nearly a year now."

"A year? Shit, I'm sorry, Cara. I've had my head so far up my own butt, I didn't know."

"It's okay. It's the job."

"It shouldn't be."

We both fall silent, and my eyes seek out Piper, chatting and laughing with her mom and Mia.

"She's super nice," Cara says. "They all are."

I sigh. "Yeah, I know."

OUTSIDE, the sky has clouded over, but the snow hasn't arrived yet.

The Locke Reserve sits on the edge of town, spanning a few hundred acres of land. It includes a community building, the famous Hideaway Spring, and the house George Locke and Alma Keye built for their family, now a museum.

It's less than a half-hour stroll, and with Erica, Marv, Mia, and Cara walking ahead, I have time to talk to Piper. I just don't know how to start without her shutting me down. We're almost there before I get an idea.

"Can I tell you a story?"

Her head snaps toward me. "A story?"

"Yeah. It's one from when I was a kid."

"Oh. Yeah, sure."

She gazes back at the sidewalk, watching where she puts her feet, and I take a deep breath.

"Once upon a time, in a fairytale land by the sea, lived a little boy who knew that fairytale places weren't always magical, and no matter what something looked like on the outside, sometimes the inside wasn't so pretty."

My gaze is fixed ahead, but in my peripheral vision, I see Piper's head turn to me.

"Okay ..."

"But what the little boy *did* have was a best friend, and that best friend also came with a family who loved him almost as much as if he were one of them."

"You *are* one of us. And we, *my parents* love you just as much as me, Ethan, Hudson, and Harper."

I give her a confused look. "This isn't about your family."

She rolls her eyes. "Yeah, right."

"Do you want to hear the rest of the story?"

"I'm not sure I do."

"I'll take that as a yes."

I get another eye roll, and she gazes ahead again.

"So this little boy grew up into a very handsome young man—"

"And modest."

"But as this *extremely* handsome young man got older, he realized that he had a few problems that seemed as insurmountable as scaling Mount Everest in his pajamas or fighting dragons armed only with a wooden sword."

"Go on."

"Well, the first problem was that he was poor, and he knew how difficult it was to live without money. He wasn't clever enough to do a lot of jobs—"

"Not true."

"Hey, whose story is this?"

"I know how it ends already."

"You do?"

"Yep. The handsome and big-headed young man realized that other people liked looking at him, and so if he left Hideaw —the magical kingdom by the sea—he could get a job modeling ye olde latest fashions."

"That's not the whole story. You forgot to mention how the young man didn't feel worthy, and so, by gathering wealth and admiration, he could prove to himself and everyone else that he had made something of his life."

"You didn't need to prove anything to us. You were perf— fine, just the way you were."

Does she mean I'm not fine anymore?

It doesn't matter. I'm channeling Braveheart, not Faintheart, and we're nearly at the reserve. Time to go for broke.

"But that wasn't his biggest problem. He'd done something very, very bad."

"What?"

I take a breath. "The handsome young man had fallen in love with his best friend's younger sister."

Piper stumbles, and I catch her arm, hauling her against my body before she falls.

We're standing, breathing heavily. My eyes on her, hers on the snowy ground.

"He was in love with her for years," I continue quickly. "But he knew he could never do anything about it. She was too young, he needed to earn enough money before he could ask for her hand, and—"

"Come on, lovebirds!" Erica calls back to us. "The boys are up ahead with Martha!"

Temporary tents have been set up outside the community hall for registering the competitors and for serving food and drink. Piper's dad is standing by one with Hudson, Ethan, and Martha, who's being held by her father.

Still clutching my arm, Piper leads us forward, her feet kicking the snow like she's forgotten how to walk properly.

"I don't understand," she finally says. "You never … I never … Why?"

"I never said or did anything because I knew I couldn't."

"Why not?"

I don't answer immediately, and she pulls on my arm, forcing me to look at her. Her face is pinched with pain and confusion.

"Why not, Brody?"

"Because I promised Ethan I wouldn't."

CHAPTER 18

PIPER

"*Y*oo-hoo!" Mom calls over to Dad. "We're here!"

I'm having an out-of-body experience, watching my legs move like they belong to someone else, while every cell inside me screams, "Brody was in love with me!"

I don't even stop to question whether he was talking about me or Harper. I just know.

The memory of our almost-kiss on the porch when I was sixteen hums in the air. It echoes from the past, like I could reach out and touch it. He *did* want to kiss me back then. I hadn't imagined it. And the reason he didn't—well, one of them, anyway—is standing in front of us now.

My teeth grind together as rage floods my mouth, crystallizing into hard words of anger.

How fucking *dare* he? Brody wasn't some high school jock who saw me as a notch on his hockey stick. He was a good guy, Ethan's best friend. And my saintly older brother has no leg to stand on. He and Olivia were having sex when they were both sixteen, so why deny me someone I loved, just as they loved each other?

I'm shaking now. *All this time*. Twelve years that I could have been with Brody. Over a decade spent trying to find someone —*anyone*—who could make me feel even ten percent of what I felt for him.

If Ethan hadn't stepped in, we would have been together. I know this in my bones. I would have shown him that he didn't need to chase fame the way he has, or run from Hideaway. We could have grown together, and it would have been a beautiful adventure for both of us. He wouldn't have acted out because he would have known he was loved. He was perfect, just as he was.

Yes, Brody left Hideaway and never came back, and why would he when his best friend in the whole world told him he wasn't good enough?

"Oh, look, Martha, honey! It's starting to snow!" Mom says, catching a snowflake on her glove and holding it out for her to see.

And that little girl is the only reason I bite my tongue and swallow my fury. I can't even speak right now, so I hang back as everyone greets each other, gripping Brody's arm as if it's the only thing stopping me from launching myself at my brother.

"Daddy took me to the spring to make a wish!" Martha is telling Mom.

"And what did you wish for?"

"I can't tell you, or it won't come true!"

"But the Hideaway spring is magical," Mom replies. "Every wish comes true, so you can tell me."

Martha doesn't sound convinced. "I'll think about it."

She looks up at Ethan and pokes the end of his nose. "Daddy, don't you have something to say?"

He faces Brody and clears his throat. "I ..."

"We had *words*," Martha says to Brody. "And now he's going to say sorry. Aren't you, Daddy?"

Ethan nods. "I was out of line yesterday, and I want to apologize."

"No need," Brody replies. "We're cool."

My grip on his arm intensifies, and he puts his hand over mine, stroking the back of it.

"I wondered if you wanted to come to my place after the race for a bit, watch the game?" Ethan asks.

Brody looks at me as if he needs my permission.

Using all of my willpower, I force a smile.

"Yeah," Brody says. "That would be great."

Martha claps. "And I can give you the tour, Uncle Brody."

He gives her a genuine smile. "I'd like that."

"Great!" Mom says enthusiastically. "Now, I don't know about you, but I need a hot dog and some spiced cider."

"Let me get them," Brody says. "What does everyone want?"

Mom raises her hands as if to stop him, but Dad gives her a look, and she puts them in her pockets. He knows that Brody needs this. This is him saying thank you to all of us and building bridges with my brother.

Brody takes everyone's orders, then goes to the food tent with me and Cara so we can help carry it all back.

The snow is still falling, but not enough to make it impossible to be outside, and the hot food warms us up from the inside out. There's no chance to talk to Brody right now, so I listen to the chatter about the race. Hudson has been training all winter and is pumped.

"You'd better be ready at the finish line to take my picture when I win," he tells Mia.

She scoffs. "I've got more important people to be photographing."

"I've got the mistletoe in my bag!" Mom calls over. "And

some white string to tie it up with so no one will see it against the snow."

"You'd rather shoot a Hallmark Christmas card than me?" Hudson asks Mia.

"Well, duh! One of our generation's finest actors, or someone who thinks fart jokes are funny?"

"I don't need you anyway," he replies. "Channel 6's *Down East News Now* is sending a crew to cover it."

"That's exciting, honey!" Mom says. "We'll all be there cheering you on when you cross the line!"

Woven rugs have been placed at the start and finish lines of the race to help with traction, and marshals are verifying the socks that competitors are wearing. Hudson takes off his boots and puts on two more pairs of socks.

"How many are you allowed to wear?" Brody asks him.

"As many as you like, but three are recommended," he replies. "And the outer one must be 100% wool and either knitted yourself or made by someone in Hideaway."

He pulls the socks up his calves and secures tape around the top so they won't fall down while he's running.

"There's a two-kilometer or a six-kilometer race," Dad tells Brody. "With different categories, as well as prizes for the best outfits. The faster runners usually compete in the longer distance, meaning the two races don't finish too far apart in time."

Hudson gets his socks checked, has a number pinned to his front, and then joins the fastest at the front for the beginning of the longer race.

Despite claiming not to want to photograph him, Mia still gets into position to shoot the runners as they set off.

The gun fires, and Hudson sprints away, leading the pack as we all shout and cheer. The marshals give them a five-minute head start, and then the two-k race begins.

"Photo time!" Mom cries, brushing snow off the top of her

bag. "I've got the mistletoe right here."

I swallow. Yes, of course I want to kiss Brody, but even more than that, I want to talk to him. To untangle our history now that there's a new lens on my memories.

"We don't have to do this," he says quietly to me.

"It won't take long, and we've got time to kill before the runners return."

He nods, seeming as unsure as I am. The photo Mom has planned feels wrong. It's not that it won't be pretty; it's just too staged. Like something you'd do to celebrate an engagement.

"John!" An older man runs toward us from the direction of the town, one arm raised.

Dad strides to meet him, and we all follow.

"Walter, is everything all right?"

"No!" He reaches us and bends over, his hands braced on his thighs as he catches his breath. "My grandson's missing."

"Cathy! Bryan! Pete! Get over here!" Dad yells at the race marshals. Then he turns back to Walter, who's still struggling to breathe. "What can you tell us? Have you called the police?"

Walter shakes his head. "Not yet. He was spending the afternoon with me, you know my house is at the edge of the reserve, and I fell asleep."

He covers his face with his hand as he sobs. "John, I'll never forgive myself if anything happens to him."

Mom rubs his back. "I'm sure he hasn't gone far. We'll find him. I promise."

"What was he wearing, and where do you think he went?" Dad asks.

"He had on his boots and coat and took his backpack. He came this way with his dog. Have you seen them?"

Brody goes rigid beside me. "What's the dog's name?"

"Lucky," Walter replies. "That's what Billy called her. She's a golden retriever puppy, about seven months old."

"Jesus Christ," Brody mutters, then looks at me. "It's the kid from the library this morning."

"Why would he come this way?" Dad asks as Mom relays what happened to the people Dad called over.

"In the summer, I started teaching him how to track animals. We went on the trails through the reserve, so I guess he thought he'd see what he could find in the snow."

Ethan's on the phone. "Yes, I'd like to report a missing child. Let me give you to his grandpa." He passes the phone to Walter. "The signal isn't great."

Dad addresses Ethan. "Round up anyone dressed for the weather, and we'll start searching now."

Ethan gives him a grim nod, then hands Martha to Mom.

"Daddy?" she asks him, a frown puckering her forehead.

He kisses her. "It's gonna be okay, sweetie, but I need you to stay with Grandma right now. Can you do that for me?"

She nods, and he sprints away.

"It's my fault," Brody mutters under his breath.

I draw him aside. "How on earth do you figure that?"

"That damn book. We were talking about how to track down a yeti."

"Brody, that's crazy. You cannot take responsibility for this!"

He looks around the snowy landscape, then up at the wintry sky. The snow is falling faster now, and I'm trying not to panic.

"I'm just going to check something out," he says, then sprints off in the opposite direction of the main trails, toward the steep slope of the mountain.

In the next few minutes, Ethan and Dad have a plan in place. The police, Warden Service, and the fire department are on their way, along with the volunteer search and rescue team that Ethan helps with when he's not on duty. People have also been sent to fetch Billy's parents.

But they don't want to waste time waiting for the services,

so Ethan organizes a line search. He's giving people their positions when Brody runs back and straight up to him.

"I don't think they went on the trails," he says. "I think they went that way, up the mountain."

"He wouldn't have done that," Walter says. "We always stick to the trails."

"Ethan," Brody pleads. "Just let me show you something."

Ethan hesitates, then faces the group assembled around him. "Set off now, and I'll follow as soon as I can."

He gives Brody a nod, and they run off in the opposite direction. I follow, even though I'm so much slower than the two of them, and we head into the tree line to the edge of a gorge.

It's not deep, maybe twenty-five feet, but the sides are steep, and you wouldn't want to fall down them. The area was always strictly off-limits to us kids when we were growing up, and not many people trek through it.

"Look," Brody says to Ethan as I arrive. "He could have gone this way."

A large tree has fallen, creating a bridge across the gorge, but it's not straightforward. The side we're on involves a climb up the tangled root structure to the trunk, and the other end is a mess of snow-covered branches.

"Why?" Ethan asks, his tone clipped. "He's seven. It's far too high and difficult for him to get up there, let alone across safely. There's no way he'd have gone this way."

"But if you cross to the other side, there's a cave up on the mountain."

"And?"

"Billy's trying to find a yeti, and yetis live in caves."

"Have you lost your goddamn mind?" Ethan shouts. "This isn't a fucking movie. This is real life, and a little boy's life is on the line."

"You think I don't know that? I'm trying to help!"

"Well, you're not. You're just wasting time. If you want to do something useful, you can help Mom keep people calm. You can distract them by signing autographs and taking selfies."

"Shut up, Ethan!" I yell.

He turns to me, looking surprised I'm even here. "Piper, go back—"

"No. Why don't you listen to what Brody's saying instead of dismissing him?"

"Because he's an actor, Piper. His life is a game of let's pretend. It's not real. And he doesn't know these woods like I do. Hell, he hasn't even *been* here for the past twelve years!"

"And why the fuck do you think that is, huh? When the one person he loved like a brother told him he'd never measure up? That he wasn't worthy? That he didn't deserve happiness?"

"What are you talking about?"

"Piper …" Brody begins.

"You told him I was off-limits. So, being the best friend he was, he did what you said. Of *course* he did. He had no one apart from his mom, and then not even her by the time you graduated. And what did you have? *Everything.* A large, stable family with a dad who's the fucking mayor. How dare you make decisions about our life? What about what *I* wanted, huh?"

"You were only sixteen."

"So? You'd been sleeping with Olivia since you were sixteen yourself. What makes you so special compared to us?"

His face darkens at the mention of Olivia, and my heart stutters inside my chest. But he's not going to use her death as a get-out-of-jail-free card for the rest of his life.

"Do you know how lonely I've been?" I cry. "You stole twelve years of happiness from me, Ethan. From Brody. What do you think Brody's life would have looked like if you hadn't stuck your sanctimonious nose into our lives?"

My heart is hammering so fast I think I might faint, but I'm not done yet.

"You're making Brody out to be the bad guy for never coming back, but you need to take a good, hard look at how you were part of the reason. You called yourself his best friend, but then told him he wasn't good enough for me. What message do you think he took from that about his worth as a person?"

"It wasn't like that—"

"Yes, it was."

"Ethan—"

Ethan cuts Brody off.

"Screw this. I've got better things to do than stand around arguing when a child is missing. You two do whatever the fuck you like, but I'm heading somewhere useful."

Brody's shoulders slump as Ethan runs off. I throw my arms around him as we watch my brother disappear through the trees.

We stand for a moment as the snow falls silently around us, then I pull back. "Okay, tell me why you think Billy went this way."

He straightens, and the fire returns to his eyes.

"From the top of Seller Hill, you can see a cave partway up this side of the mountain. When we were kids, we made up stories about ghosts, or bears, or bandits that lived up there. What if Billy and his friends do that too? And he told me he wanted to hunt a yeti."

"Okay, let's climb up and see if there are any tracks."

We hoist ourselves up through the roots and reach the trunk of the tree. It's wide enough to walk along, but I can't see any sign that Billy came this way.

Dropping to his knees, Brody brings his face almost level with the snow and carefully brushes some of it away.

202

"Piper! Look!"
Holy shit. A footprint.

CHAPTER 19

BRODY

*P*iper kneels beside me and helps brush away more snow. It's hard to see, but there are clear indentations from a small boot, along with paw prints.

"He did go this way!" she cries.

"Most likely, but there's no guarantee." I take out my phone to check for a signal.

Nothing. "Do you have any coverage?"

She shakes her head at her phone. "This is one of those times when Hideaway's lousy cell coverage is definitely a problem."

"Why don't you run back and tell everyone what we've found?"

"No way. Most people have already gone in the opposite direction, and I don't want to risk them not believing me. If he did go this way, you might need help to get him out. I'm going with you."

I nod and help her to her feet. "Okay. I'll go first in case there's any ice. Walk slowly and steadily behind me. Small steps, and keep your eyes fixed on a point up ahead."

My heart is thumping painfully in my throat as I set off along the trunk. I might not die if I slip and fall, but I'd most likely break both legs.

And the same goes for Piper …

The snow crunches under my feet as I inch my way forward. I know it's safe if I stay on the center line, but I'm petrified I'm going to hear a cry behind me as she slips and falls.

At the spot where the tree has crashed onto the other side of the gorge, I grab a snow-covered branch and turn, extending my hand to draw Piper toward me. Her face is ghost-white.

"You okay?" I ask.

"Yeah. Let's go."

We scramble through the branches down to the ground, and I scan for tracks, brushing aside the layer of freshly fallen snow until I find what I'm looking for.

"How did you know what to do?" Piper asks as we run through the trees toward the mountain. "Did you learn this on *The Tracker Man*?"

We come to an area where Billy might have gone in a different direction, so I lean down to sweep the new snow away until I find where his tracks lead.

"You saw that?"

She gives me a look, then points at herself. "Google Alert and your number one fan?"

Despite the cold, heat rushes to my cheeks. *I love you so much.*

I clear my throat. "Uh, yes. I did a ton of research and got really into the skills trackers have." I point at the boot print. "So, we know he went this way."

We run on, and after a few yards, arrive at a clearing. I know immediately something's not right. There's a branch, the length of a sword, lying on the ground with only a thin covering of snow on it. Nearby, almost obscured, I can make out—

"Oh, my God, is that *blood*?" Piper cries.

I fall to my knees, brushing the snow away. The red is vivid against the white.

My heart is racing, and sweat trickles down my back as I move the fresh snow away and try not to freak out, talking out loud as I notice things.

"There's another set of tracks … animal … coyote, probably … It looks like only one, but it was all over Lucky. Billy must have grabbed the branch to fend it off. Can you see if there's any more blood that way?"

Piper dashes through the trees, and I follow, brushing away snow as I go to make sure we're heading in the right direction.

"Brody!" she yells. "This way!"

I run to her side.

"Why didn't Billy just head back home?" she asks as we rush on.

"I guess Lucky bolted, and he ran after her," I reply, praying that they went in a straight line.

Ahead is a creek. When we reach it, my heart plummets.

"What is it? What can you see?"

I point at the ice forming at the edges. "See how it's broken here and on the other side? They went this way."

"It's not deep, though. They should be okay, right?"

"Not deep for us, but for a seven-year-old and a puppy who's low to the ground? And the ice on this side is much more damaged. One of them might have fallen in."

I look at Piper's snow boots. Like mine, they rise halfway up her calf.

"We can't afford to get wet ourselves," I say. "I'll go first."

I don't wait for her to reply, stepping carefully into the

creek and choosing a path where the water runs quickest, where it's shallowest.

"You doing okay?" I call over my shoulder.

"Peachy!"

We make it safely to the other side, and I bellow Billy's name as loud as I can, then wait for an answer.

I don't get one.

Piper grabs my gloved hands as my fear spirals out of control.

"Brody! Look at me! Breathe with me."

Holding her gaze, I claw myself out of the panic. Her eyes are my focal point. My anchor.

"You've got this, Brody. You can find them. I know you can."

I let out a shuddering breath and give her a nod.

"Okay," she says. "Where next?"

I figure out which way they went, and we race on, pausing every few strides to yell Billy's name.

There's a big tree up ahead, its branches heavy with snow reaching all the way to the ground. If I was a little kid and wanted to make a den, I'd choose there.

I dash forward and lift the lowest branch.

Thank fuck.

"Brody?" Billy asks, his voice faint.

I nod. "We've got you, buddy. Everything's going to be all right."

Piper drops to her knees beside me and lets out a gasp when she sees Billy. He's shivering, and his face is so pale it's almost blue. His coat is around a young golden retriever, who's whining and licking his hand.

"Okay, bud, we're going to get you both out of here, but you need to tell me real quick what happened and who's hurt."

"We went to find a yeti. In the cave."

"Yep, figured as much, but what went wrong?" I try not to let my fear show, but he needs to cut to the chase.

"There was a coyote. He attacked Lucky."

"Did he hurt you?"

"I found a stick and chased him off."

Okay, so Billy's not hurt. "Did you both fall into the creek?"

"Lucky did when she ran away, and then I did too when I was helping her."

Billy's trousers are soaked, and as I touch them, they crack where they've frozen.

"I'm not gonna lie to you, buddy. We need to get you to safety, but we also need to get you warm," I say, trying to keep my voice calm. "Now, this might sound a little strange, but I need you to trust me. I'm going to get you out of your wet clothes, then I'll give you my socks, my shirt, and my sweater, and carry you out of here under my coat."

"I'm not leaving without Lucky."

"Can she walk on her own?"

"I don't think so anymore."

Fuck! "Then I'll carry you both."

"What can I do to help?" Piper asks.

"Carry all his wet clothes," I say, ripping off my coat, sweater, and shirt. The shirt is soaked with sweat, so it's no good for him to wear.

"Brody?" Billy asks, his voice so shaky I can feel another panic attack coming on.

"Yes, bud?"

"Grandpa says if you're cold, you should take your clothes off and cuddle someone in a sleeping bag."

Even in this dire situation, the corner of my mouth still twitches.

"So, give your sweater to L-Lucky, and I'll just wear my b-briefs," he continues.

"You don't have a fur coat like she does so I want you to wear it. Okay?"

He nods and tries to undress.

"Let me help," Piper says. "I'm Piper, by the way."

He nods. "You were at the library."

"Sure was."

As soon as Billy is out of his wet clothes and into my sweater, socks and gloves, I pull him out of the hollow and against my chest. Then Piper drapes my coat over his back and ties the sleeves behind me.

Lucky is now on her feet, whining.

"There's blood on her neck and back leg," Piper says to me.

I nod. I need to see if she can walk without my help, so I set off back the way we came.

"Come on, Lucky!" Piper says as she makes a ball of Billy's belongings and follows me.

Lucky limps forward after us. It's not fast, but it'll have to do.

We move as quickly as we can back to the creek, stopping at the edge.

"I can carry Lucky, I think," Piper says.

"No. If she wriggles, you'll both fall."

I'm reminded of that old riddle, the one where a man has to get a chicken, a fox, and a bag of corn across a river in a boat that can only carry two at a time, without leaving the chicken alone with the corn or the fox with the chicken.

"Does Lucky have a leash in your bag?" I ask Billy.

He nods.

"Tie Lucky up to that tree so she doesn't try to follow," I say. "Then we'll both cross the creek. I'll give Billy to you, then go back and carry Lucky across."

"Got it."

Piper ties up Lucky, who is now barking, not wanting to be separated from us, then follows me across the stream.

I swaddle Billy the best I can in my coat, and Piper holds him in her lap as I go back for Lucky.

The pup trembles violently as I carry her across the

freezing river. I can't lose her. I can't lose Billy. So I draw on every ounce of strength I have left and keep going. I thought all the hours in the gym were for health and looking good on camera. I never thought this would be the scenario where it really mattered.

On the other side I put Lucky down and take Billy back into my arms. He's quiet as we start moving again, and the stages of hypothermia go through my mind. I've got to keep him conscious. I've got to keep him talking.

"Billy! Stay awake, buddy."

"I'm so tired."

"I know, bud, but staying awake is the most important thing you can do for me right now. It's part of the mission."

"It is?"

"One hundred percent. You may not have found a yeti this time, but you've had one hell of an adventure, and you know what that means?"

"No."

"The story about it has to be even bigger. Even wilder."

I'm exhausted, and the snow seems deeper with every step. I'm out of breath, but I can't stop talking. Billy feels like ice against my chest, and it terrifies me.

"So, guess what the coyote becomes?"

"I don't know."

"A bear! Come on, Billy, you gotta think big!"

"Brody!"

I turn to see Lucky on the ground, not moving.

Piper drops the bundle of Billy's clothes and knapsack, then lifts the dog into her arms with a grunt.

"Can you manage the weight?"

"Just about," she replies, staggering forward.

"The gorge is just up ahead. We'll do what we did at the creek, okay?"

"Yep!"

I stumble down the slope toward our crossing point. With Billy in my arms, I can't see my feet, and if I can't see my feet, I don't know if I'm starting out on the trunk in the middle. And how the hell am I supposed to climb up through the branches to the trunk, and then down the other side through the root structure, without using my arms?

When we get there, Piper shuffles out of her coat and wraps Lucky in it. She doesn't need the leash this time. I don't think the pup has the strength to follow us.

"I'll go behind you as you climb up to the trunk," Piper says, "and push on your back to keep your weight forward as you lift through your legs."

She climbs behind me through the branches, keeping me upright, placing my feet when I can't feel the next foothold, and guiding me with quiet instructions. My quads are burning by the time we reach the top, and I breathe heavily, trying to shake the acid from my muscles.

"You're going to have to guide me across to the other side," I say.

She nods and sets off along the narrow trunk.

I lurch forward, alarm tightening my throat. "Piper! Wait!"

"It's better if you can see me," she replies calmly.

I can't argue with that, but my stomach is filled with dread that I'm about to watch her fall.

She smiles. "I'll be careful. Slow and safe is better than fast and—" She tilts her head toward the drop beside us and I briefly close my eyes, the nightmare scenario already playing out in my mind.

When I open them again, she's half way across, and now I can't blink, can't breathe.

"Brody?" a little voice pipes up.

"Hey, Billy. Almost forgot you were there. How's it going?"

"Are we nearly there yet?"

"Sure are. Just the gorge to cross, and then we're home free.

Piper's going first to keep you warm while I go back for Lucky."

"Okay."

My heart stutters as she reaches the other side safely and gives me a wave.

I step forward onto the snow-covered trunk. "How am I doing?" I call out.

"Great!" she yells back. "Dead center! Just keep your eyes on me, I'm right in the middle, too."

I do, inching forward, drawn to Piper like she's reeling me in on an invisible rope.

"That's it," she says. "Nearly there."

Emotion rises in my throat at the thought that we've almost made it, but I shove it down. I've got to get Lucky.

Piper takes Billy and wraps him like a lumpy Christmas present. She holds his weight as she stands, leaning against the tree roots. She's staying upright so I can still see her.

Each second feels like an hour as I force myself to go slowly and carefully back along the trunk, then through the branches, to the ground.

This time, Piper isn't there to help me back up, but Lucky's lighter, so I carry her under one arm, using the other to pull myself and hold on as my feet search for the next step.

"I've got Lucky!" I yell so Billy can hear me.

Piper passes the message along, then stands upright. I can tell by the straining tendons in her neck how difficult it is for her to do so.

Her voice is clear and steady as she calls out her instructions, then gives a whoop as I make it to her side.

"I'm going to take Lucky straight down now," I tell her. "The distance to the ground isn't as far on this side, so you could probably pass Billy to me."

She nods. "Let's give it a try."

I scramble to the ground with Lucky, then lift my arms

toward the trunk above me to reach for Billy wrapped inside my coat.

It's too far.

"Billy! Can you make yourself into a tight little ball for me, bud?"

I can't hear a reply, but Piper calls down, "He says yes!"

"Awesome. Now this is a bonus part of the adventure. You're gonna keep your arms and legs tight together, and Piper's gonna drop you into my arms, okay?"

Piper looks from Billy to me and nods.

"Tight as a ball, Billy! Piper's gonna let you go in three ... two ... one ... go!"

It's only a couple of feet, but it seems like twenty until I catch him.

"Great job, Billy! Now let's get you warmed up again, yeah?"

Piper climbs down and helps get him back in place, then ties the coat sleeves behind my back.

She then lifts Lucky and staggers forward, but immediately stumbles on a branch and nearly drops her.

"Give her to me," I say. "Run on ahead and bring help this way."

I shift Billy to one side, now holding him with only one hand, then Piper helps lift Lucky under my other arm.

"Go," I tell her. "I've got them."

She runs off through the trees, and I take a breath and follow.

"Right then, Billy," I grunt. "We gotta get our story straight for when *Down East News Now* wants to interview you, okay?"

"Yes," he replies faintly.

"C'mon now, bud, you've gotta be louder than that. Let me hear you say *YEAH*!"

"Yeah," he replies, a little louder this time.

"That's more like it. Okay, so you went on your epic trek to find the yeti, with your faithful pal Lucky. But your first obstacle was a ninety-foot-deep gorge with hungry alligators at the bottom. Your only route across? A branch that's narrower than your own foot. You like the story so far?"

He nods. "And there was a bear."

"That's right. A massive one."

Each step for me is agony. My lungs can't keep up, and the icy air is like knives in my chest. My biceps are screaming at me, and my leg muscles are about to give out.

But I can't stop. I won't stop.

I stagger out from the tree line. Piper's up ahead, running toward the community building and tents by the start and finish line of the race, where a large group of people is gathered. She's shouting at them, both hands waving in the air.

Adrenaline courses through me, giving me the help I need to move faster.

"We're nearly there, Billy," I pant. "Stay awake for me, bud, and tell me the story you're gonna tell for the rest of your life."

"Once upon a time," he begins, his voice still weak. "There was a very brave boy and his doggie, who went hunting a yeti."

"That's it. You've got it. Keep going. What happens next?"

He keeps talking as I stumble forward, people running to meet us.

Thank you, God. Thank you.

Things are happening in slow motion now, and I wonder if I'm about to faint. I see John, Erica, Billy's mom, his grandpa. There's a guy with a camera over his shoulder and a woman with a microphone.

In the distance behind them all, heading toward the finish line, is a solitary runner, Hudson. No one can see him but me.

He stops at the finish line, his arms spread as if to ask, "What the fuck?" Then he shouts, "Hey!"

No one notices. All eyes are on me as I lurch forward.

Then chaos descends.

John lifts Lucky from me, and Billy's mom, Grandpa, and

another man, who must be Billy's dad, rush to check I'm actually carrying him.

His mom tries to take him from me, but his grandpa stops her. "Judy, he needs to stay wrapped up till we can get him in the back of the rig."

She's crying. "Billy, baby, you okay?"

"Brody found me, Mommy."

"He did, baby, and we're gonna get you warm now, okay?"

"And Piper," Billy adds, "don't forget her."

"I won't, honey."

Walter brushes his own tears away and puts a hand on my back. "There's an ambulance behind the building," he says, steering me forward. "They've got warm IV fluids and heated blankets."

I'm in the center of a crowd as we move toward the building and the parking lot behind it. I can't feel my limbs anymore. It's like everyone around me is carrying me forward.

I'm barely aware of a woman right in my face, and a guy with a camera pointing my way just behind her.

A microphone is shoved toward me. "Sonia Ramirez, *Down East News Now*. Brody, you saved a little boy's life today, how does that feel?"

I don't answer. All my energy is focused on getting Billy to the ambulance.

"Sonia!" John barks, "Not now!"

But she's not giving up. "Was there a moment when you thought you wouldn't make it out? Can you talk us through what happened?"

John puts his arm between her and me, holding Sonia and the camera guy back so I can keep moving forward.

The ambulance doors are open, and there's a gurney with blankets ready for Billy. My strength almost completely gone, I step inside with his mom, grandpa, and the man I'm presuming is his dad.

The paramedics prep the IV, then help me transfer Billy to the heated blankets.

"Daddy!" Billy says. "A bear attacked Lucky, but I fought him off with a *sword*."

His father's eyes well up with tears. "I can't wait to hear all about it."

"Where's Lucky now? She needs help more than me. She's bleeding!"

"I'll take her to the animal hospital," his grandpa says.

A paramedic gets the IV line in. "Okay, we're ready to go," she says.

I move to the back door, but Billy reaches to stop me. "Will you come visit? We need to get our story straight before that lady interviews me. You know, about the bear and the crocodiles."

I smile, even as my own eyes prickle. "If that's okay with your folks, then sure, I will."

Billy looks pleadingly at them. "Mommy? Daddy?"

"Of course, baby," his mom says, then turns to me, tears streaming down her face. "Thank you, Mr King. We can't thank you enough."

Billy's dad takes my hand between both of his. "Thank you," he says gruffly, his expression strained like he's barely holding it together. He doesn't seem much older than me, and that's another sucker punch. If I'd stayed in Hideaway and married Piper, we might now have a kid Billy's age.

"I need you out now," one of the paramedics says. "Mom, Dad, one of you needs to ride up front."

"I'll go," Billy's dad says, and follows me and Walter as I open the back door.

Sonia and her cameraman are pushing through to the front of the crowd. I'm suddenly aware that I've got my coat in my hand and I'm topless.

"How did you find Billy when so many others couldn't?" Sonia yells.

I look past her, scanning for Piper, and my gaze lands on Ethan. I'm too exhausted to read his expression, and my legs are too weak to support me anymore.

I fall forward, only barely aware of John and Hudson holding me up.

My hands and arms are shaking. I can't control them. The cold is cutting down to my bones, and my teeth chatter so hard I can't speak.

Everything's spinning around me like I'm on a rollercoaster. Faces blur, and voices are fading.

Piper is screaming at people to get back. I think I hear Marv, too, but I'm falling.

My arms are shoved in my coat, and the zipper's pulled up. Then my feet leave the floor, and I'm moving.

I try to talk, but it's just a mumble.

"Don't say anything. We're taking you home."

Was that Ethan?

I'm aware of the back of a car.

"Piper!" I manage. "I need—"

"Shh," she says. "I'm right here."

She's here. Billy and Lucky are safe. Everything's going to be all right.

Then my thoughts disappear into blackness.

CHAPTER 20

PIPER

"*P*ulse still thready," Ethan says, his words clipped as he tucks Brody's hand back under the mountain of blankets piled atop him. "Temperature status?"

There's a beep, and Mom removes the digital thermometer from Brody's ear. "Ninety-four," she says. "It's rising."

Ethan takes it from her and checks the reading himself, then frowns.

Brody's on one couch in the family room, and I'm on the other. Both of us are bundled under every comforter and blanket in the house, and Ethan's made us wear woolly hats. The room is filled with people, but no one dares say anything or move a muscle. The unspoken consensus seems to be that the person in the room most at risk is my older brother. Even Martha is sitting quietly on Harper's lap as she watches her father.

Ethan strides over to me, gently tucking my hair behind my

ear so he can take my temperature. He grunts when he sees the reading.

I'm feeling fine, but I'm not going to tell Ethan that when he's driving full throttle down Panic Street and his brakes have failed.

"We need more wood on the fire," he says to Hudson.

Then, because Hudson doesn't immediately spring into action, Ethan does it himself, jabbing at the embers with the poker to produce more heat before throwing on as many logs as will fit.

Mom surreptitiously removes her cardigan and looks long-ingly at the closed window, as if she's ready to throw it open. Hudson's already down to a T-shirt, as are Mia and Cara, and Marv has his shirt sleeves rolled up and is perspiring freely.

I meet Brody's eyes across the room, and we exchange a smile. He still looks exhausted, but now that we're home and he's going to be all right, the fear that was wrapped around my heart is finally receding.

"Can the wall heaters go any higher?" Ethan asks Dad.

Ever the diplomat, Dad checks the thermostat again, even though he's already done it twice in the last hour. I bet Mom could fry an egg on those heaters right now.

"Full blast," he says.

Ethan clenches his jaw and looks around the room as if there must be something else he can do to bring the room temperature up to Death Valley in July.

With his forehead knitted in a perma-frown, he checks Brody's temperature again, then lifts a mug of steaming sweet tea from a small table next to the couch and takes *its* temperature.

Martha pulls a face, clearly thinking he's lost his mind, and I hide my grin under a blanket.

"Drink," Ethan orders Brody. "It's at the optimal temperature."

Brody shuffles as if to sit up, but Ethan stops him.

"Wait. Let me. You don't want to lose any of the heat inside the covers."

Ethan tucks the covers around Brody, trapping his arms like a mummy, then supports his back and lifts the mug to his mouth.

I'm pretty sure Brody could hold the mug just fine, but he knows, as we all do, that Ethan needs this. It's not just his apology for not trusting Brody's instincts; control is the only way he can cope when someone he loves is in any form of danger. That's what he trained for as a search-and-rescue pilot, and, in his eyes only, he failed to prevent Olivia's death from sepsis.

When Ethan's happy with how much Brody has drunk, he lays him back down and turns his attention to me, lifting me up, and making me drink my mug of hot tea like I'm an invalid.

"Daddy," Martha begins in an authoritative voice.

"Yes, sweetie?" Ethan replies, not looking her way as he heads back to Brody with the thermometer.

"You told me that if people are dangerously cold, then they have to be naked and cuddle."

"That's one of the ways to restore body temperature safely," he replies, his attention on the thermometer.

"Then why doesn't Aunt Piper take *her* clothes off and Uncle Brody take *his* clothes off, and they can cuddle on one couch?"

I catch Brody's eye again, and he raises an eyebrow.

Screw the tea and blankets. That one tiny gesture makes heat whoosh through me like a flamethrower.

Not content with the first reading, Ethan takes another. "It's easier to monitor their vitals this way," he says to Martha.

"But *Daddy*, if they were lying on *top* of each other, then you wouldn't have to keep *moving*," she says, as if the logic is inescapable.

Mia snorts and turns it into a cough.

"Are *you* sick, Aunt Mia?" Martha continues.

"Only in the head," Hudson mutters.

Martha's interruption breaks the spell Ethan has cast over the room.

"I'm gonna get a pot of clam chowder on," Mom says. "There's enough for everyone twice over, so I hope you all stay for dinner. If anyone wants a drink, just holler."

"I'll help," Mia says.

"Me too," Harper, Cara, and Marv say at the same time.

Within a few seconds, everyone runs from the hottest room in the house, leaving Brody and me on our respective couches with Ethan hovering.

He takes Brody's hand out to check his pulse.

Without anyone in the room watching me, I shamelessly eye-fuck the man who told me he was in love with me when we were growing up.

The look Brody gives me in return takes my breath away. It promises that the kiss that rocked my world last night was only a taste of what he intends to unleash as soon as we're alone.

"Hmm," Ethan says, staring at Brody's wrist. "Much stronger."

Brody raises an eyebrow at me again, and I shove my hands under my backside to stop them from moving between my legs.

Ethan tucks Brody's hand back under the blankets like he's trying to buy time.

Now that Billy's safe, my anger toward my brother is receding, replaced with empathy for the man he is now and everything he's been through. He's far from old, but the lines around his eyes speak of the grief in his heart that never seems to lessen.

"I'm sorry for what I said to you," I begin. "I—"

Ethan holds up a hand. "No. Don't apologize."

He's still on high alert, his gaze fixed on the floor, the muscles in his forearms tensed as his hands form into fists.

"I … I need to think about what you said, but I can't do it now. There's no space," he says.

I know what he means. The shock and stress of the day is going to take time to fade.

"But I need to apologize to both of you for not listening to Brody. I was wrong. I was panicking and shouldn't have dismissed you the way I did."

"It's cool, man," Brody says.

"No, it's not. I'm sorry."

Ethan's gaze flicks to the door leading to the kitchen, and I know he's finding it difficult to have Martha out of his sight.

"What's Brody's temperature right now?" I ask.

"Ninety-six."

"So no longer mildly hypothermic?"

"No. But—"

"What about mine?"

He checks it again. "Ninety-eight."

"So normal, then."

"It should be ninety-eight point six."

I resist the urge to roll my eyes, and reach a hand out from the covers to squeeze his. "We'll be fine. Go see Martha."

Ethan doesn't immediately reply. I can sense his hesitation, so I squeeze his hand a little harder. "It's okay. And thank you for taking such good care of us."

He stands and drags a hand down his face, but his feet don't move.

"We'll be fine. I promise."

"Thanks, bud," Brody says.

"You need to keep resting. Keep warm. Fluids. Hot food. More rest," Ethan tells him, ticking off each point on his fingers.

"We will."

"And game night is canceled. Sorry."

Brody glances at me, and I nod. "Tomorrow?" he says.

My brother's shoulders relax a little. "That'd be great. But only if you're better."

"I'm sure I will be."

Ethan nods, then gives the room another once-over to make sure there are no hidden dangers, like an open window.

As soon as the door closes behind him, Brody's on his feet, the mountain of covers tumbling to the floor.

"What are you—"

He takes the top comforter off me and bundles it into a ball. "This one's in the wrong place."

"And where should it be?" I ask, my heart rate rising.

"On our bed."

He tears off his woolly hat, then holds out his free hand. "I don't know about you, but I'd quite like to ignore Ethan's advice right now and follow Martha's."

I drop my own hat to the floor and take his hand, a zing of electricity running up my arm at the contact. Brody pulls me to my feet and brings my body flush with his.

"You sure?" I ask breathlessly. "Are you fully recovered?"

His answer is to pull me closer against a part of him that's operating at peak efficiency. "I never would have chosen for this to happen with a houseful of people downstairs, but right now, nothing's more important to me than being alone with you."

My heart is beating double time, and all I can do is nod. I can't think about the future. All I can do is run headlong into the moment I've dreamed of my whole life.

Brody steps back and frowns at his bare chest, still dirty from rescuing Billy. "I'm gonna have to take a quick shower."

I lean into him. "Need any assistance?"

His breath hitches, and then he growls, "Fuck yeah."

EVIE ALEXANDER

He kisses down my neck, his lips like fire, and my legs begin to buckle.

A loud laugh erupts from the kitchen, and I push him back. "Quick! Before one of them comes back to check on us."

Like teenagers sneaking around, we stifle our own laughter and tiptoe upstairs. Brody tosses the comforter into our room, then takes my hand and pulls me into the bathroom.

The moment the door closes behind us, I'm on him like my pussy's got an itch, and he's my scratching post. I wrap my arms around him and crush my lips against his.

His tongue meets mine, and I swear my mouth is having an orgasm right now. It's like fireworks, with every fizz and bang ricocheting inside me until I'm shaking.

Brody's got one hand threaded through my hair, keeping my mouth on his, and the other tugging down the zipper of his pants. I help by reaching inside to free his cock, moaning when I finally wrap my hands around it, like I've found the Holy Grail of dicks after a lifetime of searching.

It's perfect: long, hot, hard, and thick. My rechargeable toyfriend is nothing compared to what Brody's packing, and I stroke him from root to tip with both hands, swiping the pre-cum from his slit and spreading it over the whole shaft.

Brody's taking multitasking to the next level, somehow managing to growl the word "fuck" repeatedly while stepping out of his pants and performing the kind of oral gymnastics that deserve a gold medal.

Now his hands are on my clothes, tugging my sweater and T-shirt up, before getting distracted by my tits. He palms them through my lacy bra, his thumbs rubbing the hardened peaks of my nipples as his tongue thrusts into my mouth, stifling my cry.

The pleasure is nuclear, and I can't get enough. I may not have climaxed yet, but the sensations he's giving me are hotter and more powerful than any orgasm I've ever had. My body's

224

no longer my own. Brody owns it, and I am a-okay with him moving in, starting with his wicked tongue and ending with his monumental cock.

It's like hot silk over a rod of iron, weeping so much pre-cum that my hands slide over it effortlessly. I grip him harder as electricity arcs from my nipples to my clit.

"Fu—oh fuck!" he cries, jerking away from me, his fingers digging into his thighs, all of his muscles straining like he's maxing out at the gym.

I don't need to ask to know he's barely holding on; his cock is red and swollen, slapping against his washboard abs as if seeking my hands again.

I use the brief respite to unclip my bra, pulling it off along with my sweater and T-shirt, then tug off my jeans and sopping panties.

Brody slowly raises his head, his gaze raking over my naked body as if he's going to devour me. I've never felt so sexy before, so fucking hot and horny, that even a million orgasms wouldn't dull the hunger I have for him.

He lifts me up, and I wrap my arms and legs around him, grinding into him as our lips crash together. I'm gasping and moaning, and he's making growling sounds that vibrate into my clit better than any toy, because they're coming from *him*.

Walking us into the shower, Brody turns on the faucet without breaking contact between us, then stands with his back to the water as it slowly warms, shielding me.

Droplets trickle over my arms and legs, and as the steam envelops us, I stroke my fingers through his hair, feeling the water soaking through his locks, running down our faces, slipping between our bodies.

His mouth is hot and wet, his body hot and hard, his skin smooth over the ridges of muscle. I trace his shoulders, the curve of his biceps, the corded steel of his forearms.

I can't stop touching him, kissing him, drinking him in. I'm drowning in the sensations flooding my body. I've craved him for so long, even when I lied to myself that I didn't.

His fingers thread through my hair again, tugging my head back so his lips can find my neck—the sensitive spot just beneath my ear that makes me shiver despite the heat. I tilt my head back further, offering myself to him as his teeth graze my skin.

"Brody," I pant, my nails scoring across his back, his scalp. His name on my lips is my ultimate fantasy. I've only ever cried it in my head, imagining his body covering me, his cock thrusting deep inside my pussy as I bring myself off. But now, each time I say his name, there's an answering growl that sends thrills through every nerve ending.

My nipples ache, my breasts swollen and hypersensitive, desperate for his touch. He raises his head, pinning me with a gaze ferocious in its desire.

"I wanna take my time," he says, his voice a low rumble. "But I'm so fucking horny for you right now, I'm about to blow my load. So, you're gonna have to be a good girl and help me out here."

I nod, reaching underneath me for his cock, but he shakes his head and lifts me off him, holding me steady as my feet find the shower tray. I start to kneel, wanting so badly to suck his cock, but he stops me with a shake of his head.

"But I want to—"

"Can you stand?"

"Yes, but—"

Brody moves me so my back is against the far wall of the shower. His expression is so intense I can hardly breathe. The energy he's bringing shatters all my wildest, most illicit imaginings, and I am so here for it.

"Spread your legs," he commands. "Show me what I'm desperate to taste."

Panting with desire, every inch of my skin burns. Holding his gaze, I step my feet apart.

His breath hitches, but he nods his approval and extends a hand, caressing my cheek before running the pad of his thumb along my lower lip. I suck the tip, swirling my tongue around it, showing him exactly what I want to do to his cock.

"Fuck, Piper," he growls, then runs his fingers down my neck, circling my breasts.

I arch my chest toward him, but he doesn't touch my nipples. "Brody," I whimper.

"Look at you," he murmurs, his gaze following his hand as it sweeps over the curve of my stomach. "So fucking perfect. Are you wet for me, Piper?"

"Y-yes." I'm trembling now, desperate to grab his hand and push it between my legs. But I stay still, my palms pressed against the tiles as the water runs down them.

"Good girl," he says, one hand holding my hip to keep me in place, the other inching lower, his middle finger leading the way through my sodden curls. I can't look away, silently begging him to keep going.

The tip of his finger grazes my clit, sending a jolt of electricity through me. I gasp for breath, then shudder and cry out as he sinks his middle finger deep inside me.

He pumps it in and out, his breath ragged. "You're so tight. Fuck, Piper."

His finger is so thick, and I'm squeezing so hard, chasing my orgasm, but then he pulls out.

I gaze up at him helplessly, silently pleading with him to continue.

He shakes his head. "You're not coming this way," he murmurs, then slowly licks the length of his finger, his eyelids closing briefly.

Mesmerized by the sight of his tongue, pleasure winds tighter and tighter inside me.

"Please, Brody," I beg.

He sinks to his knees, water raining down on his back, then taps my inner ankles, urging me to widen my stance. Now that I know what's coming, my heart races even faster.

He's staring so intently at my pussy as he parts my folds. "So pretty," he says, then looks up at me, imprisoning me in his gaze.

My breath catches, and time seems to freeze. Then he leans forward, his dark eyes still holding mine, and places a soft kiss right on my clit.

Pleasure shoots through me like lightning, making my hips buck.

"Oh, my—"

"Eyes on me, Piper," he growls, holding me in place as I shake.

He's like a wolf, ready to pounce as I draw in shuddering breaths. It's so hard to look at him. I've never known this level of arousal before, and I'm not sure I can survive it.

But I can't stop my gaze from being drawn to the sight of him between my legs, the feel of his breath ghosting over my clit.

"Good girl," he rumbles, then licks the full length of my slit.

"Fuuuuckkkkkk!"

I brace my hands against the shower wall, my orgasm forming at the edges of my being like a great wave I can only watch helplessly as it bears down on me.

Brody's magic tongue swirls around my clit, winding me up to the point of no return. I'm so sensitive right now, so swollen.

He ups the pace and stars dance behind my eyes. My hands tingle, electricity sparking across my skin as my breath quickens.

"Brody! I'm, oh my god, I'm gonna—"

He thrums the tip of his tongue against my clit, and the orgasm crashes through me, obliterating everything into brilliant light. Pleasure pounds through me in waves, and I grab Brody's head for support. He growls into my pussy, sucking my clit and rockets me into a second orgasm.

I'm gasping, crying his name, gripping handfuls of his hair as the sensations roll through me over and over.

My legs give out beneath me, and I fall forward.

Brody catches me, drawing me onto his lap with my legs wrapped around his waist. He kisses me, holding me tightly to him, as the water falls around us like warm rain.

I'm still shaking, but I need his mouth on mine, my tongue speaking without words, tangling with his as I pour out my love for him.

We're both out of breath, kissing with a desperate urgency, like it's the end of the world. Everything in me is alive, shimmering with energy. I've never known anything like it before, and it almost scares me. But in Brody's strong arms, I feel held. Protected.

Breaking the kiss, I rest my forehead on his, my body heavy. "Now you."

He huffs a small laugh. "Already did."

"Huh?" I raise my head from his, confused. His smile is so sexy, an involuntary shiver runs through me.

"When you came, I did too."

"But you weren't touching yourself."

"Didn't matter. I was touching you. That's all it took. I told you I was about to shoot my load."

Without thinking, I glance around, like I'm expecting to see ropes of cum splattered on the fogged-up glass.

Brody chuckles. "Down the plughole."

I turn back to him, my cheeks heating.

He strokes a lock of hair from my face, his gaze running over my features reverently. "You're so beautiful."

My heart squeezes. *This man.* How did I get so lucky?

"That was the hottest experience of my life," he continues.

"Me too," I say shyly.

"And the day's not over yet."

I ignore the prickle of anxiety in my stomach, the reminder that my whole family is downstairs, and Brody might be leaving for New Zealand in less than two weeks. Instead, I focus on the man in front of me.

"I don't have any condoms with me," I begin. "I never thought …"

He smiles. "Me neither."

"But …" I swallow. "I've got an IUD fitted, and I got tested after my ex cheated on me, so …"

Brody blinks, looking stunned. "I, er … I've always used condoms, but I got tested anyway after my last relationship."

I love that he doesn't say Marisa's name, like she doesn't even factor into his life anymore.

"If you'd rather use one, then we can wait," I say.

He shakes his head so fast that water droplets fly off his hair.

I laugh. "You look like a wet dog."

He grins. "I feel like a dog, one that wants to hump you at every opportunity."

"I'm down with that."

We smile at each other. I've never felt so happy before. I wriggle in his lap, his cock hard again beneath me.

"Told you, I'm so fucking hot for you."

I shimmy off his lap and kneel in front of him. The shower cubicle is big enough for two, so I've got space to admire the cock of the century.

The silence between us is electric. His eyes bore into mine as I slowly lower my head and sink my mouth onto him, taking as much as I can.

"Fuck! Piper!" he shouts.

"Hmmm?" I hum around his cock.

He jerks away from me and pulls me to my feet, his chest

230

heaving as he breathes. "Piper …" Huffing an incredulous laugh, he rubs his forehead. "You … Jesus Christ."

"But I want to."

He pins me with a gaze that makes my heart flutter.

"As do I," he rumbles. "You have no idea how many times I've fantasized about having those pretty lips stretched around my cock."

I reach down and take him in my hands, stroking as he speaks.

"Jesus—ahhh! Piper! But … I don't know how much hot water is left in the heater, and, *fuck!*"

"Yes?" I answer, feigning innocence. His dick is so thick, my fingers and thumb don't meet as I pump his length.

Letting out another strangled cry, he pries my hands away, holding them in his.

"But there's something I want even more than that."

"You do?"

He nods. "To feel your pussy squeeze around my cock. To watch your face as you come apart underneath me."

I let out a squeak as my pussy tightens, demanding to know why this isn't happening right here, right now.

"So, let's get you clean before I get you dirty again."

He stands and helps me to my feet, then reaches for the shampoo. But instead of handing it over, he squeezes some into his palm and slowly massages it through my hair.

CHAPTER 21

BRODY

*T*he low moan Piper makes as I work the shampoo into her hair nearly makes me come again. Her eyelids have fluttered closed, and fuck me, there's not a better sight than this. Suds glide down her neck, over the curve of her spectacular tits, dripping off her hardened nipples.

My shaft is rock solid, my balls aching to unload again—but this time, it'll be inside her tight pussy. *Bare.*

The thought makes me light-headed. I've never fucked anyone without a condom. Ever. But with Piper, it's different. It's *everything.*

I massage her scalp and she moans again, her head dropping back. I move her around so she's leaning back against me, then slide my soapy hands over her breasts, tweaking her nipples and being rewarded with a mewling cry that makes my head spin.

My cock's yelling at me to bend her over and fuck her until she's screaming my name, but our first time isn't gonna be like that—so I force myself to focus on washing her hair, even as my mouth waters with the memory of her sweet pussy.

Fuck... The Seven Wonders of the World have got nothing on my girl—and yes, she *is* my girl—always has been and always will be. I don't know how we're going to make this work, but Ethan's not going to get in our way ever again. Nor will my career. Nothing is more important than having Piper by my side.

I shield her face with one hand as I angle her head into the spray and rinse the shampoo out. Then I squeeze out as much water as I can and apply conditioner.

She hums her appreciation, her lips turned up in a lazy, satisfied smile. I want her always this happy, looking so content, so well-fucked that everyone knows how good I am to my woman.

Maybe it's the afternoon spent facing death to rescue Billy that's putting these thoughts into my head, but right now I'm running on testosterone, and all my inner caveman wants is to love and protect Piper with everything I've got.

While the conditioner soaks into her hair, I lather up shower gel and glide my palms over her front again, then down her spine and between her butt cheeks.

She arches her back, pushing into my hand.

"Fuck," I growl. "Piper ..."

She undulates her hips, then glances over her shoulder at me with those big blue eyes that are my complete undoing. My hands are gripping her hips, the brain in my head and my cock arguing about what's gonna happen next.

Then Piper pivots, gets a blob of shower gel, and works it between her palms. "My turn."

I've lost all words, so I just stand there, every muscle strained as she sweeps her small, soft hands over every hard part of me.

Her touch is liquid fire, sending pleasure pulsing through

my veins. With one hand, she's rolling the weight of my balls; the other glides over my length, swiping her thumb through the slit.

"You like?" she asks breathlessly.

I catch hold of her wrists. "Too much," I manage.

Pinning her hands behind her back, I move us both under the flow of water, careful to keep her face clear of the spray. When I'm sure she's steady, I run my fingers through her hair until it's silky and clean.

Even though I want to stay here forever, I switch the faucet off, sluice as much excess water as I can from our bodies, then open the shower door to retrieve a towel. I rub it over Piper's body, then wrap it around her. Her face is pink, her eyes alive but drowsy with desire.

I quickly dry off, tuck the towel around my waist, and check that the corridor is clear. Then I take her hand and lead her back to our bedroom, locking the door behind us.

It's already dark, but there's enough illumination from the Christmas lights outside for us to see. I tug the towel from Piper's body and drape it over a chair, then stand back so I can take her in.

Her blonde hair and pale skin are glowing in ever-changing colors. She's a goddess, and I'm gonna worship the fuck out of her.

I point at the bed. "Lie down."

She doesn't hesitate, lying in the middle of the bed, her eyes following my every move.

I ditch my own towel and come to stand at the foot of the bed, gazing at her. The picture's almost perfect.

"Spread your legs for me. I wanna see that perfect pussy."

She swallows, then her ankles inch apart.

"Don't stop."

She keeps going, and my cock swells even harder. I give it a tug, as if that would relieve the pressure, then lift my chin. "Touch yourself. Show me what you like."

Her breasts are rising and falling as she breathes, her teeth biting into her plump lower lip. Her hands slide lower, the fingers of one hand spreading her pussy wide as the middle finger of the other circles her clit.

I stroke my length. "That's it, baby girl."

Her thighs are tightening, and I imagine them gripping my head as she comes, her fingers tugging my hair like she did in the shower. It's the biggest rush, and I need another fix.

"Now touch your breasts." I stalk forward and pull her ankles down the bed so her legs dangle off the mattress.

"Touch them for me, Piper," I repeat, then drop to my knees on the floor and hook her legs over my shoulders. "I want to watch you."

Her body glows in the shifting colors of the lights, but I can still make out the flush in her cheeks as she obeys, her fingers fluttering to her perfect tits, then pinching the nipples.

"Good girl," I rumble, then lower my head to her sweet, sweet pussy and kiss it like I would her mouth, my tongue teasing, tasting, exploring.

"Brody!" she gasps.

Yes, yes, yes, I chant in my head as I feast on her, pushing my tongue inside her, feeling the squeeze of her inner muscles, then licking her clit, figuring out exactly which movements drive her wild.

Piper's breath is coming faster and faster, her fingers tugging and rolling her nipples. The sight is painfully erotic, and I pull my hips away from the end of the bed so there's no pressure on my cock. I'm not shooting my load unless it's deep inside her.

I press a finger inside her pussy, curling the tip up as if beckoning her orgasm toward me.

EVIE ALEXANDER

The effect is instantaneous, her hips bucking off the bed as she cries my name.

Easing another finger inside, I gently scissor them, stretching her so she's ready to take my cock, all the while circling and licking her swollen clit.

She's so tight, so wet, her pussy clenching around my fingers as her legs begin to tremble.

I want to tell her how perfect she is, how she makes me so hot that I'm burning up and losing my mind. But words get in the way of pleasuring her with my tongue, so I hum my approval instead.

"Bro—" Her voice cuts off in a silent scream as her orgasm hits, and the rush that washes through me is like no other. I thrum the tip of my tongue against her clit, thrusting my fingers in and out of her pussy as I rub the upper wall of her tight channel.

She's convulsing on the bed, her pussy contracting as the waves of her release roll through her. Now that I know she can climax more than once, I ease off my pace, only to build it up again as she catches her breath.

She threads her fingers through my hair, gripping like she's holding on for dear life, telling me with her hands that she wants me to stay exactly where I am.

I ain't going anywhere...

I increase the speed of my tongue and the pressure of my fingers as they move back and forth inside her, leading her toward another orgasm. I know it's coming, by the way she squeezes around my digits and the shuddering of her thighs.

I love you, Piper. I fucking love you.

Her legs clamp around my head like a vise as her release smashes through her. I can't hear, can barely breathe, but I've never felt happier, more powerful, and potent.

I keep the intensity up, pushing her orgasm on and on, until

236

her legs collapse back to the bed and her breath returns in fitful gasps.

Carefully pulling my fingers out, I press a gentle kiss on her clit, then pull her back up the bed and take her in my arms, kissing her damp hair.

"Oh my God, Brody," she manages between breaths. "That was ... incredible. Beyond incredible ... beyond anything."

I hold her tighter. I want to tell her I love her, but it's too soon. She needs to trust me. Trust that this time I'm back for good.

But one thing's certain: I'm going to make up for the twelve years we lost, starting by making her come for every day we've missed since I left Hideaway.

Piper's hand drifts down to my cock, her lips finding mine. Her tongue sweeps into my mouth as she grips me more firmly, and—*fuck me*—it feels so good.

"Brody," she murmurs. "I need ..."

"What do you need, baby girl?" I ask.

Her cheeks darken. "You know ..."

"Tell me. Tell me exactly what you want."

She tugs my cock. "This."

"And where do you want it? Buried deep inside your tight pussy?"

Her breath hitches, her eyes widening, then she nods.

"Nothing between us," I continue. "Me, bare inside you."

She nods again, quicker this time.

"And do you want me to come inside you? Fill you up with my cum? Mark you as mine?"

"Yes," she says without hesitation. "Please, Brody."

This is it, the moment I've fantasized about for years.

"Spread your legs for me again, Piper," I say as I position myself above her.

She does, her body opening to me, her hips lifting slightly in invitation. She's so beautiful. So perfect.

Mine.

I position the fat head of my cock at her entrance and slowly push against the resistance. She's so tight.

Her forehead puckers with a frown. "I don't know if I can—"

"Shhh," I murmur, gently circling her clit with the pad of my thumb. "Just breathe. Relax. You can take me, I know you can."

She gives me a hesitant nod.

"Good girl."

She relaxes around me at my words, and I press a tiny bit deeper.

"You're doing great," I murmur. "Look at your pretty pussy taking my cock."

My words are working as she stretches a little further with everything I say.

I thrust another inch deeper. "Touch your tits."

Gasping, she brings her hands to her breasts, rolling the nipples between her fingers and thumbs.

"Good girl. That's it. Now see how much of me you've taken."

She glances down, and I follow her gaze, my head light as I take in the sight of her pussy stretched around my cock.

"You want me to keep talking like this?" I ask, needing to know if this side of me is one she's on board with.

"Yes," she says immediately. "I like it." Her voice quietens, like she's shy. "It's really hot."

Thank fuck.

I nod. "Then you'll like it when I tell you how fucking sexy you are. How many thousands of times I've jacked off imagining you just like this, spread out beneath me."

She whimpers, her hips bucking up to press herself a little further onto me.

"That's it. You can do it." I spit on my fingers, then continue rubbing her clit. "You gonna come for me again, Piper?"

Her nod is erratic, her breathing more labored.

"Just feel," I murmur. "Your hands on your perfect tits. My fingers on your swollen clit. My cock filling your needy pussy."

I'm on a knife's edge, but I won't fall until she shatters around me.

"Don't hold back. I want to hear what I do to you," I continue, pushing a little deeper. "And when you're ready, I'm going to fuck you hard and fast. You want it like that?"

"Yes," she gasps. "Oh, yes."

"Good girl."

My thumb circles faster on her clit, and I apply more pressure. I'm almost fully inside her, and nothing has ever felt so right.

She's shaking beneath me, eyelids fluttering like they're trying to close.

I thrust. "Yeah, that's it, baby."

Now balls deep, I grit my teeth to stop myself from exploding.

"Look, Piper," I growl. "Look how you've taken every inch of my cock."

She tugs harder on her nipples, panting, but still follows my direction, her eyes locked on where I'm buried inside her.

That's her tipping point. Her eyes roll back, and her chest arches off the bed.

I jerk my hips forward as I rub her clit. "That's it, baby. Come all over my cock like the good girl I know you are. Take it. Take it all."

My jaw is so tight I can barely speak, the tendons in my neck straining as I fight not to come.

Piper's sobbing, moaning, convulsing around me as I keep her pinned to the bed. I've never seen anything hotter, more mind-blowingly beautiful.

As she gradually comes down from her high, her eyes find

mine, her fingers tracing the lines of my abs. "Brody," she murmurs.

"Yes, sweetheart?"

"I'm ready." She glances to where my cock disappears inside her. "I need …"

"Me to …"

"I … I need you to fuck me," she whispers. "*Hard*."

I close my eyes for a second, summoning every ounce of self-control. Then I take a steadying breath and hold her gaze.

"Tell me to stop if it gets too much. Promise?"

"I will."

She stretches her arms over her head, and I almost lose it. She's so open. So trusting. I love every perfect inch of her.

I pin her wrists gently with one hand, and brace the other on the mattress beside her head.

"You ready?" I ask.

She nods, her pussy tightening around me.

"Eyes on me, Piper. If anything doesn't feel good, just say so."

"I promise."

I pull out slowly, take a controlled breath, then slam back into her.

She immediately cries out.

I still. "Too much?"

"No! It was … Oh my god, Brody. Please. Do it again."

So, I do—pulling back, then snapping forward with a grunt. Piper lifts her hips to meet me.

I keep going, slowly building speed, my attention fixed on her face, catching every tiny shift in expression, needing to know she's with me all the way.

Even in the low light, I see the flush blooming across her chest as it rises and falls. I want her to come again. More than I want my own release.

"That's it. Let me fuck you, baby girl. Let me fuck you hard."

"Yes! Yes!" she gasps.

Lights spark at the edges of my vision, my focus narrowing to Piper writhing beneath me. I snap my hips faster, drilling into her, desperate to push her over the edge before I fall. I've never known pleasure like this—sharp, sweet, and so intense I'm not sure I'll survive it.

Dropping my weight onto one forearm, I reach down and take a nipple into my mouth, roughing my tongue over the hardened tip.

Piper stiffens beneath me, crying my name before shuddering as her orgasm crashes through her.

I fuck her harder, her pussy so tight around my cock it triggers my release. There's no stopping it.

White-hot pleasure shoots up my spine, obliterating everything. I can't breathe. Can't see. Can't think. I just hold on, torn apart by the force of it.

Over the pounding in my ears, I roar Piper's name. My balls contract, pulsing as I fill her with my cum—over and over. It's fucking perfect.

I release her wrists, but she wraps her arms around my back, holding me tight. I shift to move off her, and she tightens her grip.

"Not yet," she whispers. "Stay inside me."

So, I cradle her face, kissing her lips, her cheeks, the corners of her eyes while her pussy squeezes my cock like she wants to keep me inside her forever.

And I'm down with that, because there's nowhere else I'd rather be.

CHAPTER 22

BRODY

*T*he moment my eyes open, I know something's wrong.

Piper's chewing on her bottom lip, her brow furrowed as she stares at her phone screen.

She's sitting up in bed beside me, her hair unkempt in a way that reminds my cock what we've been doing all night, but the sexy smile she's been wearing is gone.

I can't help feeling I'm to blame for whatever's on that screen. It's an immediate guilt that eats away at my stomach like acid.

"Hey," I murmur.

She jumps a little. "Oh, I thought you were asleep." She's smiling again, but there's pain underneath.

I raise my chin toward the phone. "What have I done this time?"

Piper's cheeks are pink. "It's not you. It's nothing."

Even though I'm still bone-dead tired from rescuing Billy

yesterday, then fucking Piper six ways to Sunday last night, I sling an arm over her legs, drawing tiny circles on her hip bone through her pajamas.

"Can I see?" I ask.

"I know it's not true," she says firmly, but there's still an edge of insecurity in her voice.

"You're probably right," I reply, even as my pulse kicks up a notch at the thought of what new bullshit the gossip mags have dredged up this time.

I turn my hand over, palm facing up in invitation, and she places the phone on it.

"Brody King's Fake Fairy Tale: Ex-Girlfriend Says He Badmouthed Hideaway, Saw Piper as Sister."

Fuck.

I exhale with a heavy sigh, roll onto my back, open the search bar, type in my name, and click on "News." There are headlines and videos about my rescue of Billy yesterday, which are more than favorable. However, there are also plenty of others that make my blood run cold.

"King of Pretenders: Ex-Girlfriend Calls Brody King's Relationship with Piper a Hollywood Fake."

"Small Town, Big Lie: Brody King's Ex Exposes the Fake Romance with Piper."

"King of the Publicity Stunt? Ex Claims Cheater Brody Is Incapable of Love."

Marisa. She *has* been busy.

"What should we do?"

I switch the screen off and pass it back, then sit up in bed and take her hands. "Nothing."

"But do we have to put out a statement? A press release?"

Stroking her hands with mine, I try to soothe away her stress.

"Marisa's hurting that I've moved on. On some level, she felt guilty for cheating and deflected the blame for our breakup onto me. That was okay when I wasn't in another relationship, but now that I am, she's lashing out."

Piper's cheeks flush, her gaze dropping. "So, have you … I mean, are we …"

"In a relationship?"

She nods.

I place a finger under her chin and lift it so her eyes return to mine.

"I sure hope so."

The color in her cheeks deepens.

"If that's what you want," I continue.

"Yes, please."

"Good. Because now that I've finally got you, I never want to let you go."

She blinks, her eyes glassy with unshed tears, and my heart expands so much there's not enough room to breathe.

Can I tell her I love her? Is it too soon? Will she believe me?

"Kids!" a cry comes from the hallway.

Piper jumps off the bed and opens the door a crack. "Hi, Mom. Do you want us down for breakfast?"

I pull on my gray sweatpants and adjust myself for decency, then pick up a tray from the dresser. Erica must have realized we didn't want to be disturbed last night and left food outside our door.

"Does she want this?" I ask. "I can bring it down now if she does."

"I'll have that," Erica says, opening the door wide and taking the tray from me.

"Mom!" Piper begins.

"What, honey? You're taking a break from snuggle time. I'm not interrupting anything."

I resist a glance at the molding where the wall meets the ceiling, trying to find the hidden cameras I'm paranoid she's installed.

"I just wanted you to know that Judy Lowell called this morning. Billy's mom," Erica continues. "Apparently, Billy got out of the hospital last night and isn't taking well to enforced rest. He's asked if you both could visit today."

"Of course," Piper replies. "Unless you and Marv have another packed schedule for us today?"

"I don't know, honey. There's plenty going on in town, but Marv hasn't come by yet this morning."

"Maybe he thinks we've done enough to get Brody in the press?"

"Perhaps. You did create quite the stir yesterday with Billy. I expect Sonia will send you a basket of fruit."

"Sonia?"

"Hernandez. The reporter from *Down East News Now*. I think she's hoping for a call from one of the big networks after her scoop with you yesterday."

Erica leans forward like she's about to impart a big secret.

"And that's another thing. Little Billy is desperate to be interviewed by her. Judy says his account of the rescue now includes a polar bear."

I chuckle. "I told him his story had to be more exciting than what actually happened."

Erica's eyes widen. "Are you kidding me? Grant and Walter trekked back to retrieve Billy's belongings first thing this morning, and—"

She thrusts the tray back into my hands, then crosses herself like she's in church.

"What you two did … Lord bless you and keep you. Judy said you were one slip away from plunging to your deaths at the bottom of that gorge! Grant went across that fallen tree on his hands and knees. I don't know how—"

Erica pulls a handkerchief from her pocket and dabs at the corners of her eyes.

She shakes her head. "You're heroes, and I hope everyone

knows it. You'll be on the front page of *The Almanac* at the very least."

She takes the tray back from me. "You just take your time coming downstairs, and I'll let Judy know you'll come by sometime today."

As Piper closes the door behind her mom, I let out a long breath and run my hands through my hair. I've just spent the last eighteen or so hours of my life either lost in Piper or dead to the world asleep. There was no space to process the search and rescue of Billy and how fucking terrified I'd been for him.

Piper puts her arms around me and rests her head against my thudding heart.

I hold her close. *Billy and Lucky are safe. We're alive. All is okay*.

"It certainly puts everything into perspective," she says softly into my chest.

"Sure does."

Thinking of Marisa now, all I feel is empathy. She's not happy, but it's not my problem. I relax into the warmth and softness of Piper in my arms. *This* is where I need to be. *This* is where I'm at peace.

"I think maybe I should turn my phone off for a few days," she says.

"Good idea. And maybe the Google Alert with my name on it?"

Piper gazes up at me and grins. "I don't need it anymore, now that I've got my news straight from the horse's mouth."

"You saying I'm a horse?"

She palms my cock and smirks. "Well, you are hung like one …"

I slowly shake my head and smile, then I have a thought that makes my good humor fade. "You feeling okay this morning? Not too sore?"

Her cute little nose wrinkles. "A little. To be honest, I'm surprised I can walk in a straight line after last night."

"I'm sorry."

"Don't be! It was …" She blushes again but still keeps eye contact. "It was the most incredible experience of my life, and I can't wait to do it again."

My ego, as well as my dick, swells. "See how you feel later. I don't want to put you under any pressure."

"You're not. And anyway, if we can't have sex, I can always suck your cock?"

I take a breath as fireworks explode behind my eyes. When my vision clears, all I see is Piper's cheeky grin.

"And if your pussy's sore," I rumble, "then I'm gonna kiss it better."

She swallows.

"In fact," I continue, reaching behind her to lock the door. "If your sweet pussy would like an appointment with my mouth, then the doctor is ready to see you now."

Her nostrils flare as she nods.

"Good." I undo the buttons of her pajama top, slip it off her shoulders, then palm her breasts, rolling the hardened peaks of her nipples between my fingers and thumbs.

"Now take off your pajama pants," I growl, "and get back on that bed with your legs spread like the good girl I know you are …"

It's afternoon by the time Piper and I are ready to leave the house. Marv and Cara haven't shown up, so I hope this means Cara's on her way back to Milwaukee and Marv's happy with whatever publicity I've gotten so far. John's out on mayoral duties, and Erica and Harper are looking at possible sites for Harper's perfume store.

"Have you seen my phone?" I ask Piper as we're about to leave for Billy's house.

"Not since yesterday. Have you lost it?"

"I know I had it in the family room when we got back here from the Locke Reserve. Your mom took it from me."

We glance around the room and spot it tucked behind a photo on the mantelpiece. I change my number frequently, but anxiety always prickles my belly each time I look at the notifications. For my own sanity, I've switched off most of them, especially now that I don't have access to my own social media accounts.

There's a message from Cara.

> Cara: Traveling to Bangor this afternoon to fly home. I'll be online if you need anything. Please thank Piper and her family for how kind they've been to me, and thank you for the holiday. You're the best boss (and don't tell Marv that I said that, since he's technically my boss)!

"Cara's on her way home, but I don't have anything from Marv," I say to Piper.

"No news is good news?"

I rub my forehead. "I suppose I should be grateful for small mercies. It just feels weird when he's not all up in my business."

"He's a good man."

"I know. He drives me up the wall, but he's never steered me wrong and always has my back."

We bundle up and leave the house hand in hand, making our way toward the center of town.

"I know so many actors who get ghosted or dumped by their agents," I tell her. "When they can't land new jobs, or one doesn't work out for whatever reason, they suddenly can't reach their agent on the phone. Because they're not making the agent money, they get deprioritized. Then it's like they don't exist anymore. They aren't invited to the Christmas party or the Fourth of July barbecue. It's brutal."

Piper squeezes my hand.

"Marv may be a lot of things, but he's not like that. He's ferociously loyal. Like a pit bull."

"I can see that."

"You should see him at press junkets. Agents never come; it's usually a manager or an assistant. But I don't have one. I just have Marv and Cara. And if a journalist starts asking questions he doesn't like, he goes at them like a rabid honey badger."

Piper giggles. "I can imagine."

"He's a short king with a big heart. We don't often get real with each other, but I know he thinks of me and Cara like the kids he never had."

"So you've changed your mind about firing him, then?"

I stop in the middle of the street so I can gaze down at her. "How could I fire him when he brought you back to me?"

Piper's gloved hand touches my face, her lips parting like she's about to say something, but my phone interrupts with the theme from *The Godfather*.

"Speak of the devil," I say, showing her the screen.

She snorts. "*The Godfather*?"

"It was either that or 'Money, Money, Money' by ABBA."

I take the call as Piper cackles with laughter.

"That Piper? She good?" Marv barks. "You good?"

"Yeah. We're on our way to visit Billy."

"He outta the hospital?"

"Yeah, and Lucky's back from the vet as well."

"Awesome, man. That's great news. I just wanted to tell you Cara's on her way home."

"Thanks for getting that sorted. She didn't need to be here."

"Not when we've got Piper's mom and her gang on our side."

"Did you want us to do anything today?"

There's a brief pause before he replies, "Nah. The Billy story's gonna run for weeks and bury any other crap out there."

"I saw what Marisa's been saying."

"Ha! She can't beat a shirtless you, saving a little boy and a freaking puppy. She must be kicking herself after yesterday. She shoots her mouth off, and a couple hours later you turn into Wolverine after a trip to the barbers."

I grin. "So, what about you? Going to head back to New York?"

"Dunno yet. Maybe. It's nice here. Festive without the risk of getting mugged for your Rolex, y'know?"

Piper nudges me. "Ask him if we've done enough to get you the job."

I hesitate. Yes, of course I want the job, but if I get it, what does this mean for Piper and me?

"Piper wants to—"

"Yeah, yeah, I heard. Tell her I dunno, okay?"

"Will do."

"Okay, be good. I gotta bounce."

When Marv hangs up, I face Piper. "He doesn't know."

She nods, but there's something behind her smile—probably the same thoughts I've been having: If I *do* get the job, how can we make a relationship work when we're on opposite sides of the planet?

CHAPTER 23

BRODY

"*B*rody! Piper!"

I blink as a bright-eyed kid launches himself at me.

"Billy?" I stutter, lifting him into my arms.

"Who did you think it was?" he asks, giving me a look like I'm the class idiot.

His cheeks are flushed, and he seems excited. *This* is the kid I remember from the library, not the one we pulled from a hollow under a snowy tree.

I glance past Billy to his mom.

"Children get sick very quickly," she says. "And they also recover just as fast."

Billy wriggles out of my grip, slides to the ground, and grabs my hand. "I *told* Mom I was better." He gives an exaggerated sigh. "Now come and see Lucky. She's not allowed outside the house for a few days."

Piper and I take off our boots and follow him through to

251

the family room, where Lucky body slams me, her tail swooshing madly and her tongue attempting to give me an all-over bath.

"Hey Lucky!" I say to her, and she barks in reply.

The space is filled with warmth and family love, with photos of Billy from when he was a baby adorning the walls and festive decorations everywhere. There's a Christmas tree in one corner of the room, surrounded by a metal enclosure, like it has to be corralled.

Billy lets out another over-the-top huff as he follows my gaze. "That's Lucky's fault."

"Not entirely," his mom adds. "There was that time you tried to climb it."

I bite the inside of my cheek to stop my laugh, but Billy can see it in my eyes and grins at me.

"I never knew what to expect, having a little boy," Judy says. "I only had sisters."

"My best friend and I once pretended the stairs at his house were Mount Everest and tried to scale it with ropes, crampons, and ice axes," I say apologetically to her, as if Billy and I are linked by our desire to bring the adventure of the outdoors inside.

"Awesome!" Billy shouts.

"No, buddy, we could have gotten into a lot of trouble."

"Can I offer you both a drink?" Judy asks.

"A glass of water would be lovely, thanks," I say.

"Brody! Let me show you my room!" Billy doesn't wait for a reply, dragging me toward the door. He glances over his shoulder at Piper. "It's guy stuff," he says apologetically.

"That's okay," she replies. "I'm gonna hang out with your mom."

He nods. "Good idea."

I jog up the stairs behind him and Lucky to the very top of

the house. Billy has the attic, with skylights facing the ocean on one side and the mountains on the other.

"This is the coolest kid's room I've ever seen."

Billy nods. "It's got everything."

He proceeds to give me the tour, showing me his toys, his Legos, the glow-in-the-dark stars on the sloped ceiling, and finally, a telescope mounted on a stand.

"I watch the boats at sea on that side," he says, pointing at the window behind us. "But through this one, there's something way cooler."

"And what's that?"

"You'll have to bend down, but I've set it up for you."

I crouch and put my eye to the end of the telescope. "No way ..."

"*Yes* way," Billy replies. "Can you see it?"

"Yup." A third of the way up the snowy slopes of the mountains that encircle Hideaway Harbor, I see the cave.

"When I was your age, we used to think pirates lived there."

"Only in the summer," Billy says authoritatively. "In the winter, it's too cold, so the yeti lives there."

I take a knee so I'm face-to-face with him. "You know, buddy, you can't go there again on your own."

He swallows, and the serious expression on his face tells me he understands. "I know. And I won't ..."

I breathe a sigh of relief.

"Maybe, in the summer, we could go on an expedition to the cave with Grandpa?"

"Only if we find a different route across the gorge, okay?"

"Is that a yes?"

"If I'm back in Hideaway, then it's definitely a yes."

Billy fist pumps, then grabs my hand again. "Let's go get cookies. And if Mom doesn't let you have two, you just need to say you feel weak or something." He shrugs. "That's what's working for me."

I shake my head as I smile. Being around Billy reminds me of Ethan and me growing up.

"Come on!" he shouts, and I follow him back downstairs.

"Mom! Did the reporter call yet?" Billy demands as soon as we're in the room.

"Well, it's not that easy to get in touch—"

"And Brody wants cookies," he interrupts. "He's feeling weak."

Judy's eyes move to me in confusion. "Oh, well, in that case—"

"Very weak," Billy continues, then makes the mistake of winking at me.

Piper snorts with laughter, and Judy's expression turns from one of alarm to understanding.

"Okay, Billy," she says. "If that's the case, then maybe he needs to try the Christmas ones."

"Yesss!" Billy fist pumps again, then runs full tilt toward the kitchen, Lucky following.

"I'm sure the reporter would love to interview Billy," Judy says to Piper and me under her breath, "but she won't be very happy when he insists he saw everything from Bigfoot to a polar bear."

She looks over her shoulder to make sure Billy's still out of the room, then continues. "He just won't let it go."

"What if Piper films me interviewing him?" I suggest. "I could then send you the footage for him to watch."

"Would you mind? That's very generous of you."

"Not at all. It'll be the best interview I've ever been involved with."

She smiles warmly. "It can't be easy being in the public eye."

"It's not, but it's not all bad."

Billy comes running back into the room, a plate held in both hands, piled high with cookies.

"Hey, buddy, I've had an idea," I say to him. "I think that

reporter might be a bit too busy to pop by, so why don't *I* interview you?"

His eyes light up. "Will it be online? For everyone to see?"

"Er …"

"*Could you do that?*" Judy mouths.

"Well, I could edit a little film and put it on my social accounts, if your mom agrees."

Billy swivels on the spot, not noticing a cookie flying off the plate, to be caught mid-air by Lucky. "Mom? Please?"

"We'll see."

"Yesss!"

He hands the plate of cookies to her, now no longer important, and launches himself onto the couch, patting the space next to him.

I hand Piper my phone, and Judy pulls up a chair opposite us for Piper to sit on.

Lucky leaps onto the couch next to Billy, and they both sit up straighter.

"Okay," Piper says. "I'm filming."

I gaze down the lens, raising my hand as if holding a microphone.

"I'm here today to interview two best friends about their epic adventure yesterday in the mountains of Hideaway Harbor: Billy and Lucky."

I swing my invisible microphone toward Billy. "So, what can you tell us about how this all started?"

Lucky barks and Billy puts both of his hands over his mouth as he giggles.

"What was that, Lucky?" I continue. "Did you see the tracks of an unidentified animal?"

"It was a yeti," Billy says, and Lucky barks in agreement.

"So, what was your plan? What happened next?"

Billy continues his tale, prompted by me. His sentences are surprisingly short and succinct. He's either a naturally gifted orator, or he's been practicing telling this tale ever since it happened.

"Wow," I say as he finishes the part of the story about us running from a pack of wolves to safety. "Is there anything else you want to add?"

He nods, his voice turning serious. "Lucky and I want to thank you and Piper for saving our lives."

The tale he's just spun is more fiction than fact, but he knows that the last line is true.

I don't know how to respond, so I clear my throat, buying myself a moment.

"Well, thank you, Billy and Lucky, for sharing your tale," I begin, making sure my voice doesn't wobble. "This is Brody King for Hideaway News Today."

Piper hands me the phone, blinking rapidly, as if she's also struggling to hold back her emotions.

"Lemme see!" Billy says, having moved on from the moment quicker than the rest of us.

I play it back and he watches in rapt silence.

"You know, I don't think that's going to need any editing," I say when it finishes, then turn to Judy. "Are you happy for me to post it, or would you like me to make any changes?"

She wipes her eyes. "You can post it."

"Thank you, Mommy!" Billy cries, leaping off the couch to hug her.

"I just need to make a call first," I say, suddenly mortified that I don't even have access to my own social accounts. I pull an apologetic face. "My agent thinks it's best if he controls my access to the internet."

"You and me both," Billy says, shaking his head.

"Am I your agent now, too?" Judy asks.

Billy nods, a cheeky look in his eye. "And my servant …"

As they laugh, I slip into the hall and call Cara. She's waiting to board a plane but gives me the new password so I can post the video of Billy and me. Then I rejoin everyone in the family room, and we eat spiced Christmas cookies as it uploads.

When it's online, Billy insists on watching it again on my phone. Afterwards, we say our goodbyes.

Billy hugs Piper, then gives me a baby bear hug. "Don't forget our expedition. Promise?"

"If I'm in Hideaway next summer, your grandpa and parents agree, *and* we find a safer route to the cave, then yes, I'll come on an adventure with you."

"Yesss!"

I take Piper's arm as we walk away. It's dark now, and every house we pass is lit up with lights.

"Thank you for doing that with me," I say.

"My pleasure. I'm so glad we saw him. It helps get rid of all those bad memories. And Judy was a grade above Ethan and you, so we had a nice chat while you did your boys' stuff."

I smile. "He's got a telescope in his attic room trained on the mountain cave."

"So you were right."

"Lucky guess."

We continue in silence, and I wonder if Piper's thinking about whether I'll be back in Hideaway next summer or not.

Outside her parents' house, we stop.

"You sure you're okay with me going to Ethan's for the evening?" I ask.

"Absolutely. You both need this. Him, probably more than you. I'm going to have a chill evening with Mom, Mia, and Harper, then—"

"Chill?"

She laughs. "It won't be a late one. I'll be keeping the bed warm for you."

I lean down and capture her lips with mine. My cock immediately stirs, wanting more.

For a few moments, Piper softens, opening to me, her tongue darting into my mouth and making me groan.

Then she pulls back and moves to the front door. "I'll be waiting …"

I repress a growl of frustration, then touch my fingers to my lips and extend my arm as if blowing her a kiss.

The words "I love you" are waiting in my throat, but Erica opens the door for her daughter, and Piper's gone.

I head back down the snowy sidewalk. I've never been to Ethan's house before, but Piper showed me where it is—only a couple of blocks away.

With each step forward, memories of the past bear down on me. With Piper, I feel lighter than air but now, on my way to see Ethan, the ghosts of Olivia and all my regrets feel like weights around my ankles.

Walking up the path from the street, I note the subdued Christmas decorations on Ethan's house—there, but not chaotic or oversized, and the perfectly maintained family home.

It's only when my hand is on the door knocker that I realize I've come empty-handed. What a fucking shitty friend I am, not even bringing him a beer?

The door opens and the first thing I see are Ethan's dark eyes, then my heart stops as I notice what's over his shoulder.

A six-foot-tall, four-foot-wide photo hangs facing the entrance. It's of Olivia, and she's looking directly at me.

"Uncle Brody!"

I force my eyes down to mini-Olivia, vibrating with excitement at my arrival.

"I …" I pause, dragging my gaze back up to Ethan's face. "I didn't bring anything."

"Didn't need to. Come on in."

I stumble into the hall. There's a rack for shoes and coats, and two doors leading further into the house, but I can't stop staring at the photo of Olivia.

It's not how I remember her. She was always laughing, full of life, but in this photo she's too composed, almost distant. Sure, she's smiling, but she looks like an ice queen silently judging anyone who passes by.

I already don't feel worthy.

"Don't be scared of Mommy," Martha says in a matter-of-fact voice. "She's just making sure we keep the hall tidy."

I take off my boots and line them up on the mat, then Ethan takes my coat and hangs it up, brushing his hand down the sleeves to make sure they're hanging straight.

He leads me into the family room. It's immaculate. Martha's coloring books and pens are on a low table. The pens are stored nib-down in a pot, and the books are stacked neatly in a pile. Toys are in a woven basket to one side. There's a modest Christmas tree, but it looks like it was trimmed by an anally retentive elf. Photos of Olivia are everywhere. You can't turn without seeing her face.

It's been four years since her death, and it's clear Ethan has no intention of moving on.

"We're having pizza!" Martha exclaims. "Now come see my bedroom!"

Without waiting for a reply, she takes my hand and pulls me out of the room, leading me up a flight of stairs, Olivia watching my every step.

"It's okay," Martha says gently.

But I don't feel okay. If I feel overwhelmed by guilt after less than five minutes here, how must Ethan feel living in this house every day? Is this his way of punishing himself for not saving her from sepsis?

Martha stops outside a door with her name on it in bright wooden letters. "Yesterday, Papa told Nana our house is a ..."

She wrinkles her button nose, thinking hard. Then she beams: "A shine!"

"A shine?"

She nods.

"Did they maybe say a *shrine*?"

Her eyes light up. "Yes, that."

She pauses, frowning again. "Uncle Brody, is that a cuss word?"

"Why do you ask?"

"I don't think I was meant to hear it."

I crouch down. "It's not a cuss word, sweetie, but ..."

Damn. How do I explain something this complicated to a five-year-old?

Martha waits patiently, her big blue eyes locked on mine.

"Your Nana and Papa, they're your mommy's parents, right?"

"Yes. They look after me with Grandma and Grandpa when Daddy has to work."

So even Olivia's folks think Ethan's taken the self-flagellation too far.

"You know how churches have a special place where people light candles?"

She nods.

"That's a shrine."

"But my mommy isn't Jesus."

"I know, sweetie, but your daddy doesn't want to forget her."

"How can he when she's always here?" She points at her heart.

My hand rubs the center of my chest, trying to soothe the ache there. It's not just for Olivia, but for the pain Ethan endures every day.

"That's true. But this is just what your daddy needs right now."

She presses her lips together, clearly unhappy, then nods. "Okay. Come see my room now."

I follow her into a space that, thank god, is untidy, and she shows me all her favorite toys.

After about fifteen minutes, Ethan calls us down. We sit on cushions on the family room floor, eating pizza from large white plates. This is clearly a rare treat for Martha, who can't contain her excitement.

When we've eaten, I help Ethan clear up, and he puts Martha to bed.

Downstairs, I shift on the L-shaped sectional, trying to avoid facing Olivia, as my stomach ties itself into a tighter and tighter knot. Not for the first time, I wish I had alcohol to take the edge off my tension.

But I can't go there, so I sip my water and let my knee jiggle up and down as I wait for the sound of Ethan's feet coming down the stairs.

"So, apparently you hate Hideaway," he says, putting on the game but keeping the volume low so we can talk.

What the fuck?

My head snaps toward him, but he keeps his eyes on the screen.

"No, I do not hate Hideaway," I reply sharply, "and I never have. Marisa's hurt that I've moved on and is lashing out. And I never cheated on her. She was the unfaithful one."

Ethan nods. "I ... I always knew you were in love with Piper," he admits quietly.

Huh? "How?"

The corner of his mouth lifts. "Because you weren't that good an actor back then."

I rub a hand over my jaw, stunned. "I thought I hid it from you."

"I'm observant. And when you thought I wasn't aware, you looked at her the way I looked at Olivia."

Well, shit.

"Olivia argued with me about you that summer. She couldn't understand why I wouldn't let you near Piper."

I will my hands to relax.

"Why didn't you? Why wasn't I good enough?"

Ethan's head finally turns to me, his expression filled with bleak regret.

"It wasn't you. It was never about you. I saw kids who didn't graduate because they'd gotten pregnant or caught up in some stupid drama, and I didn't want that for Piper."

He sighs. "I know what I can be like. Rigid. In control. I didn't understand myself enough back then. I just wanted Piper to be happy. And when you left, I believed it justified the decision I made, that I'd done the right thing."

I can't speak. Even after all this time apart, he's still my best friend, but that doesn't mean I can easily forgive him.

"And I knew you had to leave. Even before your mom passed, I knew you had to prove something to yourself, and you wouldn't have found that by staying in Hideaway Harbor."

"Maybe. But maybe not," I reply bitterly. "I would have had a different life if I'd been with Piper, and I believe it would have been happier."

There's a weighty silence between us, interrupted only by the game commentary.

"And that's why what Piper said to me yesterday was right. I *was* wrong. And I'm sorry."

His gaze moves around the room, lingering on the pictures of Olivia. "You've got your second chance now. Don't waste a second of it."

"I won't." I take a breath. "You're the same age as me. What about *your* second chance?"

He shakes his head with a sad finality. "No one could ever replace Olivia, and I wouldn't want anyone to."

"They're not replacing her. You think your folks loved you

any less when Piper came along? Hudson? Harper? There's room in your heart to fall in love again."

"No, there isn't. I've got room for Martha and my family, and that's it."

"Even in Hideaway Harbor? The town founded on true love?"

He huffs. "I had my one true love. There isn't going to be a number two."

But what if Martha wants a mom who can talk back, not just gaze at her from a photo frame?

I don't ask the question. I may not agree with Ethan's decision for himself, but if there's one thing I know about him, once he's made up his mind, it doesn't often change.

"I love Piper," I say, just to make sure he knows. "I always have, and I always will."

Taking my wallet from my back pocket, I open it and show him the photo I've had in there for the past twelve years. The one taken by Mia at our graduation party, the same one on his parents' wall.

"You think I'd be carrying this around with me if I didn't care about her, or you?"

Ethan's hand reaches out, and he touches Olivia's face. I don't even know if he's aware he's done it.

Then he withdraws and takes a drink. "But what about your job? Constantly flying all over the world? The shit Piper's going to get from the press."

And he doesn't even know my next job might be in New Zealand ...

"We'll make it work. I'm not losing her again."

We watch the game in silence till the next ad break, then Ethan clears his throat.

"I also need to apologize for what I said to you about your job. It was an ignorant dick move. I spoke to Walter earlier about how you found Billy. You could only have done it if you knew what to look for."

I nod. "I did a TV show and spent months with a professional tracker and bushcraft expert learning as much as I could. During the filming I then went a bit method and built my own shelter and lived outside."

Ethan's eyebrows raise. "When you could have been in a hotel suite?"

"I did take a bar of soap from the bathroom. I didn't want to stink like an animal around my colleagues."

He smiles. "Do you remember when we built a tree house and claimed we would stay the night in it?"

"Hey, that owl was right on top of us and hungry."

"Don't forget we were convinced the coyotes had learned to climb."

"I stand by that. They're wily."

Ethan lets out a small laugh, and I remember that was his natural state when we were growing up. He was always upbeat and happy.

"What else have you learned for a role?"

I puff out my cheeks as I think. "Tons. I'm proficient in sword fighting, both rapier and broadsword, archery, horseback riding, precision driving, and rock climbing. I'm also a black belt in Brazilian Jiu-Jitsu, a G5 level in Krav Maga, and have a smattering of Muay Thai and Karate knowledge. It's enough to qualify me for stunt jobs, but I'm too attached to my face to do that kind of work."

Ethan lets out a whistle. "That's a lot. Tens of thousands of hours of work."

"I suppose so."

"No wonder you could find Billy and have the strength to carry him and his dog back."

I don't reply, suddenly seeing myself as if I were Ethan, someone who understands just how much hard work I've put in, and what skills I've acquired over the years.

I shouldn't look down on my career as somehow lesser. I'm not just a pretty face who's good at pretending to be other people, I've gained and retained knowledge across a vast range of subjects. And that's not due to some contractual obligation, but down to my interest and dedication.

"I volunteer for the local search and rescue service," Ethan says, not noticing I'm having a moment of deep self-realization. "You should come to the next meet-up if you're around. You could teach a few old dogs some new tricks."

"I'd like that, although I expect it would be the other way around."

"Not at all. Don't sell yourself short. You'll have so much value to share with the team."

I take a sip of water to buy myself a moment.

"I'll never be able to forgive myself for not being at your wedding, Martha's birth, and Olivia's funeral," I begin quietly.

Ethan gives me a small nod, his jaw set.

"I left Hideaway to make something of myself. Prove I wasn't like either of my parents. And after Mom died, I didn't want to be around anything that reminded me of her. And I was also terrified each job would be my last. That I couldn't ask for time off, or call in sick. I nearly got peritonitis on a job because I wouldn't see the medic until we wrapped."

"Jesus, Brody!"

I raise my hands. "I know. It was fucking stupid. When I woke up from the op, the surgeon said my appendix was about an hour away from bursting."

Ethan shakes his head, his gaze passing over the photos of Olivia on the wall.

"I wanted to become someone who was good enough for Piper, even though I pretended she wasn't who I was thinking about all the time. I'm good at denial," I continue.

"I know we spoke after Olivia passed, but every day after that my guilt grew, until it seemed impossible to ever come back. I didn't have the guts to face you. And I'm sorry. I truly am."

"Me too," Ethan replies. "I missed you. And I never realized I'd made you feel you weren't worthy. Because you are. And I want you to be with Piper. If you can love her for this long then I'll know you'll love her forever."

"I will."

He nods, seeming satisfied, and we settle back to watch the game.

But even as my eyes follow the action on screen, my mind is with Piper, wondering how we can make it work, and counting the minutes until I'm back in her arms.

CHAPTER 24

PIPER

"**H**ey."

Brody's voice startles me, and I glance up to see his head poking around the bedroom door.

I've been so focused on the drawing I was making of him that now, seeing the real thing, my brain short-circuits and words fail me.

"Earth to Piper Locke?"

"Oh, um, sorry!" I gesture at the tablet on my lap. "I was …"

He closes the door behind him. "Can I see?"

Nervous excitement whooshes from my belly to my cheeks. "It's not finished," I hedge, then show it to him.

"Holy shit! That's incredible!"

His genuine delight and astonishment fill me with champagne bubbles of pride. "You like it?"

"I love it. Wow, this is fucking hot."

I've drawn him as a smoldering elf lord, one hand braced on

a stone arch as he leans down to gaze at an elf princess who might, perhaps, look a little like me. His other hand rests on my, I mean, *her* back, the flowing dress bunched up as if he's about to pull it off completely.

"You should post it to your art account."

"Do you think it would help get you the job?"

"No idea, but that's not the point. You should post it for yourself. I mean, look at this. It's awesome."

"I wanted to use my charcoal pencils, but I didn't bring any of my art supplies with me."

Brody looks from the tablet back to me. "You're so talented. You've got a gift. I mean, I'd do elf me and I'm as straight as they come."

I laugh.

"Actually, I'm Pi-sexual," he continues.

"What?"

He places the tablet on the bed, crouches in front of me, and takes my hands. "I'm Piper-sexual. I'm only attracted to you."

"Does that make me 'Bro-sexual'?"

He grins. "Hope so."

We smile at each other, the air seeming to hum with happiness. Then Brody breaks away and digs into one of his bags.

"I know it's early," he says, pulling several wrapped packages from the bottom and handing them to me. "But I do like giving you what you want."

I turn them over in my hands. "You got me Christmas presents. A *lot* of them."

"I didn't know what to get, so I guessed. And Cara helped me."

"But I haven't gotten you anything yet," I say, my stomach tightening. "I didn't know what you would like. I thought I might find something in town."

He takes my hand again, rubbing his thumb over the back.

"You don't need to give me anything. You've already given me the greatest gift of my life. You."

His gaze is so sincere, so pure, so full of love, I blink as my eyes prick with emotion.

"Now go on, open up."

I rip the paper, squealing when I reveal pencils, pens, a watercolor block, brushes, pads, pastels, and artist erasers. "Brody! These brands are the best!"

His smile lights up his face. "They're okay then?"

"Yes! They're amazing!" I give him a pointed look. "Did you go into the shop and ask for a selection of the most expensive things they sell?"

Spots of color appear on his cheekbones. "I asked for their advice."

I stroke the boxes and tins. "Well, they steered you right. I can't wait to use them. Thank you."

My brain buzzes. I'm like a child on Christmas morning, given everything I asked for and more. I'm torn between ripping Brody's clothes off or tearing the cellophane off the art supplies on my lap.

"Do you want to draw a picture now?" he asks. "Maybe I could model for you?"

"Would you? Really?"

"Of course. I'd do anything for you." He shrugs, like it's no big deal.

"Eek! Okay, I've had this idea …" I leap out of the chair, sit him down, then pull the sheepskin rug over and place it under his feet.

"I want to draw you as the Emberking of Draventhorne on his throne. It's at the coronation after the Battle of Ashmyre, and he's at the peak of his powers."

Pulling open my closet doors, I find a blanket on the top shelf and drape it over Brody's shoulders, arranging the fabric so it billows to the ground like a cloak.

"You can talk, to begin with," I continue. "Just try to stay still."

At the back of my closet is my old field hockey stick. I pass it to him. "Hold that in your left hand like it's a sword. And ..."

I pull a tub of moisturizer from my wash bag. "Hold this in your other hand like it's the orb of Veyruyne."

"How did you draw all the other pictures when you didn't have a model?"

"I had to use my imagination, so it took much longer. This will be a breeze by comparison."

I can't hide my excitement as I settle on the corner of the bed and rip the plastic wrap off a large pad of cardstock.

"Why did you choose that one?"

"It's got a very fine grain, and even though I'm going to be drawing partly in charcoal, which is a bit messy, I want the edges of the lines to be relatively clean. You'll see what I mean when I'm done."

"So. I'm in the right pose now?"

"Yep, perfect. I'm going to sketch very lightly first."

I select a soft pencil, my gaze flicking between Brody and the pad. Having him here, actually in front of me, is a gift: the difference between climbing a mountain in flip-flops and whizzing up in a cable car.

My hand moves quickly over the paper, outlining the pose.

"How did it go with Ethan?" I ask, picking up a charcoal pencil.

Brody lets out a long breath. "I didn't realize quite how bad he was."

"I'm so sorry. We're used to it. I should have warned you."

"I nearly had a heart attack when he opened the front door."

I pull a face. "That photo is ... I don't know. Not how we remember Olivia."

"No. It's so severe. Like she's watching and judging."

My hand slows. "We call the house the 'shrine.'"

"Martha told me she overheard Eleanor and Garrett calling it that too."

"Fuck." I meet his gaze. "They want Ethan to stop punishing himself more than anyone. It wasn't his fault Olivia died."

"I can't see him changing his mind about that. He's so ... so black and white about it all."

"It'll take a miracle to get him out of it."

"Or a miracle woman?"

I smile. "Hideaway Harbor's the home of miracles and true love, so let's cross our fingers."

"We could go to the spring and make a wish on his behalf?"

"I'd like that."

My hand returns to drawing, adding detail. I've never created a picture this fast, but having Brody model for me makes it easy. I sketch a faded background of Khalduïn Hall's throne room behind him, keeping the contrast low so it doesn't compete with the central figure.

I leave his face until last so we can talk. It's so easy, chatting with him, like two parts of a puzzle that always fit together, no matter what.

"I'm going to draw the details of your face now," I say. "So, if you could keep still, that would be great."

"What kind of expression do you want?"

"You've just been victorious at the Battle of Ashmyre and know that no one dares oppose you. I want you to look at me like you know the power you have over me."

He raises an eyebrow, and my whole face flushes.

"Your wish is my command," he replies in a British accent, and my pencil immediately slips out of my hand onto the bed.

"Holy shit," I mutter under my breath as I pick it back up and force myself to concentrate on the drawing.

But when I glance up from the paper to his face, the look in his eyes makes my fingers shake. His expression is so intense, so hot, I feel like I might combust on the spot.

"Is this working for you?" Brody continues in a British accent.

"Oh my god, yes!" I exhale heavily, fanning my face. "But if you keep that up, I won't be able to finish the drawing."

"If you're experiencing a discomforting rise in body temperature," he says, sounding like the Earl of Fuck-Me-Now Abbey, "then perhaps you should disrobe."

I tug my sweater off and toss it to the bed.

Fire flashes in Brody's eyes. "Good girl."

His words hit my clit like a spark.

"Look," I say, my voice trembling, "just give me five minutes to finish this before you reduce me to a puddle."

He nods, still eye-fucking me, and I look down, blinking at the drawing as I try to focus.

Brody stays silent, and I manage to stay detached enough to finish the picture. It's the best one I've ever done. It has a vitality and energy none of the others possess. Maybe only I can tell what makes this picture so good, but it doesn't matter. All I know is I've never been this excited about my art before. Now, with the best model in the world, anything is possible.

I clear the bed, then pass the drawing to Brody so he can see it.

His eyes widen as he takes it in. "Fucking hell, Piper. This is … wow."

"Don't touch it. I need to spray it with fixative first."

"I didn't get you any."

"We can get some in town tomorrow. I'm just going to wash my hands."

I slip into the corridor before he can grab me and head to the bathroom to clean up.

Staring at my lust-drunk features in the mirror, all I can think about is Brody's thick cock driving deep inside me. My hands tremble as I dry them on a towel. Taking a steadying breath, I walk calmly back to the bedroom.

The main lights are off, the room illuminated by three candles on the dresser and the colored lights from the neighboring houses that dance across the far wall. Brody is still seated in the chair, but the blanket, hockey stick, and tub of cream are gone. His legs are spread, his hands resting on his muscular thighs.

My pulse pounds through my body, from my throat to my pussy. I want him so much.

"My lady," Brody begins in a cultured rumble, "you're late."

His voice has always done something to my insides, but in a British accent? Hoo-ee, I'm done for.

I swallow. "I apologize, my lord. What would you have me do?"

His gaze roams over me possessively, as if he owns every inch of me and I exist solely to satisfy his needs.

"Disrobe," he says. "Slowly."

My fingertips feel like fire as I undo the tiny buttons down the front of my top. My breath quickens as I glance at Brody's hands, the tendons flexing as if it takes all his willpower to keep them still.

When Brody was out with Ethan earlier, I showered and changed into a lingerie set I'd packed in Brooklyn during a rare moment of wild optimism. Judging by the way Brody's eyes bulge when I reveal my bra, he approves.

"I've changed my mind," he growls. "Remove your pants now. Do not keep me waiting."

I open the top button, pull down the zipper, and sit on the edge of the bed to slide them off.

"Come here," Brody commands, and I step closer until I'm standing between his legs.

He slowly runs a finger up the inside of my thigh, then cups my pussy through the lace of my panties.

"Mine," he states.

I nearly come undone right there as the heat of his palm

EVIE ALEXANDER

radiates through my core. My hips twitch, desperate to buck into his hand, chasing the friction my clit craves.

"Who does this pussy belong to, my lady?"

"You," I whisper.

His middle finger strokes over the gusset. "Are you this wet for me?"

I give him a shaky nod.

His finger continues stroking me in slow, steady circles, never quite where I need him most. "Do you want me to ascertain just how wet you are, my lady?"

"Please."

"Please, what?"

"My lord."

"Good girl."

I hold my breath as his finger hooks under the seam of my panties, and shudder when it pushes into my tight heat. The heel of his hand bumps against my clit, and I rub against it. I'm tingling from the depths of me to the edges of my skin.

Brody's still fully clothed, but I stand before him in my lace bra and panties, and the contrast is intensely erotic. The only physical connection between us is his finger slowly fucking my pussy, yet I feel him everywhere.

He lifts his chin in the direction of my bra. "Off."

I fumble with the clasp, then let it fall. My breasts ache, the tips desperate for his touch.

But instead, he slowly pulls his finger from me and holds it up. "Suck."

I take him into my mouth and swirl my tongue around his finger, tasting the sweet tang of myself on his skin.

"See how good you taste?"

He pulls his finger out, spins me around, and cups my ass, tugging me back until I feel his breath through the lace and his teeth nip at my skin.

Need floods me, slick and heavy, my juices soaking through my panties.

He drags them down and I step free. I can't see Brody, but I feel him behind me, his mouth trailing kisses across my ass, his hands guiding my ankles farther apart. The air hits my pussy, cool and teasing, then his fingers are back. One eases inside me while the other circles my clit, slow and sure.

I cry out, tensing around him. I'm a hair-trigger away from release. But just as I reach the point of no return, he pulls away and spins me around to face him again.

His dark eyes glitter, and his breath is heavy. "I haven't decided how I want you to come yet." He inclines his head toward his lap. "Sit."

I do. Brody spreads his legs, forcing mine wider. I'm completely naked, open to him, his gaze scorching across my skin like a flame.

He loops my hands around his neck. "You are not to move, my lady. Do you understand?"

I nod, trembling, wishing I had one of his muscled thighs between mine instead of just aching, empty air.

"You will come when I say so."

I shiver with anticipation.

"My lady?"

"Yes," I stammer.

He raises an eyebrow.

"My lord."

"Good girl," he growls, then reaches for my breasts, cupping their weight. "Mine."

I gasp, arching my chest into his touch.

His thumbs graze across my nipples, and I shudder.

"Mine," he repeats, increasing the friction.

Darts of sensation shoot down to my clit. The pleasure inside me is like a fever that needs to break. I'm burning for him, desperate to climax.

One hand stays on my breast, rolling and tugging my nipple, while the other cups my pussy again.

"Mine," he states, then thrusts his middle finger deep inside me.

"Oh, my god!" I cry out, the orgasm hovering just out of reach, so close I'm already trembling with anticipation.

"Mine," Brody growls, then sucks hard on my neck.

"Jes—fuck!"

I can't breathe. I can't keep pace with the sensations shooting around my body.

Brody falls on me, kissing and biting with feral snarls of ownership. His control is gone, and I am so fucking here for it.

Pushing another finger inside my pussy, he thrusts as the pad of his thumb circles my throbbing clit. Then he draws one nipple into his mouth while his other hand twists the other one.

I'm holding on to the back of his neck for dear life, my climax rushing toward me like a tornado I can't escape.

"Come, Piper," Brody commands, then lightly bites the tip of my nipple.

I shatter around him with a scream, jerking as the orgasm breaks me apart. I feel it everywhere, from deep in my pelvis to the crown of my head. Every part of me expands outward, then collapses in on itself in endless waves of pleasure.

Just when I think it's subsiding, another release crashes through me, sharp and sweet, battering my body all over again.

I'm struggling to breathe, gulping in air. Brody eases his fingers out of me, then wraps his arms around my back, stroking and soothing as he murmurs words of praise in my ear.

I'm still shaking with the intensity of it, not sure whether I need to laugh or cry.

Brody seems to realize I'm barely holding it together, so he carries me to the bed. He lays me on my side in a fetal position, then spoons me. His large form curves around mine, covering and protecting me as he nuzzles and kisses my neck.

I don't know how long we lie like this; I only know I'm safe, and that I love him. I can taste the words on my tongue, but something inside me keeps them from spilling past my lips.

At this moment, I am his forever and ever. But the thought of his job hangs over us like a shadow, keeping me from telling him how I truly feel.

As I slowly return to my body, there's an aching loneliness inside me, as if Brody's already on the other side of the world. I need him to fill me, to join his body with mine, to make me whole again.

Reaching behind me, I fumble to undo his pants.

"You want my cock, baby girl?" he murmurs.

"Please don't make me beg," I whisper. "I need you inside me."

He kisses the hypersensitive spot below my ear, then shucks off his clothes and curls around me again.

I sigh with relief at the feel of his hot skin, the hair on his legs tickling the backs of mine, and the heavy thickness of his cock pressing against the crease of my ass.

His hands drift over my breasts, my stomach, my pussy. His touch is still gentle, still soothing, but it stirs something deep, reigniting the flames until every cell in me burns with need.

I lift my top leg and arch my lower back, undulating against the solid heat of his cock.

Brody's breath hitches. He grips my thigh, adjusting me with care until I'm open and ready for him.

The thick head of his cock nudges at my entrance, and I exhale, forcing myself to relax, to let him in.

"That's it, sweetheart. You can take my cock. Yeah, just like that."

Letting go of my leg, his fingers move to my clit. The pleasure is immediate, and I pant.

He pushes in another inch and draws a tight breath. "Good girl," he murmurs. "Feel me inside you, baby. Feel how well your pussy takes my cock."

The stretch is stinging and delicious, sending prickles of light shooting out from my core. Brody's fingers keep circling my clit. His other arm snakes beneath me, his hand closing over my breast, teasing my nipple.

I cry out at the pleasure and bear down, wanting every inch of him inside me.

"God, Piper. You're so fucking hot. So fucking tight."

He's still not all the way in, but I squeeze around him, another orgasm rising like a tide.

"Fuck, baby, you're killing me," he growls.

Clinging to his forearms, I soak in his strength, the hardness of him everywhere. I melt in his arms, soft and fluid, my body molding to his as if I were made to fit there.

His hips jerk, and his cock fills me further.

"Yes!"

"That's it. Let me in, Piper." His words are low and raspy. "Let me fuck you. Let me fill you up."

My eyelids flutter closed as I drown in his voice, in the heat between my legs, the ache in my nipples, and the throbbing pulse of my clit.

I push down onto him, taking everything he has to give, feeling the coarse hair at the base of his cock as he fills me completely.

"Fuck ..." We breathe together, our bodies locked in pleasure.

Brody hasn't stopped playing with my nipple and clit, and my release is almost here. He doesn't even need to move his cock, just the feeling of being impaled on it is enough to take me to the edge.

He exhales, his breath hot against the back of my neck. "You gonna come for me, baby? You gonna come on my cock?"

I nod, my breaths coming faster. I don't have to search for my release or fight for it. Brody's taking me there. All I have to do is surrender.

His hips shift, nudging his shaft a few millimeters deeper, and electric shocks shoot along every nerve.

"Oh, my god!"

"Good girl," Brody murmurs, his own breath as unsteady as mine. "Look how well you take me." He thrusts again. "Feel my cock filling your sweet pussy."

My fingernails dig into his arms as I squeeze harder around him.

"That's it," he says, his hips jerking forward. "Feel me fucking you, Piper. Feel me fucking you deep."

And with my name on his lips, I'm gone. I thrash on the bed as he holds me tight, the release barreling through me, knocking the breath from my lungs. My core is the epicenter of the explosion, blinding light and pleasure radiating from where he fills and stretches me. Stars flash in my vision as the boundaries of my skin disappear, lost under the waves of sensation crashing through me, out into the universe.

Still buried inside me, Brody rises and guides my leg around him, shifting until he's on top, face to face.

I hook my legs behind his, anchoring him to me, then tangle my fingers in his hair and drag his mouth to mine. The kiss is hot and messy. His tongue is all fire, and I can't get enough.

He withdraws an inch, then jerks his hips forward.

I tear my mouth from his with a cry. "Keep going. Don't stop."

His cock shunts forward again, and sparks burst behind my eyes and inside my pussy.

"Yes, more."

He drops his weight onto his forearms and thrusts hard into me. Again, and again.

I'm delirious with desire, my words slipping into an incoherent babble of, "Yes, yes, more."

Nothing compares to the feel of him inside me. He burns any comparison, any past memory, to dust. All my body knows and wants is him.

Then he shifts onto his knees, pulling me with him, and my eyes open to take in the sight.

In the candlelight, every ridge of muscle is starkly defined. His body is a blend of burnished gold and smoky darkness, his eyes hooded but still burning as they devour me. My gaze drifts down his abs, over the cut V at his hips, to where his cock pounds into me.

"You're so fucking hot. Look how well you take me. Every inch inside your tight pussy."

We breathe together as he thrusts hard and fast into me. Another climax builds in my core, and each time his cock drives forward, it stokes the fire that's going to take me there.

Bringing his fingers to his mouth, Brody spits on them, then rubs the slickness over my clit. It's so filthy, and I love it.

"Touch your tits," he says, his jaw clenched and his neck tight.

Holding his gaze, I lick the tips of my fingers and brush them over the hard buds of my nipples. Pleasure arcs down to my clit, lighting the fuse of my orgasm. I suck in one last desperate breath, then it crashes through me.

"Fuck!" Brody growls as he pistons his hips.

I cry his name as I'm broken apart with pleasure, forcing my eyes to stay open so I can watch him shatter with me.

"Piper!" he roars as his hips jerk, his cock pulsing as he fills me with his cum.

The sight is so raw, it amplifies every sensation. He's so strong, yet so vulnerable in this moment, and my heart overflows with love for him.

He collapses forward onto me, his breath heaving as he alternates between saying "fuck" and my name.

I hold him tightly to me, a smile splitting my face even as tears sting my eyes.

I love you. I love you. I love you.

I don't know what the future holds, but I pray that we can find a way for this to work, for what we have now to remain unbreakable, no matter what happens.

CHAPTER 25

PIPER

"*H*ave you heard a word of what I just said?"

My mother's hands are on her hips as she stands in the middle of the kitchen.

Cramming another cookie into my mouth, I nod, even though I have no idea what she's just been talking about. I tuned out the moment Brody put his hand on my thigh under the breakfast bar. With the sweetness of a homemade cinnamon cookie crumbling on my tongue, and my super-hot, fake-now-real boyfriend's palm on my jeans, I was gone. Lost in memories from last night, with the warmth of arousal once more flooding my body.

My mom's stance is stern, but her gaze is soft as she looks at us. Touching her heart, she lets out a happy sigh. "My baby's in love."

The heat that had been making my panties wet now rushes to my cheeks. I swallow the bite, then wash it down with a mouthful of cinnamon latte when the cookie sticks in my throat. Yes, I know *I* love Brody, but I need him to say those three words before I have the confidence to. It's still all so new, and I keep having to pinch myself that we're actually together.

"You were talking about Eileen," I say, even though that's the only word I can remember her saying.

"Only at the beginning."

Mom lets out the kind of over-the-top sigh that Martha loves to copy, then starts up again.

"So we have to go to Hard to Find this morning for the calendar reveal, because no one else is going to be there."

"Why not?"

"Because the owner, Fredrik, hasn't advertised it and doesn't want anyone showing up. His sister, Felicity, from our crochet club, put his name forward to try and force him, I don't know, out of his shell a bit? You know, after his personal tragedy."

I raise my eyebrows in question. My mom knows everyone in Hideaway Harbor and always assumes I do, too.

She moves forward, lowering her voice as if we're in a public space and might be overheard.

"His wife died two years ago," she whispers. "But we're not allowed to talk about it, so pretend you don't know."

"Even though everyone *does* know? It's not like he's Hideaway's only villain and buried her body in the backyard."

Mom straightens and crosses herself as Brody chuckles beside me. "Oh my Lord, no. He's the sweetest man. Just a little … withdrawn. And we've also got to support Noelle. She's the one we're pinning our hopes on."

I'm lost already. "Who's Noelle?"

"I told you about her, honey. New in town and running the Christmas pop-up shop next to Frederik's bookstore. She's the sweetest thing and seems to have a connection with him, so we need to, you know, help them along."

"By going to the calendar reveal this morning?"

"Yes! Noelle spent the night making pulla in Fredrik's range after Ida had to leave town because her daughter gave birth early."

I resist the urge to rub my forehead as my brain tries to make sense of it all. "And what does any of that have to do with the—"

"It's Pulla Appreciation Day today!" she tells me, like I ought to have known. "And Ida was in charge because she's Finnish." Mom turns to Brody. "Pulla's a sweet bread with cardamom from Finland, topped with pearl sugar."

He nods slowly. "I think I had it once. It's delicious."

"But Ida had to leave to be with her daughter, and Noelle offered to step in because her grandmother's Finnish and has a family recipe. She's using the old range in Fredrik's house to make it, then giving it away outside Hard to Find this morning to try and tempt people inside. Felicity's bringing the trestle tables in her van."

"Okay. Let me get this straight," I say slowly. "You need us to show up at the bookstore because you don't think anyone's going to come to the calendar reveal or eat any of the pulla that Noelle spent all night baking, and because you're trying to set up Noelle and Fredrik?"

Mom claps her hands like I've just won a spelling bee. "Yes."

"You had me at 'pulla,'" Brody says, then squeezes my thigh. "What do you feel like doing?"

Er, *you?* I hide my face behind the coffee mug as my cheeks flush again. "Sounds great," I mumble.

"Wonderful!" Mom says happily, then takes the landline phone from the wall. "I'll let Eileen and the other girls know I've got you two on board."

"Where's Harper?" I ask.

"With Lola," Mom replies as she taps on the screen. "There's a unit opening up next door in the new year, so they've gone to look at it."

Her eyes move from the phone to us. "What was in the gift bag Lola gave you?"

"I haven't opened it yet," I mutter into my drink as Brody's fingers move to the inside of my thigh, stroking upward.

Mom's face falls. "Well, that's a missed opportunity for bringing a bit of extra excitement to snuggle time."

"Mom!" I splutter, as Brody's hand moves higher.

She shrugs like a teenager. "Just saying."

Brody's middle finger presses at the seam of my jeans, and I leap off the stool.

"Wow!" I squeak. "Look at the time! Maybe we should get going?"

"You ARE SO BAD," I mutter under my breath to Brody as we make our way toward the town center.

Mom's walking ahead, chatting away on her phone with Eileen, although most of the conversation seems to be her loudly asking, "Can you hear me now?"—thanks to Hideaway's patchy signal.

"You make me want to be bad," he murmurs.

I tug my scarf away from my throat as a hot flash arrives twenty years too early.

"It's the last week of the Christmas market," I say, trying to steer the conversation back to neutral ground before I drag him back to bed. "I want to look for a present for you."

"I don't need anything."

"Please?"

He smiles at me, and butterflies take off in my stomach. "We'll see."

"Good."

"Oh, my gosh!" Mom exclaims as she pockets her phone. "Eileen heard from Felicity, who heard it from Summer Whittaker, that Marv was three sheets to the wind last night. Had to be carried back to the Hideaway Hotel."

"What?" Brody asks.

"Summer works shifts at The Shore Thing, and apparently Marv came in after nine, already a little tipsy. He kept drinking, and then couldn't walk! Have you heard from him today?"

Brody shakes his head. "I haven't turned on my phone yet."

"Has he messaged you, honey?" Mom asks me.

"My phone's been off, too."

Mom presses her lips together and frowns. "Should you get in touch?"

"He's probably still asleep," Brody replies. "I'll call him after the calendar reveal."

"Okay, but it does make me worry. That doesn't seem like the kind of thing he would do."

I look to Brody for confirmation.

He rubs his free hand over his jaw. "It's not. I'm sure he's fine, but we'll check up on him when he's slept it off."

Mom taps on her phone. "I'm sending him a message telling him where we're going to be, in case he sees it."

When Mom's done, we continue down Hideaway Avenue toward Hard to Find as a bitter wind whips the bottoms of our coats. I glance up at the darkening sky, and a pellet of ice hits my eye.

"Ow!"

"You okay?" Brody asks immediately, his voice laced with the same concern Ethan might show if Martha cried out.

"Yes, fine," I reply, blinking the pain away. "But I think it's about to ha—"

"Quick!" Mom cries, as hailstones lash down like God's unloading a dump truck full of gravel on us.

We run forward, dodging patches of ice on the sidewalk toward the store, where people are rushing two folding tables inside along with baskets of pulla bread.

Inside the bookstore, it's carnage. Mom said no one would show, but the place is packed, and there's no room to breathe. My favorite bookstore in Brooklyn is light and airy, with attractive displays of the latest social-media-trending reads. The interior of Hard to Find looks like it belongs to a book hoarder from a Charles Dickens novel, with haphazard piles of books, dark wood shelves filled with leather-bound classics, and small, awkward spaces that force strangers to stand uncomfortably close.

Eileen is helping Fredrik, whose face is harried, like he'd rather be anywhere else than in his own business right now. A pretty woman, wearing a peach-colored fluffy jacket over an emerald green dress, who I presume is Noelle, is balancing a stack of baskets that look about to tip.

As a team, we go to her side, taking them from her so she can help Eileen and Fredrik clear space for the tables among the crowd.

"Here, you can carry mine," Mom says, dumping hers into Brody's arms, then shouting to Eileen that she's coming.

We edge back toward a bookshelf as the smell of pulla makes my stomach gurgle with excitement.

Brody grins. "So much for no one turning up."

"It looks like Mom and Eileen told everyone the same story and made them promise to show."

"Fredrik looks thrilled."

I snort with laughter. "Poor guy. He'll either have to leave town or marry Noelle just to get Mom and Eileen off his back."

Despite the chaos inside, people soon spot Brody, and within a couple of minutes, we're hemmed in by a sea of excited female faces.

"Oh, my gosh! *The Almanac* didn't say you would be here!"

"Do you remember me from the Perfect Package?"

"Can I get a selfie?"

Brody smiles, but there's tension in it, and his eyes dart to the entrance.

"I'd love to, but my arms are a bit full right now," he says.

"We'll take them!" a woman replies, and a few seconds later, there's nothing between us and his adoring fans.

A younger woman, maybe in her early-twenties, stares at me, then puts her hand on her heart and gasps. "You're Piper!"

"Er, yes?"

"You're the one who did those pictures of Brody!"

I'm utterly confused. Is she talking about photos I've taken of him?

"Oh my gosh, they're lit! You're like sooo talented!"

"I think they're even better than AI," another woman chimes in. "You should definitely get your own account and post them there."

Icy fingers of panic tighten around my throat. "W-what pictures?"

The first woman takes out her phone. "The ones Brody posted to his socials." She shows me the screen, swiping through image after image. "Of him as the Emberking of Draventhorne and the Warlock of Zhash-Dhrog. They're next-level hot."

My gut is rolling, threatening to bring up my breakfast. I can't believe what I'm seeing. All the pictures that only the two of us even knew existed are now plastered all over his social media.

It's my worst nightmare made real. I never drew these for anyone's eyes but mine, and now the man I trusted with my heart has put them on display for anyone to pick apart.

I can't focus or think straight. My head's too full of fire.

"How could you?" I manage.

Brody's eyes widen. "What?"

I can't breathe fast enough. It's like someone's standing on my chest. "You're the only other person who's ever seen them! How could you betray my trust like that?"

"You think *I* did this?"

"Who else?" I shout. "You're the only person other than me who has copies of them!"

Through the fog of my anger, I'm dimly aware of people around us watching the show.

"I would *never* do that!" Brody runs a hand through his hair. "I don't even have access to—"

"Yes, you do. Cara gave it to you yesterday so you could post the video of you and Billy."

His expression stills, then he shakes his head. "It wasn't me. I promise."

But I'm not listening. Every part of me is howling with rage and anguish. I've never experienced pain like this. And the worst part of all? I'd trusted Brody enough to fall in love, to hope and dream of a future with him.

"Is it because of the job?" I cry. "Did you think it would swing it for you?"

"No! Jesus Christ! I couldn't give a shit about that right now. It's the last thing on my mind."

"Why? Marv said you wanted it more than anything. I thought it was all that mattered to you."

"No! *You're* all that matters to me!"

"Why?"

"Because I love you!" he shouts.

The silence that follows is deafening.

"What?" I whisper.

"I love you," he repeats. "I loved you when we were growing up, and I love you even more now. You're my everything, Piper. I would never do *anything* to hurt you."

"You … you love me?" I ask, my heart tripping over itself while my brain struggles to catch up.

Brody nods, and his eyes are so full of tenderness that mine prickle with tears.

"Every part of me loves every part of you," he says, and the sound of women sighing with happiness ripples through the air.

He cups my face. "It's not the job I want anymore," he murmurs, then brushes a kiss across my lips. "It's you. It's always been you."

My breath catches in my throat, and I swallow. "You love me," I repeat, clearly not as up to speed as everyone else.

Brody nods, then kisses me gently again, like he's sealing a promise.

"Oh." I blink at him, and a tear rolls down my cheek. "But ... then who—"

I jump as the front door to the bookstore is flung open with an almighty crash and a jangling of bells.

Marv staggers in wearing shades, his usually slicked-back hair disheveled and his coat buttoned up like he got dressed in the dark.

"Piper! Brody!" he calls across the crowd to us before lurching forward like a drunk Frankenstein. "I'm so fucking sorry!"

EVEN NOW, at twenty-eight, when things go wrong and I'm hurting, I want my mom. However, I didn't expect to have to share her with a guy in his sixties who reeks of cologne and whiskey, and is having a "come-to-Jesus" moment.

We're all gathered in a booth at Love at First Sip, Brody by my side, and Mom and Marv across from us. Eileen took us to her coffee shop after we dragged Marv out of the bookstore, and is currently fussing over him as much as Mom.

"I brought back pulla for you," Eileen says, placing an entire loaf in front of Marv like a religious offering. "And considering your current state, Lucy's made you a Heathcliff. It's our strongest black coffee."

She sets a mug down in front of him that looks like crude oil. "It's dark, intense, and a little dangerous. But you're a New Yorker, so you can handle it, right?"

"I'm a shitty person!" Marv wails, tears tracking down his cheeks from under his sunglasses.

"No, you're not, honey," Mom says, stroking his back. "Whatever's happened, we can fix it. It's gonna be okay, I promise."

I grind my teeth as I gaze at them. This was meant to be *my* pity party, but Marv's stealing the presents and eating all the cake.

"I'm so sorry!" he continues, then grabs a handful of napkins and blows his nose with the dexterity and grace of a toddler.

"There, there," Eileen says, quickly cutting slices of Pulla. "Your blood sugar is just a little low and you're tired and emotional. This should help."

She pushes a plate toward him. "Go on, eat."

Hand shaking, Marv picks it up and takes a bite.

There's a brief moment of quiet, then he lets out another wail, his mouth stuffed with bread. "Ih astes oh ood!"

From Mom and Eileen's delighted reactions, you'd think he'd just walked on water.

"There we go! Pulla makes everything better!"

"Chew and swallow, sweetie, then have some more."

Lucy brings over the rest of our drinks, and I cup my Lord Byron cinnamon latte, the scent taking me right back to Espresso Yourself and the first time I met Marv. I can't help being moved by how upset he is, but I'm also furious with him.

And I'm reeling from what Brody said: *he loves me.*

Mom's still rubbing Marv's back. "So, what's happened? You know you can tell us anything."

His head lifts, and I see the shadow of his eyes behind his shades, then he drops his gaze back to the plate of pulla.

"Piper had drawn pictures of me that were private," Brody says, his voice hard and clipped. "Marv took my phone, most likely when I was recovering from rescuing Billy, sent them to himself, then posted them to my social accounts last night."

Mom and Eileen's eyebrows nearly reach their hairlines as they exchange a knowing look.

"Oh," Mom says, then swallows. "And, uh, these *pictures* … were they—?"

"They weren't nudes!" I snap.

Mom gives a relieved laugh. "Well, what *were* they then, honey?"

Brody gazes across at me as if asking my permission.

I nod. The damage is already done, and at least I'm not trying to hide my feelings for him anymore.

He passes his phone to Mom, who scrolls through the carousel while Eileen peers over her shoulder.

Mom sighs with pride. "Oh, sweetie! These are brilliant!"

"And they're private," Brody growls.

"I don't understand why," Eileen says, her brow furrowed. "They're wonderful!"

I search for a reason that would make sense to them but come up empty. I can't tell them I've been drawing Brody for years, nor that our so-called "relationship" only really started a couple of days ago.

"They were only meant for us to see," I say.

"Why?" Mom asks. "You should be proud of what you've done. Show the world! I don't understand what all the fuss is about."

"He stole them and posted them without Piper's permission," Brody says directly to Marv.

"I'm s-sorry!"

Eileen puts another slice of pulla on his plate.

"And he's apologized," Mom says firmly. "He knows he did something wrong and is atoning for it."

"Why did you do it?" Brody asks him.

All heads turn Marv's way. Taking off his shades, he rubs his red-rimmed eyes.

"I was mad," he begins, his voice tired and subdued.

"At me?" Brody asks.

Marv's gaze immediately flicks up. "Fu—god no. You're solid. The best ..."

"Then who?"

He takes a sip of his Heathcliff and grimaces before swallowing. "The showrunners of *The Chronicles of the Sword and the Flame.*"

"Why?"

Marv lets out a heavy sigh. "You didn't get the job. They chose someone else to play the Warlock of Zhash-Dhrog."

CHAPTER 26

BRODY

For a brief moment, there's silence. Time seems to stop inside me. But I can't think or process the news because Erica and Eileen are clucking their tongues in disappointment like mother hens.

"Oh, honey, I'm so sorry," Erica begins. "We should have tried harder."

"They don't know what they're missing out on," Eileen adds, shaking her head. "You're the best actor in the business."

"I don't know about that," I try, but they're having none of it, either continuing to find fault with themselves for not getting enough publicity for me over the last few days or berating the showrunners.

Under the table, Piper's hand reaches for mine.

"I'm so sorry," she murmurs.

"It's okay," I say quietly to her, then look at her mom and Eileen. "It's nobody's fault. These things happen. It's part of the job."

"Have some more pulla," Eileen says, cutting me another slice. "Those silly producers wouldn't know talent if it kicked them in the butt."

I smile. It's good to have these women on my side. They're like substitute moms since I no longer have mine around.

"I'm sorry, Brody," Marv says. "And Piper, I should never have done it. I just got mad and then got drunk. Then madder and stupid. I wanted them to see what they were missing. How Piper drew you … I dunno, man. She just gets you, y'know? Those pictures were the bomb, and I wanted them to see how fu—crazy they were to have turned you down."

"When did you find out I didn't get the gig?"

"A couple of days ago."

"Why didn't you tell me?"

He shrugs. "You were so happy. I didn't want to ruin it."

I mull over his words for a moment. Sure, I'm disappointed, but this door closing opens another one. And what lies behind it is a future where I don't have to spend the next year on the other side of the world from Piper.

Putting my free arm around her, I drop a kiss on the top of her head. There's a lightness in me now that the weight of our potential separation has been lifted.

She tilts her face to look at mine. "I'm sorry."

"Don't be." Leaning down, I brush a kiss across her lips. "It's not a crisis; it's an opportunity."

A slight crease remains in her forehead, as if all she can think about is my feelings of rejection. And in that moment, just when I think it's impossible, I fall even deeper in love with her.

"Do you want to visit the Christmas market?" I ask, wanting to be alone with her so we can talk.

She gazes at her mom and Eileen like she's asking to be excused.

Erica makes a shooing motion with her hands. "You two go on. Eileen and I will look after Marv."

Getting up, I take out my wallet, but Eileen pushes it back into my pocket with surprising strength. "On the house, honey. Now off you go. It's the last week of the market, so you might get some good bargains."

Marv starts to stand, but I place my hand on his shoulder. "It's okay, man. We can talk later."

He looks at Piper. "I'm sorry."

She nods. "Apology accepted."

Collapsing back into the booth, Marv reaches for a paper napkin to mop up fresh tears.

Erica rubs his back like she's trying to warm him up. "I think we should take you to the spa. You need an organic detox juice, a sauna, and a hot stone massage."

"Ooh, yes," Eileen pipes up. "And there's a discount today for seniors!"

"I'm not a se—" Marv says before being drowned out again by Erica and Eileen as they plan their own version of a twelve-step program.

Taking Piper's hand, I lead her out of Love at First Sip and onto the snowy street. Thankfully, the hail has stopped as quickly as it began, and patches of bright blue are now breaking through the clouds.

I draw in a deep lungful of the crisp air, glad to be outside and relatively alone with Piper.

"I'm sorry you didn't get the job."

Guiding her to the side of a building, I take her in my arms. I can't stop wanting to touch her. I may have lost the job of a lifetime, but I've got the woman I've always dreamed of.

"It's all good. I promise. And it means I'll be on the same side of the world as the woman I love."

Her cheeks flush adorably, and I kiss her again.

She makes a soft sound, halfway between a gasp and a moan, and I'm instantly hard.

I slant my head, deepening our kiss, my tongue sliding against hers. I don't care where we are right now. I just need to taste her sweet mouth and underline my words of love with my body.

Her fingers run up the back of my neck into my hair, tugging me closer. She's hot and needy, and I'm so here for it. Desire roars through me, demanding I back her up against the stone wall and fuck her until she's coming apart on my cock and screaming my name.

"Get a room!" a man quips, and people laugh.

Reluctantly raising my head, I gaze at Piper and raise an eyebrow.

She giggles. "Maybe we should go to the Christmas market?"

"It's that or give the good folk of Hideaway Harbor a show they weren't expecting."

WE WALK UP MAIN STREET, then take a right down Lobstah Lane where the Christmas market is. Wooden huts line the street, and food stalls fill the air with the smell of roasting chestnuts, Glühwein, clam chowder in bread bowls, and cinnamon churros.

Our pace slows as we take in the sights. There's the odd glance of recognition, but no one comes to ask for a selfie, and I'm glad. I can pretend I'm just a regular guy out with his girl.

"Have you deleted the photos?" Piper asks.

"Fuck! No, sorry." I come to a halt and pull out my phone. "It got so crazy back there, I totally forgot."

She folds her hand over mine. "Wait a moment."

I do, not sure where she's going with this.

"I've been thinking about what Mom and Eileen said," she

begins hesitantly. "That I should show people my drawings and be proud of them. What do you think?"

"That's not my decision to make."

"But if someone else had done them, say Harper or Mia, and the guy wasn't you, what would you say to them in this situation?"

I don't reply. I don't want to sway her decision either way. It took enough guts for her to show them to me; I don't want to pressure her to open them up to the rest of the world, and people who would only criticize out of petty jealousy.

"Brody, please."

"This has to be *your* call."

"It will be, I promise. But I value your opinion, and they are of you, so you need a say as well."

I take a measured breath. "I think you should put them out there. They're incredible. But on *your* terms. How *you* would want them to be posted."

She nods. "I've spent most of my life drawing you in secret, but now that we're ..."

"Together."

Her cheeks flush with color, but her eyes brighten with excitement. "Together," she repeats as if she can't quite believe it. "I don't have to hide my obsession any longer."

"You can be obsessed with me as much as you like, Piper Locke. Bring it on."

She grins. "Your number one fan."

"The best."

"And I've had an idea ... about my art."

"Go on."

"I've seen these adverts online for companies that you can build a website with. They handle everything from the domain and design to security. They have templates you can pick from, and it's meant to be really intuitive.

"Now we're excused from enforced public outings, I

thought I could create one. It would be a better platform for showcasing my work, and I could advertise for commissions. So, if I don't hang onto my job, then this could help cover bills until I find a new one. What do you think?"

I want to tell her that I'd happily support her for the rest of our lives if she wanted to quit tomorrow, but I keep my big mouth firmly shut. If she's passionate about her job, then I want her to keep it.

"I think it's an awesome idea. You can link to it from your socials, and I'll link to your socials and your site from my accounts to help drive traffic to it."

"You'd do that?"

"Of course! I love you and want to show the world how amazing you are."

She blushes. "Thank you. And now it doesn't matter about hiding all the pictures I've drawn of you because there's a backlog to post."

"And I can always pose for more ..."

"I'd like that."

I kiss her again, and she sighs as our lips meet, then she breaks away.

"Come on. We need to choose a present for you."

"I don't need one. You've already given me you, and that's everything I've ever wanted. Plus, you've drawn me looking way hotter than I actually am."

"There's no one hotter than you, Brody King."

She pulls me toward a stall festooned with Christmas tree decorations, all laser-cut from wood and depicting different scenes of Hideaway Harbor.

"Look at these," Piper says in a hushed tone. "They're beautiful!"

"If there's a view of Hideaway you want and don't see, I can always create it," the woman inside the hut tells us.

"Thank you," I reply as Piper's eyes flit from ornament to ornament.

"Look! There's the wishing bridge over the spring! The harbor, Larry the Lobstah, Skippy the dog, the museum, the town square." She faces me. "Would you like one of these for Christmas? Would they work on your tree back in New York?"

I tense, as if I've just been punched in the gut. "Yeah, that'd be nice," I reply. "Perfect."

Piper's excited expression falters. "You sure?"

"Absolutely." I force a smile. "I'll turn my back, so it's a surprise."

I don't wait for a reply, facing the street as memories of Christmas past come back to haunt me.

A minute later, Piper threads her arm through mine, and we set off again.

"Do you want to talk about it?"

No, I don't, but this is Piper, and she deserves the truth from me, no matter how hard it is to talk about.

"I don't have a tree. Never have."

"That's okay. I only have a tiny artificial one in Brooklyn."

"I don't decorate at all."

"Nothing wrong with that."

"Maybe. But I don't celebrate Christmas at all."

She stops in her tracks. "What do you mean? Surely you go somewhere on Christmas Day?"

I shrug, allowing myself to feel the sadness and emptiness of my life.

"If I could have worked over the holiday season, I would have. But even Hollywood shuts down for a couple of days. So, I either took myself on vacation and got wasted, or went to some celebrity party and got trashed with people like me. Lonely folks getting drunk and pretending they're happy not having to deal with families."

"What about Marv? Where does he go?"

"He used to go to his sister's place in Missouri, but she died a few years ago. He always invited me, but I think it was more for protection, as she was a drunk and lived with about fifteen semi-feral dogs."

"Jeez."

"Yeah. I don't know what he does now. Probably the same as me, just stays in his apartment and binge-watches shows."

"There's nothing wrong with that," Piper says firmly. "But from now on, both your Christmases are going to look a little different."

"You're inviting Marv as well?"

"Yes. Mom already said he's going to be with us, and I know his heart's in the right place, even if his brain got lost yesterday."

My own heart's so full it's pressing into my throat. "I love you so much."

"And I love you too."

"You do?"

"Only for about the last sixteen years," she replies with a grin. "It's old news."

A few weeks ago, all I could see in my future was work, but now all I see is happiness.

"I want to do everything Christmassy with you that I've missed out on since leaving Hideaway," I say. "Roasting chestnuts, movies, midnight mass, ice skating, sledding—"

"Sledding?"

"I bet you've still got the sleds your dad made when you were kids."

She grins. "Yup. Think you can still handle Seller Hill?"

"Hell yeah." I hold up my hand. "Last one to break their leg is a loser?"

She high-fives me as she laughs. "You're on."

. . .

A HUNDRED YEARS AGO, there used to be a market at the base of Seller Hill, hence the name. Now it's also known as Cellular Hill, since the top is the only place you can guarantee mobile reception.

After getting a sled from her folks' garage, Piper and I take the salted path to the top and peer down the smoothest slope to the bottom.

"If we were alone, I might consider wussing out," she says. "I haven't done this since I was a teenager."

The air is filled with shouts and excited screams as kids throw themselves down the hill.

"I don't do my own stunts," I say. "But the guys I know who do would love this. They'd go down headfirst."

Piper shudders. "That's the kind of thing Hudson and Mia might do. But only in an attempt to show the other up."

"We don't have to do this. We could just watch everyone for a bit?"

I put the sled down and sit on one side, patting the other for Piper.

She perches next to me, and I sling an arm around her, holding her close.

"I've had an idea," I say.

"Should I be worried?"

I grin. "Hope not."

"Okay, what is it?"

As I gaze at her, my heart races. Not just because I'm constantly hot for her, but I'm worried what I say next might scare her off.

But then again, what have I got to lose? And I don't want to waste any more time.

I swallow. "I was thinking of giving up my apartment. Getting one across the river in Brooklyn."

Her eyes light up.

"And because I'll save a bunch of money moving out of

Manhattan, I thought I'd get a three-bedroom place. So, there'd be room for family and friends to come stay, and a dedicated studio for you, my favorite artist."

Now her eyes are glossy. Are these happy or sad tears?

"And I don't want you to pay any rent," I say quickly. "Save that money. You don't know what's happening with your job, and I'd rather you spend it on yourself."

"You ... want me to move in with you?" Her voice is a whisper.

Shit. "Yes," I reply firmly. "As soon as you're ready."

She gulps in a breath, her lower lip quivering, then lets out a breathless laugh even as a tear streaks down her cheek.

"Is this a good thing?"

Piper throws her arms around my neck, peppering my face with kisses. "Yes! Oh my God, Brody, it's a *very* good thing."

My shoulders sag with relief. "Thank God."

She laughs again. "Best. Christmas. Ever."

Then her mouth slants greedily over mine, and my whole body roars *yes*.

I don't think or care about anyone who might be around us as she shifts to straddle my lap. My blood as well as my brain has rushed south, and my cock is now in the driver's seat.

Our tongues slick against each other and pleasure fizzes across my skin. It's like we're floating on a cloud of lust, the ground no longer stable beneath my feet.

I growl as I thread my fingers through her hair, anchoring her mouth on mine. This incredible woman rocks my world and no other woman has ever made me feel like this. Like I'm flying.

Piper rips her mouth from mine with a gasp, and I realize with a jolt of fear that the Earth is literally moving.

Or rather, *we're* moving.

Straight down the hill.

"Brody!" Piper screams as I dig my heels into the snow, trying to slow our descent.

Snow and ice arc into the air from my heels like spray from a jet ski. However, gravity is not our friend right now, and the weight of two people on the sled means we're hurtling faster and faster.

Piper's clinging to me tighter than a barnacle on the bottom of a lobster boat, screaming so loudly my eardrums scream back. I don't have a hold of the rope, so I can't steer, and there are a dozen trees at the bottom that all have our names on them.

Engaging my quads like I'm maxing out on the leg press, I dig my heels in harder, feeling the resistance as we begin to slow.

At the bottom of the slope, people scatter out of our way. We're not going to glide to a graceful stop anytime soon.

"Hold on tight!" I yell, even though if she clasped my neck any harder, it'd break.

Then I throw myself off the sled, keeping her on top of me, and slide the rest of the way down, finally coming to a stop with a thud against the trunk of a tree, whose branches promptly dislodge all the snow they were carrying onto us.

Piper's making an awful sound, like she's having an asthma attack.

I push up out of the snow, brushing it from her face in panic. "You okay? You hurt?"

People rush to our side, adults concerned, kids whooping with excitement.

My heart restarts as I realize Piper's laughing.

"You sure you're alright?"

She nods. "That was a once-in-a-lifetime experience."

I grin. "Meaning you never want to do it again?"

"Yup!" She glances at the crowd around us. "Please tell me someone got that on film?"

A kid comes forward, and we all squeeze around the phone screen to watch, laughing at the sight that was so terrifying just moments ago.

Piper gets the kid to send the video to her, then we turn for home.

"One and done?" she asks as we step onto Bay View Road.

I wince. "Now that the adrenaline's wearing off, I'm starting to ache in all the wrong places."

"Epsom salt bath?"

"Only if you join me."

"Deal."

The bumps and bruises no longer bother me. I've got my girl by my side, and she's going to move in with me after Christmas. Nothing can burst my bubble.

CHAPTER 27

PIPER

> Colin: Please can we talk for five minutes? I'd
> rather do this on a voice call

*M*y backside hits the bed as I stare at my phone screen.

What does he want? Surely he isn't going to tell me I don't have a job come January? Right before Christmas?

The scent of morning coffee filters along the landing from the kitchen downstairs. Brody went down ahead of me this morning to make cookies with Mom while I had a leisurely shower.

Get it over with.

I call Colin before I can talk myself out of it and he answers immediately.

"Piper! Hey, thanks for calling me back. How are you?"

Amazing, thank you for asking. I'm moving in with my hot new boyfriend, and I have thousands of new followers on my socials. You know, for the pictures I draw that you look down on? Oh, and I've built a website over the last few days and already have two commissions. So, I'm doing great!

Of course, I can't say any of that as he's the son of my new boss, so I settle for, "Fine. How are you?"

"Er … not so good. I miss you."

How does he expect me to reply to that?

"Oh."

"Lacey and I broke up. And she's not working for us anymore. We should never have been together in the first place. She was a mistake."

I cringe, immediately feeling sorry for the young woman who helped break up my relationship with Colin.

"And with Christmas coming up, it reminds me that I was going to come back to Hideaway Harbor with you. Meet your folks."

Oh my fucking god. He's not outside the house is he?

"I've got a new boyfriend," I say quickly.

"You have?"

"Don't sound so surprised!"

"No, I'm not. Sorry, that came out wrong. I'm uh … glad you're happy."

"Thank you."

"Is it serious?"

"Yes."

"Oh. Okay. That's probably for the best."

"Why?"

"Well, we'll be working together for hopefully a long time. I wanted to call to let you know that next year your job's secure. I'm taking a management position after we merge companies and we want to offer you the position of head of graphic design, overseeing and training two graduates to work under you."

Oh my god.

"And the new role comes with a twenty percent pay rise."

"Wow. That's ... amazing."

"We want you to be an integral part of the leadership team with full autonomy."

Colin's offering me everything I've ever dreamed of at Parker and Overton, and then some.

"And I promise I'll be professional. But if you ever break up with your new guy, please consider giving me a second chance."

I make a non-committal sound in response because I don't want to be rude when he's offering me such an amazing opportunity.

"So, uh ... Merry Christmas, Piper."

"You too."

"What are you up to today?"

"It's the town dance and we're spending the day decorating the room, so I'd better go. Mom's calling me."

"Okay, no problem. I've gotta go too and shovel snow with Dad. So ... see you in the New Year?"

"Yep. See you then."

I ring off and leap to my feet, running out of the room.

I need to speak to Brody.

Bang! Bang! Bang! Bang!

My heart jumps into my throat as I'm halfway down the stairs. The urgency of the knock makes me panic that something awful has happened.

Mom reaches the front door at the same time I do, and I stand back so she can open it.

Marv barges in. His eyes are manic, the broken capillaries livid in his cheeks as he struggles to breathe. It looks like he sprinted all the way from the Hideaway Hotel.

"Where's Brody?" he pants.

"In the kitchen, honey. What's happened?"

He staggers further into the house. "Brody! Brody!"

Mom guides him through to where Brody is wiping his hands on a dish towel.

"What's going on?"

Marv spreads his arms wide like he's announcing the arrival of the Second Coming.

"Bro! You're not gonna fu—believe it!"

"Take a seat," Mom says, guiding him to a stool at the end of the breakfast bar. "You can't tell us anything if you have an aneurysm."

My hand reaches for Brody's. I have no idea what Marv's going to say, but I suddenly fear his words are going to destroy my blissful happiness.

Brody gives my hand a reassuring squeeze as Mom bustles around Marv, getting him coffee and a cookie.

My tablet sits open on the breakfast bar, Brooklyn rentals on the screen, smudged with floury fingerprints. I power it down. It feels like bad juju to leave it open when I don't know what bomb Marv's about to drop.

His hands tremble as he pats his sweating forehead with a handkerchief.

Mom rubs his back. "Take all the time you need. We're not going anywhere for an hour or so."

Marv nods, then tries to speak, but it comes out as a high-pitched laugh.

"You okay?" Brody asks.

"Yeah, just—" Marv shakes his head and holds out his quivering hands. "Look at me."

Mom takes the mug of coffee away from him. "Maybe this isn't such a good idea. Let me get you a chamomile tea."

Marv glances at Brody, then away as if he's trying not to cry. "I'm just so happy for you, man. No one deserves this more than you."

My pulse quickens. Something tells me Marv isn't talking about our relationship.

Brody's thumb on the back of my hand stops moving.

"Deserve what?" he asks warily.

"The showrunners got in touch. They …"

"They've changed their minds?" I ask, my heart thudding in my chest.

Marv's gaze turns to me, and something flickers in his eyes, a glitch in his fervor.

He mops his forehead again, staring at the handkerchief, then takes a deep breath and locks eyes with Brody.

"They want you to play the Emberking of Draventhorne. They've offered you the lead role."

There's a high-pitched ringing in my ears as chills race across my skin. This is incredible. And it also makes me want to crawl under a comforter and cry.

"What do you mean?" Brody asks, like he thinks it's some kind of trick. "That's for an A-lister."

"I know, but fans are losing their shit—apologies, Erica— over Piper's pictures, and now the showrunners want *you*."

"But … the Emberking is in every book," Brody continues, his words echoing my thoughts. "The studio's already confirmed three seasons, so that's three years of work."

In New Zealand …

"I know! And you should see how much they're gonna pay you. I'm losing my freaking mind right now!"

Brody turns to me. There's a question in his eyes, but also excitement. I know how much he wanted the part of the warlock, but to be offered this instead? It's more than he could ever have imagined.

"What do you—"

"Take it, you have to."

"But—"

"Opportunities like this come along maybe once in a lifetime. You've got to do it."

"Wha—"

"We'll make it work!" I say brightly, even though my heart is calcifying as I speak. "That's what technology is here for. And I've got two vacation days I'm carrying over from this year into next."

Two extra days to add to my measly ten-day annual allowance. It'll take me twenty-five hours just to get from New York to New Zealand. I know this because I checked.

"We should talk about this," Brody continues.

"We are."

His gaze moves to Mom and Marv, then back to me. "Maybe we should go for a walk."

"No need, honestly," I say with as much positivity as I can muster. "You've got to say yes."

Brody stands and takes my hand. "Come on."

I begin to protest, but he gives me a look and leads me into the family room.

"Do not even think of turning this job down," I say as he shuts the door behind us.

"Why not?"

"Because it's like the best thing ever! It's more than you could have dreamed of!"

"*You're* more than I could have dreamed of."

"And I'm not going anywhere. We can make this work. I promise. And anyway, I've got my own news about work."

"Huh?"

"I've been offered a permanent position at Parker and Overton. I'll be line managing and training two graduates, so I get my own team! Full autonomy in the role, *and* a twenty percent pay rise!"

"When did this happen?"

"Five minutes ago. Colin called me to let me know. I was on my way to tell you when Marv burst in."

"Colin?"

"Yes."

"Your *ex*, Colin?"

"U-huh, and I told him about you and that I'm not getting back together with him."

"He wants that? To get back with you?"

"I told him it's not going to happen."

I can't read Brody's expression, but he doesn't look happy.

"I trust Colin on that. He's not going to make trouble." I try to reassure Brody, reaching for his hand, but he withdraws and rubs his jaw.

"I—" he exhales. "I want us to be together."

"We will be. We've waited this long, haven't we?"

His eyes meet mine. He looks as pleased as I am about the prospect of another three years apart.

The silence is broken by another heavy sigh. "Look. I need to put this out there, even if it's not the right thing for you. The money I'll get for playing the Emberking will be way more than I could ever need ..."

Brody's expression is intent, like he wants me to read the meaning behind his words. "I've got enough to support both of us and then some."

I swallow. He wants me to quit my job and go with him, but I can't. It's not really about the money. I've worked so hard to get where I am. And if I go to New Zealand, what will I do? Wait around in Brody's trailer for him to finish filming each day?

"I know it's not fair asking you to follow me," he continues. "But the offer's there."

"And I appreciate it. I really do." I take his hands, and this time he doesn't pull back. "But I can't just sit over there twiddling my thumbs when I've been given this opportunity to advance my career. This is important to me."

He nods. "I know. And that's why I want us to talk about whether I'll accept the part or not."

I take a step back. "You can't be serious. You've got to take it!"

"Why?"

"Because—Jesus Christ, Brody!"

Frustration pricks the inside of my skin like thousands of tiny knives. I'll never live with myself if he doesn't take it.

"You cannot turn it down because of me. No way!"

I start pacing but the room feels too small to contain my angry energy. "Have you read the books?"

"Yes, but—"

"Then you'll know the story arc for the Emberking is epic! He's a multidimensional character with a hero's journey like no other! He's Henry the Fifth, meets Beowulf, meets Luke Skywalker, meets Gandalf!"

Brody's lips press together like he's forcing himself not to agree with me.

"If you say no to this, it's the equivalent of me, I don't know, refusing a book deal, a top spot at Comic-Con, *and* an exhibition at the Guggenheim. You *have* to say yes."

"But what about us?"

My feet suddenly stop moving, my anger turning into fear. Is Brody saying he won't want us to be together if we're on opposite sides of the world for so long?

"You don't want … you don't think we'll make it?"

"What? No! That's not what I'm saying!"

"Then what?"

"I want to see you every day. I want to share my life with you!"

"We can still talk! Video call!"

"It's not the same." He sounds deflated now, which isn't how I want him to be after being offered the job most actors would kill for.

"I know, but it'll be worth it. I promise. If I get my dream job, then I want you to have yours."

"I don't know."

"For me?"

"That's not fair."

"You said you'd do anything for me. So do this. Take it."

He pauses, then nods.

I let out a breath of relief. "Good. Now let's go back and tell Marv, then get to the hall so we can help set up for the dance tonight. We should be celebrating!"

He doesn't reply, so I drag him out of the room and back to the kitchen. My heart may be breaking, but I have to hold it together for the both of us. I'm not going to be the reason he turns this opportunity down.

"AUNT PIPER," Martha says, handing me two small branches for the evergreen garlands she's helping me make.

"Yes, sweetie?"

"Are you and Uncle Brody going to get married?"

I shoot a quick glance at Brody. He's on the other side of the main room in the town hall's community building, helping my dad and brothers fix an enormous tree into place.

I don't know how to reply to her. It's what I've always wanted, but now our future seems so unsure. I can already feel the distance between us, like a yawning chasm.

"Because you should," Martha continues.

"Why's that?"

She gives me a look like I should already know the answer. "Because that's what grown-ups do when they fall in love. And I want to be a flower girl."

I smile at her simple logic. "Sometimes life isn't straightforward. Things get in the way."

"Then you should move them. Tidy them up."

If only …

I rub fir needles between my fingers, then lift them to my

nose. The woodsy oils smell like Christmas and home, a scent that always makes me happy. However, now it's tinged with sadness. I'll always associate it with Brody, and the perfect few days when our stars finally aligned. But now our worlds are drifting apart, and my heart is trying to protect itself by withdrawing.

Martha copies me, then sniffs her hands. "It smells like the candle stall at the Christmas market where I helped Daddy buy presents for you."

"Isn't that meant to be a surprise?"

Her big blue eyes widen comically. "Oops!"

I laugh. "I promise I won't tell."

"Thank you. Are you going to Australia with Uncle Brody?"

"Australia?"

"Grandma was telling Daddy, and he told me it's near Australia."

"Do you mean New Zealand?"

She shrugs. "Maybe?"

"Uncle Brody's got a job there, but I can't go with him because my job's here."

She perks up. "In Hideaway Harbor?"

"New York."

"Oh." She scrunches her nose. "Can you move it?"

"I don't think so, sweetie."

"Have you made a wish at the spring about it?"

"Not yet."

"Well, you should. They always work out. I made a wish the other day, and I know it's going to come true."

Hideaway beliefs and legends have more staying power than Santa, the Easter Bunny, and the Tooth Fairy combined. Objectively, I know it's all probably nonsense, but the intention behind it is what matters.

Martha takes my hand and presses a sprig of fir into my

palm. "This came from near the spring, so it has the same magical powers. Make a wish now."

Her face is so serious, I don't know whether to smile or weep at how sweet a kid she is. So I close my eyes, feeling Martha fold my fingers over the foliage.

"Now think of what you want more than anything in the whole wide world."

In my mind's eye, the image appears instantly. It's Brody and me together, holding hands and smiling at each other. He's dressed as the Emberking of Draventhorne, and we're standing in one of those sweeping, timeless landscapes the South Island of New Zealand is famous for. The picture is so vivid, it feels like I'm already there.

This is what I want, to be with Brody and to travel the world. Two things I've always dreamed of but never done.

"Now open your eyes," Martha instructs.

I do, and the first thing I see is Brody striding across the room toward me.

When he reaches us, he leans down. "A tree's fallen, blocking the mountain road into Hideaway. I'm going with your dad, Ethan, and Hudson to help clear it."

"Is anyone hurt?"

"No, thank God, but it might take a few hours." He glances at his watch. "I don't know if we'll be back in time for the start of the dance, so don't wait for me at your folks'. I'll meet you here later."

I nod. "Is there anything I can do to help?"

"Decorate the tree? It's up and secure, and we've placed it by the stage so there's more height to reach it. A couple of people can easily rotate it so you can dress it all the way around."

"Okay."

I gaze at him, trying to read his expression. His eyebrows knit together like he's worried. And I know it's not just about decorating or clearing a tree.

His fingers reach out to cup my cheek. "I love you."

I press my lips together as tears instantly sting my eyes. I can't speak, or I'll bawl, so I just nod.

He hesitates, then leans in and kisses me softly. "I love you," he murmurs again, like we're already saying goodbye.

"What about me?" Martha asks.

Brody stands and smiles at her, even though his eyes are glassy. "I love you too."

"Good. Just checking."

He chuckles, and I surreptitiously wipe my eyes.

"Make sure you look after Daddy," Martha continues.

He salutes. "Yes, ma'am."

"And hurry back, because I'm only allowed to stay at the dance until eight."

"I'll do my best."

Martha's little hand takes mine. "Don't worry, Aunt Piper. You've made your wish now, so everything's going to be all right."

I don't know how, but for one night at least, I'm going to put my trust in the faith of a little girl, and her belief in the magic of Hideaway.

CHAPTER 28

PIPER

"*H*oney, can you run to Making Whoopie for me?" Mom asks.

It's mid-afternoon, and we haven't stopped since we arrived at the town hall community building this morning. Brody, my brothers, and Dad are still out clearing the fallen tree, and we have no idea when they'll be back because there's no cell service in that area.

I finish clipping a festive paper tablecloth to a trestle table, and stand. "Sure, what can I get?"

Mom pushes a fifty-dollar bill into my hand. "Whatever Audrey's got left. We just need a pick-me-up to get through the next hour or so."

I nod. It's always down to the wire getting the main room ready, but without half my family and Brody pitching in, it's taken even longer.

The tree is decorated, and thousands of feet of string lights hang across the ceiling. Evergreen garlands line the middle of the tables and are attached above the doors and along the bottom of the windows. However, the band is still performing a sound check, the food and drinks haven't arrived, and there's a mess everywhere.

Throwing on my coat and scarf, I make my way out of the building, hang a right, then turn left when I reach Main Street. It's chilly, and the light is fading fast, but I'm glad to be outside, the crisp air clearing my foggy head. When Brody left, I threw myself into getting the main room ready, not wanting a moment of peace to reflect on the double bombshells dropped this morning.

But now, as I cross the road and join the line outside the bakery, reality settles on me like gently falling snow. I've been given a choice to make. Not by Brody, but by the universe, God, a higher power, destiny, or whatever label I want to use.

Colin's call this morning offered me everything I thought I ever wanted: stability, security, and knowing that I had a clear career path. But is that really what my soul desires?

The other path before me is the one less travelled. A chance to turn my artistic passion into a new career, even though the risk is so much higher. I need the courage to try something new, believe in myself, and be proud of what I draw.

And, much as I hate to admit it, Mom and Mia are right. My heart isn't in advertising staplers and office chairs.

I've loved my time in Brooklyn, but I've also been lonely. If I follow Brody to New Zealand, we'll be together and happy, and I'll have plenty of time to look for online design jobs while also working on my art.

My skin tingles as I make my decision, and the further my mind travels in this new direction, the more I know it's the right one for me. I'm scared, but in an excited way, like the feeling you get on a roller coaster as it cranks its way up to the first drop.

And Brody? He's going to be by my side as I create a new future for myself.

Making Whoopie is my favorite bakery in Hideaway Harbor, and on a Friday afternoon, everyone else in town seems to share the same opinion. I stamp my feet to keep warm as the line slowly shortens, then take out my phone to see if there's anything from Brody.

Still nothing.

I go to my socials, my mind boggling at the number of new followers, likes, and comments. It's too much to take in, let alone reply to, so I check my email to see if any more commissions have come through.

My gaze snags on a name I don't recognize and a subject header that doesn't immediately make sense.

I open it and read the contents.

Then read it again.

Is this a joke? A prank? A mistake?

My heart is racing, and I'm burning up under my layers. The email has an attachment, and I click to open it, terrified it contains a virus that's about to drain what little is left in my bank account.

But it's just more text, pages and pages of it that I don't have the expertise to understand.

I call Brody again, but once more it goes to voicemail.

Glancing around the street, as if the answer lies nearby, I recognize someone inside Making Whoopie—Jack Lourd, Amanda Willis's agent.

"Excuse me, excuse me," I say as I cut to the front of the line and enter the bakery.

Jack's standing behind the counter, and I suddenly don't know what to say.

"Help!" I shout, then cringe as everyone stops what they're doing to stare at me.

"I need your help," I say to Jack.

He glances behind him, then points at himself. "Me?"

"Yes, it's an emergency."

I tug my hat off as sweat trickles down the back of my neck. I'm creating a scene in my hometown that's going to keep the gossips going for days.

"I'm not a first-responder, you know." He leans in as if sharing a secret. "I'm a lawyer."

"Yes." I nod. "That's exactly what I need."

SMOOTHING my hands down the sides of my red satin dress, I scan the crowds. For the past hour, I've been two people in one body—the smiling, chatty daughter of Mayor Locke on the outside, and someone freaking the fuck out on the inside.

Where is he?

It's now seven o'clock, and the town dance is in full swing. Christmas tunes play over the excited chatter, and people are enjoying drinks before digging into the food.

Everything's picture-perfect, but I'm a bundle of nerves and excitement. Mom keeps reassuring me that everyone's all right, but she doesn't know what's on my mind. No one except Jack Lourd does.

Mia's set up a photo booth with a snowy backdrop and holiday-themed props so she can take fun pictures of people as they arrive. Harper's admiring the Christmas tree with Martha, and Mom and Eileen are introducing Marv to people like he's a debutante in his first season.

Every second feels like an hour as I wait, constantly moving to get the best view of the door.

Then, just as I'm about to push through the crowds and go out onto the street, Brody enters the main room. Dressed in black tie, he's so devastatingly handsome, I have a mini-orgasm on the spot.

His eyes are searching the room, his forehead furrowed, but

when his gaze catches on mine, the tension in his face dissolves.

Brody. My Brody.

My feet move me forward without any input from my brain, and we meet in the middle of the floor under the sparkling lights, holding each other's arms as if we're lost at sea.

I can't stop smiling, and neither can he. There's a lightness in his expression, a relief, as if he's just unloaded a heavy burden from his shoulders.

For a moment, we just stand there, grinning like fools. Then he takes me in his arms and holds me tight. I can feel the love pouring off him. I've never felt so cherished before. This is a hug of heart and soul, of the past, present, and the future. It's a promise, and it's home.

"You're so beautiful," he murmurs in my ear. "I love you so much."

"I love you too," I reply, then pull back. "And I need to talk to you."

"Me too." His forehead creases again. "I'm not taking the job."

"What? No! You have to!"

He shakes his head and smiles. "I don't. I've just spent the last few hours hauling wood, and that was too much time away from you. We could have been together for the last twelve years, and now that I've finally got you, I don't want to spend another minute away from your side if I can help it."

"But—"

"It's just a job. Nothing is more important than you. Nothing."

Panic has its claws in my chest. "Have you told Marv yet?"

"Not yet." He glances around the crowded space. "Have you seen him? I'll tell him now."

"You'll do no such thing!" I hiss, dragging him away to put more distance between us and Marv.

"I've made up my mind," Brody says calmly.

"Well, you've got to unmake it. Because I'm coming with you."

He stops. "You can't give up your career just to follow me. It's not fair."

"I'm not giving up anything! I'm getting more than I ever imagined!"

"Is your company letting you work remotely?"

"No. I'm quitting!"

"But—"

"I got another job, in New Zealand!"

He blinks, then glances around us. "How have you managed to do that in the last few hours while handling all this?"

I'm bouncing on the balls of my feet, excitement bubbling inside me. "I got an email from the showrunners of *The Chronicles of the Sword and the Flame*. They want to hire me as a concept artist for the series!"

"What?"

"After all the fans went crazy for my drawings, the showrunners said they want me to work with the production team on art to promote the series. They even sent me a provisional contract, which I signed a couple of hours ago!"

Brody's staring at me like I just told him I met Santa and accepted a six-month contract to work at the North Pole.

"You *signed* something?"

"Yep!"

He rubs his forehead. "I feel like a total asshole right now, but do you even know if it's legit? There are so many sophisticated scams out there. And you should never sign anything without an entertainment lawyer looking it over first."

"I did."

"Did what?"

"Got an entertainment lawyer to review it. He called the showrunners, requested a few amendments, which they made and emailed back before I signed."

"Who? Marv?"

"Jack Lourd."

"Amanda Willis's agent?"

"Uh-huh. And he's my agent now, too. I'm not sure how to break the news to Marv that I'm not going with him."

Brody's still staring at me. "Is this for real?"

I nod, my cheeks hurting from smiling so much. "Jack was amazing. He went through every paragraph, every clause, every word. And he knows one of the showrunners anyway, so it was easy to get the changes done right then and there."

There's a beat, then Brody's blank expression breaks, and he pulls me into the tightest hug. "Oh my God, Piper, I love you. I'm so fucking proud of you. You're coming with me. We're doing this together."

I don't get a chance to reply, because he's kissing me like his life depends on it, like I'm the oxygen keeping him alive.

My body instantly responds, electricity crackling across my skin and liquid fire pooling deep in my abdomen. I love him and need him, and nothing can keep us apart now.

"Not in front of the children!" Mia yells, and we slowly break the kiss.

She holds up her camera. "Now let's get a family-friendly version."

I tuck into Brody's side and smile for the photo.

Mia snaps a couple, then looks at the back screen and snorts. "That's the picture of the night."

Turning it around, she shows us the last one she took. We've got cheesy grins on our faces, our hair is sticking up in all directions, and my lipstick is smeared around both our mouths.

I burst out laughing. "That's terrible!"

"It's perfect," Brody says. "Absolutely perfect."

"Not so fake anymore, then?" Mia asks with a smirk, wagging her finger back and forth between us.

Brody's eyes meet mine. "It was never fake for me."

"Me neither," I say as I smile up at him, my heart bursting with happiness.

"Well, no shit," Mia says. "I just wish I could've bet on this outcome. I would've won big."

"Aunt Mia!" Martha cries as she runs over. "Daddy, Grandpa, and Uncle Hudson are here!"

"That's great, sweetie," Mia replies, running a hand over Martha's blonde curls.

Martha raises her eyebrows at Brody and me. "Have you been kissing?"

"I'm afraid so," I reply.

"Why are you afraid?"

I laugh. "It's just—"

She waves her little hands, cutting me off. "Grandma will have a handkerchief in her purse. You need to clean up, because you both look silly."

Brody chuckles beside me, then flattens his hair back down. "Any better?"

Martha purses her lips. "You still look like a clown. But a handsome one." She turns back to Mia. "Uncle Hudson is wearing a suit, like Uncle Brody. He looks like a mighty fine piece of ass."

"What the f—heck?" Mia splutters as Brody and I crack up. "Where did you hear that?"

Martha shrugs. "Some ladies were talking about him. Do you think Hudson is a mighty fine piece of ass, Aunt Mia?"

My best friend's cheeks flush scarlet. "You can't say that."

"Why not? Should I say he's a mighty fine piece of bottom instead?"

Brody and I collapse with laughter, and Martha gazes crossly at us.

"How do I know what's right or wrong if you just keep laughing?"

"Sorry, sweetheart," I manage.

She throws her hands in the air. "Is he a mighty fine piece of tush?"

Hudson chooses that moment to weave through the crowd behind Mia. For a second, his gaze burns hot as it flicks down and back up Mia's body. Then the fire disappears as if it was never there, and he pulls a face at me.

"You look like you're auditioning for the circus," he says as he approaches.

"That's what *I* thought, Uncle Hudson," Martha says. "They look like clowns."

Hudson chuckles deeply, and Mia takes a step back.

"But you look like a mighty fine piece of—"

"Martha!" Mia, Brody, and I interrupt quickly.

Hudson has a wicked glint in his eye as he slowly rotates like he's on stage at a bachelor auction.

Yes, he's my brother, so automatically gross, but I know he's handsome, and tonight, in a tux, he looks like a Navy SEAL turned model.

"What do you think, Mia?" he asks. "The finest piece of butt in the room?"

"Butt *head*, more like," Mia mutters, her eyes on her camera as she fiddles with it.

"Want to put your name down for a dance later?" Hudson continues. "My card is almost full, but I can save a space for you."

Mia doesn't reply, and something subtle shifts in the air between them. But before I can question it, a handkerchief appears in my face.

"Oh, honey, the two of you need to save all that for snuggle time!" Mom exclaims as she dabs around my mouth.

"Mom!"

She grabs Brody by the ear like a schoolboy and tugs him down. "Come here, young man."

The corner of his mouth twitches as he lets her wipe lipstick from his face, then she lets him go.

"There, much better. Now, how about some food? John and Harper have saved us a table. Come on, everyone."

She takes Martha's hand, and we follow them across the floor to the buffet.

"When do you want to tell them?" Brody asks me.

"Tomorrow. At the Christmas Eve dinner, when everyone's there. I just want to keep it between us tonight."

"It still hasn't really sunk in."

"I know. I can't believe it!"

He stops to kiss me softly. "I can't wait to get you alone," he murmurs.

An excited shiver ripples through me. "Can we leave early?"

He nods. "Food, one dance, then back for snuggle time?"

I grin. "And would you like a surprise gift as well?"

An eyebrow arches. "What is it?"

My face heats. "Well, to be honest, I've got no idea. I just thought we could see what's in the gift bag we got from The Perfect Package."

His eyes flash, and a spark of heat pulses between my legs.

"Oh yes," he rumbles. "I like the sound of that."

CHAPTER 29

PIPER

The house is dark and quiet as Brody and I slip inside. It's only nine, plenty of time before anyone else gets back.

The thought makes my mouth run dry with anticipation.

Brody grabs a couple of glasses of iced water, and we pad upstairs. My heart thumps as I take the gift bag and tip its contents onto the bed.

"Hmmm ... what do we have here?" Brody asks, lifting two cellophane-wrapped packages.

Opening them, he pulls out a lilac leather eye mask and silky-soft lilac cuffs.

Our eyes meet, and I swallow at the smoldering power of his gaze. Holding the cuffs in one hand and the eye mask in the other, he raises an eyebrow in question.

"Yes," I whisper. "To both."

"Good girl," he murmurs, and I suck in a breath as his words zing straight to my clit.

He makes short work of the other boxes, checking that everything's pre-charged, then lays out the selection of colored silicone toys before me.

I have no clue how some of them work, but I can't wait to learn. There's one shaped like a rose, another that looks like a teardrop-shaped pebble, and a curved one I presume is for both inside and out. There's also a pack of wipes and a bottle of lube.

"You can use them all," I say, my voice breaking slightly.

He nods, and the air crackles between us. I don't know what he's going to do, but my pussy is screaming, *Do everything!* and my dress suddenly feels too tight to breathe.

Brody takes out a cleansing wipe and carefully cleans the toys, then lays them in a neat line across the bed.

"Are you ready, Piper?"

"Yes."

"Yes …?"

"Sir," I breathe out.

His nostrils flare slightly, and I swallow again, arousal humming through every cell. I'm so turned on right now, my panties are soaked through.

Brody stands, then lights the candles on the dresser and switches off the main light. The room fills with flame and shadow, his powerful form backlit by the colored lights outside.

He removes his black jacket and drapes it over the back of the chair. Then, facing me, he slowly and deliberately rolls up the sleeves of his white dress shirt.

I watch him hungrily, taking in his strong hands and his muscular forearms with their thick veins and dark hair. I want to lie back and surrender, to let him unleash all of that power onto me.

He loosens his bow tie, then pulls it off and tosses it onto the chair.

Walking to the closet, he takes out a clean towel and lays it across the bed.

"What … what's that for?" I ask, my mind racing at a million miles an hour.

"Do you trust me?"

"Yes."

"If at any point something doesn't feel good, or isn't what you want, you tell me, okay?"

I nod.

"I mean it, Piper. Don't wait. Tell me."

"I promise."

"Good. Now take off your dress."

It's got a long zipper down the back, so I turn around and hold my hair up so he can help.

The warmth of his breath ghosts across the back of my neck, raising goosebumps, but he doesn't touch me, he just eases the zipper down. Shrugging the capped sleeves from my shoulders, I let the dress drop to the ground and step out of it.

His breath catches in his throat as I reveal the same lacy underwear set I wore a few days ago.

My hands go to the clasp, but then freeze when he says, "Stop. Keep them on."

Desire floods through me, begging me to pull him on top of me, but I don't move. I'm submitting to him, and nothing has ever felt so hot.

"Turn around," he commands.

I do, my nipples hard and aching, poking through the lace of my bra and pointing directly where they want to go.

Brody's eyes rake down my body, and I swear to God I feel the fire of his gaze burning through my skin.

His cock is tenting his dress pants, and the sight makes me even hotter for him. Knowing he wants me as much as I want him only amplifies my desire.

"On the bed," he says. "On your back."

I climb onto it, and he straddles me, attaching the cuffs to each wrist, then tying them together with the ribbons so they're above my head. The whole time, he's doing his best not to touch me, and it's driving me wild.

Then he takes the blindfold and secures it on my face. I'm suddenly plunged into darkness, no light even coming in around the edges.

"Good girl," he murmurs in my ear, then nips the lobe.

I gasp, angling my head toward his, but he's already gone.

"You gonna stay still, Piper?"

I nod.

"You're gonna take what I'm gonna give? Come as many times as I say? Beg me to finally fuck you? Scream my name when I do?"

"Yes," I moan. "Yes, already."

He taps the inside of my ankles. "Spread them, baby girl. Show me how wet you are."

Spreading my legs wide, I'm rewarded by the sound of Brody's ragged inhale.

"Such a pretty sight."

His finger drags up the gusset of my panties, and I jump.

"Soaking."

I twist, trying to get his finger to my clit, but then it disappears.

"Brody," I whine.

"You're gonna come when I say so," he rumbles.

I pout. "But I need it now!"

He gives a dark chuckle. "I promise I won't edge you for long, just enough to make it worth it."

The bed shifts, and I can feel his warmth even though he still isn't touching me.

"You're so beautiful," he murmurs in my ear. "So fucking hot. You think this is frustrating for you? You have no *idea* what it's like for me. My cock's hard as fucking steel, and all I want is to suck on your sweet tits and thrust into your tight pussy until I'm so deep in you the whole world disappears."

I moan at his words, already so close to coming, my inner muscles clenching around nothing as I chase my orgasm.

"But I'm not gonna fuck you till you're stratospheric. So lie still and let me take you there."

"O-okay," I manage, then bite my lower lip as if it might release some of the pent-up energy coiling inside me.

The bed moves again, and I hear the clinking of ice cubes.

"Wha—ah!" I cry as a single point of cold touches my nipple.

But before I can adjust to the sensation, Brody draws it into the wet heat of his mouth.

"Oh my God," I moan. "Oh, my—"

My words break off as the ice cube rubs the tip of my other nipple, followed by the fire of Brody's tongue.

Between the shock of the cold, the soothing warmth, and the scratch of lace against my hypersensitized flesh, I'm struggling to keep track of the feelings. My breath is coming faster and faster, my chest arching into his touch.

But then there's a buzz on my inner thigh, and I nearly jump out of my skin.

"Don't move," Brody says, then lightly bites a nipple.

I let out an incoherent cry, my hips angling to get the buzz higher.

He moves it to my other leg, and I twist to follow.

"You gonna stay still?"

"I can't!" I cry.

"Then I'll help you."

He bites my nipple again, almost making me come, then he's gone. Fabric and heat press against my inner thighs, like he's using his legs to keep mine braced apart.

The buzzing trails up one inner thigh, then the other, never quite getting high enough to where my pussy is begging for it.

Pinned beneath him, I can't move as pleasure crackles across my skin like lightning. The orgasm hovers just out of reach, every cell screaming for release.

"Please. Please, Brody. I need to come," I gasp.

"Hmmm ..."

The vibe moves higher, teasing above and below my mound. My nerves fire and misfire, my body a chaos of pleasure and desperation. But I can't move my hips or direct my pleasure. All I can do is submit to Brody.

His free hand comes to my right breast, rolling the nipple between his fingers, and electricity shoots straight to my clit.

"Yes! Oh, my go—"

Then he finally puts the vibe right *there*, and I shatter into a million pieces of light. The release shudders through me, even more powerful because I can't move. Stars explode in the darkness behind the mask, a ringing in my ears almost as loud as my scream.

The climax keeps pulsing through me with the vibration of the toy on my clit. No vibe has ever felt like this. But then again, it's one thing to fantasize about Brody when using a toy by myself, and quite another to have the man himself using one on me.

As I lie boneless on the covers, panting, my mind and body broken, the weight of his legs lifts. Then he takes my underwear off and spreads my legs again.

"So beautiful," he murmurs right next to my pussy, and I'm hit with another jolt of pleasure.

"Please."

He blows a stream of cool air across my clit, and I buck my hips, trying to meet his mouth.

"You want me to lick this sweet pussy?" he asks, his voice deep and husky. "Because you know I want to. I want to taste you on my tongue, feel you fall apart."

"Yes!"

Just as I think he won't, he gives my pussy an open-mouthed kiss, his tongue thrusting deep inside me.

"Oh my God, yes!"

He groans as he eats me out, as if he can't get enough, and, hot on the heels of my first climax, another one barrels toward me.

But then he stops, leaving me panting and lost.

"Keep those legs spread for me, Piper. I'm gonna try something."

I nod, my heart thumping in my chest, pleasure prickling across my skin.

There's another buzzing sound, then he attaches a toy to my clit, and suddenly I'm racing so fast for the edge of the cliff I can't even breathe.

His tongue thrusts back inside me as he turns the vibe up to eleven, and I'm gone. The release shoots me through heaven and out the other side into an endless ocean of orgasms, each one building on the other until I don't know how I'm still in one piece. My pussy feels like a waterfall of light, like—*holy shit, am I squirting?*

But I can't follow the thought because Brody's mouth and the toy are gone, and now he's easing another one inside me, already vibrating.

This must be the—oh my fucking God!

One end is buzzing inside me, and the other end is suctioned onto my clit like a horny octopus.

Brody's free hand finds my breast, and the moment he tugs my nipple, I'm screaming once more, my pussy convulsing with another climax even more powerful than all the others I've just had.

He thrusts the toy inside me, and I gush again, my muscles contracting as pleasure crashes through me.

Every breath is a cry, the sensations breaking me apart until I'm shaking.

Brody eases the toy out of me, removes the cuffs and blind-fold, then covers me with his body, murmuring how much he loves me and how perfect I am as he strokes my hair and soothes me.

My arms are still trembling as I hold on to his back, feeling the dampness of his shirt from his sweat.

"I …"

"Shh … it's okay. You don't need to talk."

I don't know how long we lie like this as I continue to float somewhere between heaven and earth. I have no aware-ness of time. It's just endless bliss, with no beginning and no end.

But eventually I become aware of two things: one, I'm lying on a wet towel, and two, my pussy wants Brody's hard cock inside her.

"Did I squirt?" I murmur.

"Yes," he replies, nuzzling my ear. "And it was hot as fuck."

"You almost broke me."

He raises his head. "And what do I have to do to finish the job?"

"I think you know."

"I do?"

I undo the top buttons of his shirt. "Yeah, you do. It starts with you taking your clothes off and ends with me screaming your name."

He rises to his knees and undoes the rest of the buttons. "Is that so?"

"Yep," I reply, tugging open his trousers.

Brody's busy with his shirt, so I don't waste time, reaching inside for his cock, then taking it into my mouth with an appreciative hum.

"Jesus—fuck!" he shouts, throwing his shirt to the floor, then threading his fingers through my hair.

I lick and suck the head as deep as I can, working the rest of the shaft with both hands as Brody tenses and growls above me like he's about to shift into a bear.

The sound of his pleasure is the ultimate turn-on and the sexual energy pouring off him is elevating every sensation. The toys only took me beyond the edge of the universe because he was using them. Now, nothing's touching me, but my clit is still throbbing with need.

He eases me away. "I need to be inside you, baby."

I raise my head to meet his searing, desperate gaze. With everything that's happened today, I understand his need to join our bodies this way. We're sealing our promise to each other for the future, something we couldn't truly do before.

Straddling him, I bring my arms around the back of his neck and sink an inch down onto his cock.

Our eyes lock as we breathe together. Even after countless orgasms and the last vibe, I'm still so tight around him. Using my weight, I push down, but he only slips in a tiny bit further.

I make a noise of frustration.

"Hey, you've got this." He tucks a lock of hair behind my ear. "Just breathe. We've got all the time in the world."

His hands reach between us, cupping my breasts and teasing the nipples with the pads of his thumbs. The pleasure is sharp and immediate, and I gasp as I take a little more of him.

"That's it, baby girl."

I moan with pleasure, everything inside me primed for another release.

"You feel so fucking good," Brody murmurs. "So tight and wet."

He rolls the sensitive buds of my nipples, increasing the pressure, and my head drops back with a cry.

"Eyes on me," he rumbles, and I raise my head to meet his gaze. "I want to see your face as you take me."

My toes curl with desire, electricity tingling across my skin. He's not fully inside me, but I feel him everywhere. There's a direct line between my nipples and clit, and every time he tweaks the ends, another orgasm builds.

I undulate my hips, rocking him a little deeper until I feel the coarse hair at the base of his shaft.

"Good girl. That's it," he grits out. "Feel how your pussy's taken every inch of my cock."

I rock forward and back, losing myself in the rhythm and the endless darkness of his eyes. My release creeps closer with the inevitability of the tide. All I need to do is hold on until it washes over me.

"You gonna come, Piper?" Brody's voice is rough and ragged, like he's barely holding on. "You gonna come on my cock? Let me feel you come undone."

I nod, stars already dancing at the edge of my vision.

"And when you've come, you're gonna let me fuck you?"

I cry out, his words the tipping point for my release.

His hips jerk up. "You're gonna let me fuck you hard?"

"Brody!" I wail as my pussy spasms around the girth of his cock and he thrusts deeper.

I cling to him for dear life as the climax burns through me, scorching every cell, then tug him down onto the bed. I need to keep him inside me. I don't want him to take off his pants. I don't want to lose this connection.

As my back hits the mattress, he braces himself above me, withdraws an inch, then slams his hips forward.

"Yes! More!" I cry, not wanting him to stop and check in with me, because right now, being railed by him is the only thing in the world I want and need.

He pulls back, then snaps his hips forward, thrusting deep inside me.

"You want this? You want my cock?"

"Oh my God, yes!"

He pumps faster, harder.

"Touch yourself. I need you to come for me one more time, Piper. You can do it."

I don't know if I can, but as one hand moves to my left breast and the other to my clit, I know this is going to end exactly as I promised—with me screaming his name and shattering again.

The orgasm crashes over me so fast I barely catch a breath before it's there.

"Brodyyyy!" I scream, my voice raw as he pounds me into the mattress.

He's roaring my name back, and nothing has ever felt so right.

Then he collapses on top of me, and I hold him with every ounce of strength I have left. Because he's mine, I'm his, and this is our forever.

CHAPTER 30

BRODY

"*S*hubrum, mub dum."

I press my lips together so a laugh doesn't escape and wake Piper. She's sprawled in the middle of the bed, an arm slung over my chest and a leg tucked over one of mine.

"Brum mubdub, hummm."

My cheeks ache from smiling, and my chest feels full of pink cotton candy. I've never known happiness like this—bone-deep contentment and excitement that gives me goosebumps.

She's coming to New Zealand with me. We're doing this together.

I'd talked myself out of the job and made peace with the decision to turn it down. But now it's actually happening, all thanks to my girl, I know I'm the luckiest guy alive. Piper's right: it's the role of a lifetime, and I'm the fortunate bastard who gets to make it his own.

And this beautiful woman is going to be by my side, today, tomorrow, and forever if I play my cards right.

"Crosshatch shading!" Piper says with the clarity and diction of a British art teacher who can't wait to leave the classroom behind.

I can't stop the snort that escapes.

Piper shuffles in bed, then stills, her breathing stopping.

"You awake?" I ask.

"Did I just shout something about drawing?" she mumbles.

"Cross-hatch shading, to be precise."

She pulls the comforter over her head and groans. "So embarrassing."

I lift the covers and smooth her hair from her face. "It's cute. I'm learning so much."

Opening her eyes, she blinks at me. "How do you get to be so gorgeous this early in the morning?"

I grin. "Not as gorgeous as you. And it's nearly nine."

She lifts onto her elbows. "What? Seriously?"

"Yup."

Flopping back onto the mattress, she lets out another groan. "Not enough time for snuggles."

I trail a finger down her shoulder. "I don't know about that. What else is planned for Christmas Eve?"

Piper gives me a look. "In less than five minutes, we're going to have a visitor."

"Santa?"

"Not this morning."

My hand stops as a baby elephant runs up the stairs and along the corridor.

There's a loud knock at our door, followed a millisecond later by Martha, who dashes up to the bed and throws a bag and a bundle of wood onto the comforter, right where my own wood was looking forward to some "snuggle time" with Piper.

"Fu—aghhh!" I cry, hands darting under the covers to protect my junk.

340

"The elf came to visit!" Martha shouts, ignoring me completely.

Piper shoots me a worried look. "You okay?"

I nod as stars dance in my eyes.

"The elf left this!" Martha repeats. "At the front door! Look, Aunt Piper!"

The bundle contains a few small branches, and a net bag containing pinecone fire-starters made with colored beeswax.

"Grandma says they'll make pretty flames when they burn!" Martha continues excitedly. "And we can try them tonight!"

Everything is tied together with a festive ribbon, and a gift tag is attached.

"*To the Locke family, from the Hideaway elf.*"

"See?" Martha says. "The secret elf came to *us*!"

"Did you just arrive with Daddy?"

"No, he got called to work last night, so Nana and Papa came to look after me and bring me here this morning."

"Do you think I'll meet the Hideaway elf this afternoon?" Martha continues.

I raise an eyebrow at Piper in question.

"It's the elf treasure hunt in town," she says to me. "But it's absolutely nothing to do with the secret do-gooder. And Mom said Martha was coming here this morning to bake cookies for Santa tonight."

Martha frowns at us. "Why are you still in bed?"

"Well—" Piper begins.

"You need to hurry up. Downstairs in five, okay?"

Before either of us can reply, she runs out of the room and down the corridor, leaving the secret Hideaway elf's present on the bed with us.

I chuckle. "Why do I get the feeling she'll be back up in four minutes to check on us?"

Piper kisses me on the cheek. "Because you know her well. How's the King's jewels? Still in one piece?"

I huff. "Only just."

"Want me to kiss them better?"

I glance at the wide-open door just as Martha's voice floats up the stairs, yelling, "Hurry up!"

Piper giggles. "Maybe later." She hops out of bed and goes to the window. "Snowing already," she says, grinning at me over her shoulder. "Merry Christmas Eve, boyfriend."

I smile back. "Merry Christmas Eve, girlfriend," I reply, even though inside I'm thinking, *Merry Christmas Eve, wife.*

"Don't say a word," Marv says, his palm raised as if he's stopping traffic. "Not a f—fudging word."

He's wearing his camel-colored greatcoat and cashmere muffler, but a lurid green-and-red elf hat with a bell at the end is perched on his head, and bright red circles have been painted on his cheeks. He looks like a member of the mafia trying to hide out in Santa's workshop.

"Go ahead, laugh," he continues testily as Piper and I crack up. "You should look in a mirror yourself."

Both Piper and I are also wearing elf hats and have rosy red circles on our cheeks, courtesy of Harper's face paints. Piper looks so cute I can't stop sneaking kisses from her.

We're in the town square, getting briefed on the elf treasure hunt by John and Erica, who are dressed as Mr and Mrs Claus. I realize now why John grows a beard for Christmas. I think he's been in that red-and-white suit more than his regular clothes since we arrived.

"You'll be at your stations between two and three this afternoon," John says. "You've been given your scripts, but feel free to embellish them. When each child works out the answer to your riddle, give them a magical token and stamp their treasure map. And remember, you can always help the little ones out."

Mia's taking photos and is currently up in Hudson's face,

whose cheeks are rapidly turning the same color as the spots Harper painted on them ten minutes ago.

"Then back here for hot chocolate and cookies at about five past three," John continues. "Okay, any questions?"

Mia raises a hand. "What's Hudson's elf name this year? Frownie, Cranky, or Grouch?"

John laughs. "You're going to hurt his *elf*-esteem. This year he's Sparky."

Erica claps her hands. "Let's do a roll call! Do we have Tinsel?"

A woman waves. "Here!"

"Doodle?"

"Here!" Piper says.

"King Jingle?"

I give Erica a wave. "Present and accounted for."

"Sprinkle …? Fizzle …? Twinkle …? Bubbles …? Glimmer …? Snickerdoodle …? Pickle …? Nibbles …?" Erica continues as people around us raise their hands.

"Sparkle …? And finally, last but by no means least, Big Apple?"

Marv reluctantly raises a hand.

"All here, Mr Claus!" Erica says to John.

"Ho, ho, ho-mazing!" he replies. "Right, off to your stations!"

Piper and I are posted outside the offices of *The Almanac*, and Marv's set up on the opposite corner of the town square outside the bookstore. As soon as Piper and I get to the steps of the *Almanac* building, she turns to me.

"I really think I should tell Marv about the job and the fact that I've asked Jack to be my agent. I don't want him finding out at the same time as everyone else."

I nod. "We can tell him together later if you like?"

"I'd rather do it now. Are you okay for five minutes?"

"I'm a moderately famous actor, dressed as an elf, in the

center of Hideaway Harbor on Christmas Eve," I reply. "What could possibly go wrong?"

"You spend your whole time taking 'elfies' with fans?"

I laugh and pull her in for another quick kiss. "You're adorable."

She beams up at me. "So are you. Now have fun, and I'll see you in a bit."

My gaze follows her as she makes her way across the road and into the town square, love filling every part of me.

Out of the corner of my eye, I see a family slowing their pace as they approach. I smile, trying to place how I know them.

"Mr King?" the man says.

He's pushing a stroller with a toddler wrapped up inside, and the woman holds the hands of two older children.

"I don't know if you remember us," he continues. "You gave us your rooms at the Hideaway Hotel."

"Yes! Great to see you all again. How's your stay been?"

"The best. We can't thank you enough."

"Absolutely," his wife says, then turns to her older children. "Say thank you to Mr King."

"Thank you, Mr King," they dutifully parrot.

"Are you here for the treasure hunt?" I ask them.

They shyly hold out printed maps.

"You ready to solve my riddle?"

Two heads nod.

"Okay, here we go. I'm curved and sweet, with stripes of red, a treat for the season that's often widespread. I hang on the tree or stick in your cup. What am I? Take a guess, don't give up!"

"A candy cane!" the girl cries.

"That was quick!"

"It was *easy*," her younger brother says, then holds out his map.

I stamp both their maps, then give them one of the "magical tokens" Erica gave us to hand out.

"Good luck on the rest of the treasure hunt," I say, then crouch down next to the kids for a photo as their mom holds up her phone.

"Thank you so much, Mr King," she says. "You're the best."

I wave her words away. "It's the least I could do. I'll catch you folks again in the square at three for hot chocolate?"

They nod and thank me again, then move on to the next elf, leaving me feeling warm and fuzzy inside.

I strain to see the other side of the square where Piper is with Marv, but there are too many people, so I focus instead on the steady trail of kids with their parents, who come to take photos and solve the riddle.

It's laid-back and festive, but just as I'm getting into my stride, a dog blindsides me, barreling out of nowhere, barking wildly, and jumping up like it wants to kiss or eat me.

"Brody!"

I wrestle the overexcited dog, only to be attacked by an overexcited little boy.

"Lucky *knew* it was you before I did!" Billy cries. "She's so clever. Good dog! Good Lucky!"

"Hey, Billy! How's it going?"

"Awesome! I'm on a hunt!"

"For elves?"

"Nah. Well, kind of." He beckons me down to his level, then cups his hand over his mouth and whispers loudly, "The treasure hunt is my cover story."

Lucky barks loudly in agreement.

"Hello, Mr King," Billy's mom says as she reaches us.

"Brody, please," I reply and shake her hand. "Billy tells me he's on another hunt."

"SHUSH!" Billy whisper-shouts as his mom rolls her eyes.

"So, what are you hunting?" I ask quietly.

"Jack Frost. I saw *The Santa Clause 3* last night, and if anyone's gonna ruin Christmas, it's him."

"I like your logic. So what's your plan for when you meet him?"

Billy narrows his eyes. "Mom ruined it."

"Honey," she says with a barely concealed smile, "you can't bring your Nerf gun into town."

I laugh, then immediately cough to disguise it.

"See?" he says, pointing at me. "Brody thinks it's a good idea."

"Your mom is right," I say, using every actor's trick in the book to keep a straight face. "But that doesn't mean there aren't *other* ways to handle Jack Frost."

"Like what?" Billy asks breathlessly, as his mom's eyebrows raise in alarm.

"A snowball?" I suggest quickly.

Billy pumps his fist. "Yes! Now all I need to do is find him."

"Well ..."

"Is he here?"

I lower my voice. "I've heard a rumor that he's at the treasure hunt disguised as an elf ..."

"No way!"

"*Yes* way."

"What does he look like? Does he have white pointy hair, like the guy in the movie?"

"Not really. He doesn't have much hair at all."

"And where is he?"

"Apparently, he's been seen skulking outside the bookstore."

Billy gives me a serious nod, then gathers a handful of snow from the side of the steps leading up to the front door of *The Almanac*.

"Honey, you can't walk around with that," his mom protests.

"Okay," he replies, then squeezes the snow into a ball and shoves it in his pocket.

"Billy!"

"What?" He doesn't wait for an answer, scraping more snow from the steps, compacting it together, then filling his other pocket.

"Do you want to get your map stamped?" I ask, attempting to deflect him from his armament project.

He shrugs. "Sure. What's the riddle?"

I tell him, and he immediately gets the answer.

"So, where's your map?"

Rummaging in his pocket, he pulls out a wet and battered piece of paper and hands it to me.

"Maybe I should look after that?" Judy says after I stamp it.

"Thanks, Mom!"

I give her the map and a magical token for safekeeping, then turn back to Billy. "So, where are you going next?"

"Oh, I dunno," he replies artlessly. "I was thinking about the bookstore."

He gives me an enormous wink, and I fake another coughing fit to cover my laughter.

"Come on, Lucky! Come on, Mom," he says, then gazes at me. "You'll be there for hot chocolate at the end?"

"Wouldn't miss it for the world."

"Good, I'll let you know how I get on *at the bookstore*." He gives me another wink, then dashes off with Lucky, his mom running after him, yelling at him to slow down.

"Was that Billy?" Piper asks as she crosses the street a few moments later.

I kiss her. "Yeah. Full of energy and on the hunt for Jack Frost."

"We don't have anyone playing him. Maybe we should have that next year."

"I told him he was disguised as an elf."

She gives me the side eye. "And who is that, then?"

I grin.

EVIE ALEXANDER

"Oh, you didn't! Not Marv?"

"See, you picked him first too."

She giggles. "Poor guy. He won't know what hit him."

"I think he will. Billy's got snowballs in his pockets."

"Brody! You are—" She shakes her head, but she's still laughing.

"How did it go with Marv?"

She sobers up a little. "Okay, thank goodness. He's just happy that we're happy. He told me he was worried you were going to change your mind and turn the job down."

"He knows me well."

"I said we're going to tell everyone tonight after the treasure hunt, when we're home. And Mia's going to be there too, for the family photo and presents."

"You still do presents on Christmas Eve?"

"Just one or two. It's nice and chill before the big day, which is mostly about Martha."

"She must love it."

"She does, and that just makes us love it even more as we see it through her eyes."

I wrap my arms around Piper and kiss her, because I love this woman, and I can't wait to spend forever by her side. The kiss is relatively chaste, but one turns into two, and two into twenty, and I completely forget we're both dressed as elves, with a job to do.

"Beautiful!" Mia cries, and we break apart. "And another one with just smiling. Please?"

We pose for her with ridiculously cheesy grins on our faces.

"You photographing all the elves?" Piper asks.

"Pretty much. I got a great one just now of some kid lobbing a snowball at Marv."

Piper digs her elbow in my ribs as I crack up. "See you for hot chocolate at three?" she asks Mia.

"Maybe not. I've got a few errands to run first." Mia catches my eye, then gives me a tiny nod.

Good. My plan is in motion.

"But you'll be at ours at four?" Piper continues.

"Sure, but I've gotta shoot now," Mia replies, then jogs up the steps into *The Almanac* building.

My heart beats a little faster in my chest. If Mia comes through, I'll have a present for Piper that she won't be expecting.

CHAPTER 31

PIPER

"*M*arv! Get in here!" Mom calls out as we all assemble next to the tree in the family room for the annual Christmas Eve photo.

The house smells of cinnamon cookies and coffee, with the faint scent of wood smoke from the fire. With the colored lights illuminating the tree and reflecting off the decorations around the room, it's more festive than a Hallmark movie.

"Nah, this is for family," Marv says, flapping a hand in her direction and taking a step back.

"You *are* family," Mom replies briskly, then drags him to stand next to her.

I lean back against Brody, warmth suffusing every part of me as he nuzzles my neck, occasionally nipping at my skin and making me shiver.

"Hey, you two in the back row. Stop making out!" Mia calls to us, then shifts the camera to her face. "Okay, say 'jingle bells'!"

"Jingle bells!" we say, and she takes a few pictures, then checks the screen on the back.

"It's—"

"Perfect except for me?" Hudson says, and everyone laughs.

Mia grins. "Busted."

Marv steps forward, his hands outstretched. "Let me take one with you in it."

"Yes!" Mom says. "Come on, Mia."

Mia looks between her camera and Marv like she doesn't trust him with her baby.

"I went to film school," he tells her. "I know my way around a camera."

She reluctantly hands it to him, and he moves it in his hands, checking it out. But as Mia edges toward us, he cries out and pretends to drop it.

Mia shrieks, lunging for him, then shakes her head as he winks at her and says, "Gotcha!"

We all crack up, and Mia rolls her eyes and shakes her head. "That's a Hudson-level prank."

"And you still fell for it," Hudson replies with a smirk.

"Come on, honey," Mom says to her. "Stand here." She puts Mia next to Hudson. "Now, son, put your arm around her."

"This isn't going to end well," Ethan mutters behind me.

"Why not, Daddy?" Martha asks.

Hudson flinches as if he's just been poked. "Hey," he says to Mia. "Cut that out."

"You need to smile for the camera," she says to him.

"I know how to—will you *stop*?"

"Stop what?" she asks, but her hand is behind her back, her finger already poised to poke him again.

Suddenly Hudson grabs her in a headlock and gives her a noogie.

Mia shrieks, then executes a move straight out of the WWE, grabbing his legs and sweeping them out from under him, bringing them both to the floor. We scatter as Mia and Hudson grapple on the rug.

My best friend is really strong, but you'd have to be a bull to get the better of Hudson.

"Submit!" he shouts.

"Never!" she yells back, twisting to free herself like a snake having a seizure.

Both of them are red-faced and out of breath. I don't think they realize we're all still here until Ethan hands Martha to Dad and steps forward with Brody to separate them.

"How old are you?" Ethan asks as if Hudson were his son, not his younger brother.

Hudson's chest heaves. "She started it!" he protests, jabbing a finger at Mia.

"Me? You're the one who gave me a noogie!"

"Say sorry," Ethan says to Hudson.

"Why do I—"

"*Both* of you say sorry," Ethan continues with the kind of authority no one dares question.

"Sorry," Hudson and Mia mumble at each other.

I sneak a glance at Harper, Mom, and Dad. They're grinning like this is the best form of Christmas entertainment. Marv, meanwhile, is still taking pictures of the drama.

"Now you need to kiss and make up," Martha says, her tone imitating that of her father.

"What?" Mia and Hudson exclaim together.

"If you're really sorry, then you'll kiss each other and make everything better."

There's an electric silence as Mia and Hudson stare at each other. Then Mia shakes her head.

"I'm good, thanks," she mumbles and goes to the far end of the group, running her hands through her hair.

Hudson smooths his own hair down, then goes to the opposite end from Mia.

"Let's try again, shall we?" Marv says. "Say 'jingle bells'!"

"IS IT PRESENT TIME YET?" Martha asks Mom as we all settle into couches and chairs a few minutes later.

"Almost, sweetie," Mom says. "Grandpa just went to look for Santa."

"Grandma," Martha says patiently. "I know it's really Grandpa."

"Really?"

"Yes. The real Santa is too busy preparing for tonight, so he needs his stunt doubles. Like Grandpa."

"Okay, but you must remember to play along. Don't let Grandpa know you know."

"I won't. I promise."

She climbs onto Ethan's lap, and he drops a kiss on her head.

"So, you do presents on Christmas Eve, then?" Marv asks.

"It's a nod to my Nordic heritage," Mom says. "We still open some presents on Christmas Day, but it can get a bit busy, and it's really—"

"About the children," Martha interrupts seriously, then adds. "Like me."

"And what do *you* want for Christmas?" Marv asks her.

"A new mommy," she says firmly.

I freeze, and Brody stops breathing beside me. My gaze darts to Ethan's tight expression.

"You've already got a mommy, sweetheart," he says quietly.

"I know," she replies calmly, as if this is a speech she's been practicing for a long time. "But I want a mommy who talks. One who gives me kisses and cuddles."

I grip Brody's hand as tears prick my eyes.

Ethan clears his throat. "It's not that easy."

Martha shifts on his lap to look at him directly and puts a

little hand on his cheek. "I know, Daddy. But don't worry. I've taken care of it for you."

His eyebrows knit together in confusion. "Huh?"

"I made a wish when we went to the spring."

Martha glances from him to Marv. "If you make a wish at the spring, it always comes true. Especially if it's about love."

She looks around the room at the rest of us. "I know she's not going to be here for Christmas. That's too soon for the magic to work. She's coming *next* year."

Silence. I don't know what to say, and it seems no one else does either. I want to hug Martha and Ethan, take away the pain on my brother's face, and reassure his little girl that it's okay to want a mom who's alive.

"Well, um …" Mom begins. "Just as long as she doesn't arrive when Grandpa and I are on our cruise."

Martha's face falls. "I forgot about that. When are you going?"

"Fall, sweetie. Not for ages yet."

"How long will you be gone?"

"A month," Mom says, then winces as Martha's mouth falls open.

"But that's forever!" she gasps, her chin wobbling.

"No, no, sweetie! It's not long, I promise!" Mom says, getting out of her chair and taking Martha's hands. "And Nana and Papa will still be here."

Martha nods. "Okay." She takes a breath. "They can meet my new mommy first."

"Sweetheart—" Ethan starts, but the door opens, cutting him off.

"Ho, ho, ho!" Dad says loudly. "I hear some people want to open their presents early!"

"Santa!" Martha yells, sliding off Ethan's lap and running to his side. "Look, everyone! It's Santa!"

Everyone except Ethan chimes in excitedly.

I glance his way and mouth, *"You okay?"*

He nods, then forces a smile and turns to Martha, who's pulling Dad into the room.

"You have to give out our presents first," she says, holding up a bag. Dad reaches for it, but she hugs it close to her chest. "You can help me."

"Okay," he says, his eyes twinkling. "Who's first?"

Martha pulls out a present. "For Grandma and Grandpa."

He follows her across the room so she can give it to Mom.

"Thank you, honey. Can I open it now?"

"Not yet, because everyone got the same. Kind of. You'll see."

She hands out the rest of the gifts to each of us, then claps with excitement as we open them, revealing candles.

"We got them from the Christmas market. And I decided which one was best for each of you."

We all thank her as she twirls in a circle, basking in the appreciation.

"Who's up next?" Dad asks.

Harper raises her hand.

Martha skips over. "Can I help you, Aunt Harper? I'm Santa's little helper."

"Sure you can, sweetie." She gives Martha a bag. "But before you open them, I've got a small announcement."

I sit up straighter, conscious that I've still got my own announcement to make.

"I'm going to open my perfume shop next year!" she says, an excited grin splitting her face. "I signed the lease yesterday."

"Oh honey, that's wonderful news!" Mom exclaims, leaping up to hug her.

Then we're all on our feet, showering her with congratulations. It's what she's always wanted, and I'm thrilled her dream is becoming a reality.

"I'm in the unit next to Lola," Harper tells us. "And we're going to work together to bring more love into people's lives!"

"I can't wait to tell everyone!" Mom exclaims. "They're going to be so excited, especially Eileen!"

"I made you all a scent to celebrate," Harper continues.

"Have you made one for me?" Martha asks.

"Sure have. It's got top notes of unicorns and candy canes."

Martha dives into the bag Harper gave her, rooting through it until she finds the one with her name on it. Then she hands the bag off to Dad, saying, "You can do the rest, Santa."

Dad gives us our gifts, and I unwrap the tissue paper around mine to reveal a beautiful glass bottle with my name written in calligraphy on the side. Popping the stopper, I smell cinnamon, coffee, and vanilla. My clever sister has created a scent that will always make me feel happy and remind me of home.

"Some of them have your name on them," Harper says. "Others have a word that I thought would be a good representation of you."

"Power," Marv reads on the side of his bottle. "Thank you, Harper! This is neat. I'm gonna wear it to all my meetings."

"Fire," Hudson reads. "Love it." He looks at Mia. "What did you get?"

She shows him. "Light. Thank you, Harper!"

Brody takes the stopper out of his bottle and hands it to me to smell.

"Oh, my," I murmur as the scent travels through me like olfactory Viagra. "I thought you smelled divine already, but with this …"

He raises an eyebrow, then sprays a puff of the scent above our heads, the fine droplets floating down like mist.

Suddenly, I'm in a sex forest at dawn, and I'm here for wood. My lips meet Brody's, and my body lights up. Desire scorches through me like wildfire. I can't get enough. I need—

"Is your perfume called 'Snuggle Time,' Aunt Piper?" Martha asks loudly.

Brody and I break apart as everyone laughs.

I glance at Harper. She's got the smuggest expression on her face. She's a genius and she knows it.

Fanning my face, I take a bag from beside my feet. "Okay, I'm going next, but first I've also got an announcement."

"Oh my Lord, you're pregnant!" Mom shrieks.

I blink at her.

"Erica ..." Dad says.

Mom's cheeks turn bright red. "I mean ... er ..."

"I'm not pregnant," I say. "That's not ... we haven't ..." I glance at Brody.

"It's not something we've discussed yet," he says smoothly.

"Oh," Mom continues. "But you *will* discuss it—"

"Erica ..." Dad says, more firmly this time.

"Yes, yes. Sorry," she mumbles, then folds wrapping paper in her lap as if nothing just happened.

"Grandma wants more grandkids," Martha says to Marv. "And Aunt Piper and Uncle Brody are her best bet."

"Is that right?"

"Yes. But next year, when my new mommy arrives, she'll have a baby with Daddy, and I'll get a little sister."

"What?" Dad stops in his tracks, and I remember he was out of the room when Martha told us about her wish at the Hideaway Spring.

"I'm quitting my job and my apartment in Brooklyn to move to New Zealand with Brody," I say loudly. "The showrunners offered me a job as a concept artist on the production, and I've accepted."

The room erupts—Mom crying, Mia whooping, and most others clapping or cheering. Martha scans the room, trying to decide how to react, while Brody gazes at me like I'm his entire universe.

"Oh, honey, I'm so happy for you!" Mom cries, rushing over to envelop me in a tight hug. "You have to tell us everything!"

Excitement bubbles out of me like champagne from a shaken bottle as I recount how the showrunners reached out after fans went wild for my drawings.

"And so they should," Harper says with a proud smile. "You're truly gifted."

Everyone is thrilled, and their love and support make me even more excited about the future.

Presents are forgotten as I'm bombarded with questions. I thought Mom would be upset about me being away from Hideaway so long, but she seems to think this means I'll be home more than when I was working in Brooklyn.

"Your mom's right," Mia says. "You'll have more time off, so we'll see more of you, not less."

"Yay! And you'll be right next door to us!" Martha says, clearly picturing New Zealand as just another neighboring state, like New Hampshire.

"We can chat more at dinner," I say. "We're forgetting the presents."

"Yes," Martha agrees, grabbing Dad's hand. "Come along, Santa."

I sit back down, and Brody puts his arm around me, pulling me close. Contentment runs through my veins like warm molasses. I've got the best family and friends, and now, the best boyfriend, too.

He unwraps the Christmas tree ornament I bought him at the market like it's the most precious gift he's ever received, his face lighting up with a smile.

"Thank you. I love it." Then he pulls a flat package from behind the couch and hands it to me.

"What's this? You've already given me all my presents."

"This is an extra surprise my elf friend and I have been working on."

"Your elf friend?" I glance around the room. Marv looks innocent enough, but Mia wears a knowing grin. "What did you do?" I ask.

She shrugs. "The usual—was awesome and made people's dreams come true. Same old, same old."

It feels like a hardback book, but when I tear off the paper, I gasp, then burst out laughing.

It's a photo book, and the cover is the picture Mia took of Brody and me at the town dance, right after I told him about the New Zealand job. We're grinning at the camera like we might burst with happiness, our hair tousled and lipstick smudged around our mouths.

"Oh, Aunt Piper ..." Martha says, wrinkling her nose. "You look like clowns."

"Very happy clowns," I reply, smiling, before opening the book.

It's a collection of every photo taken of us since we arrived in Hideaway Harbor as fake boyfriend and girlfriend: the first-night family photo, the calendar reveal at The Perfect Package, us hugging at Love at First Sip, our first kiss in the town square during the carols.

I leaf through the pages, my heart overflowing. Our relationship may have started as fake, but anyone looking at these photos would see two people deeply in love.

The last pages hold pictures from today's elf treasure hunt. I wipe my eyes as I take them in.

"Thank you," I say softly to Brody. "And thank you, Mia. This is incredible."

"There's one more picture," Mia says.

I turn the final page to find a copy of the photo taken at Ethan, Olivia, and Brody's graduation party. The one where I'm standing next to Brody, the backs of our hands touching.

But this copy isn't scanned from the photo hanging in the dining room. Its edges are worn, and the colors are faded.

EVIE ALEXANDER

I glance at Mia, then Brody, my brows drawing together. "Why does it look like this?"

Brody shifts, pulling his wallet from his back pocket and opening it carefully to show me what's inside.

My hand flies to my heart and my breath catches. "Have you …?" I look up at him. "How long have you had this?"

"Mia gave it to me the day before I left Hideaway," he says quietly. "It's been in my wallet ever since."

My throat is too tight to speak, and my eyes flood with emotion.

Brody wipes my tears away with the pads of his thumbs, then gathers me into his arms. "Don't cry, sweetheart," he murmurs. "We're together now."

But everything is spilling out at once, and I can't stop.

"Come on," he says, helping me to my feet. "Let's get some air."

We leave the family room, and Brody helps me into my boots and coat, then leads me out onto the porch. It's cold and still out here, snow falling gently and muffling every sound.

The peace and quiet settles over me, and I start to calm. I blow my nose, then snuggle into Brody's side.

"I remember standing here when you left Hideaway," I say softly. "The moment we almost kissed. And not knowing if I'd ever see you again."

Brody lets out a sigh. "I thought I'd come back once I'd made it, but 'making it' kept turning into just one more job. And then I figured it was too late."

He gently lifts my chin, and I lose myself in the liquid warmth of his eyes.

"I'll never be able to thank Marv enough for his meddling," he says, "because it brought me back to you. And now that I've got you, I'm never going to let you go."

His lips find mine, and I kiss him with all of my heart. I kiss him for the woman I am now, and for the sixteen-year-old girl who loved him just as much then as I do today.

Breathless, I break the kiss just to gaze at him again, to remind myself this is real, and the start of the rest of our lives together.

"I love you," I whisper.

He touches his forehead to mine. "I love you, too."

In the distance, sleigh bells ring softly, reminding me that no matter the season, Hideaway Harbor is a magical place.

I smile. "Merry Christmas, Brody King."

"Merry Christmas, Piper Locke," he replies, love shining in his eyes. "And here's to the happiest New Year ever."

Then he kisses me again, and I melt in his arms, knowing our stars have finally aligned and will shine together on the same path forever.

EPILOGUE

PIPER

"Yep, that's it. Perfect," I say as Brody adjusts his stance. "Are you okay holding that pose for the next twenty minutes or so?"

"Sure, no problem. What's my motivation again?"

"Champion of the sword, master of magic, king of all he surveys. You're gazing down at the battlefield of Ashmyre after your victory over the Skarthven, knowing you've vanquished your enemies, and no one dares challenge you to the crown."

"So, just a normal day at the office, then?"

I grin. "And you're also the hottest elf lord around."

"Even dressed like this and splattered in fake blood?"

"*Especially* like that."

He gives me a smoldering look that promises even more earth-shattering sex tonight when we get back to our hotel, then adopts the stance I'm after.

We're perched on one of the massive limestone boulders along the slopes of Castle Hill in Arthur's Pass National Park, at the end of a long day of filming. Most of the crew has already headed back to Christchurch, but Brody and I stayed behind so I could sketch him in this incredible landscape.

Massive boulders, some larger than buildings, are scattered across the rolling green hills, as if tossed carelessly by the gods. From our vantage point, we have a full 360-degree view of the surrounding mountains. It's an epic setting, featured everywhere from *The Chronicles of Narnia* to *The Lord of the Rings* and *The Hobbit*.

When we got to New Zealand four months ago, the production of *The Chronicles of the Sword and the Flame* gave me a folding chair, a table, and a small portable easel to use on set so I can either draw by hand or on a large tablet. Each morning, I pinch myself that this is my life now, and with every bit of positive feedback I receive, my confidence grows.

My pencil moves fast over the paper, sketching out Brody in full costume, hair, and makeup. My inner nerd is officially out of the box and I'm leaning into every "Brody as a warrior elf" fantasy I've ever had. Luckily, he thinks it's cute, and the hair and makeup team doesn't ask too many questions when he leaves the set still wearing his pointy ears …

Right now, I wonder if he's ever been hotter. He's dressed for battle in an outfit of supple leather and hardened metal plating adorned with intricate filigree. His shoulders are capped with elaborate pauldrons shaped like the wings of a bird, and his arms are protected by articulated gauntlets, etched with an alloy pattern of vines and leaves.

He's wearing leather leggings and boots, his gold-and-silver helm lying on the ground, and his bloodied sword still in hand. His hair is longer than usual, and fake blood and dirt streak his face.

It takes all my self-control not to let go of my pencil and jump him.

It's golden hour, and the sun is setting in the west, casting

Brody in an ethereal glow and glinting off the metal of his costume. I quickly take a few photos for future reference, then keep drawing, capturing his energy and power at this pivotal moment in the story.

I'm so in the zone, I don't notice time passing until I come to a natural stop and take a cleansing breath.

"Can I see?" he asks.

I nod, suddenly bone-tired, and glance at my watch. "I'm so sorry! I didn't realize it had been so long."

"It's all good. I was enjoying the view."

He lets out a long whistle as he gazes at my drawing. "Holy shit, Piper. That's incredible!"

My chest puffs with pride. "I'll make more tweaks when we're back, but I'm so pleased with how it's turned out. It makes such a difference doing it out here."

I gaze at the landscape around us, the very one I imagined last Christmas when Martha asked me to think of what I wanted more than anything in the world, then blink, reminding myself I'm really here.

Standing to stretch my limbs, I face Brody and smile, but then falter. There's something in his eyes, a hesitancy or worry. I'm so finely attuned to him that I know something's up, and it doesn't look good.

"What's wrong?" I ask. "You okay?"

He's gazing at me intently, his expression so serious that my heart flutters.

"Brody?"

He drops to one knee.

"Piper. I love you, and I've always loved you."

He takes my hands in his. "For me, it's always been you, and it always *will* be you. I know it may seem sudden, but this has been on my mind for over a decade. When you're ready, and if you're ever ready, will you marry me?"

My brain stops normal function to throw a party to which my vocal cords have not been invited.

"Shit, I almost forgot," he mutters, his hands shaking as he reaches into an inside pocket of his costume and pulls out a ring, holding it out to me.

"Is that ...?" I croak.

"It's a copy, but made of gold and platinum, and set with real diamonds and rubies."

I stare at the ring of the Queen of Draventhorne, based on a picture I'd drawn for the production when I arrived on set in January.

"It's your design, so I hoped you'd love it," Brody continues. "And in this universe, you're *my* queen. You're my other half, my partner in life, and my one true love."

My mouth is still in shock, refusing to articulate my thoughts, so I take the ring from him and slip it onto the fourth finger of my left hand.

The gems catch the light of the setting sun, making the ring sparkle and glow on my trembling finger like it's alive.

"Is that a 'yes,' then?" Brody asks.

I nod faster than a bobblehead on a bumpy road and drag him to his feet.

He gives me a relieved smile. "Are you sure?"

"Y-yes!" I finally manage. "Yes, yes, yes, yes, yes!"

Then I throw my arms around his neck and hold him so tight I can't breathe.

A distant wolf-whistle breaks us apart, and I turn to see a few crew members down in the valley clapping and cheering.

"Did they know?"

He smiles. "I don't think so, but the whole 'going down on one knee at sunset on top of a rock in a national park' might have given the game away."

I laugh, happiness making me lighter than air. "I can't wait to marry you. I've been doodling 'Piper King' in my sketchbooks since I was a teenager, so I'm finally going to make it official."

"Fall wedding in Hideaway, then?"

"Yes! Mom's gonna freak out. I need to call her."

"At one a.m.?"

I pull a face. "She won't mind being woken up with that news, but then she won't be able to get back to sleep, so we'd better wait."

"And in the meantime, I'm gonna take you to bed and show you just how much I love you. And you're only allowed to wear one thing: that ring."

I sigh. "Sounds perfect."

He rubs the end of his nose against mine. "Just like you."

Then he kisses me, and I lose myself in him and this perfect moment. Brody's my first love, my greatest love, and the man I can't wait to spend the rest of my life loving.

THE END!

Ready for more holiday fun in Hideaway Harbor?
Next up is ...

The Holiday Whoopie by Sara L. Hudson

Jack Lourd didn't plan to stay in Hideaway Harbor—or fall for Audrey Nouel, the woman in cranberry Crocs who bakes like a dream and glares like a sport.

But between mistletoe mishaps and pastry-fueled chaos, he starts to wonder if he's ready to make whoopie...pies.

The Holiday Whoopie is a grump vs. grump holiday romcom featuring a jaded Hollywood lawyer and a small-town baker with zero patience and a menu full of suggestive desserts.

Read The Holiday Whoopie now!

Christmas at Hideaway Harbor series

1. The Holiday Hate-Off by Angela Casella
2. The Holiday Fakers by Evie Alexander
3. The Holiday Whoopie by Sara L. Hudson
4. The Holiday Post by L.B. Dunbar
5. The Holiday Grump by Enni Amanda

All books are interconnected standalones and can be read in any order.

REVIEW THE HOLIDAY FAKERS

WRITE A REVIEW & MAKE MY DAY!

Thank you so much for reading The Holiday Fakers! I hope you enjoyed reading it as much as I enjoyed writing it!

Even if just a few lines (or star rating), writing a review is the most amazing thing you can do! It helps people find my books, and lets them know what you loved about them.

You can review The Holiday Fakers at:
Amazon
Bookbub
Barnes & Noble
Goodreads
The StoryGraph
And any other storefront or platform you use!

And, if you want to share more about The Holiday Fakers on social media or your blog, please **help yourself to our library of graphics, elements and more by going to:**

www.eviealexanderauthor.com/the-holiday-fakers/

Thank you!

Evie♡

READ MORE OF EVIE'S BOOKS!

Want to check out Evie's other books? Why not start with the **Kinloch series**. Laugh-out-loud steamy romcom that's heating up the Scottish Highlands!

Start with the multi-award-winning **Highland Games** (available in all formats) by going to:
www.eviealexanderbooks.com

And you can also dive into the **Foxbrooke series**. Laugh-out-loud steamy romcom with an outrageous aristocratic family in Somerset!

Start with the multi-award-winning **Love ad Lib** (available in all formats) by going to:
www.eviealexanderbooks.com

NEWSLETTER SIGN-UP

Want free books and audiobooks? Sign up to my newsletter to get your copies today, plus so much more...

In my newsletter you get Evie news before anyone else, as well as exclusive content and goodies.

Newsletter subscribers are my extra special friends, and get everything from bonus epilogues, 19,000 words of deleted sex scenes, free books and audiobooks, extracts from my current work-in-progress, and exclusive offers and giveaways.

Sign up now!

www.eviealexanderauthor.com/subscribe/

SEX INDEX

(AKA THE GOOD BITS)

There have been many great contributions to the world of literature. Gutenberg invented the printing press, Shakespeare invented romantic comedy, and J K Rowling invented Harry Potter. However, all of these achievements pale into insignificance compared to my contribution – the sex index.

Using this sex index, you can easily find the steamier moments from The Holiday Fakers. Enjoy...

Page 157 – Let's practice kissing ...
Page 223 – When you've cheated death, it's time to re-affirm life
Page 272 – You have a date with the Earl of Fuck-Me-Now Abbey
Page 328 – She's pickin' up good vibrations ...

And if that wasn't enough, don't forget I've got nineteen thousand words of super-hot deleted sex scenes from Highland and Hollywood Games available exclusively for newsletter subscribers.

If you want some extra action, then click here to sign up to my newsletter today!

www.eviealexanderauthor.com/subscribe/

ACKNOWLEDGMENTS

Yay! Here's where I say a massive THANK YOU to all the amazing people who helped get The Holiday Fakers out into the world!

This book is dedicated to Enni Amanda. She's a truly beautiful human inside and out, and a gifted writer, artist, designer, and loyal and supportive friend. When we had the idea of creating a shared world romance series and the world of Hideaway Harbor back in 2024, I knew it would be an incredibly fulfilling project, and I've loved every moment we've spent together planning it all out.

Enni also gets an extra thank you for designing this stunning cover. If you want her to design a cover for you, find her at www.yummybookcovers.com!

Thank you to Dr Tonya for always being there to answer medical questions, and to Dr Suzanne Belton for teaching me so much about the clitoris and also making such fabulous models. Get yours now by going to www.anatomicaleducation.org

Thank you to my editing and proofing team — Aanchal Jain, Margaret Amatt, Tori Ross, Barbara Kellyn, Heather Kelley, and @babewithbigbooks, as well as Pash Baker for being the most epic alpha reader.

My team at Emlin Press: Victoria and Liezl. Thank you for doing everything I can't, won't, or don't have time for. Thank you for tolerating my foul mouth, laughing at my unfunny jokes and sticking around.

Thank you to my husband—the best decision I've ever made, and to my daughter—the best luck I've ever had. I love you both to the ends of the multiverse and back.

And last, but by no means least, I want to thank my fabulous ARC team, the incredible online community of book lovers and YOU, the reader! Thank you for your continued support and for reading my first book in the Hideaway series! Each time you read my books, write me a review and recommend me in countless different ways, my heart gets a little fuller. Thank you!

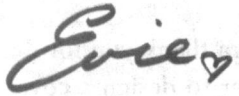

Ps - I love love LOVE hearing from my readers so please get in touch via email or social media to ask me anything or just tell me about your day!

ALSO BY EVIE ALEXANDER

Get all of Evie's books in print, audio, or eBook format, as well as special offers, early releases, and exclusive deals at www.eviealexanderbooks.com

THE KINLOCH SERIES

HIGHLAND GAMES

Zoe's given up everything for a ramshackle cabin in Scotland. She wants a new life, but her scorching hot neighbour wants her out. As their worlds collide, will Rory succeed in destroying her dream? Or has he finally met his match? Let the games begin…

<u>Tropes</u>

Small Town, Enemies-to-Lovers, Grumpy/Sunshine, Fish-out-of-Water, Opposites Attract, Forced Proximity

HOLLYWOOD GAMES

In a last-ditch attempt to save Kinloch castle, new lovers Rory and Zoe throw open the doors to a Hollywood superstar. But when it all goes south, it's up to them to rewrite the script, save the castle's future, and find their own happy ending.

<u>Tropes</u>

Small Town, Soulmates, Grumpy/Sunshine, Fish-out-of-Water

KISSING GAMES

Bodyguard Charlie has a new mission: teach workaholic Hollywood actress Valentina how to play, one wild adventure at a time. But when no-strings fun turns into something more, they have to face some hard truths. Can they find a future together, or will their love remain a Highland fling?

<u>Tropes</u>

Small Town, Dark Secrets, Bodyguard/Actress, Forced Proximity, Alpha-roll hero, Dating Game

MUSICAL GAMES

After lying to a Hollywood megastar, Sam needs Jamie to write an album with her in just ten days He's got the voice of an angel and the body of a god, but fame is the last thing on his mind. Will he help make her dreams come true?

<u>Tropes</u>

Small Town, Grumpy/Sunshine, Male Virgin, Cinnamon Roll Hero, Opposites Attract, Fish-out-of-Water, Forced Proximity

WEDDING GAMES

Rory and Zoe want to get married. Not easy when their mothers are mortal enemies and Rory's step-father is a Hollywood star with a death wish. Can they unravel the tangles in time to tie the knot, or is eloping the only answer? Get ready for Scotland's wedding of the year!

<u>Tropes</u>

Small Town, Grumpy/Sunshine, Opposites Attract, Soulmates, Fish-out-of-Water

CHRISTMAS GAMES

Having a baby's easy, right? Until wayward in-laws, an out-of-control cow and mad Santa get in the way. All Rory and Zoe want is a relaxing Christmas before their baby arrives, but straightforward is not their style…

<u>Tropes</u>

Small Town, Grumpy/Sunshine, Opposites Attract, Soulmates, Fish-out-of-Water

THE FOXBROOKE SERIES

ONE NIGHT IN FOXBROOKE

When chef Ben 'Kenobi' Walker gets the call to help save a VIP dinner at Foxbrooke Manor, he doesn't expect to run into old flame Leia Perry. She's all grown up and even more attractive than when they were teenagers – but she hasn't forgotten what happened ten years ago, and she *definitely* hasn't forgiven him. Will one night give Ben the second chance he needs to prove himself and win back Leia's heart?

Tropes

Small Town, Second Chance, Return to Hometown, Enemies-to-Lovers, Bet, Brother's Best Friend, Work Colleagues, Forced Proximity, First Love, Reverse Grumpy-Sunshine, Opposites Attract

LOVE AD LIB

Shy and reserved Lord Henry Foxbrooke needs a fake girlfriend. Free-spirited actress Libby Fletcher needs a job. But when they arrive in Somerset for Henry's birthday celebrations, neither are prepared for their reception. As friendship blurs and faking it starts to feel a little too real, disaster strikes. Can Libby and Henry stick to the script, or has their entire act just bombed?

Tropes

Small Town, Fake Dating, Grumpy/Sunshine, Opposites Attract, One Bed, Different Worlds, Fish-out-of-Water

AN UNHOLY AFFAIR

Gorgeous Jack Newton has fallen in love with Eveline Shaw. But she's a female vicar dreaming of marriage and kids, and he's a male escort heading out of town. Can Jack show Eveline heaven and keep his secret safe, or are they both headed straight for hell?

Tropes

Small Town, Forbidden Love, Love at First Sight, Sworn off a Relationship, Priest, Different Worlds, Opposites Attract, Dark Secret

THE UPPER CRUSH

James Hunter-Savage is a cocky city boy who isn't used to anyone else taking the reins. Lady Estelle Foxbrooke is a fiery country girl who's about to show him who's boss. Can they learn to fight for love rather than with each other, or will their love hate relationship destroy everything they're working for?

Tropes

Small Town, Enemies-to-Lovers, Alpha Hero, Love/Hate, Playboy in Love, Different Worlds, Workplace Romance, Fake Dating

THE LOVE POSITION

Beautiful academic, Sophia Hunter-Savage, has run away to an ashram to reinvent herself. Hot yoga teacher, Isaac Hayward, has left town to avoid the only woman able to tempt him off the spiritual path.

But karma sucks.

Now Isaac's teaching Sophia and they're finding themselves in all kinds of unexpected positions. Will their forbidden love bring inner peace and happiness, or end in a tangled mess?

Tropes

Forbidden Love, Opposites Attract, Teacher/Student, Sworn off a Relationship, Forced Proximity, Love at First Sight, Different Worlds, Fish-out-of-Water

CHRISTMAS OFF SCRIPT

Best friends, Leo Foxbrooke and Ella Chamberlain, have never been single at the same time. Until now… Playing Cinderella and Prince Charming in the Christmas pantomime, their on-stage chemistry kindles an unexpected spark behind the scenes. Can they rewrite their friendship this festive season and finally unwrap true love?

Tropes

Small Town, Friends-to-Lovers, Best Friend's Ex, Oblivious to Love, Unrequited Love, Fake Relationship

ONE NIGHT ONLY
Coming soon

Pop star Avery Taylor craves a break from her public life, and a one-night stand with a stranger feels like the perfect escape. A year later, while recovering from an injury, she's stunned to find her nurse is Connor Foxbrooke, the man who touched her soul that night. Avery is ready to break the rules for love, but Connor, who values his quiet life, fears heartbreak. With Avery set to return to the spotlight as soon as she's recovered, can they bridge their worlds and turn their one night into forever?

Tropes

Second-Chance, Mistaken Identity, One Night Stand, Different Worlds, Opposites Attract, Injury, Forced Proximity, Fish-out-of-Water, Celebrity, Pop Star, Small Town

RIGHTING MR WRONG

Coming soon

Mooning a party of nuns is bad for anyone, but for TV star Aiden Wilder, it's catastrophic. Enter Willow Foxbrooke, a quiet PR worker who's tasked with saving his reputation through a fake relationship. As Willow teaches him how to recover his image, they start to fall for each other. But how can true love grow from something that was never real to begin with?

Tropes

Small Town, Fake Dating, Grumpy/Sunshine, Celebrity, Opposites Attract, Different Worlds, Fish-out-of-Water

UNDER THE INFLUENCER

Coming soon

Sunny Summer Foxbrooke's career as an Influencer is over. Now she's forced to work with grumpy Finn Oakley, the man who's avoided her for years. Will Finn finally return her love, or will she always just be his best friend's little sister?

Tropes

Brother's best friend, Grumpy/Sunshine, Beauty and the Beast, Age Gap, Unrequited Love, Rivals, Different Worlds, All Grown Up, Small Town

THE HIDEAWAY HARBOR SERIES

THE HOLIDAY FAKERS

I promised my mom I'd bring a boyfriend home for Christmas.

Instead, I'm fake-dating Brody King—Hollywood heartthrob, tabloid train wreck, and the reason I have a folder of fantasy fan art I'll never admit exists.

He's also my brother's best friend, the guy who ghosted me twelve years ago… and now we're sharing a bed.

This was supposed to be fake.

So why does it feel dangerously real?

<u>Tropes</u>

Small Town, Fake Dating, One Bed, Brother's Best Friend, Found Family, Celebrity, Different Worlds

❄

By Evie Alexander and Kelly Kay

EVIE & KELLY'S HOLIDAY DISASTERS SERIES

Evie and Kelly's Holiday Disasters are a series of hot and hilarious romantic comedies with interconnected characters, focusing on one holiday and one trope at a time.

CUPID CALAMITY

Featuring **Animal Attraction** & **Stupid Cupid**

Patrick and Sabina have ditched their blind dates for each other. Ben's fighting a crazed chimp for Laurie's love. Insta-love meets insta-disaster in these laugh-out-loud Valentine's day novellas.

COOKOUT CARNAGE

Featuring **Off With a Bang** & **Up in Smoke**

Cute farm boy Jonathan clings to a love ideal, blissfully ignoring what the universe has planned, while keeping track of his pet pig. Posh Brit follows his heart into the American Midwest in search of Sherilyn, his digital dream love.

CHRISTMAS CHAOS

Featuring **No way in a Manger** & **No Crib and No Bed**

In Scotland, Zoe and Rory attempt to have a civilised and respectable rite of passage, but straightforward is not their style. In Sonoma, Bax and Tabi attempt to throw a meaningful Christmas celebration. But there are too many people involved and it's nothing like they expect.

Get Evie's books in all formats as well as special offers, early releases, and exclusive deals direct from her website:

www.eviealexanderbooks.com

ABOUT THE AUTHOR

Evie Alexander is a multi-award-winning author of sexy romantic comedies, blending snort-laugh humour and panty-melting chemistry into unputdownable stories that will steal your heart.

When she's not dreaming up swoony heroes and relatable heroines, Evie can be found in the beautiful West Country of the UK, where she lives with her ridiculously patient husband, miracle daughter, and two dogs who think they run the show.

eviealexanderbooks.com

eviealexanderauthor.com

- instagram.com/eviealexanderauthor
- facebook.com/eviealexanderauthor
- bookbub.com/authors/evie-alexander
- amazon.com/Evie-Alexander/e/B08ZJGLP29?ref=sr_ntt_s-rch_lnk_1&qid=1630667484&sr=8-1
- pinterest.com/eviealexanderauthor

THANK YOU FOR READING
THE HOLIDAY FAKERS!